DOWNFALL

ALSO BY J. A. JANCE

J. P. BEAUMONT MYSTERIES

Until Proven Guilty
Injustice for All
Trial by Fury
Taking the Fifth
Improbable Cause
A More Perfect Union
Dismissed with Prejudice
Minor in Possession
Payment in Kind
Without Due Process
Failure to Appear
Lying in Wait
Name Withheld
Breach of Duty
Birds of Prey
Partner in Crime
Long Time Gone
Justice Denied
Fire and Ice
Betrayal of Trust
Ring in the Dead: A J. P. Beaumont Novella
Second Watch
Stand Down: A J. P. Beaumont Novella

JOANNA BRADY MYSTERIES

Desert Heat
Tombstone Courage
Shoot/Don't Shoot
Dead to Rights
Skeleton Canyon
Rattlesnake Crossing
Outlaw Mountain
Devil's Claw
Paradise Lost
Partner in Crime
Exit Wounds
Dead Wrong
Damage Control
Fire and Ice
Judgment Call
The Old Blue Line: A Joanna Brady Novella
Remains of Innocence
Random Acts: A Joanna Brady and Ali Reynolds Novella

WALKER FAMILY NOVELS

Hour of the Hunter
Kiss of the Bees
Day of the Dead
Queen of the Night
Dance of the Bones: A J. P. Beaumont and Brandon Walker Novel

ALI REYNOLDS NOVELS

Edge of Evil
Web of Evil
Hand of Evil
Cruel Intent
Trial by Fire
Fatal Error
Left for Dead
Deadly Stakes
Moving Target
A Last Goodbye: An Ali Reynolds Novella
Cold Betrayal
No Honor Among Thieves: An Ali Reynolds/Joanna Brady Novella
Clawback

POETRY

After the Fire

DOWNFALL

A BRADY NOVEL OF SUSPENSE

J. A. JANCE

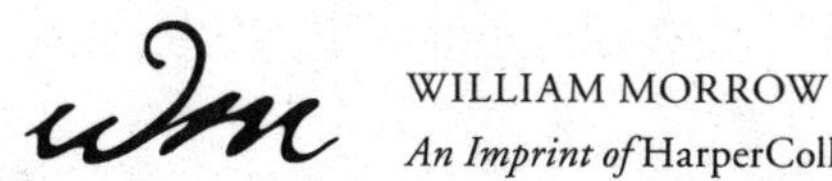

WILLIAM MORROW
An Imprint of HarperCollins*Publishers*

This is a work of fiction. Names, characters, places, and incidents are products of the author's imagination or are used fictitiously and are not to be construed as real. Any resemblance to actual events, locales, organizations, or persons, living or dead, is entirely coincidental.

HarperCollins books may be purchased for educational, business, or sales promotional use. For information, please email the Special Markets Department at SP-sales@harpercollins.com.

FIRST EDITION

Library of Congress Cataloging-in-Publication Data has been applied for.

ISBN 978-0-06-229771-6

16 17 18 19 20 RS/RRD 10 9 8 7 6 5 4 3 2 1

Thank you to Oscar Soule, David Dettman, and William Peachey—
for keeping me on the straight and narrow

DOWNFALL

PROLOGUE

SHERIFF JOANNA BRADY PULLED INTO THE PARKING PLACE IN front of the Higgins Funeral Chapel, put her Buick Enclave in park, and then sat staring at the storefront before her, only vaguely aware of her surroundings. Lowering clouds blanketed the Mule Mountains in southeastern Arizona. It was the last day of August. The summer monsoons had arrived early and stayed on, leaving the desert grassland valleys of Cochise County lush and green.

A flash of lightning off toward the east roused Joanna from her reverie with a warning that the skies might open up at any moment. Still she lingered, unready to go inside and face down this awful but necessary task. She was relieved when her phone rang with her husband's name in the caller-ID window. Answering a call gave her an excuse to stall a little longer.

"Hey," she said. "Where are you? I thought you'd be here by now."

"So did I, and we would have been," Butch said, "if not for the huge backup caused by a semi rollover on the I-10 bridge over the Gila. We're in Tombstone right now. If I come straight there, I could arrive before they close, but—"

"No," Joanna said firmly. "Take Denny home. A funeral home is no place for a five-year-old. I'll handle this on my own."

"You're sure?"

"I'm sure," she said, reaching for the door handle. "I'll see you at home."

She switched her phone to silent and stepped out of the SUV just as the first fat raindrops splattered down on the hot pavement. As soon as the moisture dampened nearby overheated creosote bushes, the air came alive with the unmistakable perfume of desert rain. Most of the time, Joanna would have rejoiced at that distinctive aroma, but not today. Instead, she crossed the sidewalk and opened an all-too-familiar door.

She had come to the Higgins Funeral Chapel for the first time as a teenager, arriving there with her mother, Eleanor, in the aftermath of her father's death. D. H. Lathrop had been changing a tire for a stranded family when he had been struck and killed by a passing vehicle. Then Joanna had come here alone nine years ago. On that occasion she had been a widow, making funeral arrangements for her newly deceased husband, Andrew Roy Brady. And this time?

A week earlier, in the dead of August, life had been as normal as Joanna's life could be, considering she was a busy county sheriff with a daughter heading off to college, a five-year-old son starting kindergarten, and a baby girl due to arrive in early December. That normal had been shattered by a three A.M. phone call that had rousted her out of bed with the news that her mother, Eleanor Lathrop Winfield, and her stepfather, George Winfield, had been involved in a serious vehicular accident while driving their RV home to Bisbee from a summertime sojourn in Minnesota.

George died at the scene; Eleanor had perished after being airlifted to a Phoenix-area hospital for treatment. In the ensuing investigation, Joanna discovered that what had originally been regarded as a simple traffic accident was anything but. A troubled kid, wielding a high-powered rifle with a laser scope, had stationed himself on a highway overpass south of Camp Verde, where he had fired at passing vehicles. With the help of a relatively new friend, Ali Reynolds, Joanna had helped search for and eventually find the shooter.

While attempting to elude his pursuers, the boy had crashed his 4x4. Less than twenty-four hours after George and Eleanor's murders, Joanna had found herself kneeling on the ground at the injured boy's side, comforting their dying killer. Now she was left cleaning up the rest of the bits and pieces. The remains had finally been released by the Yavapai County Medical Examiner's Office. The mortuary had called earlier that day to say that the bodies had arrived in Bisbee shortly after noon.

A discreet chime sounded in a distant room as Joanna opened the funeral home's Main Street door. Norm Higgins, dressed in his customary suit and tie, appeared silently in the doorway of an office just to the right of the entryway.

"I've been expecting you, Sheriff Brady," he said, giving her a stiff half bow. "So sorry for your loss. How can we be of service?"

He ushered her into an old-fashioned wood-paneled office where a single file lay on the polished surface of an ornate antique desk. "I took the liberty of glancing through your mother's file," he said. "At the time of your father's death, your mother purchased two adjoining plots at Evergreen Cemetery. According to this, she was opposed to cremation and wished to be buried in the plot next to your father's. As far as your stepfather's wishes are concerned, however, we're completely in the dark."

"That makes two of us," Joanna said, withdrawing a piece of paper from her purse. "In going through George's things, I located this letter saying that he wished to be cremated and have his ashes scattered near his cabin at Big Stone Lake in Minnesota. The problem is, this letter predates his marriage to my mother. Just today I've learned that my mother has been negotiating with the Rojas family, the people who own the plots next to my parents' plots, in hopes of purchasing the nearest one for George's use. Presumably he had changed his mind about cremation."

She didn't mention how she had learned about the cemetery-plot situation because, the truth was, it hurt like hell. Joanna certainly hadn't heard about it from Eleanor herself. No, that bit of vital intelligence had been gleaned in a phone call with her brother, Bob Brundage—a brother born to her parents out of wedlock and given up for adoption long before Joanna was born. After the deaths of both his adoptive parents, Bob had come looking for his birth family. Once reunited, he and Eleanor had gotten along like gangbusters. And the fact that her brother had been privy to her mother's final wishes when Joanna herself had not was something that still rankled. In fact, Joanna had heard about the cemetery situation for the first time earlier this morning, mentioned in passing when Bob had called to let her know when he and his wife, Marcie, would be flying in from DC on Tuesday.

What am I? Joanna had wanted to ask while they were still on the phone. *Chopped liver?* Why had her mother chosen to tell Bob all about what was going on when it was Joanna, the daughter with boots on the ground, who would most likely be expected to oversee the arrangements? Why was she the one who had been left in the dark? Joanna's feelings had been hurt, but she hadn't said anything to Bob about it. After all, it wasn't his fault.

"Did it work?" Norm Higgins asked, bringing Joanna back to the present conversation and perhaps repeating a question he had asked previously.

"Did what work?"

"The negotiations to buy the plot."

"More or less," Joanna said. "I mean, my brother was able to reach an agreement on the deal this morning. He expects to have the certificate of purchase in hand by tomorrow afternoon, but I'm not at all sure that's how I want to handle this, and that's what I need to discuss with you. My mother specifically said she wanted to be buried rather than cremated? You're sure about that?"

"Yes," Norm replied, patting the file but not bothering to open it and verify the information. "Her position in that regard is quite clear."

"What am I supposed to do, then?"

Norm Higgins drummed his fingers on top of his desk. "We have a situation where we have reason to believe that Dr. Winfield and your mother wanted to be buried together even though there was no separate plot currently available. On the other hand, we have a handwritten document indicating his wish to be cremated."

"So what do you suggest?" Joanna asked, rephrasing her earlier question.

Norm shook his head. "Quite frankly, Sheriff Brady, these

kinds of issues are usually resolved by what we commonly refer to as 'the last person standing.' They're the ones who have the final say, as it were."

"In other words, it's up to me."

"Exactly."

Joanna took a deep breath. "All right, then," she said. "Here's what we're going to do. Go ahead and cremate George's remains. Put his ashes in an urn, reserving a small portion that Butch and I can scatter at Big Stone Lake later on. I want you to have both the urn and the casket on display during the funeral. At the end of that, we'll put the urn in the casket with my mother. That way Mom and George can be buried together. If my father objects, the three of them will need to sort that out among themselves when they get to the other side."

Norm withdrew a piece of paper from his desk, a form of some kind, and began filling in the blanks. "I trust you're not expecting to have an open-casket service or a viewing, are you?"

Joanna was adamant. "Absolutely not. I saw the damage," she said. "My mother wouldn't be caught dead looking like that."

The unthinking words were out of her mouth before she realized how absurdly true they were. Eleanor Lathrop had always put her best foot forward. Remembering that and the appalling way her mother had looked in the hospital, Joanna forced herself to bite back a sob. If Norm noticed her discomfort, he didn't acknowledge it. No doubt he was accustomed to dealing with people who blurted out inappropriate comments because their emotions had been strained beyond the breaking point.

"Yes," he said, nodding. "That's my assessment, too. There's only so much we're able to do. But placing an urn in the casket is a creative way of handling a complex issue. I believe you mentioned the word 'funeral' rather than 'funerals.' Does that mean you're anticipating a joint service?"

Joanna's cell phone buzzed in the pocket of her blazer. She had turned the ringer to silent when she came inside. Over the course of the last several days, she had been overwhelmed with condolence calls. She appreciated all of them, of course, but the sheer number made it hard for her to think straight. Right now she needed to deal with Norm.

"Yes," she said. "A joint service."

"Here in our chapel or at your mother's church? I believe Eleanor attended the Presbyterian church."

"Here," Joanna said, "and with my friend Marianne Maculyea officiating. How soon could you schedule it?"

Norm leaned back in his chair. "We keep a very limited number of caskets and urns in stock," he said. "If you were to make your selection from those, we would have more flexibility. Otherwise, scheduling would depend on how soon we could receive the shipments."

"Assuming I find something suitable in your inventory and choose from those?"

"In that case, I would suggest scheduling the funeral for late Friday morning—say, eleven or so," Norm suggested. "Doing it as early as Thursday would make it difficult to get notices to the local media. We handle all of those, by the way," he added. "The notices, I mean. That's part of our comprehensive service. And I'll need to get bio information from you on both your mother and Dr. Winfield in order to write the obituaries. Or would you rather do that yourself?"

"I'll provide the info," Joanna said, "but I'd rather someone else did the writing. And when you post those notices, please mention that the service itself will be private, by invitation only. I'll give you a list of the people who should be there. What I don't want is to have a bunch of outside gawkers show up just for the fun of it."

Joanna's phone buzzed again. Whoever had called earlier had just left a message. She ignored the message notice just as she had ignored the call.

"How much will all this cost?" she asked. "And how soon do I need to pay?"

"Let's worry about that after you've selected the casket and urn," Norm said, rising to his feet. "We expect payment in advance, of course. Once you've made casket and urn selections, I'll be able to prepare an invoice, and since we'll be holding only a single service, I'm sure you'll find the charges reasonable. This way, please."

Back in the mortuary's warehouse section, Joanna found precious little to choose from—at three distinct price points. Knowing her mother would have been pissed if any expense had been spared, and since Bob had agreed to split the funeral expenses fifty-fifty, Joanna opted for the high-priced version—for both Eleanor and George, putting the whole bill on her Visa. Finished at last, she staggered out of the mortuary an hour and a half after entering. It was dark now—well past closing time. Norm unlocked the front door to let her out and then locked it from the inside and closed the security shutters behind her.

Relieved that the funeral-planning ordeal was finally over, Joanna stood on the sidewalk and took a deep breath. The air was cool and fresh. The rainstorm had come and gone, leaving the streets wet and shiny under the glow of recently illuminated streetlights. Runoff from the rain was still draining away, flowing down Brewery Gulch, across Main Street, and into the storm gutter—known locally as the Subway—where Joanna had once done hand-to-hand battle with a killer.

Her phone buzzed with a text from Butch:

> Come home. Making dinner. You need to eat to keep up your strength.

After sending a text back saying she was on her way, she scrolled through her recent calls. The last one had come from her chief deputy, Tom Hadlock.

She listened to his voice mail. "Sorry to bother you at a time like this, but we've got either a double homicide or a murder/suicide. Can't tell which. Can you give me a call?"

Joanna ground her teeth in frustration. Tom had served admirably as her jail commander, but she worried that promoting him to chief deputy had been a mistake on her part. He was still out of his depth in certain situations, and this was clearly one of them. She dialed him back immediately.

"What's up?"

"A couple of kids out climbing Geronimo east of Warren late this afternoon found two bodies at the base of a cliff—two females. No visible gunshot or stab wounds. Looks like they either jumped or were pushed. One of them seems to have had a campsite set up near a water hole at the base of the peak, and we found ID in a purse at the campsite. The name on the ID is for one Desirée Wilburton. Apparently she's a grad student from the University of Arizona. The other victim had no identification of any kind. I know you're on bereavement leave, but—"

"Never mind that," Joanna said. "I'm coming. Who all is at the scene?"

"Right now, just the original responding deputy. The two boys who found the bodies are still there as well. Dr. Baldwin is on her way, coming from the far side of Benson. Dispatch is in the process of notifying the on-call detectives, the Double C's."

Kendra Baldwin was Cochise County's relatively new medical examiner. The term "Double C's" was departmental shorthand for Detectives Ernie Carpenter and Jaime Carbajal, Joanna's longtime homicide investigators.

"All right," Joanna said, looking down at her clothing. "At the moment I'm not dressed for hiking either to or around a remote crime scene. I'll need to go home to change and maybe grab a bite to eat. You should probably call in a couple of extra deputies as well. Who all is on duty?"

"Jeremy Stock is close by. He's in the process of finishing up a traffic stop on Highway 92 near the San Pedro. Armando Ruiz is somewhere between Elfrida and Willcox. I'll call both of them and let everybody know that you're coming. The ME is still more than an hour out, so there's no big hurry. You know the way?"

"The front side of Geronimo or the backside?" she asked.

"Front side," Tom answered.

For generations of Bisbee kids, climbing that distinctive double-humped limestone peak east of town had been a rite of passage. Locals referred to it either as Geronimo or else by the name Anglo pioneers had given it—Black Knob. In official topo-map parlance, however, it was referred to as Gold Hill. Too short to be officially labeled a mountain, the limestone peak with a humped top that resembled the top of a valentine, clocked in at

5,900 feet, 400 higher than the desert surrounding its base. Viewed from the streets of Old Bisbee, Gold Hill stood in the distance like a lonely gray sentinel, towering in the background over the flat expanse of a rust-colored mine-waste tailings dump.

Joanna was personally acquainted with Geronimo, having climbed it twice—once with a long-ago Girl Scout troop and once with her first husband, Andy Brady, shortly before the two of them married. Both times she had scrambled up the rocky front of the mountain on her hands and knees and slid back down, most of the way on her butt. Both times she'd been in trouble with her mother afterward for wrecking her clothes.

The front side of Gold Hill was accessed through an old cattle ranch whose entrance was, unsurprisingly, at the end of a street called Black Knob. The backside was approached via a primitive dirt track that ran past a now mostly deserted rifle range. Both routes required four-wheel drive most of the way and a hike for the last half mile or so.

"Okay," she said. "Where are you right now?"

"Still at the Justice Center."

"Give me half an hour to go home and change, then come out to the ranch with my Yukon and we'll drive to the crime scene in that. No way am I going to take my Enclave there. It doesn't have a scratch on it at the moment, and I fully intend to keep it that way."

CHAPTER 1

"DO YOU HAVE TO GO?" DENNY WHINED, PUSHING HIS MACARONI and cheese around on his plate. "Why do you always have to work?"

"Your mommy has an important job," Butch explained. "People are counting on her to do it."

Changed into a regulation khaki uniform augmented by a pair of sturdy hiking boots, Joanna shot her husband a grateful glance. She'd called him on her way home, and he'd had her dinner on the table when she arrived.

Butch, more than anyone, understood Joanna's unstinting commitment to her job. She hadn't run for office with the intention of being sheriff in name only. From the moment she was elected, she had made it a point to be at the scene of every homicide that had occurred inside the boundaries of her far-flung jurisdiction. Just because she had spent most of the day grieving the deaths of her mother and stepfather and planning the funeral service didn't mean she was going to abandon her official duties, especially when a possible double homicide had turned up less than ten miles away from her home on High Lonesome Road.

On the other hand . . . the disappointment registered on Denny's face represented every working mother's all-too-familiar tug-of-war.

"Finish your dinner, Denny, and get your jammies on," Joanna suggested. "Maybe I'll have time enough to read some Dr. Seuss to you before Chief Deputy Hadlock comes by to pick me up."

With a gleeful shout, Dennis hopped down from his chair, cleared his dishes, and then scampered off toward the bedroom with their two dogs—a rescued Australian shepherd named Lady and a stone-deaf black Lab named Lucky—hot on his heels.

"He's tired," Butch remarked, "and so am I. It was a long haul back and forth to Flagstaff, but I think we did the right thing. It's a lot more important to have Jenny settled in her dorm and Maggie in her new stable in a timely fashion rather than expecting Jenny to hang around here for the funeral and end up being late for her first college-level classes. Starting her freshman year that way might leave her feeling like she's behind everyone else from the very beginning."

Joanna nodded. The truth was, it hadn't required all that much effort to talk Jenny into taking a pass on her grandparents' funeral. Not that she didn't care about them—she did. In fact, she had doted on George, and in many ways, she had enjoyed a better relationship with Eleanor than Joanna ever had. By the end of August, however, most of Jenny's friends had gone off to school, and she was ready to follow suit.

"But will she feel guilty later about missing the funeral?" Butch asked. "That's what worries me."

Joanna smiled at him. "She's a freshman in college. She'll be far too busy to feel guilty for very long."

Dennis returned with his book, his "blankie," and two very devoted dogs. "You go read," Butch said. "I'll clear up."

Joanna and Dennis snuggled into an easy chair in the living room. *Green Eggs and Ham* was Dennis's all-time favorite book, and it wasn't so much a case of Joanna reading the book aloud as it was a responsive reading, with Joanna beginning each sentence and Dennis finishing it. At this point he wasn't actually reading the printed words. He simply knew the whole book by heart.

Two pages from the end, Chief Deputy Hadlock turned up. He stayed in the kitchen with Butch long enough for Joanna and Dennis to finish the story. Then, even though it was still a little before seven, Dennis was ready to brush his teeth and go to bed.

"You do that," Joanna told him, kissing him good night. "Daddy will come tuck you in." Out in the kitchen, Tom Hadlock, hat in hand, stood just inside the back door as if uncertain of his welcome.

"Any news?" Joanna asked.

"The storm we had this afternoon played havoc with the roads. Right now Gold Gulch is running bank to bank, so going by way of the rifle range is out of the question, and from what I hear, the other route isn't much better."

"We should get going, then," Joanna said, giving Butch a quick hug. "See you later."

"Stay safe," he said.

She nodded. It was what he always said when she headed out for duty, and she knew he meant it every single time.

Dusk fell as they drove back toward the highway on High Lonesome Road. There had been enough rain this summer that usually dry washes had been running trickles of water most of the time. Forty-five minutes earlier, after the drenching but fast-moving storm, swiftly flowing muddy water had been hurtling through several recently installed culverts. Now the high water had mostly subsided—at least right here. That was one of the things that made flash floods so dangerous. They were unpredictable. They could arrive with no warning and with no rain in sight, flowing downhill from a storm miles away. The good thing about them was that they disappeared almost as quickly as they came.

"Sorry about calling you out on this," Tom apologized.

"Don't give it another thought," Joanna assured him. "After all, a potential double homicide counts as serious business, and we'll need all hands on deck on this, mine included."

As they drove toward the crime scene, Tom brought her up to speed. Earlier in the afternoon, two boys, thirteen-year-old Marcus Padilla and his younger brother, Raul, had left their home in Bisbee's Warren neighborhood and set out on a hike, planning on doing a little skinny-dipping in the water hole that summer rains had left behind in a natural basin near the base of Geronimo.

According to Tom, Marcus and Raul had evidently pulled the same stunt several times over the course of the summer, and they were accustomed to having the area all to themselves. This time, however, they discovered a red Jeep Cherokee parked at the end of the roadway. Closer to Geronimo itself and near the water hole, they had come upon a seemingly deserted campsite that included a tent, bedroll, and camp stove along with a selection of cooking and eating utensils. Worried about running into the camper, the boys had given up on the idea of skinny-dipping. They decided to climb the mountain instead, hoping to get up and down before the threatening rainstorm arrived. As they started their ascent, they discovered the two bodies, lying one on top of the other at the base of a rocky ledge. With no service available on his phone, Marcus climbed high enough on the mountain to locate a cell signal. Once he had one, he called 911.

"That was when?" Joanna asked.

"About four," Tom said.

"But if the ME just now got there . . ."

"My fault," Tom said. "When Larry Kendrick called me from Dispatch and told me he had a couple of kids on the line, I thought at first it was a prank. It's the end of summer when bored kids can get up to all kinds of mischief. So I asked for someone from Patrol to drop by and check it out. By then it was raining pitchforks and hammer handles. Took some time for Deputy Marks to get there. The Jeep was unlocked and the kids had taken shelter inside it to get out of the rain."

"With a thunderstorm like that brewing, those kids shouldn't have been up on the mountain in the first place," Joanna said.

Tom nodded. "There is that," he agreed, turning off Highway 80 and onto the Warren Cutoff. Once in town, they turned a wide left, drove up and over Yuma Trail, and then turned left again onto the dirt-track ranch road. As soon as they did so, they could see the bright glow of generator-powered work lights used to illuminate crime scenes.

Tom's cell phone rang. With effort, he wrestled the device out of his hip pocket and glanced at caller ID. "Oh no," he groaned. "Not her again."

"Marliss Shackleford?" Joanna guessed.

Marliss was a reporter for the local newspaper, the *Bisbee Bee,* which, against all odds, was still going strong both in print and online. At the paper, Marliss functioned as both star reporter and columnist. In her column, *Bisbee Buzzings,* Marliss often took issue with local public officials, and Joanna's department was a common target for her derogatory coverage, even though she and Joanna's mother had been close friends for years.

"Yup," Tom replied. "The very one."

"Don't answer, then," Joanna advised. "Until we have a better idea of what we're up against, we're better off ignoring her."

"What if she shows up at the crime scene?"

"Considering current road conditions, that doesn't seem likely," Joanna said. "If she does show up, we'll deal with her then."

A mile and a half later, the dirt track ended abruptly in a clutch of parked official vehicles. The last one in line was the ME's Dodge Caravan. "The Jeep on the far side of the wash evidently belongs to one of the victims," Tom explained, putting Joanna's Yukon in park. "She must have hiked in from there, and we'll have to do the same."

"How come?"

"The wash," Tom answered. "A little while ago I was told it was running four feet deep."

Taking Tom's Maglite with her, Joanna hopped out and walked forward to see for herself. Shining the beam into the wash, she saw that the water had subsided. If it had been running four feet deep earlier, now it was down to only a foot or so. It could most likely be forded on foot, but that entailed climbing up and down perpendicular embankments on either side of the running water. Once a vehicle splashed down one of those steep edges, driving up the other side would be impossible. No wonder all the vehicles were parked on this side rather than closer to the crime scene itself.

Joanna returned to the Yukon and to the luggage compartment, where she retrieved her own Maglite as well as a pocketful of latex gloves. When she stepped off into the swiftly flowing water, she gratefully accepted Tom's offered hand, which kept her from being swept off her feet. Once on the far side, both she and Tom had to sit down and empty sand and water out of their boots before continuing on to the crime scene.

By now, the clouds had rolled away. Pinpricks of stars gleaming in the dark sky did little to illuminate the rock-strewn pathway. Neither did the tiny sliver of waning moon. As they approached the grove of trees surrounding the water hole, Joanna caught a glimpse of crime-scene tape.

"We need to go around," Tom explained. "That's where the campsite is."

Beyond the water hole, the ascent began in earnest. It was gradual at first, but as the path became steeper, Joanna found herself panting. Not only was she eating for two these days, she was evidently breathing for two as well.

Partway up the mountain, they had to halt and step off the path in order to make way for several people who, armed with their own flashlights, were making their way down from the crime scene. The momentary pause gave Joanna a much-needed chance to catch her breath. Once the newcomers drew near, she recognized Deputy Jeremy Stock accompanied by two dark-haired boys.

"Meet Marcus and Raul Padilla," Deputy Stock said. "They're the witnesses who found the bodies."

"I'm Sheriff Brady," Joanna said, moving the Maglite from one hand to the other in order to greet the boys properly. "Which of you is Marcus?"

"I am," the taller one said.

"And I'm Ruly," the second one chirped. "I'm the one who saw them first. It was gross."

"I'm told their mother is beside herself with worry," Deputy Stock explained. "The detectives are still busy at the crime scene. The ME just got here, and Ernie is too busy to talk to the boys right now. He asked me to take them home. Ernie and Detective Carbajal will stop by their house later to do an official interview when their parents can be present."

"It's just our mother," Ruly volunteered. "Our parents are divorced. Dad doesn't live with us anymore."

The older boy jabbed the younger one with his elbow as if to silence him. "They don't have to know that," he said.

"You go on home with Deputy Stock," Joanna urged. "I'm sure your mom is worried sick, but thank you for calling 911, Marcus. Some people would have just walked away from something like this without reporting it for fear of getting involved."

"It's okay," Marcus mumbled.

"All right," Deputy Stock said. "Let's get moving."

While the three of them continued down, Joanna glanced up toward a place where the artificial glow cast by work lights illuminated the crime scene, leaving the enormous shadow of Geronimo looming in the background. Another quarter mile of hard climbing brought Joanna and her chief deputy to the base of a massive limestone cliff that soared skyward. Just outside the circle of light, they ran into Deputy Armando Ruiz, who was dutifully stringing crime-scene tape from boulder to boulder.

Stepping into the light, Joanna joined a busy group of people hard at work on their appointed tasks. Dr. Kendra Baldwin, the ME, was on her knees next to what looked like a heap of bloodied clothing but that, on closer examination, proved to be something barely recognizable as two intertwined human forms. Detective Carpenter hovered in the background, keeping an eye on everything, while Dave Hollicker—the male member of Joanna's two-person CSI unit—snapped an unending series of crime-scene photos.

"Evening, Joanna," Kendra said, rising to her feet and coming forward to greet the newcomers while stripping off a pair of latex gloves. She was a tall, spare African American woman with a ready smile and a down-to-earth way about her. "So sorry to hear about your mom and George," she added. "Are you sure you're up for this?"

Joanna nodded. "Thank you," she said. "I appreciate your concern, but I'm here to do the job. What have we got?"

"Two females," Kendra replied, looking back at the bloody tangle of victims. "One, Desirée Wilburton, is age twenty-seven. The other probably is midthirties or maybe a little younger. Rigor suggests they've been dead for twenty hours or so, but I'll be able to give you a more definitive time frame once I have them back at the lab. The stage of decomp suggests that both victims died at about the same time. Desirée wore a watch, which is still running, by the way. She wasn't wearing a wedding ring, but the other one was. Probably the easiest way to sort out who she is would be to check missing-persons reports."

Joanna nodded. "You mentioned a name—Desirée Wilburton. You already have a positive ID on her, then?"

"Tentative," Kendra corrected. "ID was found in a purse

inside the tent back at the campsite. In addition to her driver's license, she was carrying ID that identifies her as a teaching assistant for the University of Arizona. Detective Carbajal is in the process of contacting the campus cops there to see what, if anything, they can tell us. So far we have no information at all on the other victim."

"Cause of death?"

"Initially, I'd have to say multiple blunt-force trauma to the head for both of them."

"From being hit with something?"

Kendra shook her head. "No, the injuries I'm seeing so far are all consistent with a fall. No visible gunshot or stab wounds that would indicate the use of a weapon."

Joanna nodded, thinking about how, once George had been extricated from the tangled wreckage of the RV, the immediate assumption had been that his injuries had been caused by the wreck itself. Only Eleanor's insistence on the presence of a "red dot" had convinced Joanna that George Winfield had been shot by someone using a laser sight, and a subsequent autopsy had proven that to be true. Perhaps something similar would occur here, and further investigation of the remains would reveal the use of a weapon of some kind.

Joanna stood in silence, studying the distorted heap of tangled limbs and clothing. Years earlier, encountering sights and smells like this would have sent her racing for the nearest restroom, retching her guts out. Tonight, though, she stood her ground. Carrion eaters and insects had been hard at work devouring the remains for what seemed to be the better part of forty-eight hours. Remnants of clothing revealed that one of the victims—the one on top—was apparently dressed in sturdy hiking boots, jeans, and a long-sleeved khaki shirt. The one on the bottom wore a pair of shorts, a tank top, and a single lightweight tennis shoe. One was dressed to be outdoors roughing it; the other was not.

Jaime Carbajal entered the circle of light, descending from somewhere on the hillside and pocketing his cell phone as he came.

"Had to gain some elevation before I could get a signal," he explained. "According to the U of A, Wilburton is a Ph.D. candidate in microbiology. She's originally from Louisiana. She came to Arizona first as an undergrad and stayed on to earn a master's and is close to finishing up her doctorate. The guy I spoke to says he'll get back to me later with whatever next-of-kin information they have on file, but probably not before tomorrow morning."

"Thanks, Jaime," Joanna said before turning her attention to Ernie. "Any theories, Detective Carpenter?" she asked.

"I'm coming down on the side of murder/suicide," he replied. "From the looks of things, I'd say Desirée had been camping here for a while—a day or two at least and possibly more. The other victim, her girlfriend maybe, drops by. They get into some kind of argument—a lovers' quarrel perhaps. One thing leads to another, and they both end up dead."

"Is there any way to figure out exactly where they were when they fell?"

Jaime shook his head. "Before that rainstorm there might have been physical evidence—maybe even footprints—that would help us determine that. As it stands, we've got nothing." He glanced back at the cliff face rising straight up behind him and then at the ground below. "The thing is, when you're dealing with such hard-packed, rocky terrain, you don't have to fall very far to end up with this kind of catastrophic outcome."

"What about the boys?" Joanna asked. "Is it possible they were involved in some way?"

Ernie shook his head. "I don't think so. The kids look like innocent bystanders to me," he said. "Because they took shelter in the Jeep during the storm, we went ahead and took their prints for elimination purposes. Just to be sure, Casey ran them through AFIS. Not surprisingly, nothing turned up on either of them."

Casey Ledford was the other member of Joanna's CSI team—her resident fingerprint expert. With newly upgraded computer capability installed on all the patrol cars, it didn't surprise Joanna to hear that the fingerprints of both boys had already been run through the national Automated Fingerprint Identification System.

"What about the vics'?" Joanna asked.

"Considering the decomp, those may or may not be retrievable. In any case, Dr. Baldwin prefers to take prints once she has the bodies back at the morgue."

"Her job, her rules," Joanna conceded.

"Hey, how about somebody giving us a hand here?" Ralph Whetson asked, coming into view while lugging a metal-framed stretcher designed to transport bodies.

Ralph was Dr. Baldwin's morgue assistant and a constant complainer. He dropped his load just inside the circle of light, as if carrying it another step was more than he could manage. Seconds later, someone else appeared behind him. The newcomer was Deputy Stock, also loaded down with a stretcher.

"Hey, Jeremy," Ernie called out, his tone stern and thunderous. "I thought I told you to take those boys back home to their mother."

"You did," the deputy agreed. "I was on my way to do that very thing when I ran into Ralph here and Detective Howell. I could see that Ralph needed a hand. He was trying to carry both stretchers by himself and wasn't making much progress. Deb offered to take charge of the boys so I could help Ralph with the stretchers."

Deb Howell was Joanna's third homicide detective. She hadn't been on call that night, but Joanna knew she was a self-starter. It was hardly surprising that she would turn up at the scene on her own.

Ernie Carpenter, on the other hand, tended to be a bit of a grouch on occasion. From his point of view, orders weren't something that could be casually handed off to someone else. Given that he was close to the top of the department's pecking order, his grumbly bear persona meant that he wasn't always on the best of terms with Joanna's patrol deputies. Knowing this, she stepped in to smooth things over.

"Good thinking," she said. "Carrying those stretchers may be challenging now when they're empty, but it'll be a whole lot more difficult once they're loaded. Seems to me we're going to need all the help we can get."

Ernie favored her with a grudging nod. "Okay," he said.

Dr. Baldwin moved away from the bodies. "Glad you're here, Ralph," she said. "I think we're ready to rock and roll. Let's load 'em up and head 'em out."

CHAPTER 2

JOANNA'S PREDICTION ABOUT THE LOADED STRETCHERS BEING unwieldy turned out to be one hundred percent accurate. In the end, everyone at the crime scene had to lend a hand—including Joanna and Kendra Baldwin herself. The rough terrain and the need to use flashlights made for slow going. Getting the two bodies across the still-running wash wasn't easy, either. Once again Joanna's boots filled with sand, making every step more painful than the last.

Back at the makeshift parking lot, the first body was quickly loaded into the back of the ME's Dodge Caravan. The problem was, the minivan was only equipped to carry one body at a time. That meant everything had to grind to a halt until an aid car, summoned from the city of Bisbee, arrived to transport the second one.

While they waited, Joanna sank down on the Yukon's running board long enough to catch her breath and empty her boots.

While she was doing so, Kendra looked down at her with visible concern. "Are you all right?" she asked. "You didn't overdo it, did you?"

"You mean for someone in my delicate condition?" Joanna asked.

Kendra smiled. "Well?"

They were both women doing jobs that historically belonged to men, and they had established a natural camaraderie from the very beginning. Coming from Kendra, the comment felt like what it was—a joke—rather than a form of politically incorrect criticism.

Joanna shook her head. "No, I'm fine. As far as the autopsies are concerned, what's the game plan?"

Kendra looked at her watch, some kind of electronic device that glowed in the dark. "It's almost nine," she said. "By the time we get the bodies back to the morgue, it'll be too late to start processing them tonight, but I should be able to collect fingerprints. If I get decent prints, I'll shoot a copy of them over to you so your people will have access to them sooner rather than later. I'll also take dental X-rays and ship those along as well, in case dental records work better than prints."

Joanna gave the ME a weary smile. "Thanks," she said. "Once were done here, I'll be going back to the office while Ernie and Jaime go interview the two Padilla boys. Deb Howell wasn't supposed to be on duty tonight. I hate to run up the overtime, but once Deb dropped off the two boys, I asked her to start working on finding Desirée's next of kin. Pima County property-tax rolls say that the address listed on Desirée's driver's license belongs to one Roberta Wilburton."

"Mother/daughter maybe?" Kendra asked.

"Or maybe two sisters," Joanna answered. "We'll know soon enough. Deb is on her way to Tucson to speak with Roberta right now."

"And all the while Detective Howell is driving to Tucson, she's getting overtime, but you're not, right?" Kendra observed.

"You should know," Joanna said, nodding in agreement. "Neither do you."

"Which is another reason I won't be doing those autopsies tonight—to hold the line on staff overtime. Let's say we'll set the first one for tomorrow at nine A.M. In the meantime, what's the deal with the crime scene?"

"Both the crime scene and the campsite are mostly cordoned off," Joanna replied. "Dave Hollicker will have the Jeep hauled to our impound lot at the Justice Center. I believe a tow truck is en route. I've also made arrangements for one of my on-duty deputies to stay at the campsite overnight. Tomorrow my CSIs will come in, dismantle it, and take everything into evidence."

"Speaking of evidence," Kendra said, reaching into her pocket and pulling out a cell phone wrapped in a clear evidence bag. "When we separated the two bodies, I found this caught between them, and I'm sure that's the only thing that kept it from being smashed to pieces. The problem is, the battery is discharged. It's dead as a doornail."

Joanna held up the bag and peered at the phone. "It's the same model as mine," she said. "I have a charger in the car, but without a pass code, I doubt that charging it will do us any good."

Back at the Yukon, Joanna donned a pair of latex gloves and plugged in the charger. Still inside the evidence bag, the phone came to life with a flashed warning of very low battery life. As expected, a six-number security code was required to access it.

"Do you happen to have Desirée's date of birth?" Joanna asked.

Kendra consulted her notes. "Yes, I do. June sixth, 1990. Why?"

Using the point of a stylus she dug out of her purse, Joanna carefully keyed in the number 060690, and the phone lit up immediately. She went first to the recent calls and found seven in a row from "Mom," all of which had come in the course of the day and had gone unanswered since Desirée was already dead. There was a string of messages, too. No doubt all those calls and messages had contributed to draining the battery.

In the contacts list, Joanna located the ICE category—In Case of Emergency. The top name on the list was Roberta Wilburton along with the same 520 phone number she had found in the recent-calls list. The listing, however, also contained an address: 587 North Fourth Avenue, Tucson, AZ.

Knowing her phone most likely wouldn't function any better than Jaime's had, Joanna climbed inside her Yukon and used the radio to be patched through to Detective Howell. "Is the address you found for Roberta Wilburton at 587 North Fourth?"

"Yes, ma'am," Deb answered. "It sure is. How did you learn that?"

"Dr. Baldwin located a cell phone that belonged to Desirée Wilburton, and I managed to unlock it. Roberta Wilburton's name was at the top of the list with the same phone number as the one listed in recent calls under 'Mom.'"

"Good to know," Deb responded. "I'm just passing the Sonoita turnoff on I-10. I'll get back to you as soon as I've had a chance to speak to the woman. Anything else of interest?"

"Nothing more just now. We'll need to study everything that's on the phone, but not until after we have a properly sworn warrant in hand. In the meantime, an ambulance just arrived to help transport the second body."

"Do you want me to call you tonight or wait until morning?" Deb asked.

"Call tonight," Joanna answered. "I'm planning on going back to the office for a while. I'll be awake."

Again using the stylus, Joanna turned off the phone, removed the charger, and then offered the phone—still in the evidence bag—to Kendra. "Do you want to take this to Ernie or should I?" she asked.

"I'll take charge of it," Kendra said. "In the interest of maintaining the chain of evidence, I'd best be the one who hands it over."

Joanna nodded. "Fair enough," she said.

Standing beside the Yukon, Joanna watched the activity unfolding around her as the second body—she was unsure which one—was loaded into a newly arrived ambulance. Thinking she'd use the relative quiet to update Butch on what was going on, she pulled out her phone. Only when Joanna saw that she had no bars and no service did she remember that Jaime had had to climb partway up Geronimo before he had a signal.

Tom Hadlock turned up about then. "Do you want me to drive you back home or are you going to drive yourself?" he asked. "Deputy Stock is about the head out. I can catch a ride back to the department with him. Tica tells me media calls are already coming in, and I should be there to handle them."

Tica Romero was Joanna's nighttime dispatcher.

"Good thinking," Joanna said. "I'm going to hang around here until the Jeep is towed, then I'll come there, too."

After Tom left with Deputy Stock, Joanna went to the back of the Yukon and rummaged through the box of just-in-case clothing she kept there, retrieving a pair of dry socks and tennis shoes. She had just finished changing out of her still-sodden boots when the tow truck arrived. The driver, Mel Jackson, was an old-timer in coveralls with the stub of a cigar jammed in the corner of his mouth. He got out and surveyed both the wash and the vehicle stranded on the far side of it. Water still ran, but not quite as furiously as it had before. As the sand gradually settled out, the bed of the wash would rise. In the meantime, the two abrupt edges remained, with no gradual way in or out.

"So near and yet so far," Jackson muttered, speaking around his cigar. "If I go off that sheer drop-off, my truck'll land in that sand, come to a dead stop, and won't ever get up the other side. Since I can't get at the Jeep from here, I'll have to come around the long way, past the rifle range."

Joanna knew better than to argue the point. "You and Dave do whatever you have to do."

Mel and Dave Hollicker set off at once. With Deputy Ruiz on hand to oversee the Jeep until they returned and then remain at the crime scene overnight, Joanna headed for the Yukon, intent on going back to the department, when another vehicle arrived on the scene—an all-too-familiar white Toyota RAV4. It pulled in next to her and stopped. The driver darted out onto the ground, leaving the Toyota's engine running and the headlights on. The high beams backlit the wild mane of hair that could belong to only one person, Joanna's least favorite reporter—Marliss Shackleford.

"You've got no business being here," Joanna told the new arrival abruptly. "Chief Deputy Hadlock is on his way back to the department, where he'll be preparing for a press briefing early tomorrow morning. If you're looking for information, that's where you need to be."

"But can't you tell me something tonight—a little something that will give me a head start on everybody else?" Marliss wheedled. "It's the least you can do since I've gone to all the trouble of coming out here. That should count for something."

It counts for your being a total pain in the ass, Joanna thought, but she did her best to keep a civil tongue in her head. "You know the drill, Marliss. Details of the incident will be released once the bodies have been identified and next-of-kin notifications have been made. No information will be provided before that time."

"So you are confirming that there are at least two victims, then?" Marliss asked.

Joanna hadn't meant to acknowledge that. Now, not wanting to give away anything more, she didn't respond one way or the other.

"Where are they?" Marliss persisted.

"The victims are on their way to the morgue," Joanna said. "A vehicle belonging to one of them is about to be towed back to the department, and that's where I'm going, too."

"But didn't I meet a tow truck just now? It was going out as I was coming in?"

"Mel couldn't cross the wash here," Joanna said, gesturing with her Maglite. "He's having to go the long way around."

"I understand all this happened over on Geronimo," Marliss said, looking first at the hillock looming in the background and then peering down into the sandy wash. "How did you get them out?"

"We carried them," Joanna answered. "On stretchers."

"Wouldn't it have been easier to use a helicopter for that kind of operation?" Marliss asked.

Joanna recognized the seemingly innocent question as a minefield the moment she heard it. An organization focused on law enforcement issues along the Mexican border had offered the Cochise County Sheriff's Department a grant that would have paid the entire cost of leasing and operating a helicopter for the period of a year. On the face of it, it was a very generous gesture, but Joanna had turned it down. Accepting it would have been a lot like taking in a free-to-good-home long-legged colt without having any understanding about the long-term implications of caring for and feeding a full-grown horse.

Yes, having the helicopter available tonight would have made retrieving the bodies a much simpler procedure, but after years of running the department, Joanna understood that once the people of Cochise County became accustomed to the idea that the sheriff's department had a helicopter at its disposal, they would expect that availability to continue from one year to the next. The problem was, once the grant ran out, there was no way Joanna's budget could afford such a luxury item without having to take a substantial hit in terms of the number of officers on duty at any given time.

Unfortunately, Donald Hubble, Joanna's opponent in the current reelection cycle had made "revisiting the helicopter decision" a major part of his program and the centerpiece of each campaign speech, although whenever he brought up the subject, he conveniently failed to acknowledge the ongoing budget problems operating the helicopter would entail.

"Since we don't currently have a helicopter, there's no point in debating that issue," Joanna replied. "Now, if you'll excuse me . . ."

But Marliss wasn't finished. "Considering what happened, I'm a little surprised to see you working tonight."

"You're referring to what happened to my mother and George, I suppose?"

"Well, of course."

"What makes you think either one of them would expect me to turn my back on a serious incident like this? My mother would expect me to do the job the people of Cochise County elected me to do, and so would George—George probably even more so. And now, as I said earlier, I have business to attend to."

With that, Joanna climbed into the Yukon, pulled a U-turn, and then drove off, leaving a frustrated Marliss Shackleford standing alone in the desert. Halfway back to town, once Joanna reconnected with the cell-phone network, a whole series of message announcements arrived. Not wanting to hang around long enough for another encounter with Marliss, Joanna continued to drive without stopping to look at any of the incoming messages, but when Butch called, she answered.

"How are things?" he asked.

"I'm on my way back to the office. Two dead females. No sign of a weapon. No immediate signs of wounds on either victim other than what you might expect from falling off a cliff onto a pile of boulders. Could be either a suicide pact or else homicide/suicide. Dr. Baldwin has the first autopsy scheduled for nine A.M. tomorrow. We've got a tentative ID on one of the victims, and Detective Howell is off to Tucson to speak to someone we believe to be that victim's mother."

"I take it I shouldn't wait up," Butch said resignedly.

"Correct," Joanna replied. "The media barrage is already under way, and I expect Tom will need some backup."

"You know my thoughts on that score."

And Joanna did know his thoughts, chapter and verse. Butch firmly believed that Tom Hadlock was incapable of ever growing into the job of chief deputy, especially when it came to handling media relations. Sometimes Joanna thought so as well.

"I know," she agreed, "but one crisis at a time, please."

"Okay," he said. "Don't stay at the office too late. The last few days have been hell on wheels. You need your rest."

"Yes, sir," she said. "Got it. Good night."

"See you in the morning."

CHAPTER 3

DUE TO GEORGE AND ELEANOR'S SUDDEN DEATHS, JOANNA HAD now been out of the office for a solid week. During the years she'd been sheriff, she'd taken a day or two off here and there, but the only times she'd been away for extended periods of time had been when she and Butch had gone on their honeymoon and when Dennis was born. Both times, Frank Montoya had been her chief deputy, and he had carried the load with no difficulty, which probably accounted for why the city of Sierra Vista had lured him away from the sheriff's department to be their chief of police.

Joanna parked in her usual spot behind the building and entered through the private keypad-activated door that opened directly into her office. When she turned on the light and saw stacks of paper covering the entire surface of her desk, she was heartsick. Paperwork was the bane of her existence. It appeared on her desk every day, generally properly organized by her secretary, Kristin Gregovich. Joanna made it a point to handle that day's dose that very day, if possible—but once a week's worth had accumulated, it seemed utterly overwhelming.

Without bothering to touch even so much as a piece of paper, Joanna sat down, pulled out her phone, and looked at her waiting messages. The most recent was from Deb Howell. *Interview with the victim's mother is done. Call me.*

Joanna did so at once. "What's the story?" she asked when Detective Howell answered.

"I don't like doing next-of-kin notifications," Deb said.

Having recently been on the receiving end of one of those, Joanna understood why. "Nobody does," she murmured. "They're no fun."

"No," Deb agreed. "Not at all, especially since Desirée was Roberta's only child. She was evidently a brilliant girl. Somewhere along the way, the husband and father announced that now that his daughter was grown, he had lived a lie long enough. He was gay and he was out of there. See ya."

"Tough on everybody involved," Joanna said.

"Roberta took her divorce settlement, hired a mover, and came west to join her daughter. She had enough money that she probably could have bought a house up in the foothills. Instead, she purchased a run-down apartment house on Fourth Avenue—a place that had been a mansion back in the early 1900s which had later been carved into separate units. Roberta paid cash for the place and then rehabbed it from top to bottom. In the process, she created separate living spaces for both her daughter and herself, along with three additional efficiency units that, because of the house's proximity to the university, she's able to rent out with no difficulty."

"Sounds like a smart woman as well as a smart daughter," Joanna observed, "but what's a microbiologist doing camping out at the base of Geronimo?"

"Studying hedgehog cactus," Deb answered. "Fendler's hedgehog in particular."

"Never heard of it," Joanna replied.

"Roberta told me about them. They're sort of like barrel cactus, only skinnier. From what I understand, when it comes to being studied, cactus are pretty low on the totem pole. They've been sorted out and given names and species assignments based on a somewhat arbitrary basis without taking into consideration differences in genetic makeup between samples that are similar but should have been assigned to an altogether different species."

"This whole discussion is over my pay grade," Joanna said, "and what does the Finger's hedgehog—"

"Fendler's," Deb corrected.

"What does whatever it is have to do with our victim?"

"Desirée Wilburton has spent most of the summer traveling and camping in southeastern Arizona and southwestern New Mexico taking DNA samples of whatever Fendler's hedgehogs she could find. She called her mother two days ago and was really excited. Desirée said she had climbed to the top of a small knoll near Bisbee and found a group of cactus that were so isolated from any others growing in the nearby desert that she thought she may have stumbled upon a brand-new species. Desirée told her mother that she was calling from up on the knoll itself because she didn't have any cell service down at her campsite."

"That's for sure," Joanna said.

"That phone call, made about four o'clock on Friday afternoon, was the last time Roberta heard from her daughter. She said Desirée usually called her on Sundays when she'd go into town long enough to clean up, buy groceries, and do laundry. When she didn't call on Sunday, Roberta didn't worry about it all that much because her daughter had, what she called, an independent streak. But then today, when Roberta realized she hadn't heard a word since Friday, she did start worrying—afraid that something out of the ordinary might have happened—that Desirée might have taken a fall or been bitten by a rattlesnake, something that has actually happened on two previous occasions."

"Two rattlesnake bites and she was still out camping on her own?" Joanna said. "Not only did Desirée have an independent streak, she must have been tough as nails."

"I'll say," Deb agreed. "Rattlesnakes scare the hell out of me. Anyway, Roberta had made up her mind that if she didn't hear something from Desirée by tomorrow morning, she was going to run up the flag to us and ask us to go looking."

"Which was at least three days too late," Joanna said.

"Did Dr. Baldwin give you a preliminary time of death?"

"Estimated only, sometime Saturday night or early Sunday morning. Autopsies are scheduled starting tomorrow, nine A.M. Did Roberta mention anything about her daughter being involved in any kind of romantic relationship?"

"She told me some but not much," Deb replied. "Desirée was engaged last year to a fellow grad student. He got his Ph.D. and went off to work in Australia. She wanted to finish her degree and wasn't all that wild about Australia, so they broke off the engagement. The way Roberta told it, I gathered that the breakup was fairly low-key and amicable—no huge drama. I have the ex-fiancé's contact info, though, and I'll be verifying that he was safely on the other side of the pond when all this went down."

"Any hints from the mother that Desirée might be AC/DC and play both sides of the fence?"

"No, none," Deb replied. "Why?"

"That's Ernie's pet theory at the moment—that the two victims were involved in some kind of romantic relationship. Once we have a warrant and gain access to Desirée's phone records, they may lead us directly to the identity of the second victim."

"Have you checked missing-persons reports?" Deb asked.

"We have. So far there's nothing showing in our department," Joanna said, "but as soon as you and I are off the phone, I'll have someone do some checking with other nearby jurisdictions. I'm also expecting Dr. Baldwin to send fingerprint info any moment—if she can lift them, that is. With any kind of luck, that may lead to an identification on victim number two."

There was a lull in the conversation. "I'm sort of surprised that you're working tonight," Deb said tentatively.

"Funny," Joanna replied. "That's the same thing Marliss Shackleford said to me a little while ago, and I'll tell you the same thing I told her. Neither my mother nor George would want me to turn my back on the job I was elected to do—no matter what.

"They're gone, Deb," Joanna continued. "George and Eleanor Winfield are no more. I've already been off work for more than a week. My staying home any longer or maybe taking to my bed isn't going to do a thing to bring them back. Believe me, I shed buckets of tears before Butch and I ever came home from Sedona after the shooting. As far as I'm concerned, I'm all cried out. I also spent the afternoon making funeral arrangements. So right now, when I suspect I won't be able to sleep anyway, I'm better off being here, wading through paperwork and keeping an eye on the investigation, than I would be at home, tossing and turning and accomplishing nothing."

"Got it," Deb said. "I hear you loud and clear."

"But thanks for your concern," Joanna added. "I really do appreciate it."

"If you're going to be at the office, do you want me to come by there when I get to town?"

"Go on home," Joanna urged. "I believe the Double C's are going to handle the autopsy situation. We'll have a briefing here about noon tomorrow to figure out what's to be done."

"Okay," Deb said. "Good night."

Joanna hung up the phone and turned to the papers littering her desk. Front and center was a stack of yellow sticky phone messages. Leafing through them, she discovered they were all condolence calls of one kind or another from people who didn't necessarily have access to either her home or mobile number. Next to the messages was a pile of sympathy cards as well. Kristin had already slit open all the envelopes. Joanna went through the cards one by one, reading the thoughtful notes that often accompanied them. Most were from people who had been friends of her mother's rather than friends of Joanna's, but many of them expressed similar sentiments, saying how proud Eleanor had been of her daughter and of the great job she had been doing as sheriff of Cochise County.

Instead of offering comfort, the messages in the notes did the exact opposite. They made Joanna cry again. If Eleanor Lathrop Winfield had been so busy telling her friends how proud she was of her daughter, why had she never expressed those same sentiments to Joanna herself? Joanna and her mother had been at odds for much of Joanna's life. Recently, she had hoped they were finally moving beyond all that old stuff, but now Eleanor's sudden death had obliterated all opportunities for long-term détente. And that was what Joanna grieved for more than anything—that the closeness she had one day hoped to achieve with her mother would never happen.

Her e-mail notification alert sounded, first once and immediately thereafter a second time. Unlike paper communications, she'd been able to respond to online ones on the fly, so the listing of unanswered messages had only started earlier this afternoon when she had shut off her phone before entering the mortuary. The sender of the two most recent messages was Kendra Baldwin, copying Joanna with the same sets of computerized fingerprint images the ME was sending to Casey Ledford.

Joanna picked up her phone and dialed the lab. Casey answered immediately. "Just wanted you to know that I'm in my office if you get any hits on the prints," Joanna said.

"I'm looking at them now," Casey replied. "Dr. Baldwin does good work. These will require only minimal enhancement before I submit them to AFIS. I'll let you know if anything pops."

"Great," Joanna said.

"And how are you?"

Same question but slightly different words. In this case "How are you?" substituted for "Why the hell are you working when your mom just died?" But Joanna's people were all concerned about her well-being, and she could hardly fault them for that.

"Okay," Joanna answered. "Hanging in."

"It's got to be tough."

"Yes, it is," Joanna agreed, "but I'm better off working than I am not working."

Once off the phone, Joanna asked the nighttime watch commander to have someone check the missing-persons situation. Then she turned to the mess on her desk. She moved the condolence messages and cards off to the side to be dealt with later, then she waded into the paperwork jungle, scanning through summaries of briefings and police reports. There was nothing outrageous—mostly traffic stops along with a few domestic violence situations. The fates had held off on dealing Cochise County a possible double homicide card until Joanna at least was back in town.

Tom had sorted the end-of-the-year vacation schedule requests, making sure that shifts would still be adequately covered over the holidays. He had attended the board-of-supervisors meeting in her absence and had come away with a voluminous set of notes. He had approved jail menus for all of September, and had interviewed several people and narrowed the field from ten down to two for the soon-to-be-vacant position of head cook in the jail. Joanna had just launched into her nondepartmental correspondence—including a request for her to speak at the next meeting of the newly formed National Association of Female Sheriffs—when her phone rang.

"Got something," Casey said.

"I'll be right there," Joanna answered. Abandoning her desk, she hurried down the corridor to the lab. It was close to midnight by then, but Casey Ledford was still on the job and so was Dave Hollicker.

"What?" Joanna said.

"Look at this," Casey said, turning on her PowerPoint and projecting two-foot-high images of two fingerprints onto a screen over a worktable. "What do you think?" she asked.

"They look the same to me," Joanna said.

"That's because they are the same—the print from the right-hand index finger of the unidentified victim. When I ran Dr. Baldwin's prints through AFIS, I got nothing," Casey explained. "Then I tried the FBI's Integrated Fingerprint Identification System. And voilà—here were are—Susan Marie Nelson, of 4440 East Busby Drive, Sierra Vista, AZ. Her prints went into the system during a routine background check for something called the Sierra Vista School for Scholastic Excellence. It says here that she's married to one Drexel Maynard Nelson of the same address."

"By the way," Dave Hollicker put in, speaking from behind a computer screen that completely obscured his face. "The SVSSE is a charter school that's been in business for about ten years now. Very highly rated. They've walked off with the title for the Arizona Debate Team Challenge three out of the past five years. I only mention that because Susan Marie Nelson is listed as the debate coach."

"This is Monday night," Joanna said thinking aloud. "The victim died on Saturday or Sunday at the latest. Has anyone filed a missing-persons report, and if not, why not?"

"No missing-persons reports so far," Casey answered. "Someone already checked."

"And there's no mistake about the ID on this," Joanna said, reaching for a phone. "The print for sure belongs to Susan Marie Nelson?"

"Yes," Casey said. "I ran it by a criminalist at the crime lab up in Tucson just to be sure."

"All right, then," Joanna said, dialing Detective Howell's number. "Are you back yet?"

"Close," Deb answered. "I'm on the far side of the divide. How come?"

"Don't go home," Joanna advised. "I'll need you to come to the department. You have another next of kin to do tonight, and I'm doing a ride-along."

"You've identified the second victim?"

"We believe so. Casey made the ID using fingerprints from an old background check. The victim's name is Susan Marie Nelson. She's a married teacher at a charter school in Sierra Vista."

"If she's married, why no missing-persons report?" Deb asked.

"That's exactly what I want to know," Joanna said, "and I'm going to wake up Sierra Vista's chief of police and ask him the same question."

"Won't Frank Montoya mind your dragging him out of bed at this ungodly hour?"

"He'll mind a lot more if we end up conducting an investigation inside his jurisdiction without letting him know beforehand."

"Okay," Deb said. "See you as soon as I can get there."

"Thanks, guys," Joanna said to Dave and Casey. "You did good work."

Back in the corridor, she located Frank's cell number and punched it. A very groggy Frank Montoya answered. "Hello."

"Sorry to wake you," Joanna said. "Hope I didn't disturb anyone else."

"LuAnn's at the hospital," Frank said. "And the kids could sleep through an atomic bomb blast."

Joanna always blamed the city of Sierra Vista for luring Frank away from her department, but the situation was more complicated than just a job offer. Frank had fallen hard for and married Dr. LuAnn Marcowitz, an emergency room physician at the hospital in town. And the kids in question were LuAnn's two teenagers, Greta and Gabriel.

"So what's up?" Frank asked.

"We're investigating a suspected double homicide that happened east of Warren. We're pretty sure both victims died sometime Saturday night or Sunday morning. Fingerprints have identified one of them as being a Sierra Vista resident named Susan Marie Nelson, but we can't find any trace of a missing-persons report."

"Crap!" Frank Montoya muttered.

"What do you mean, 'crap'?" Joanna asked.

"Reverend Nelson tried to file a missing-persons report on Sunday afternoon after church, but when he started filling us in on the details, the detective taking the information determined that it was likely his wife had gone off on her own. The detective is the one who made the call not to file the report until after my department's suggested forty-eight-hour wait had elapsed."

"Did you say *Reverend* Nelson?" Joanna asked.

"Yes, Drexel Nelson runs a small nondenominational church called Holy Redeemer Chapel out of a mobile home on Busby Drive here in town. Susan is his wife."

"Filling in what details exactly?" Joanna asked.

"The marriage has evidently been going through a rough patch. Reverend Nelson told my detective, Ian Waters, that he and Susan had a huge quarrel on Saturday afternoon. Not quite knock-down-and-drag-out, but close. At least that's how he described it. He said she left the house in a huff to go to school for a tutoring session and never came home. Based on that information, Ian concluded that it was likely she had gone missing of her own volition."

"The school in question being the Sierra Vista School for Scholastic Excellence?" Joanna asked.

"That's the one. She teaches there—taught there—during the

school year and held weekend tutoring sessions with students from there on a year-round basis. Detective Waters did have a patrol car go by the school to check. No sign of her vehicle. When he mentioned the situation to me, I couldn't fault his assumption that Susan Nelson probably went off on her own somewhere to cool off."

"And ended up getting murdered," Joanna observed. "As for Reverend Nelson? What did he have to say concerning his whereabouts on Saturday and Sunday?"

"Claimed he was home alone on Saturday night, working on his sermon, and on Sunday morning he was at church."

"So once the ME gives a time of death, it's likely he has no alibi," Joanna asserted.

"Not so much," Frank agreed.

"Deb Howell is coming by the department to pick me up, then we'll be coming your way to do the next of kin. Given the couple's marital history, this incident may or may not have started inside your city limits. For the time being, however, we should probably consider it a joint investigation. You might want to have one of your detectives on hand at the upcoming interview. What was the name you just mentioned?"

"Waters—Detective Ian Waters. When are you coming?"

"As soon as Deb gets back from Tucson, where she went to speak to someone we now know to be the other victim's mother. Deb should be here any minute."

"Okay," Frank said. "I'll call Ian and let him know you're on your way, then we'll saddle up and meet you there. The house isn't easy to find. It's set way back on what looks like a vacant lot. The church is right next door, and you access the driveway to the house from the back of the church parking lot."

"See you there," Joanna said. She had returned to her own office by then. As she ended the call with Frank, Deb Howell appeared in her doorway.

"Knock, knock," the detective said.

Joanna glanced down at her uniform. It was a little the worse for wear, having been through both water and mud as Joanna went back and forth to the crime scene. With her still sodden boots in the luggage compartment of the Yukon, she was dressed in a pair of shabby and very unofficial-looking tennis shoes, but at this point, she was reluctant to go home to change into anything else. If she stopped by in the middle of the night, she'd probably wake the whole household.

"Let's go," she said. "I don't exactly look my best, but I doubt Reverend Nelson is going to be studying my feet."

"My car or yours?"

"Yours," Joanna said. "I have a few calls to make, starting with Dr. Baldwin. She doesn't yet know that we've managed to identify the second victim."

CHAPTER 4

DURING THE HALF-HOUR DRIVE FROM BISBEE TO SIERRA VISTA, JOanna's first call was to the ME. Her second was to Chief Deputy Hadlock, letting him know that both victims had now been positively identified and that next-of-kin notifications either had been or were in the process of being done. She knew this would make a huge difference in the kind of briefing paper he was preparing for release the next morning. Tom sent her a copy of his rough draft of the press release. Feeling like one of her old high school English teachers, Joanna edited it on her iPad, going through the material sentence by sentence, correcting grammar and making suggestions to improve the flow. Butch was right, of course. Media relations would never be Tom's strong suit.

Once that was done, Joanna leaned back in her seat, closed her eyes, and actually dozed off for a moment while the GPS in

Deb's dash guided them to the address for Holy Redeemer Chapel on Busby Drive. When the car came to a stop, Joanna started awake and saw that they had pulled up next to a solitary streetlight standing in a bare dirt parking lot. A humble three-foot-tall wooden sign, painted white with black letters, said HOLY REDEEMER CHAPEL. In much smaller letters in the bottom right hand corner were the words *visitors welcome*. Behind it sat a fourteen-by-seventy mobile home—a single-wide. How that functioned as a place of worship was more than Joanna could imagine.

Two unmarked Sierra Vista cop cars pulled up silently beside them. Frank Montoya exited one and came over to knock on the passenger window of Deb's marked Tahoe. Joanna buzzed down the window.

"Sorry to hear about your folks," Frank said. "Should you even be working?"

Joanna sighed. "Thank you," she said, "and yes, I should be working. I'm pretty sure that given the circumstances, you would be, too."

Frank thought about that for a moment before he nodded. "Okay, then. We'll lead you over to the house. Since Reverend Nelson knows Ian, we'll have him knock on the door and introduce you. After that, it's up to you."

"Deb has already done one notification tonight, so I'll handle this one," Joanna said. "It's only fair."

When the other two vehicles pulled out, Deb's Tahoe fell into line behind them. Joanna couldn't help but notice, somewhat enviously, that both Sierra Vista PD vehicles were sleek, almost new, all-wheel-drive Ford Interceptors. Deb's aging Tahoe was almost an antique by comparison, but then the sheriff's department wasn't nearly as flush with cash, and Joanna's people had to deal with far more rugged terrain.

They drove to the far end of the lot and then onto a narrow dirt track that led to a house. It was a small wooden affair, long and narrow, and painted white. It was about the same proportions as the church itself, only this one sat on a permanent foundation. As headlights lit up the house, Joanna noted the old-fashioned windows and doors, realizing that the reasonably well-maintained house, sitting in the middle of a mostly empty block, probably predated the city by decades. Joanna suspected that the structure had been part of the local landscape during the lean years some sixty years earlier when Fort Huachuca had been a shuttered derelict and the sleepy town next door had been called Fry rather than the sprawling bustle of current-day Sierra Vista.

Once the three pairs of headlights shut down, it was clear there were no lights visible inside the house. "If Reverend Nelson is sitting up worrying about his missing wife," Deb observed dryly, "he's doing so in the dark."

The sarcasm in the remark was obvious. "Sounds like you've already made up your mind," Joanna replied.

Deb shrugged. "He's the husband," she said. "It's always the husband. Shall we?"

They got out of the Tahoe together, slamming their doors in unison. At once a window toward the back of the house lit up. By the time Joanna and Deb followed Detective Waters up onto the small front porch, lights had come on in what, through gauzy sheer curtains, was clearly the living room. Detective Waters barely had time to tap once on the door before the porch light next to it flashed on and the door flew open.

"Did you find her, Detective Waters?" demanded a man dressed in a pair of blue-and-white pajamas.

"Sorry to disturb you," Ian said respectfully. "These are Sheriff Joanna Brady and Detective Deb Howell with the Cochise County Sheriff's Department. And this is Frank Montoya, Sierra Vista's chief of police. May we come in?"

Reverend Nelson glanced back over his shoulder as though looking for a reason to say no. A moment later, though, he stepped back and opened the door wider, allowing them entrance, eyeing each of them suspiciously as they walked past. "You still haven't answered my question," he grumbled. "What's this all about?"

"You may want to take a seat, Reverend Nelson," Joanna began. "I'm afraid we have some very bad news."

"She's dead, then?" he asked.

Joanna nodded. "I'm so sorry for your loss," she said.

Joanna remembered all too clearly exactly what had happened to her when Jaime Carbajal had shown up at her house a little more than a week ago to deliver the terrible news that George Winfield was dead and her mother gravely wounded. That news had come completely out of the blue, and it had hit her so hard that it had been all she could do to remain upright. Since Susan Nelson had been missing for several days, news that she was dead might not come as a total shock. Nonetheless, Joanna expected some kind of emotional outburst from the bereaved husband. That wasn't what she got.

"All right," Reverend Nelson said, nodding. "All right, then." He stepped farther into the room, lowered himself into a nearby rocking chair, and gestured for his visitors to take seats themselves in a tiny room stuffed with too many pieces of oversized furniture.

"All right?" a dismayed Joanna asked, settling in the easy chair closest to his rocker. "What do you mean by 'all right'?"

"'Let no man put asunder,'" he intoned.

"You mean you and Susan were married 'until death do you part'?"

"Exactly," he responded, without the slightest trace of grief. "Susan was out there doing all kinds of ungodly things and wouldn't consider atoning for her sins. She refused to go even so far as to pray for forgiveness. Our Lord may be able to forgive Susan her sins, and maybe eventually I will be able to as well. Right now, though, there's no forgiveness in my heart. None. She betrayed me, and what I'm feeling is something close to relief, now that I know she's dead. I suppose I could have divorced her, you see. In fact, I probably should have divorced her—but then I wouldn't have been practicing what I preach, now would I. And all those people sitting there in the pews listening to my sermons would have been able to call me a hypocrite, and rightly so."

Reverend Nelson leaned back in his chair and studied Joanna expectantly while she studied him in return. He was a paunchy man, with a balding pate and sagging features. From the looks of him, Joanna placed him as being somewhere in his early fifties, which would have made him a good fifteen years older than his late wife.

"Well?" he demanded impatiently. "Are you going to tell me what happened or are we just going to sit around the rest of the night looking at one another? I suppose Susan must have totaled her car someplace, hopefully not with one of her lovers right there in the car with her. That wouldn't surprise me, though, not a bit. What can you expect from such a shameless hussy?"

This was unlike any next-of-kin notification Joanna had ever done. The anger and bitterness in the air were almost palpable. Even family members who eventually turned out to be killers usually had the good sense to at least pretend to be grief stricken. There was no such charade going on here. Reverend Drexel Nelson was pissed. He wasn't going to take it anymore, and he was obviously happy to have been spared the shameful necessity of publicly divorcing an erring spouse.

Was that enough to turn him into a suspect? Joanna wondered. Absolutely, especially since the man had already admitted to someone else that he had no alibi for the time when the murders were thought to have taken place. Right now, though, in the midst of what was clearly a next-of-kin interview, Joanna was under no obligation to tell him that he had just landed on the suspect side of the equation. In fact, her purpose now was to keep him talking for as long as possible.

Joanna glanced in Deb Howell's direction, and gave her a nod. To her relief, the detective pulled out her cell phone and adjusted it before replying with an answering nod. The unspoken message that had passed between them meant that from this moment on, the next-of-kin interview would be recorded.

"The reason Chief Montoya and myself, along with Detectives Waters and Howell, are here tonight is not only to deliver this news but to learn whatever you can tell us about your wife's last days as well as about her friends and associates—anything at all that would help us determine who might be responsible for what happened."

Reverend Nelson nodded. "Of course," he said. "I understand."

"That being said," Joanna continued, "do you have any idea of someone who might wish to harm your wife?"

"Besides me, you mean?"

"Yes," Joanna said. "Besides you."

"Not really," he said with a shrug. "Maybe one of her boyfriends. I know she's had several, but for the most part, I don't know who they are."

"For the most part?" Joanna echoed.

"I know that for a while she was whoring around with the guy who used to be the principal of the school where she works, but he left town two years ago. She wasn't his only interest, and the board gave him a choice of leaving or being fired for cause."

"It turns out your wife wasn't with another man when she died," Joanna said. "She was with a woman. Both victims died at approximately the same time on Saturday night or Sunday morning. They were found at the base of a steep cliff east of Warren."

Reverend Nelson's jaw literally dropped. "Another woman? Are you serious?" He ran one hand across his forehead in apparent disbelief. "I never saw that one coming. Who was she?"

"A graduate student from the University of Arizona. Her name is Desirée Wilburton, and she was a doctoral candidate in microbiology. Have you ever heard the name? Do you know of any connection between them?"

Reverend Nelson shook his head. "Never heard of her. I have no idea how they might be connected."

"So as far as you know, your wife's extramarital interests didn't extend to other women?"

"I knew there were men involved, but nothing about any women."

"How did you know?" Joanna asked.

"Easy," he said. "I had a headache one day and went looking

for a bottle of aspirin. There weren't any in the bathroom, so I checked Susan's bedside table, and that's where I stumbled on a boxful of condoms. That's what gave me my first clue. Now, I ask you, why would the wife of a man who had a vasectomy twenty-five years ago need to have a supply of condoms on hand? Once I knew that, everything went downhill. Oh, she still showed up at church every Sunday, sitting there in the second row, smiling up at me like she was sweetness and light itself. Sometimes it was all I could do to remember where I was in the service let alone stay on track during the sermons."

"When was the last time you saw her?"

"Saturday afternoon. We were out working in the yard. She was wearing skimpy shorts and a too-tight tank top. I told her she needed to go inside and change. I suggested that it was about time she figured out that she wasn't a teenager any longer and maybe she should start dressing accordingly. I also told her that just because she was acting like a whore didn't mean she should dress like one. She drove off in a huff."

I wonder why? Joanna thought. "Did she say where she was going?"

"She didn't have to. I knew where she was going," Reverend Nelson replied. "To school. She did tutoring sessions there most Saturdays, working primarily with kids from her debate team. She was the debate coach, you see, and one of the reasons her teams always won is that she worked with them on a year-round basis, even during summer and winter vacations."

"The students she generally worked with," Joanna said. "Do you happen to know any of them by name?"

Reverend Nelson shook his head. "Nope. She mostly talked about them by first names only—Jimmy, Patrick, Bobby, Rochelle, Andrew. For all I know, that could be last year's team rather than this year's. You'd have to check with someone at the school to find out the names of the kids on this year's team."

"We'll do that," Joanna said. "How long has she been at SVSSE?"

"About eight years now, I think. She had worked as a substitute teacher there and at other schools in the area while she was working on her degrees. Once she had her master's degree, they hired her full-time."

"How old was your wife?" Joanna asked the question even though she already knew the answer

"Thirty-six."

"And how long have the two of you been married?"

For the first time in the whole process, Reverend Nelson looked somewhat uncomfortable. He squirmed in the chair and rocked several times before he answered. "Twenty years," he said finally.

"You married her when she was sixteen?"

Reverend Nelson nodded.

"Her family kicked her out when she was only fourteen. She showed up at the church, homeless and destitute. My first wife and I took her in and gave her a place to live. And then things just . . . well, you know . . . sort of got out of hand."

"Your first wife's name?" Joanna inquired.

"Anna," he said.

"So you and Susan had an affair?"

"We fell in love, but I never touched her. Not like that—not once before we married. Anna could see where things were going, though, and so she left. She went home to her family in Michigan and got a divorce, which I didn't contest, by the way."

"You said you and your wife gave Susan a home. Does that mean she lived with you?"

"Yes," he said. "Right here in the second bedroom."

"Did she continue to live here after Anna left?"

"Yes, but as I said before, nothing untoward happened between us until our wedding night. I made sure of that."

Of course you did, Joanna thought. Her initial opinion of Drexel Nelson which had been low to begin with nosedived to reprehensible. A homeless juvenile had shown up on the good reverend's doorstep, seeking help, and he had taken unfair advantage of the situation. There were many ways for a thirtysomething adult male to manipulate an impressionable teenager without necessarily taking her to bed right off the bat.

"What about her parents?" Joanna asked. "What became of them? They should be notified as well."

"Roger and Phyllis Judson," Reverend Nelson said at once. "He was in the military—stationed here at Fort Huachuca. They got transferred to another post shortly after they parted company with their daughter."

"Where are they now?"

"I have no idea."

"Susan made no attempt to reconcile with them or to get back in touch?"

"They didn't exactly part on the best of terms."

"You said they threw her out. Why?"

"They said she was defiant—out of control. She'd been hanging out with a bad crowd, ditching school, doing drugs, getting into all kinds of devilment."

"Including trouble with the law?"

"Some," he acknowledged.

"As in sent to juvie?"

"Yes," he answered, "but after she got her GED and was an honors student at the U of A, I was able to have her record expunged."

"Which is how she was able to pass the background check for teaching?"

"Exactly."

"She went back to school after you married?"

"Yes, I insisted on it. And for a while everything was fine."

"But then it stopped being fine?"

"Yes."

"Why?" Joanna asked.

Reverend Nelson looked uneasily from Joanna to Deb Howell. "Do I really have to talk about this?"

"We're trying to solve your wife's homicide," Joanna said. "We need to know as much as there is to know."

Nelson sighed. "When we started out, she was sixteen and I was thirty-one. At the time, the age difference didn't seem like such a big deal. But a few years ago, I developed . . . well . . . a bit of a problem. Not fatal, and something a little blue pill can fix, but they're very expensive. That's when things started going downhill.

"At first I tried to see things through her point of view. After all, she was a young woman and sex had always been important to her—to us. I thought if she strayed on occasion, it might not be that big a deal. Then I found the condoms and hit the roof. She had them hidden right there in the bedroom, and I felt like she was rubbing my nose in it. That's when I reminded her of her wedding vows. I told her my problem was the sickness part of 'in sickness and in health.'"

He paused and closed his eyes. "You know what she told me?"

"What?"

"If I thought she was going to go the rest of her life living without sex, I could go straight to hell, and I have been. I've been living in hell ever since."

For the first time in the whole interview, Reverend Nelson shuddered and broke into sobs. Not, Joanna noted, because he was sorry for his dead wife but because he was sorry for himself. She waited until he quieted and blew his nose into a hankie he had extracted from the breast pocket of his PJs.

"How long ago did you find the condoms?" she asked.

"Three years."

"Before or after Susan's affair with the principal?"

"Before."

Joanna rose to her feet and motioned to the others to do the same. "Do you have someone we could call to come be with you?"

"No, I'll be fine."

"We should go, then," she said. "In the meantime, please accept our condolences. If we require any more information, we'll be in touch."

Reverend Nelson didn't move from his rocker. Joanna and the others let themselves out, closing the door behind them before huddling next to their collection of parked cars.

"I think Reverend Nelson could bear a whole lot more scrutiny," Ian Waters said. "Three years is a long time to be packing that kind of grudge. I think he may have finally snapped."

"Okay," Joanna said as weariness suddenly overwhelmed her. "If it's okay to have Detective Waters on board, what about if we gather at my office tomorrow around noon. By then the autopsies should be complete. Maybe by then we'll be able to come up with some kind of game plan. Right now I'm done for."

"Sounds good to me," Chief Montoya said. "And as far as Detective Waters is concerned, for the time being, consider him yours."

CHAPTER 5

JOANNA AWAKENED TO THE SMELL OF FRYING BACON AND EGGS. IN the past there would have been a background aroma of brewing coffee as well. Not now, however, and not in the immediate future, either. Most of Joanna's early-pregnancy morning-sickness symptoms had abated—except for her inability to tolerate the smell or taste of coffee. As a consequence, Butch and she had recently agreed to stick to tea for the duration of her pregnancy.

That morning, for once, Joanna didn't have to worry about being late. She had left a note at the office letting Kristin know that she wouldn't be in until later in the morning—after the autopsies were over and just in time for the noontime task force meeting. That was no accident on her part. She had timed her arrival to be well after the end of Tom Hadlock's ten A.M. press briefing. Not having to encounter Marliss Shackleford played a big part in Joanna's scheduling decision.

Instead of rushing into the bathroom to shower and dress, she pulled on a robe and went to the kitchen. Denny, as Dennis preferred to be called, had graduated from a makeshift booster seat on the breakfast nook's wooden bench (a ten-pound copy of Butch's *Webster's International* third edition) to just the bench itself. His abandoned high chair, a harbinger of things to come, lurked in the corner of the kitchen.

Butch handed Joanna a cup of hot presweetened tea on her way to the nook. Slipping onto the bench next to her son, she watched as Dennis drew pictures on his plate with pieces of ketchup-drenched scrambled eggs before popping them into his mouth. Weeks earlier the sight of scrambled eggs and ketchup would have turned her stomach on end.

"You got in late," Butch observed mildly, putting an egg-laden plate in front of her.

Joanna nodded. "After midnight. Casey Ledford was able to get a positive ID on the second victim. It turns out she'd gone missing from Sierra Vista on Saturday afternoon. Deb Howell and I drove out to do the next of kin."

Butch went back to the stove, flipped another set of over-easy eggs with practiced ease, and slid them onto a plate. That was what he had been doing years earlier when he and Joanna had first met. He'd been the short-order cook in a restaurant he had owned, the Round House Bar and Grill in Peoria, Arizona, near Phoenix. Newly elected sheriff and determined to become a fully qualified police officer, Joanna had sent herself off for a law enforcement training course at the nearby Arizona Police Academy. At the time, the last thing she had expected was that she would walk into a restaurant, meet someone, fall in love, and get married again. But as she sopped up the yolk from her perfectly done over-easy eggs, she couldn't help but be thankful. Marrying a talented cook certainly had its merits.

Butch set down his own plate and cup of tea and then took his place next to Joanna. "Your brother called to give me their ETA," he said. "He and Marcie are due to fly into Tucson from DC about four this afternoon. They're renting a car and coming straight here. They've booked a room at the Copper Queen until Sunday. Bob wanted to take us to dinner at Café Roka tonight, but I told him since it's Tuesday and the restaurant isn't open, we'll have steaks here. He said that was fine as long as he can treat tomorrow night. We'll get Carol to look after Denny, so it'll be an all grown-up evening."

"I want to go, too," Denny said, pouting. "Why can't I go?"

"Because your mom will need to have some time with her brother," Butch explained. "And she won't need you interrupting every two minutes. They'll most likely be discussing the wills."

"Right," Joanna said sarcastically, "it's going to be just peachy."

Always attuned to his mother's moods and tones, Dennis looked quickly from Joanna to Butch. "What's a will?" he asked.

"Never mind," Butch answered. "None of your beeswax. Now, if you're done eating, clear your plate and go brush your teeth. We need to head out to school in five. Kindergarten isn't like preschool, where you could show up whenever you wanted to. Now you have to be there when the bell rings or else your teacher marks you tardy."

Without further objection, Denny did as he was told. Not only was Butch a great cook, Joanna thought, he was also a terrific father.

"With everything that's going on, I'm not sure that I'm up to dealing with Bob and Marcie today," Joanna said. "Couldn't we put them off until tomorrow?"

"Look," Butch said. "I know how much it hurt your feelings that Bob was privy to some of Eleanor and George's final wishes when you weren't. And I also know what a big deal it is that they named him to serve as their executor instead of you, but if you want to have any kind of relationship with your brother in the future, you need to get over these hurdles, the sooner the better."

My brother, Joanna thought bitterly. *I think I liked it better when I didn't know I even* had *a brother.*

Butch was right, of course. Learning from Burton Kimball, the local attorney who had drawn up George and Eleanor's new wills, that Bob would serve as both of their executors had been yet another bitter pill to swallow.

"Why should I have a relationship with him?" Joanna demanded. "He's my mother's son—my mother's 'perfect' son," she added, drawing air quotation marks around the word "perfect." "He's got nothing to do with me."

"He's your father's son, too," Butch reminded her. "Stop building a case. Like it or not, Bob Brundage is a blood relation, and I think it's ill-advised to cut him out of our lives."

For the better part of thirty years, Joanna Brady had thought of herself as an only child. Always at odds with her mother, she had been the apple of her father's eye right up until Sheriff D.H. Lathrop's supposedly accidental death at the hands of a drunk driver while Joanna was still in high school. Her father's untimely demise did nothing to improve her testy relationship with her mother. In fact, it had taken a turn for the worse as a headstrong Joanna began acting out against what she regarded as her mother's too-restrictive parenting style.

Part of that rebellion had included Joanna's decision to start dating Andrew Roy Brady, a local guy much older than she. In no time at all, at age seventeen, she found herself unmarried and pregnant while still in high school. There was never any question about Andy's "doing the right thing." They had married in time for their wedding to predate Jenny's birth, but only just barely, and the shame of what Eleanor called "your shotgun wedding" was something she had chided Joanna about for years.

Bob Brundage had first appeared in Joanna's life while she was in Peoria, Arizona, undergoing her police academy training. Spotting him as he approached her across a hotel lobby, Joanna had been shocked. He had looked so much like her father that for a moment she had thought she was seeing a ghost.

But Bob wasn't a ghost. He was, in fact, the spitting image of his biological father, who, she soon learned, also happened to be Joanna's father. As the story gradually emerged, Joanna had finally understood why Eleanor Lathrop had been so upset by her daughter's unwed pregnancy—Joanna had unwittingly been following in her mother's footsteps.

When Eleanor had turned up pregnant in high school, her parents had shipped her off someplace back east to have the baby, who was immediately put up for adoption. When Eleanor returned home, her parents had forbidden their disgraced daughter to have anything to do with D.H. Instead, the two of them had continued to date in secret and had married, against Eleanor's parents' wishes, the moment the bride turned eighteen and no longer needed parental permission. Her parents had responded by disowning their daughter completely, all of which went a long way to explain why Joanna had grown up with zero contact with her maternal grandparents.

Bob had been raised in a loving adoptive family. He had grown up, enrolled in ROTC in college, and joined the military. He had been a full colonel and nearing retirement when both of his adoptive parents had passed away within months of one another. Then, and only then, had he come looking for his birth parents, and Eleanor had welcomed him with open arms.

Try as she might, Joanna could never quite get beyond her resentment of her mother's hypocrisy—her insistence that Joanna should never have gotten pregnant in the first place—all the while completely disregarding and not owning up to what she and D. H. Lathrop themselves had done all those years earlier.

After Bob's surprising entrance into Joanna's life, she had maintained a cordial but rather distant relationship with him—an acquaintance relationship, really, one where they sent each other Christmas cards, but that was about it. Meanwhile her mother had gone completely gaga over the man. Once she and George married, the two of them had visited with Bob and Marcie on several occasions. Each time they had returned home with a slew of vacation photos and stories, Joanna had found herself growing more and more resentful. Why was it Eleanor was so completely enamored of a son who had been absent from her life for most of his while constantly criticizing and denigrating the daughter who had been with her the whole time?

Last week, while dealing with the aftereffects of George and Eleanor's deaths, Joanna had been forced to come face-to-face with the fact that in many ways, Bob had known more about the current realities of George and Eleanor's lives than Joanna had. For instance, Bob, rather than Joanna, had been well aware that the couple had planned to return from Minnesota to Bisbee by way of

Salt Lake City. That stop to visit some friends who were also snow-birding retirees had routed them down I-17 and into the pathway of their shooter. As far as Joanna was concerned, Bob's revelations about the cemetery negotiations had been the last straw.

"You can't let things eat at you like this," Butch advised. "Whatever arrangements Eleanor made with regard to Bob are on her head, not his. You can't blame him for your mother's short-comings."

Dennis turned up in the kitchen. "How many LEGOs do you have in your pocket?" Butch asked. Startled at being caught red-handed, Denny held up a single finger.

"Give it to me, then" his father ordered sharply. "I already told you. No LEGOs at school. Understand?"

"Okay," Denny grumbled, nodding, removing the offending piece of plastic and handing it over. Sulking, he headed for the door without giving his mother so much as a passing glance.

"I guess I don't merit a good-bye kiss this morning," Joanna said.

"You do from me," Butch said, brushing the top of her head with his lips on the way past. "Once I drop Denny off, I'll need to go by the store and pick up a few things for dinner. Be safe."

"Will," she said.

Surprised at having a weekday morning with some alone time, Joanna poured another cup of tea, led the dogs into the living room, and settled down on the couch. Lady, her rescued Australian shepherd, crawled up on the sofa next to her, while Lucky, Jenny's deaf black Lab, curled up at her feet. Clearly, both dogs were missing Jenny. So was Joanna.

She sat there for a while, absently stroking Lady's soft coat, and, inevitably, thinking about her mother—about the things that shouldn't have been said that had been said and vice versa. All those said and unsaid things were haunting Joanna every step of the way this week, along with all the condolence wishes being offered by everyone she met. She knew people were sorry about what had happened. *She* was sorry! But carrying all that sorrow around with her in public was a very tall order right about now, and she wasn't sure she was up to it.

And that was one of the reasons she had thought sending Jenny off to school on time was a good idea, rather than keeping her at home for a week of nonstop mourning. It was far more important for an eighteen-year-old college student to start her freshman year along with the rest of her peers, rather than hanging around home to help with funeral arrangements.

On the way into the living room, Joanna had stopped by the bedroom long enough to retrieve her phone from its charger. Now, on impulse, and without knowing the first thing about Jenny's class schedule, she tried calling.

"I'm busy right now," Jenny's voice mail announced. "Please leave me a message."

Joanna did so. "It's Mom," she said. "I miss you. Denny misses you. Dad misses you. Lady and Lucky miss you. Call me back when you can."

Once that second cup of tea was gone and with the baby kicking up a storm just under her belly button, Joanna roused herself from the couch. In the bathroom she indulged in a far more leisurely shower than usual. When it came time to dress, she reached into the closet, pulled out one of her two new uniforms, and peeled off the plastic cover. She had bought the uniforms and had them professionally altered the week before. The shirt was a size larger than she usually wore and had needed to have the sleeves shortened, but the shirttail was now large enough that she could fasten the bottom button. The pants featured elastic inserts on each side of the waistband that made allowances for a waist that was expanding at an alarming rate.

Putting on her shoes and socks was another issue. It was no longer as easy to do that as it had once been nor as difficult as it would be shortly, but dealing with the shoes reminded her of the most-likely-still-wet boots that were stowed outside in the Yukon. Once dressed, she went outside, retrieved the boots, and set them on the shaded porch to dry. By the time she returned to the house, it was almost time for the briefing. She reached at once for her iPad. Knowing that her presence in the room would have amounted to a distraction for Tom, she had made arrangements for Kristin Gregovich to attend the press conference and Skype the entire proceedings to her.

Once the call connected, Deputy Chief Hadlock began by reading from the prepared statement Joanna had helped him compose the night before: "The Cochise County Sheriff's Department is investigating the deaths of two women who died of multiple injuries suffered in falls while climbing a mountain peak east of Warren sometime over the weekend."

His original version had said "two homicides." Joanna had changed that to something less specific. The original version had mentioned the time of death as being "late on Saturday night." Joanna had revised those words so they were less specific as well. Tom Hadlock had yet to learn the subtleties of telling as much as necessary while, at the same time, leaving out key details. Being brusque and straightforward was fine if you were running a jail, but they weren't traits that served one in good stead when you were dealing with the media.

"The two female victims have been positively identified. The first is Desirée Monique Wilburton, a twenty-seven-year-old teaching assistant at the University of Arizona who has been in the area around Bisbee for some time studying local flora. The other victim is Susan Marie Nelson, a thirty-six-year-old teacher and debate coach at the Sierra Vista School for Scholastic Excellence. Ms. Nelson reportedly went missing from her home in Sierra Vista sometime Saturday afternoon.

"The bodies of both victims have been transported to the Cochise County Medical Examiner's Office in Bisbee, Arizona, where they are awaiting autopsies. At this time, anyone who may have seen either of the two women or who may have information that will aide us in our investigation are urged to contact the Cochise County Sheriff's Department.

"The investigation is ongoing, and we have no additional information to offer at this time. Questions?"

Kristin turned her iPad toward the audience, which consisted of three sets of Tucson-based TV crews, along with a dozen or so other local and not-so-local print reporters. Naturally, Marliss Shackleford, in the middle of the front row, was the first to leap to her feet, waving to be recognized.

"My understanding is that this happened out by Geronimo," she said. "Do you have any idea what the victims were doing there?"

That was the other reason for leaving details out of the briefing paper itself—to give the reporters a reason to ask questions so they could feel like they were doing their jobs.

"Thank you, Ms. Shackleford," Tom replied smoothly, making Joanna smile in amusement. He was learning.

"Marliss is something of a local legend around here," he said with an apologetic grin toward the other attendees. "For those of you from out of town who aren't familiar with local geography and may be searching topo maps in vain, please be advised. Those of us who live here refer to the small peak involved in this incident as Geronimo. Its official name is Gold Hill.

"As for what the victims were doing there in the first place? The answer is that we don't really know. We've learned, for example, that one victim, Ms. Wilburton, was a microbiologist and an expert in the study of hedgehog cacti, specifically the Fendler's hedgehog." Tom paused and made a show of consulting his notes. "Officially it's referred to as *Echinocereus fendleri rectispinus,*" he added, pronouncing the difficult words with what Joanna regarded as commendable aplomb and then spelling them out one slow letter at a time while the gathered reporters busily took detailed notes.

"Our understanding," he continued, "is that Ms. Wilburton had been camping in the area for some period of time while she collected specimens. We have no idea why or how Ms. Nelson joined her there."

"What about vehicles?"

"Ms. Wilburton's Jeep was found at the scene. So far there has been no trace of Ms. Nelson's vehicle." He paused again to refer to his notes. "She was reportedly driving a blue Honda Accord, Arizona license C9L8A6. Anyone spotting that vehicle is asked to contact the sheriff's office immediately."

"What about this second woman, Ms. Nelson?" someone else asked. "Were she and the woman from Tucson involved in a relationship of some kind?"

"That's unknown at this time. We have no information on that, one way or the other," Tom replied.

"When you were retrieving the bodies last night, wouldn't it have been helpful to have had the use of a helicopter?"

That pointed question was from Marliss again. Who else? Joanna couldn't help smiling when she heard it. She had seen it coming well in advance and had provided Tom with a ready answer.

"You're right, of course," he said. "There was a serious storm in the area early Monday evening—it's rainy season after all. Dealing with runoff made transporting the bodies from the crime scene somewhat challenging, but we were able to accomplish the task by simply carrying them on stretchers without having the added risk or expense of calling in a helicopter and crew."

"You said the words 'crime scene' just now," one of the TV reporters said. "Does that mean the deaths are being investigated as possible homicides?"

"That has yet to be established. We expect to know more on that once the autopsies are complete."

"When will that happen?"

"It's my understanding that the first autopsy is under way at this time."

"It's been widely reported that Sheriff Brady's mother and stepfather died as a result of an I-17 shooting incident south of Sedona last week." That comment came from another one of the Tucson TV correspondents. "I don't see her here in the briefing room this morning. Is she taking an active part in this investigation or is she out on leave?"

Tom nodded somberly. "At the moment, the unfortunate deaths of Eleanor and George Winfield last week constitute a dark cloud hanging over our entire department. Eleanor Lathrop Winfield, Sheriff Brady's mother, was the widow of our late sheriff D. H. Lathrop. Dr. Winfield served as a well-respected medical examiner here in Cochise County for a number of years. Both of them will be greatly missed. That said, Sheriff Brady takes her role as sheriff very seriously, and yes, even though this is a particularly difficult time for her and her family, she is taking an active part in heading this investigation."

"Any word on when the funeral services will be held?"

Joanna recognized the person asking that question as a reporter from the *Sierra Vista Daily News*. It was something she should have seen coming and hadn't. She should have let Tom know in advance that services for George and her mother would be private and by invitation only.

"No details on that are available at this time," Tom answered. He glanced at his watch and then purposefully picked up his papers. "That's all I have for now. I'll let you know more as those details become available."

With that he left the room, closing the door firmly behind him. That was something else Joanna had coached him on—escaping the press conference in a clean, well-defined manner without letting one of the eager-beaver reporters trap him into making comments that weren't part of the official script. Maybe he was starting to catch on after all. Finally.

"Is that all, Sheriff Brady?" Kristin's image was asking from the screen of Joanna's iPad.

"For the moment," Joanna replied. "Thanks so much for doing this and for giving me a bird's-eye view of what was going on, and please let Tom know I thought he did a great job."

"I will," Kristin agreed. "But it would probably be better if those words came from you directly rather than from me. Are you on your way into the office now?"

"In a matter of minutes," Joanna said, "but not until I know the coast is clear. Let me know when the last of the reporters and camera crews leave the area."

"Most especially Marliss Shackleford?"

"You've got that right," Joanna said. "You know me too well."

CHAPTER 6

JOANNA ARRIVED AT THE OFFICE AT 11:40, A GOOD TWENTY MIN-utes before the scheduled twelve-o'clock meeting. Knowing she would be holding the briefing during her people's lunch hour, she'd had Kristin dispatch one of the front-office clerks to Daisy's Café to collect enough Cornish pasties to go around.

Pasties had come to Bisbee back in the early days when miners from defunct tin mines in Cornwall had emigrated to Arizona's thriving copper-mining camps, where the crusty meat pies became almost as much of a staple in miners' lunches as tamales were. For years, the previous owners of Daisy's Café, as well as the one before that, the original Daisy herself, had served pasties one day a week. Liza Matchett, who had come to town recently, had correctly gauged the dish's continuing popularity and now made them available seven days a week.

Accessing her office through the private backdoor entrance,

Joanna immediately caught a whiff of freshly baked pasties and knew the conference room was fully stocked. She was grateful that she had taken the time last night to mow through the many stacks of paperwork that had awaited her. There was a new load of paperwork again, but this was only today's batch, and it looked doable as opposed to daunting.

She set down her purse and then pressed a button on her phone, calling Kristin to let her know she had arrived.

"I'm so glad you're in," Kristin said. "Deputy Stock is here to see you. He says it's urgent."

Joanna took a breath. An urgent meeting with a deputy—a private meeting—usually spelled trouble. The possibilities were endless—everything from having two deputies involved in some kind of romantic entanglement (that had happened twice) to someone reporting that a member of her department had been seen drinking on the job. (That report had turned out to be bogus. A uniformed deputy had been in a bar in Tombstone, but the security tapes clearly showed that what he was drinking was nothing more than iced tea laced with a couple of packets of sweetener.)

"Any idea what this is about?" she asked.

"None," Kristin answered. "I asked, but he said it was confidential."

"You'd better show him in, then."

Deputy Jeremy Stock came into the room, dressed in a spotless and well-pressed uniform and carrying his hat. He had been around longer than Joanna had, but he was content to remain where he was—as a deputy—and had exhibited zero interest in going after a promotion. Like so many of the younger generation currently in law enforcement, he was a product of military training and had come looking for a job in the sheriff's department after serving a couple of tours of duty in the Middle East.

Joanna knew him to be a family man—a churchgoing guy, happily married, as far as she knew, to his first and only wife. He was the father of a pair of sons, one of whom was away attending college. Joanna knew from secondary sources rather than personal knowledge that Jeremy had spent years serving as both a Little League and a soccer coach. In other words, she regarded him as one of the good guys, and she was surprised to see him enter her office looking anxious and wary. He usually greeted her with a polite tip of his Stetson and an easy grin. This time he used both hands, clutching his Stetson in front of his chest with something approaching a death grip.

Rising from the chair behind her desk, Joanna stepped forward to welcome him into the room before closing the door behind him. Deputy Stock sank into one of the visitors' chairs while she returned to her place behind the desk. If this was something serious, she needed to address it from a position of authority.

"Good morning, Jeremy," she said. "You needed to see me?"

He answered with a silent nod and nothing more.

"What seems to be the problem?"

"It's about my son—Travis."

"What about him?"

"I read the morning briefing when I came on duty and saw the part about Mrs. Nelson," he blurted. "She's one of my son's teachers and his debate coach, too."

"I can see why you're concerned," Joanna said. "Having your child come face-to-face with a homicide investigation is unsettling for all concerned. Early this morning we notified school officials about what had happened. We wanted them to be informed well before the official press conference so they'd be able to have counselors on hand to help students deal with the situation."

"It's more than just that," Jeremy said miserably. "Travis actually had his regular Saturday-evening tutoring set with her. Then, at the last minute, one of his buddies invited him to go to Tucson to see the U of A football game. He asked me if I'd call her and let her know he wasn't coming, and I did."

"You actually spoke to one of the victims on the day she died?" Joanna asked.

Deputy Stock nodded. "I did, and I thought you'd want to know about it right away."

"I do," Joanna answered with a nod. "What time did you speak to her?"

He pulled out his cell phone and scrolled through what must have been a list of calls. "It says here I made the call at four forty-five."

"Do you remember exactly what was said?"

"I told her that Trav had been invited to a ball game and wouldn't be coming to his tutoring session. She said that was fine, that she had some lesson planning she needed to finish up and that not doing the tutoring session would give her a chance to do that."

"How did she sound?"

"Fine. I mean, I don't really know the woman. I've met her a couple of times at teachers' conferences and debate tournaments. What I do know is that Travis thought she was terrific. Losing her is going to be really hard on him."

"Have you spoken to him since you found out about what happened?" Joanna asked.

Jeremy shook his head. "I thought it was my duty to let you know that I had been in touch with the victim. When we finish here, if you don't mind, I'll take the rest of the day off and go be with Travis."

"Of course," Joanna said. "I understand completely. I wouldn't want you to do anything else. Just be sure to let Chief Deputy Hadlock know so he can adjust the patrol assignments."

Nodding, Jeremy got to his feet. "Thank you, ma'am. I'll be going, then."

Watching him leave, Joanna understood all too well what the man must be feeling. She'd gone through a similar experience not long ago when Jenny's high school principal had been murdered. People in law enforcement had to face far too many grim realities in the course of the job. Parents in law enforcement naturally wanted to spare their children from having to deal with same. That strategy stopped working when a homicide landed right on your child's doorstep.

"You do know that Travis will need to be interviewed," Joanna cautioned as Jeremy reached to open the door.

He paused and nodded. "Of course," he said.

"We'll also be interviewing Ms. Nelson's other students," Joanna added. "Please let Travis know that it's strictly routine and that all he needs to do is tell the truth. You can also assure him that you and/or Allison will be able to be present during the interview."

"Thanks," Jeremy said. "I'll let him know."

He left then. Grabbing her iPad, Joanna followed him out into the reception area before making her way to the conference room. It was five to twelve, but her entire team was already assembled around a U-shaped arrangement of tables. The promise of fresh pasties had helped ensure that everyone would appear on time. A set of open boxes sat arranged on a table at the back of the room. They were mostly empty, with only one or two unclaimed pasties remaining. Next to the boxes were two thermal carafes containing reasonably freshly brewed coffee. On the table at the front of the room and next to the lectern where Joanna would be standing sat a single paper cup. Joanna knew without taking a sip that it would be filled with her favorite apricot tea. *Thank you, Kristin,* she thought as she assumed her spot, looked around the room, and silently took attendance.

Other than Dave Hollicker, her entire investigative unit was already on hand—the Double C's, Deb Howell, and Casey Ledford. As promised, Frank Montoya had dispatched Detective Ian Waters to work the case. Chief Deputy Hadlock sat at the back of the room, stationed next to the door so that, should the need arise, he could be called away easily while Joanna was running the meeting.

There was nothing in the congenial atmosphere of the room to indicate that this was anything other than an ordinary business gathering. But Joanna understood it wasn't ordinary at all. Two people were dead, and these were the folks who were required to figure out why the victims were dead, to learn who was responsible for the crime, and bring them to justice.

Joanna was about to call the meeting to order when Kristin, shorthand tablet in hand, slipped quietly into the room as well. Joanna had asked her to take notes on the meeting. Since this had been designated a joint investigation, she wanted to have copies of all the proceedings available to pass along to Frank Montoya.

"Okay, people," she said, rapping on the lectern with her knuckles to call the meeting to order. "Let's get started. First let's have a round of applause for Chief Deputy Hadlock. Great job with the press conference this morning, Tom. Your handling of Marliss Shackleford was nothing short of brilliant."

The people in the room put down their plastic silverware long enough to applaud while Tom Hadlock ducked his head and flushed with pleasure at the unexpected praise.

"Now then, on to new business. Has everyone here met Detective Ian Waters of the Sierra Vista Police Department?"

Ian raised his hand and waved to the others while Joanna continued with her introductory overview. "One of our victims, Susan Nelson, hailed from Sierra Vista. She failed to return home after leaving for school—the Sierra Vista School for Scholastic Excellence—late on Saturday afternoon. Susan had been a teacher there for a number of years and was also the coach of the debate team. Her husband told us that she often did one-on-one tutoring sessions with debate team members on weekends.

"Thinking her disappearance may have started in Sierra Vista proper, Chief Montoya and I have declared this to be a joint investigation. That's why Detective Waters is here with us today. At this point he's the only Sierra Vista investigator who is actively assigned to the case, but I'm sure we'll be able to call on other Sierra Vista personnel and assets as needed. Since we're working two cases, I suspect we'll need all the help we can get, and Ian here will be assisting with both. So what do we have and who's up first?"

To Joanna's surprise, Detective Waters was the first to raise his hand. "Last night when we interviewed Susan Nelson's husband, he indicated that his wife had been estranged from her parents for some time, but that her father had been stationed at Fort Huachuca at one time.

"As you might expect, we have a good working relationship with the folks on post. MPs were able to provide us with information on the parents' whereabouts. The father, Roger Judson, retired from the military ten years ago. He and his wife, Phyllis, then moved to Sweet Home, Alabama. Roger passed away two years ago, but his widow still lives there. I contacted the Sweet Home PD first thing this morning, asking them to notify the mother. The guy who made the notification called me later and said that Phyllis told him that she'd written Susan out of her life years ago and wanted nothing further to do with her. Then she slammed the door in his face."

"Finding Susan's mother was a good start, but I'm guessing her reaction wasn't exactly what the cop in Alabama expected," Joanna surmised.

"Exactly," Ian agreed. "He wanted to know if he should make the effort to ask her any more questions. I told him we'd let him know."

"If the mother is at home in Alabama, and if Susan died here after years of estrangement, I don't see why interviewing Phyllis any further is essential at this time," Joanna said. "But thanks for following up on that."

"In addition," Ian continued. "We put out a BOLO on Ms. Nelson's Honda Accord. So far there's no sign of it. This morning we obtained a search warrant for Ms. Nelson's classroom at the SVSSE."

"How did that go?"

"Her purse was in her desk, and her cell phone was inside it. There was nothing out of place in the room, and no sign of any struggle. But her car keys weren't in her purse, and her car wasn't in the parking lot."

"Surveillance tapes?"

"Yup," Ian said, "and I was able to obtain copies of the applicable footage." It took a few minutes and some help from Casey Ledford to get the footage on his computer locked and loaded into a PowerPoint presentation. "Here's where it starts."

Joanna studied the blurred images on the screen. The time stamp dated 8/23 at 4:45 P.M. showed a single male wearing what appeared to be a hoodie walk onto the school grounds making sure his features were obscured from the camera lens.

"A little hot to be running around in a hoodie, don't you think?" Joanna observed. "But the hoodie does exactly what he intended it to do—it hides his features completely."

Once the man entered the school grounds, he sheared off to the right and disappeared from view.

"The cameras are located at the school's front entrance," Ian explained. "Ms. Nelson's classroom, however, is off on the right in one of five portables. Unfortunately, none of those are equipped with surveillance cameras."

Ian fast-forwarded, stopping the film at 4:47 P.M. "Here's what happens next."

Two people appeared in the frame—a man and a woman. Joanna surmised that most likely the man was the same one they had seen before. He still wore the hoodie. The woman was dressed in a tank top, skimpy shorts, and a pair of tennis shoes. The man walked to the woman's left, gripping her upper arm with his right hand while keeping his left hand out of sight in the pocket of the hoodie.

"So the perp's left-handed," Casey Ledford observed. "I'm guessing he's holding a weapon of some kind in his left-hand pocket."

"If it was a kidnapping," Ian said, "why no demand for ransom?"

"Speaking of weapons," Ernie interjected, "Jaime and I came here straight from the autopsies. I have Dr. Baldwin's preliminary results. According to her, both victims died of blunt-force trauma from a fall. No gunshot wounds. No stab wounds. So here's what I don't understand. If the perpetrator used a weapon in the course of the kidnapping, why not use it again as the murder weapon once he got her on top of Geronimo?"

"Good question," Joanna said. "Maybe the perp thought that if there was no indication that a weapon had been used, we'd be more likely to write it off as an accident rather than a homicide."

"What kind of weapon are we talking about?" Casey asked. "Remember, it had to be threatening enough to hold not just one but two women captive."

"Another good question," Joanna agreed. "Go on, Detective Waters."

"On the basis of what we're seeing here, Chief Montoya said he would go ahead and notify the FBI that we're dealing with a suspected kidnapping. By now he's most likely done so."

Joanna wasn't overjoyed at the idea of working with the feds—locals never were—but over the years she had developed a better track record of working with the local agent in charge than she'd had in the beginning.

"Any ETA on when the feds will swoop in?" Joanna asked.

"Not so far. In the meantime, Chief Montoya wants you to know that he'll personally handle the process of obtaining Susan Nelson's phone records. He said to tell you he'll be glad to run point in obtaining the other victim's phone records as well."

Frank Montoya's uncanny ability to obtain phone records in

a hell of a hurry had always been one of his best tricks. That was something else that, as yet, was way beyond Tom Hadlock's skill set.

"Thanks, Detective Waters," Joanna said as Ian resumed his seat. She looked around the room. "Questions or comments?"

"Can you zero in on that hoodie for us?" Casey asked.

It took the better part of three minutes for Ian to find a frame of the two people walking away from the camera and then enhance it to the point where the lettering on the back of the hoodie finally came into focus: SVSSE.

Joanna felt as though she'd taken a blow to the gut. "Most likely a student, then," she breathed. "How many kids at that school?"

"Two hundred and fifty or so," Ian answered.

"We're going to need to interview all of them and the teachers as well," Joanna said. "I'd like to do that on a full-court press basis, and it'll be easier if we do the interviews at school in a group-grope situation rather than tracking everyone down at their individual homes. So here's another assignment for you, Ian. Let the school authorities know that we'll be coming in tomorrow morning and will need access to enough rooms for my three detectives and you as well as anyone else Chief Montoya can spare to conduct private interviews, one after the other, with both students and school personnel.

"Our goal will be to sort out anyone who may require additional screening. Since these are preliminary discussions only, I think simple audio recordings of the interviews will suffice. Even so, the school will have to work out a tentative schedule and then notify parents in writing so they can be on hand when their child is being interviewed. The students are juveniles. We won't be able to talk to them without parental units actually in attendance unless we have written permission to do so in their absence."

"Interviewing that many people is going to take time," Ian said.

"Yes, it certainly is," Joanna agreed, "but the sooner we do it the better. What time does school start?"

"Eight thirty."

"Let the school know that we'll be on hand at eight thirty sharp. Got it?"

"Yes, ma'am," Ian said. "Will do." He glanced at his watch and frowned. "School gets out at three thirty. If you want interview rooms set aside for tomorrow morning, and if you want those parental notices to go out today, I should hit the road. I can either work on that end of things, or I can stay for the rest of the meeting. Which do you prefer?"

"By all means go," Joanna urged. "We can always bring you up to speed later."

CHAPTER 7

IAN HURRIEDLY GATHERED HIS EQUIPMENT IN ADVANCE OF LEAV-ing. As he approached the door, it opened from the other side, letting Dave Hollicker into the room. He stopped off at the back table, loaded a pasty onto a paper plate, grabbed some plastic silverware, and poured himself a cup of coffee before taking a vacant seat next to Casey.

"Thanks for joining us, Dave," Joanna said wryly. "I trust you were working."

He had already taken a bite of the meat pie, so at first he could only nod. "Sorry, Sheriff Brady," he said, "I was. I've been out at the crime scene dismantling Desirée's campsite and bringing everything I could find back to the lab."

"Did you find anything interesting?"

"Not so much," Dave replied. "She had a really cool solar-powered fridge, but it didn't have a single crumb of food in it. All it held was slides, hundreds of them, all of them apparently containing DNA samples from individual hedgehog cactuses that she had been collecting all summer long. Each sample is labeled with a date and a GPS coordinate. I can't imagine why someone would be that crazy about hedgehog cactus that she'd decide to spend the whole summer out in the wilderness tracking them down."

When Joanna had first heard about Desirée's research, she had wondered if the victims' deaths might be due to some kind of professional jealousy. Maybe Desirée Wilburton had been doing some piece of groundbreaking research and someone else in the same field wanted to steal the credit. Or maybe her studies had infringed on something another researcher was already doing. In any of those scenarios, Desirée would have been the actual target, with Susan Nelson little more than collateral damage. Now, though, having seen the security tapes from the school, Joanna was pretty sure that the situation was reversed. Susan was clearly the target. Did that mean Desirée Wilburton had simply showed up at the wrong place at the wrong time?

"Aside from that amazing cooler," Joanna said, "anything else of interest?"

"Let's just say that Desirée wasn't exactly doing luxury-style camping. I know there's been some theorizing that maybe there was some kind of romantic entanglement between the two victims. From what I saw out at the campsite, I don't think that's likely. There was nothing there that would have been suitable for a romantic roll in the hay. Desirée had a tent—a small pop-up tent—capable of sleeping one, not two. Her cot was a fold-up, old-fashioned wooden sling/canvas-style affair, topped by a single bedroll, a grimy one at that."

"What about provisions?" Jaime asked.

"As far as I could tell, she used plastic milk containers to haul water to the campsite from her Jeep, a gallon at a time. I went through her garbage bag. Looks to me like she survived mostly on MREs and instant coffee. Oh, and there was only one set of tin camping dishes—one plate, one bowl, one cup, and one set of silverware."

"So she wasn't set up for hosting visitors," Joanna said, "overnight or otherwise."

"Not at all," Dave agreed. "The campsite was strictly a solo undertaking."

"So if Desirée was camped out there on her own, and if Susan was brought there under duress," Joanna mused, "what's the connection between them? Did the two women know each other from some other time or place? Did they maybe go to school together somewhere along the line? Are they longtime friends or acquaintances?"

Deb Howell rose to her feet. "Not that I've been able to discover," she said, "and not according to the background checks I ran on both of these individuals this morning. As we learned yesterday from Roberta Wilburton, our one victim's mother, Desirée came to Tucson from New Orleans for her freshman year at the University of Arizona, and she hasn't gone anywhere else. She earned both her bachelor of science and her master's there, and was close to finishing her doctorate.

"Susan Nelson, on the other hand, came to Arizona at age thirteen when her father was transferred to Fort Huachuca with the US Army. She dropped out of high school during her freshman year—at age fourteen approximately. The next official record on her that I located was two years later at age sixteen when she went to court to obtain the status of an emancipated adult. She married Drexel Nelson immediately thereafter. Susan earned her GED at age nineteen before enrolling first at Cochise College and later at the University of Arizona, but she did all her classwork at the U of A's branch campus in Sierra Vista. So, although both women may have attended the University of Arizona during the same time frame," Deb added, "I don't see that many places where their paths would have intersected."

"Was Susan's father ever stationed in the New Orleans area?" Dave asked.

"Not that I could find."

Joanna made a few notes before raising her head and asking, "What else do we know?"

Ernie Carpenter immediately lumbered to his feet, handing Deb Howell a stack of multipage handouts for her to distribute.

"As I mentioned earlier, Detective Carbajal and I came here directly from the ME's office, where we witnessed the autopsies," Ernie said. "These are Dr. Baldwin's preliminary findings."

Deb stopped next to the spot where Detective Waters had been sitting. "What about Ian's copy?" she asked, nodding toward his empty chair.

"Give Kristin a copy, too," Joanna said. "She can fax copies to both Chief Montoya and Detective Waters. Right, Kristin?"

"Will do," Kristin said. "Glad to."

Joanna spent a few moments examining her own copy of the report, including the line drawings and notations that laid out the multiple injuries found on Susan Nelson's body.

"Can you cut to the chase and summarize these for us, Ernie?" she asked.

Ernie nodded. "Both victims suffered multiple injuries, but in both cases the ME says the cause of death is blunt-force trauma to the head, consistent with a fall that she estimates to have been at least twenty to thirty feet. In addition, both victims suffered multiple contusions and abrasions, as though they had rolled for some distance before landing on a hard, rocky surface."

"Any sign of sexual assault?" Joanna asked.

"None," Ernie answered, "although Ms. Nelson showed signs of recent sexual activity. Dr. Baldwin obtained what she hopes is usable DNA evidence from that. In addition, the ME's examination revealed that Ms. Nelson was about eight weeks pregnant with a male fetus at the time of her death.

"That's interesting," Joanna said, "especially considering her husband had a vasectomy years ago. Last night, he told us that was when the marriage really came to grief—when he found condoms hidden in Susan's bedside table."

"Maybe she should have used some of 'em," Jaime suggested with a wry grin.

"Hey, you guys," Deb Howell objected. "I happen to have a son named Ben who is living proof that condoms are not one hundred percent effective."

"Okay," Joanna said, trying to put an end to what had turned into a free-for-all. "If Susan Nelson was pregnant, most likely the father isn't her husband, but the fetus should prove to be an invaluable source of DNA. What about Ms. Wilburton? Did she show any signs of sexual activity?"

Ernie shook his head. "No, she did not."

"Was there any other possible DNA evidence present?"

"The ME took scrapings from under the fingernails of both victims," Ernie answered. "What she found was mostly dirt under Ms. Wilburton's nails, which would be consistent with her being out in the desert, camping, and tracking down cactus specimens. The dirt and debris found under Ms. Nelson's fingernails would be consistent with someone trying to reach out and grasp something to break her fall. But no human DNA was found."

"So she was conscious as she went over the edge?"

"Yes."

"Still," Tom Hadlock grumbled from the back of the room, "this is all a whole lot of nothing."

"Not exactly," Ernie replied, "because here's where it gets interesting. Dr. Baldwin found tiny traces of an adhesive of some kind on one item of Ms. Nelson's skin—on both her wrists and her legs."

"Adhesive?" Joanna asked. "Like from duct tape, maybe? You're saying she was restrained then?"

"Most likely at some point," Ernie replied.

Joanna looked at Dave. "Did you find any remnants of duct tape at the campsite?"

"Not a smidgen."

"So Susan may or may not have been restrained in the course of whatever sexual act occurred, but she wasn't restrained when she fell to her death," Joanna concluded. "The problem is, from what we saw in the video, Susan Nelson appeared to leave the SVSSE school grounds without putting up any kind of fight."

"In addition, her attacker knew exactly which of the portables was assigned to her," Jaime suggested. "He also felt confident enough to approach her on the school grounds in broad daylight, so he must not have expected anyone to question his presence on campus."

"Was anyone else at the school that afternoon?" Deb asked.

"Not that we know of now, but that's one of the things we'll be trying to ascertain tomorrow in the course of interviewing school staff as well as the students," Joanna said. "What about toxicology, Ernie? Is there a possibility Susan was given some kind of knockout drug to sedate her?"

"Toxicology tests take time," the detective replied. "I'm sure Dr. Baldwin will let us know the moment she has something definitive." With that, Ernie sat back down.

Joanna glanced around the room. "So what do we have here?" she asked.

"Susan was pregnant by someone who most likely wasn't her husband. She was abducted, had sex—forcibly or not—and now she's dead," Jaime concluded. "One thing is certain. Nobody carried her up that mountain. It's too steep. She would have had to make the climb under her own power, and she wouldn't have been able to do that if she was restrained in any way."

"So did she leave the school voluntarily or not?" Joanna asked.

"After looking at the security footage, I'd say not," Jaime said. "I believe Susan Nelson was force-marched off the school grounds by someone threatening her with a weapon of some kind. It's also possible that both homicide victims were force-marched up the mountain the same way, possibly at gunpoint. What I don't understand is, why didn't they fight back? If it was two against one, why did they just do as they were told?"

"Who knows?" Deb supplied. "When someone's holding you at gunpoint or knifepoint, it's a lot easier to do as you're told than it is to do anything else."

"Was Dr. Baldwin able to ascertain if the victims jumped or if they were pushed?" Casey Ledford asked.

"Without knowing their exact launch point, there's no way

to tell," Ernie replied. He turned to Dave. "Any information on that?"

"Like I said, I spent most of the morning dismantling the campsite. This afternoon I plan to climb up Geronimo itself to see what I can find. Last evening's storm was ferocious enough that I'm sure there won't be any footprints visible, but there may be trace evidence—shreds of torn clothing or strands of hair—that will tell us something about what went on during the actual confrontation."

"I've been to the top of Geronimo," Joanna said, "and it's a mother to climb. Don't make that trip on your own, Dave. Take someone with you."

"Yes, ma'am," Dave said. "Will do."

"Did the Padilla boys give us anything?" Joanna asked.

"Not much," Jaime answered. "They've gone swimming at the water hole at the base of Geronimo at least once a week since the rainy season started—without their mother's knowledge, by the way. She was pretty pissed when we brought them home. They were able to give us some help with the timeline, though. According to them, Desirée Wilburton's campsite wasn't at the water hole last week when they went swimming, but it was this week. Other than that, nothing useful."

"This is where we are, then," Joanna summarized. "We've got two homicide victims who died at the same place at approximately the same time, but we have been able to establish no connection between them. We know that one of the two was kidnapped from her place of employment by a perpetrator who was most likely armed and who is also most likely left handed, someone who may or may not be a student or an employee at the school where the victim worked. Does that sound about right?"

There were nods all around the room. Just then a cell phone rang and Tom Hadlock grabbed for his shirt pocket. He pulled out the device and held it to his ear for a moment. Putting it away again, he glanced at Joanna then held up his hand, waiting to be recognized.

"What is it?" Joanna asked.

"That was Chief Montoya," he replied. "Susan Nelson's Honda Accord has been located in an abandoned gravel pit off Dake Road on the outskirts of Sierra Vista. Someone using the gravel pit for target practice heard about the case on the noon news and wondered if the blue Honda he saw in the gravel pit was the same one the cops were looking for. Turns out, they are one and the same."

"Is the gravel pit within walking distance of the SVSSE campus?" she asked.

A moment after passing along Joanna's question, Tom nodded. "Affirmative on that," he said.

"Okay," she said. "Here's the deal. Deb, you keep working background checks on the two victims and see if you can find any points of connection between them. There must be something. Dave, get yourself back up the mountain. Come to think of it, don't just take any deputy. Grab Terry Gregovich and Spike. Give Spike a whiff of Desirée's bedroll and turn him loose on Geronimo. A four-footed German shepherd will be able to do better on that mountain than either you or Terry. Casey, you go on out to Sierra Vista with the Double C's and take a look at that Honda. Once you finish the on-site inspection, have it towed back here to the impound lot so you can go over it inch by inch. And tomorrow morning, eight thirty sharp, I want all three detectives on campus at SVSSE and ready to rumble. Got it, people? Now let's hit the bricks."

They all nodded and began gathering up to go. Joanna followed them out. At the back of the room a single untouched pasty still lay on the tray. She looked at the crusty pastry and tried to walk past it, but that didn't work. Succumbing, she picked it up, put it on a plate, and carried it back to her office.

After all, she told herself, setting the plate down on her desk, *I really am eating for two.*

CHAPTER 8

ONCE IN HER OFFICE, JOANNA IMMEDIATELY DIALED THE ME'S OFfice. It took some time to talk her way past Madge Livingston, Kendra Baldwin's combination clerk/receptionist. In the old days, talking to gravel-voiced Madge was like running into a brick wall. While working for both George Winfield and his successor ME, Guy Machett, Madge had functioned more as a repeller of callers and visitors than a greeter of same. During the tenure of Dr. Baldwin, however, the cantankerous old woman seemed to have undergone a personality transplant. She wasn't all sweetness and light, but she was now a whole lot easier to get along with.

This time, upon hearing Joanna's voice on the phone, the usually tough-as-nails Madge promptly burst into tears. "I just can't believe that wonderful man is dead," she sobbed. "George Winfield was, without a doubt, the best boss I ever had, bar none." She paused long enough to blow her nose. "I've heard the funerals will be private. I do hope I'm invited. I'd like to be."

"Of course," Joanna said. "You're on the list."

Madge wasn't currently on the list because so far there was no list. Norm Higgins had asked Joanna to prepare one, but with everything else going on, she had yet to start. Opening her iPad, she went to notes and created a new file titled *Funeral Invitees.* As a consequence, Madge Livingston's name ended up being the first one listed.

"Could I speak to Dr. Baldwin, please?" Joanna asked. "It's about one of the autopsies she did this morning."

"You're working, then?" Madge asked in apparent disbelief. "Even after what happened to your mother and Doc Winfield?"

"Yes," Joanna said wearily. "I am working, and if I could just speak to the ME, it would be a huge help."

"All right," Madge relented. "I'll put you through."

"Hey," Kendra Baldwin said when she came on the line. "What's up?"

By then Joanna had the line drawings from Susan Nolan's autopsy sitting in front of her. "I'm looking at Susan Nolan's drawing. You noted some bruising on her upper arm on the left-hand side."

"Yes," Kendra said. "Those weren't caused by the fall. Almost a complete handprint."

"Did you swab it for DNA?"

"Absolutely," Kendra said. "We swabbed every square inch of skin we could find. Those and her clothing will need to be sent to the crime lab in Tucson for DNA testing and profiling. Even if the guy was wearing gloves, her attacker may have left some cast-off DNA on her clothing. Oh, and Terry Gregovich just called, asking if I'd let him take one of Desirée Wilburton's hiking boots and Susan Nelson's one tennis shoe so he and Spike could go back to the mountain and track down the actual crime scene as opposed to the landing site. He's coming to pick them up right now. I'm assuming that's okay with you as long as we maintain the chain of evidence."

"Yes," Joanna said. "That's just what we need."

"By the way, the bodies will be ready for release tomorrow morning. Do you want to notify the families or should I?"

Joanna thought about that, remembering Reverend Nelson's unforgiving rage when he had told them about finding condoms in his wife's bedside table. Was it possible he had also learned she was pregnant, most likely by someone other than himself? If the condoms had enraged him, it was more than possible that news of Susan's pregnancy might have pushed him over the edge. Joanna wanted at least one of the detectives assigned to the case to be there with her when Reverend Nelson heard the pregnancy news. They'd already asked him about his nonexistent alibi for the night on which his wife had died. Did he have a better one for the time on Saturday afternoon when they now knew Susan Nelson had been taken from the school grounds?

Notifying him that the body was ready to be released was as good an excuse as any to speak to him again, without running the risk of his being officially regarded as a suspect in his wife's homicide. This was a conversation Joanna could have with the man without having to read him his rights.

"No," she said finally. "My investigators and I have already spoken to him in person and to family members of both victims.

We'll be glad to handle that part of the notification process. Everyone's doing other things right now, but I'll make sure someone speaks to Reverend Nelson if not before day's end, then first thing in the morning."

"Anything else you need from me?" Kendra asked.

"Not just now."

Ending the call, Joanna looked at her watch. Telling Reverend Nelson that his wife's remains were ready for release wasn't exactly mission critical. Rather than heading for Sierra Vista right that minute, she turned back to her iPad. She spent the next half hour combing through her contacts list and creating a separate directory of the fifty or so people who would be invited to the funeral. She struggled when it came to Marliss Shackleford's name. Marliss and Eleanor Lathrop had always been great pals. Much as Joanna despised the woman, she knew that the snub of not inviting the reporter to the funeral would be far more costly to her personally than the irritation of having her present. After all, Marliss was already one of Joanna's most outspoken critics. If she was snubbed and barred from the funeral, it would make a bad situation that much worse.

Once the list of invitees was complete—or as close to complete as Joanna could make it—she e-mailed the collection of names and addresses to Norm Higgins along with a copy to Butch in case he wanted to make any additions or corrections. Then, with her people still busy at their appointed tasks, she settled in to tend to some of her own. She started by letting Tom Hadlock know that due to the funeral situation, she would once again need him to sub for her at Friday's board-of-supervisors meeting.

She contacted both of the remaining applicants for the jail chef job and set separate appointments for them to come in for final interviews the following week, interviews that would include samples of their cooking—breakfast, lunch, and dinner—prepared in the jail kitchen with the staples and supplies that were usually on hand. Joanna had learned there was often a big difference in quality between what people *said* they could cook and what they actually *could*.

She went over the briefings of what had gone on in her absence. She studied the shift schedules Tom had prepared and signed off on additional vacation requests. Finally, with most of the day-to-day stuff handled, she settled back to study the speaking request she had received from the National Association of Female Sheriffs.

There were approximately three thousand sheriffs in the country at any given time, and Joanna was more aware than most that fewer than fifty of them were female. As someone who was in the process of seeking her third term in office, she was regarded as an "old-timer." The association wanted Joanna at the gathering as an elder, of sorts, in hopes that what she related of her own experiences on the job would provide encouragement for those coming after her. The conference was being held in Phoenix in August—during the dead of summer, when hotel rates would be dirt cheap. On the surface, all of that was good news. The bad news? Joanna would be there with a babe in arms. How well would that work? And then there was that other important variable to be considered—what if she lost the election?

She had yet to make up her mind when there was a tap on the door. She looked up to see Marianne Maculyea framed by the doorway. "Anyone here interested in having a brief chaplain visit?" she asked with a smile.

Joanna and Marianne had been best friends since junior high. Not only was the Reverend Marianne Maculyea the pastor of Tombstone Canyon United Methodist Church, which Joanna and Butch attended, she was also a trained police and fire chaplain.

"Anytime," Joanna said, standing and hurrying over to embrace her friend before leading her to the visitors' chairs, where they sank down side by side.

"How are you doing?" Marianne asked.

"At least you didn't start out by saying how surprised you are to find me working under the circumstances," Joanna observed.

"You're right about that," Marianne replied. "I'm not the least bit surprised, but even for you, dealing with two funerals and a double homicide at the same time seems like a bit much."

"Maybe it is," Joanna admitted. "My brother and his wife are flying in from DC today and coming to dinner at the house. I'm not looking forward to seeing him. He has every right to be here, of course, but having him in town is going to bring up all those tired old rumors about his being a product of an out-of-wedlock pregnancy. Not that it should matter, especially with both of my parents dead, but still."

Marianne knew all about Joanna's mixed feelings concerning her long-lost brother and Eleanor's fair-haired-boy treatment of same.

"That's actually why I stopped by," Marianne said. "I wanted to show you a rough draft of what I intend to say about Bob Brundage at the service. Since it's going to be private, most of the people will probably be aware of his connection to your mother, correct?"

Joanna nodded.

"So that's the premise I'm going on," Marianne continued. "I'll simply assume that everybody in the room already has a grasp of the complexities of the situation and not make any attempt to explain it. Here, look at this and tell me what you think."

With that, Marianne handed her iPad, already opened to a document, over to Joanna, who immediately started reading:

Today we celebrate the lives and passings of two remarkable people, a loving couple who were brave enough to take a second chance on love late in life.

Eleanor Lathrop Winfield, the widow of longtime Cochise County sheriff D. H. Lathrop, was a lifetime resident of Cochise County and the mother of two children—a daughter, Sheriff Joanna Brady, of Bisbee, Arizona, and a son, Bob Brundage, of Manassas, Virginia.

George Winfield, born in Minneapolis, Minnesota, was a widower who moved to Bisbee after losing both his wife, Annie, and his daughter, Abigail, to cervical cancer. While working as the Cochise County medical examiner, George met Eleanor Lathrop. The two of them hit it off and fell in love. They eloped and were married in a private ceremony in Las Vegas.

Returning to Bisbee, they made their home in Eleanor's longtime residence on Campbell Avenue while using an RV to commute back and forth to George's cabin near Big Stone Lake in Minnesota during the summers.

They traveled many miles together and somehow it seems

right that they are embarking on this final journey together as well. Yes, their unexpected deaths last week are a tragedy to those they leave behind, but the love they shared while they were here was an inspiration and a blessing to those around them.

Handing the iPad back to Marianne, Joanna tried unsuccessfully to stifle a sob. Marianne went back to the door and closed it before gathering Joanna into her arms, soothing and rocking her as though she were a child.

"Sorry to be so stupid," Joanna murmured at last, pulling away. "What you wrote was just right. Not too sweet. None of the 'loving mother' crap. Thank you for that, by the way."

"I left those words out just for you," Marianne said. "I know Eleanor loved you, but she did so in her own peculiar fashion. The problem is, your mother was someone who wanted to do everything by the book—the way things had always been done—and she could never quite bring herself to appreciate a daughter who insisted on coloring outside the lines. Mine, either," she added quietly.

Joanna looked at her friend and knew it was true. Marianne's situation with her own mother was every bit as complicated as Joanna's had been with Eleanor.

"So here's the deal," Marianne went on. "You're not just mourning the loss of your mother. You're also mourning the loss of a relationship that never became quite what either one of you wanted. Given enough time, that might have happened one day. Now it never will. You not only lost your mother, Joanna. You also lost what might have been."

Joanna's tears flowed again, a gusher this time. "That's what I was thinking about all the way to Phoenix," she blubbered. "I kept thinking about all the things I needed to say I was sorry for. I wanted to put them all right, somehow, and I never had the chance. They took her into surgery, and she never woke up. I never got the chance to take back any of those ugly things I never should have said."

"Which brings us back to Bob Brundage," Marianne said. "I understand the whole dynamic with Bob. He shows up out of the blue and somehow forms the kind of unconditional love relationship with your mother that you never had. But tonight when you're having dinner, remember that your mother's embracing of Bob had less to do with him and more to do with her. Being forced to give up that first child must have been a terrible loss for her—an unbearable loss. So it's easy to understand her incredible joy when, by a seeming miracle and against all odds, that lost child was finally returned to her."

"You're starting to sound a lot like Butch," Joanna said.

"Butch is a smart man," Marianne replied with a smile. "None of this is Bob's fault or yours, either. So here's an idea. Tonight at dinner, instead of having to regret being unable to take back something said in anger or sorrow or whatever, how about if you try not saying it in the first place? The regrettable things you don't say are things you never have to take back later on."

"Got it," Joanna said, sniffling. "The thing is, I know Bob really is a great guy. If he weren't my brother, I wouldn't mind so much."

They both laughed then. Chuckled more than laughed, but it was a way of putting the subject to rest.

There was a light tap on the closed door. "Sheriff Brady," Kristin said tentatively, "I hate to disturb you, but Detective Waters is on the phone. He needs to speak to you. And there's an FBI agent out here in the lobby waiting to speak to you as well."

"Great," Joanna said with a sigh. "I can just imagine how well that will go."

Marianne stood up. "I'll let you get to it, then," she said, "but if you need to talk, call me."

"I will," Joanna said. "Thank you."

CHAPTER 9

RETURNING TO HER DESK, JOANNA PUNCHED THE BLINKING HOLD number on her landline and picked up the receiver. "Detective Waters?"

"Yes, ma'am," Ian said. "Thanks for taking my call. Mr. McVey is dragging his feet."

"Who is Mr. McVey?"

"The principal of SVSSE. He says there's no way he's sending out notices to the parents that their children are about to be interviewed by the cops, and he's refusing to grant permission for us to conduct any of the interviews on school property. He said, and I quote, 'Having cops overrun the school is just like what happened in Nazi Germany.'"

"Nazi Germany? Are you kidding? He thinks we're running a police state here? Is he aware that this is a homicide investigation and that a member of his faculty was murdered by someone who marched her off the school grounds wearing a sweatshirt with the school's logo on it?"

"Yes, I told him all that."

"Give me his number," Joanna said. "Let me give him a call. What's his first name?"

"Marvin."

"Okay," Joanna said, jotting down the number. "Let me handle him."

A moment later a receptionist answered, "Sierra Vista School of Scholastic Excellence, where all our students are given the tools it takes to succeed."

And no doubt they're all above average, too, Joanna thought, unimpressed by the school's overly optimistic motto.

"Mr. McVey, please," Joanna said when it was her turn to speak.

"May I say who's calling?"

"No, thank you," Joanna replied. "It's an urgent matter, and I wish to speak to him directly."

Joanna knew it was rude to blow her way past a receptionist who was only doing her job, but she needed to take control of the situation, and being rude was one way of accomplishing that goal.

"To whom am I speaking?" Marvin McVey demanded when he came on the line a moment later.

"This is Cochise County sheriff Joanna Brady, Marvin. Thank you for taking my call."

He was Marvin. She was Sheriff Brady. Establishing a hierarchy from the get-go was part of the game, and Joanna needed to be in charge.

"If this is about the interviews you expect to conduct

tomorrow morning," McVey declared, "I'll tell you the same thing I told Detective Waters. SVSSE's job is to educate our young people, not to make them available to the whims and demands of local police officials."

"Excuse me, Marvin, was or was not Susan Nelson a member of your faculty?"

"Yes, but—"

Joanna pushed on. "Did you or did you not see the surveillance tapes of her being escorted—some would say strong-armed—from your campus late Saturday afternoon?"

"Yes," Mr. McVey agreed, "I did see the footage, but—"

Joanna continued without allowing him to finish. "The fact that Mrs. Nelson's assailant kept his hand in the pocket of that SVSSE hoodie indicates to us that he was most likely carrying a weapon. So let's say Susan Nelson was escorted from your campus at gunpoint at four thirty P.M. on Saturday afternoon, and a few hours later, she was brutally murdered."

"Yes, but—" McVey attempted again.

And again Joanna took control of the conversation. "I'm afraid there are no acceptable buts as far as you are concerned, Marvin. Susan Nelson, one of your faculty members, was murdered in cold blood, most likely by someone connected to your school. Until we determine who that individual is and why this tragedy occurred, there's a possibility that more of your students and faculty may be at risk.

"Our best chance of finding the person responsible is through interviewing the people closest to our victim, including both students and teachers from your campus. Interviewing students on the school grounds with their parents or guardians present is the most expeditious means of accomplishing that goal and of apprehending the suspect in a timely fashion. If you cause even the slightest delay in that process, Marvin, and if someone else is harmed as a result of that delay, you can be sure that I'll inform the local media that you and you alone are fully responsible."

"But—" Marvin McVey said again.

"We need space to do the interviews," Joanna insisted, "starting at eight thirty A.M., and we will have investigators from my department and from the Sierra Vista Police Department on campus to conduct them. How many classes did Susan Nelson teach?"

"Five."

"And they were?"

"An advanced placement English course, two senior English classes, one junior, and one speech. Oh, and she had one planning period."

"So she interacted directly with how many students?"

"Probably seventy-five or so. But since this is only the first week of a new school year, it's likely that most of the seniors don't know her very well, at least not yet. Last year's seniors would probably know her better than this year's."

"So seventy-five plus the students on her debate team?"

"I suppose there's some overlap," McVey allowed. "Some of her speech students are part of the debate team as are some of her other students, especially the AP ones."

"Let's start with those, then. The debate team kids and the kids who are in her classes. They're who we'll be interviewing first. I'm sure you'll be able to send out text or e-mail notices on that, right?"

"I suppose," McVey conceded. At that point Joanna knew she had him.

"Okay then, Marvin," she said. "You get cracking on those notices. We'll see you first thing in the morning."

As she hung up the phone, Joanna was surprised to hear applause coming from the doorway into the lobby. Marianne had evidently left the office door open on her way out. Looking in that direction now, Joanna saw a slender woman, a tall, good-looking brunette, in a sleek black suit, a white blouse, and sensible but stylish black pumps, standing in the doorway clapping her hands.

"That's one way to get their attention," the interloper said. "Threaten them with a media crap storm. That'll bring them to heel in a hell of a hurry every single time."

"Who are you?" Joanna demanded.

The woman held up her badge. "Robin Watkins, FBI," she said. "Please excuse my barging in like this. Your secretary—Kristin, is it?—went to use the restroom. I noticed when I arrived that your office had a private entrance, and I was worried you might try to scoot out through the back door without talking to me, so I took the liberty of letting myself in."

More nerve than a bad tooth, Joanna thought, thinking of one of Jim Bob Brady's, her first father-in-law's, favorite expressions and suppressing a smile. When Kristin had mentioned that an FBI agent was waiting, Joanna had imagined someone in a suit all right, but more on the order of a *man* in a suit. Not only that, but the idea of skipping out the back door had actually crossed her mind.

"Since I'm officially on the case now," Agent Watkins continued, "how about bringing me up-to-date?" Uninvited, she settled into one of the visitors' chairs and then added, as an afterthought, "Sorry for your loss."

Obviously Agent Watkins had been well briefed. Each time someone offered their condolences, Joanna felt as though she was a thin rubber band gradually being stretched too far and too often. After a moment, though, she got a grip.

"We're dealing with a double homicide, Agent Watkins," she said. "An apparent kidnapping that ended up with two women being murdered."

Joanna's secretary, Kristin Gregovich, the wife of K9 officer Terry Gregovich, was nothing if not efficient. Breezing into the office, she delivered not one but two copies of the notes she had taken during the noontime meeting. She handed one set to Joanna and the other to Agent Watkins.

"Would either of you care for tea or coffee?" she asked.

"You have tea?" Agent Watkins asked.

"Apricot decaf," Joanna said, patting her baby bump. "I've discovered that in my current state, coffee most definitely does not agree with me or the little one."

"I won't have coffee, then, either," Agent Watkins said. "Apricot tea sounds just right."

"Make that two teas, please," Joanna said, smiling at Kristin. "Thank you."

As Kristin bustled cheerfully out of the office, Joanna realized that if she did end up speaking to those lady sheriffs—as she liked to think of them—that was something else she'd need to mention to the newbies. That if people were used to taking orders from males, they might push back against the idea of having a woman in charge. That had certainly been the case between Joanna and Kristin initially, and it had taken time, effort, and patience on both their parts for them to establish a good working relationship.

Once Kristin returned with the tea, Joanna and Agent Watkins sat quietly reading through the notes and studying the ME's findings and line drawings.

Agent Watkins spoke first. "So there was never any indication that Susan Nelson's abductor was interested in making a ransom demand?"

"No," Joanna answered. "Whoever took her did so with the intention of killing her."

"But why transport her all the way to that mountain—what's it called again?"

"Geronimo," Joanna replied, "and I have no idea. We know that the other victim, Desirée Wilburton, was camping at the base of Geronimo, but so far we've been able to find zero links between them."

"Why there?" Agent Watkins asked. "What's so unique about that particular spot? Maybe Geronimo has some special meaning to the killer."

"For kids from around here, climbing that particular peak is a rite of passage," Joanna answered. "At least it was when I did it. It's an interesting climb. Challenging enough and dangerous enough that you know the whole while you're doing it that your parents would never approve."

Agent Watkins gazed out the windows of Joanna's office at a looming wall of limestone cliffs behind a sea of bright green ocotillo. "Is Geronimo as tall as those cliffs back there?" she asked.

Joanna shook her head. "The one on the right, the tallest one, is Grassy Hill at the top of Mexican Canyon. It clocks in at something like sixty-five hundred feet. Here at the Justice Center, we're at around fifty-three hundred, which is why Bisbee is called a 'mile-high' city. I think Geronimo, or Gold Hill, as it's officially known, is about fifty-nine hundred, so we're talking a four- to six-hundred-foot climb, depending on the altitude at the base. Believe me, some of that is pretty much straight up and down."

"Could I go take a look at the crime scene?" Agent Watkins asked.

Joanna eyed the stylish but entirely unsuitable suit and the pristine white blouse, to say nothing of the shiny pumps. "Not dressed like that," she said.

Robin laughed aloud, an easy kind of infectious laughter. "Not to worry," she said. "I keep several changes of clothing handy when I'm on the road. You can never tell what might turn up."

"What are you driving?"

"A Taurus."

"Okay," Joanna said. "Change into hiking duds if you have them. You don't need to go down the hall. You're welcome to use the private facilities here in my office. After that, I'll give you a ride. Four-wheel drive is definitely called for on this venture. But about the crime scene: I won't be able take you to the exact crime-scene location. I can take you to where the bodies came to rest, but we still don't know exactly where they went airborne. I currently have my K9 unit and one of my CSIs out at the scene trying to track down that exact location."

Robin went out to her car and returned carrying a soft-sided duffel. She disappeared into Joanna's private restroom looking like a respectable corporate executive and emerged a few minutes later looking like someone who was Cochise County born and bred. Her plaid, pearl-snapped cowboy shirt, her very slender jeans, to say nothing of a respectable silver buckle on a leather belt—one that also held her badge—would have been right at home at one of the local rodeos. The lace-up hiking boots were the only items in the outfit that didn't exactly blend.

"I didn't expect you to show up looking like a total cowgirl," Joanna commented.

Robin laughed again. The more she laughed, the better Joanna liked her.

"Did you ever hear the story of Br'er Rabbit?" Robin asked.

"Of course," Joanna said.

"That's my story, too," Agent Watkins said. "Turns out I got into a pissing match with my supervisor back in DC, and he remoted me to Tucson. It was supposed to be a life lesson for me as well as a punishment, just like throwing Br'er Rabbit in the briar patch was supposed to get him to straighten up and fly right.

"Unfortunately, things didn't quite work out the way my ex-boss intended. As soon as I drove into town, I discovered that I love Tucson. In fact, I love all of Arizona. I may have gone a little overboard in terms of going native—well, not Native native—but Western anyway. Just wait until you see my Stetson. I took myself straight to Arizona Hatters the first chance I had and got the real deal."

Yes, Joanna decided, maybe Robin Watkins was one FBI agent she could actually befriend. "Come on," she said. "Let's get going."

Once they were out in the parking lot, Robin went back to her government-licensed Taurus, tossed the duffel bag into the trunk, and emerged wearing a white Stetson and grinning from ear to ear.

"See there?" she asked, climbing into the passenger seat of Joanna's Yukon. "What did I tell you?"

"All you need is a gun and holster on your hip," Joanna said.

"Nope," Robin replied. "I'm small-of-back or ankle holster all the way. So where are we going?"

"Back into town. Where are you staying?"

"The Copper Queen."

"The hotel is in a part of town known as Upper Bisbee—where the community actually started. Where we're going now is a neighborhood called Warren. In the old days, most of the businesses were located in Upper Bisbee, while Warren was designed primarily for residential use."

Robin nodded. "I liked the photo, by the way," she said.

For a moment Joanna was lost. "Photo?" she asked. "What photo?"

"The one of you back there at the Justice Center."

"You mean the one in the display case out in the main lobby?"

Robin nodded. "I noticed that, to the man—all of your predecessors looked like so many tough guys, especially the ones posing with their handlebar mustaches, guns, and horses. They were all doing their best to look, if not fierce, then at least deadly serious. And then there you are, cute as a button—a little girl in pigtails dragging around a wagon loaded to the brim with Girl Scout cookies. By the way, I'm still a sucker for Thin Mints."

"That makes two of us," Joanna said. "Too bad it isn't Girl Scout cookie season right now. I'd break out a couple of those just for the heck of it."

CHAPTER 10

JOANNA FOLLOWED THE SAME ROUTE TOM HADLOCK HAD TAKEN the night before to get from the Justice Center into town, first up Highway 80 and then turning left onto the Warren Cutoff. As they approached town, an intervening scrub-oak-covered hill kept Geronimo hidden from view. Only when they had entered the town itself and reached the top of Yuma Trail was the mountain completely visible.

"There it is," Joanna said, pointing. "That's Geronimo."

"The funny-looking one with the two bumps on the top?" Robin asked.

"That's the one."

"It looks steep."

"It *is* steep."

Joanna turned off the street onto the ranch road and then rumbled across the cattle guard. Last night, the dirt on the road had been topped by a layer of slick caliche-like mud. Today the crust had been broken, revealing red dirt underneath, which was marred by multiple tire tracks leading back and forth.

"We had a big storm late yesterday afternoon, and this was all covered with a kind of slippery muck we call caliche," Joanna explained. "Last night, too, the wash up ahead was running bank to bank. We had to park on this side of it and walk in and out, carrying the bodies by hand."

"That must have been fun," Robin said.

"Not so much," Joanna replied. "The hiking boots I wore still aren't dry."

As they approached the spot where the collection of vehicles had been parked the night before, Joanna looked around for signs of Terry's K9 Tahoe and didn't see it. Driving as far as the edge of the wash, she saw that enough sand had settled out of the water to make the entrances into and out of the wash gradual enough to be passable. Since there were already several other sets of tracks leading the way, her Yukon bounced into and out of the wash with no difficulty.

"I hope you've been here long enough to know that when you see a sign that says 'Do Not Enter When Flooded,' they mean it, and you need to pay attention," Joanna said, by way of conversation.

"Yes, ma'am," Robin replied. "I hear you loud and clear. I made that mistake last summer shortly after I got to town. I tried crossing Tucson Boulevard on Elm when water in the street was running curb to curb. It was a lot deeper than I expected, and the car almost floated away. I finally washed up on a sandbar that was solid enough for me to be able to get the wheels turning again."

"Company car?" Joanna asked.

"Yup," Robin said. "Another Taurus."

"I'll bet you got hauled on the carpet for that one."

"I did. According to the motor-pool guy, the water completely screwed up the ignition system."

"I'm sure it did," Joanna agreed.

Up a short rise, Joanna parked next to Terry's Tahoe. "Here we are," she said. "Desirée Wilburton's actual campsite was here inside this grove of scrub oak. There's a water hole nearby, on the far side of the grove. The bodies landed on the far side of the water hole and partway up the mountain."

Leading the way, Joanna held up the crime-scene tape to let Agent Watkins pass underneath it.

"Here?" Agent Watkins asked, looking around. "I don't see anything resembling a camp."

"That's because one of my CSIs, Dave Hollicker, came out here this morning, packed up everything he could find, and took it back to the lab."

When they approached the water hole, Robin looked into the brownish murk and frowned. "Those two kids you were telling me about planned to swim in this?"

"If you're a kid growing up in the desert," Joanna said, "water is water, muddy or not, and swimming in the water hole is all part of the whole rite-of-passage deal. First you climb the mountain, then you go skinny-dipping. By the way, it's a lot muddier this morning because of the storm. It's actually fed by an underground spring halfway up the mountain, so there's usually some water here year round. It's only during the rainy season, however, when there's enough to actually swim. Otherwise, it's little more than a wading pool."

Walking side by side, Joanna and Agent Watkins made their way around the water hole and then climbed to the point where forward progress was blocked by a sheer wall of rock. The rocky bank at the base of the perpendicular cliff was littered with a number of bright yellow evidence markers.

"This is where they landed?" Robin asked.

Joanna nodded. "That's where we found them, one on top of the other."

For the better part of a minute, Robin examined the surrounding dirt and rock. "I don't see any blood spatter," she observed. "Both victims had extensive injuries. Shouldn't there be blood?"

"There was," Joanna answered, "but the runoff from last night's storm was pretty fierce—enough so that it washed away most of the visible stains. However, with the help of luminol, we found evidence of blood stains scattered on the rocks down here and on the ones just above where they first landed. Those are what the other evidence markers designate."

Just then, a dog barked somewhere nearby but farther up the mountain, out of sight beyond the looming cliff. Joanna realized this wasn't just any dog, and it wasn't just any bark, either. It was the sound of Spike, alerting his partner to the fact that he'd found something.

"Hey, Terry," Joanna shouted, up the hill. "Sheriff Brady and FBI agent Robin Watkins are down here below where you are. What did Spike find?"

"Wait a minute," Terry called back. "I'll go check, but stand back from the side of the mountain. The footing up here is really uncertain. I don't want to send a rockslide raining down on your heads."

Joanna and Robin retreated back down the way they had come. Moments later, a scatter of rocks and gravel tumbled down the face of the cliff and came to rest precisely where they had been standing earlier.

"Spike found a shoe," Terry shouted. "Looks like Susan Nelson's missing tennis shoe. Remember, we only found one of them last night. Hang tight. There's a rock outcropping up ahead. Let me check that out."

"Is there any way for us to get up there?" Robin asked Joanna.

"I know how, but I'm not attempting it without my own hiking boots. I've got an extra pair still in the Yukon. Wait here."

Joanna hurried back to the SUV, switched into her extra hiking boots, and then went back, bringing along three bottles of water. "This way," she said, passing one of the bottles to Robin and heading toward the peak's northern flank. "The ascent there is a little more gradual."

"This is supposedly gradual?" Robin panted as they started up the vestigial trail. "It doesn't seem gradual to me." Eventually they passed a spot where a faded and decaying wooden cross stood semi-upright in a cairn.

"What's that?" Robin asked, huffing to catch her breath.

"It's a memorial to a kid named Michael Grady. He fell and died here in the early 1940s. His parents erected the cross here, hoping it would deter other kids from making the same mistake. I can tell you from personal experience that it didn't work."

"The early forties?" Robin remarked. "That's a long time ago, but the cross is still here? How's that even possible?"

"It's not the original cross," Joanna said. "It's sort of like George Washington's ax. It has a new handle and a new head, but everyone still claims it's George Washington's ax. When the cross gets too bad, someone comes along and replaces it, but nobody ever forgets Michael's name, because it's right here, chiseled on some of the rocks."

She paused and examined the rocks, then moved some of them around until they were arranged like puzzle pieces in proper order and read MICHAEL GRADY, B. 3/29/29, DIED 7/4/41. RIP.

"Even walking past this wasn't enough to keep kids from coming here?" Robin asked.

"Nope," Joanna answered. "We all climbed the mountain anyway, but seeing that cross as we passed meant that we were thinking about poor Michael Grady all the way up and all the way down."

Walking carefully, with Joanna in the lead, they slowed as the climb turned steeper. It wasn't until after they topped the first rise, something that had seemed like little more than a foothill from a distance, that they finally caught sight of the other officers. The two men and the dog were scrambling southward, slowly negotiating their way across the mountain's front face toward what looked like a crease at the very center. Terry and Spike seemed to be doing fine in the rough terrain, while a less fit Dave Hollicker was clearly struggling.

"I'm pretty sure we've found it," Terry called again. "They must have gone off right here. Judging by the evidence markers, it's almost a straight shot from here down to where they landed."

"Hold on," Joanna said. "We're coming."

"What do you mean 'we'?"

"I tried to tell you earlier. The FBI has joined the investigation," she told him. "Agent Watkins is here with me."

There was no reply to that, not from Terry Gregovich and not from Dave Hollicker, either. Joanna suspected their lack of response indicated a certain lack of enthusiasm. Local cops are often less than happy when federal officers horn in on cases where help isn't necessarily needed or wanted.

For the next few minutes, Joanna and Robin climbed steadily before finally drawing even with the others. The two men as well as the dog were huddled together, positioned on a small flat outcrop that seemed no larger than a regular-sized mattress. A double, yes, but not a queen and definitely not a king!

To reach the spot, Joanna realized that she and Robin would have to do the same thing—work their way across the steep face of the mountain in a place where, without a path, they would be risking life and limb at every step. The direct approach might have been shorter, but it was littered with treacherous loose hunks of limestone and low-growing scrub brush that offered no guarantee of solid footing or even a handhold should one be needed.

"We can try to make it over there," Joanna said, "or we can wait until they come to us."

"I say wait," Robin said, sounding relieved. "But while we do, what say we go on up to the top. It doesn't look very far from here."

Agent Watkins was most likely a year or two younger than Joanna, and she certainly wasn't pregnant, but if she was game, Joanna had to be, too. With a shrug of her shoulders, she led the way. Nearing the top, she reached out to use a rock ledge to pull herself up and startled a dozing horned toad in the process. It scooted downhill in a hurry, shooting past both Joanna and Robin.

"What the hell was that?" Robin demanded, dodging out of the way and almost falling backward in the process.

"A horned toad."

"Are they dangerous?"

"To flies and bugs maybe."

"I thought they were poisonous."

"You're probably confusing horned toads with Gila monsters. Those are poisonous, but they're totally different creatures. You should pay a visit to the Arizona Sonora Desert Museum and learn the difference."

"I'll do that," Robin said. "As soon as I have a chance, and assuming I can get down from here without breaking my neck."

By then, Joanna had already resumed her upward climb. Once they topped out onto relatively flat ground at the top of the knoll, both women were panting and sweating. It was midafternoon by then, well into the nineties with very low humidity. There was a slight breeze blowing across the mountaintop, and they reveled in it as they paused long enough to drink some water and look around.

"I have to admit you were right," Robin observed, turning a full 360 degrees to take in the entire panorama. "It's a pretty spectacular view."

"Yes," Joanna agreed. "And that's why generations of kids from Bisbee have climbed this mountain, dangerous or not. They do it because it's here and to savor a view that can't be had anywhere else."

After that, they stood in silence for a few moments. Robin might have been enjoying the view, but Joanna was remembering the last time she had stood in this place. She had come with Andy, shortly after the doctor—one who also happened to be her mother's doctor—had given her the bad news: Joanna Lee Lathrop was pregnant. She had opted for going to the doctor's office rather than getting a test kit for the drugstore where everyone knew exactly who she was.

She and Andy had been standing together in almost this exact place when she had shared the daunting news about her unexpected pregnancy. She had told him about it, not knowing what he would think or how he would react. Andy had stood there for a long quiet moment, looking out across the valley toward town. Then he had turned to her with one of his most engaging grins and said, "Well, then, Carrot Top, I guess you and me had better get hitched, and we'd better do it sooner than later."

She'd usually hated it when he had called her Carrot Top, but she hadn't hated it that time.

Joanna had looked down the mountain. She was standing in a small depression between the two rounded bumps that formed the peak's pinnacle. There was a natural cleft between them formed by a rocky wash that dropped straight down the front of the mountain and seemed to come to an end in a small grove of scrub oak halfway down.

"I'll marry you," she had called to Andy over her shoulder, "but you'll have to catch me first." With that she had dropped onto her butt and slid down the wash, using it like a gigantic amusement-park slide. Naturally Andy had followed her. Their downhill movement came to an end in the grove of oak, where an on-again/off-again spring provided much-needed moisture.

That was where Andy had finally caught up with her—in the grove of trees. Laughing, he had grabbed her and kissed her. Later they'd gone skinny-dipping in the water hole. Then, under the sheltering oak, they'd made love, with Joanna's body cushioned by nothing more than layers of dried leaves and a pile of their abandoned clothing.

"After all," Andy had said, just before they did the deed, "what does it matter? We're already pregnant."

Joanna was pulled out of her momentary reverie by Agent Watkins's voice. "It's not very big up here, is it," she remarked.

Joanna looked around. She had to agree that the slightly rounded top of the mountain, divided in half by that distinctive dip, was surprisingly small—not more than fifteen yards long and no more than ten across. Here and there, scattered across that tiny bit of landscape, were small clumps of what Joanna now knew to be hedgehog cactus.

"Those are the Fendler's hedgehogs," she explained. "The ones Desirée Wilburton was out here researching."

"Which means those are the hedgehogs that got her killed," Robin responded. "If you ask me, they don't look like much, and I doubt any of them were worth dying for."

CHAPTER 11

"HEY, SHERIFF BRADY," DAVE CALLED. "WHERE ARE YOU?"

Joanna and Robin sidled over to the edge and peered down to where the two men and the dog were still visible, only now their positions were reversed, with the women at the top of the peak and the two men and dog well below.

"Up here," Joanna called back, waving. "Did you find anything?"

"This is the spot for sure," Dave replied, his voice flowing up to them with almost no distortion, as if carried and amplified by the breeze blowing against the rock face from the west.

"Anything besides the shoe?"

"Affirmative."

"Okay, then," Joanna told him. "We'll meet you back at the cars."

Joanna's phone rang, letting out its unmistakable rooster crow.

"What the hell is that?" Robin demanded.

"Sorry," Joanna said, tugging the phone out of her pocket. "Hello."

"We've got the car," Casey Ledford said, "and maybe part of the crime scene."

"What do you mean?" Joanna asked.

"Let's just say there's lots of biological evidence in that backseat. I think it functioned as Susan's private no-tell motel, and not just once, either. It's on its way to the impound lot as we speak. Once it's here, we'll need to swab it for DNA and dust it for prints."

"Good," Joanna said. "We're up on Geronimo. Dave seems to have found some additional pieces of evidence, including Susan Nelson's missing shoe. We won't know what else is there until we meet up with him down at the bottom."

"You said 'we'?" Casey inquired

"I'm here with Agent Watkins. Dave is working with Terry and Spike."

"So I'm assuming it's okay to clock in some additional overtime on this?" Casey asked.

"Yes," Joanna said. "For right now we'll all need to do whatever needs to be done. See you back at the office."

"How did you end up with a rooster ring tone?" Robin asked when Joanna ended the call.

"I like it," Joanna said. "Nobody else has one like it."

"I wonder why," Robin grumbled.

They made their way back down the mountain. It was too hot to wait in the car, so they sheltered under the scrub oak until Dave, Terry, and the dog reappeared half an hour later.

"What did you find?" Joanna asked, after introducing Agent Watkins to the others.

One at a time and brimming with pride, Dave began pulling evidence bags out of the many pockets of his safari-style vest. "One shoe," he said. "Size eight and a half; found just below what we now believe to be the drop-off point."

Dave withdrew another bag and handed it to Joanna. "This one contains one tiny piece of blue fuzz."

"Blue fuzz?"

"There's a partial path from the cliff back over to the main route up and down the mountain," Dave explained. "I found the fuzz caught on a creosote branch on the way back down. I'm thinking the guy was in a hell of a hurry and didn't notice his clothing had gotten hung up on something."

"You think it's from the hoodie?" Joanna asked.

"That's certainly a possibility," Dave said with a nod. "I believe the SVSSE school colors are blue and white."

He pulled out another bag. "Here's my current favorite."

Joanna peered at the bag. It took a moment before she finally caught sight of a single strand of brown hair, approximately eight inches in length, trapped between the two layers of clear plastic.

"I believe Desirée Wilburton was described as having shoulder-length light brown hair," Dave said.

Joanna nodded. "I believe so, too. Good work—good work, all of you," she added, reaching down to rub Spike's pointed black ears. "Casey tells me Susan's Honda is on its way to the impound lot. Let's go back to the department, reconvene in the conference room for a few moments, and sort out where we are."

They were back in the Yukon and bouncing toward town when Robin broached a painful subject. "I'm guessing you'll be having to take time off for funerals later this week?"

Since this was a joint investigation, Joanna considered it to be a fair question. "Funeral, not funerals," she answered. "One only. Friday morning at eleven. I'll probably take all day Friday off, but I expect to work the rest of the time."

"Were you and your mother close?"

"Not really," Joanna said. "It's a very long story."

"And none of my business," Robin said.

And then, because Robin hadn't asked, Joanna told her anyway. Because talking about Eleanor with a complete stranger was easier than talking about her with someone who happened to know where all the bodies were buried. Even so, Joanna didn't tell all of it—there wasn't time—but she hit the high spots.

"In my family, my mother's fine," Robin said when Joanna finished. "It's my father who's the pain in the butt. He's FBI, too. It's sort of the family business. My brother chose to join the Secret Service, which sent my father into a tizzy. And my signing up to follow in Dad's footsteps was the last thing he wanted. Sounds like your mother and my dad would have been birds of a feather."

"But what about your brother?" Joanna asked. "Is all forgiven now? Is he still the fair-haired boy?"

"Absolutely," Robin said. "Ray's a good guy, and we get along fine when the folks aren't around, but Dad never lets me forget for one minute that I come in a very distant second."

"What are you doing for dinner tonight?" Joanna asked.

"Dinner? I'll eat at the hotel, I suppose. Why?"

"Because my brother and his wife flew in from Manassas today. My husband, Butch, invited them to dinner. I've had a hell of a day, and I'm not up to having some big family conflab tonight. There's enough on my plate right now, and before I deal with whatever I need to deal with as far as Bob and Marcie are concerned, I also need a good night's sleep."

"Is Butch a good cook?" Robin asked.

"He's a great cook," Joanna answered.

"And you're inviting me to dinner so I can function as a human shield?"

"Yes," Joanna admitted. "I suppose that's about the size of it."

"Let's see," Robin said. "Go to a hotel and eat by myself in a strange dining room or go somewhere else and have a home-cooked meal for a change while I help someone I like deal with an older brother who may or may not be too full of himself? Which sounds like a better deal to you?"

Joanna smiled as she swung into the parking lot. "I'll call Butch and tell him to set another place."

CHAPTER 12

BACK AT HER OFFICE, JOANNA HAD KRISTIN SET UP AN IMPROMPTU video conference call during which everyone, including Ian Waters and Frank Montoya, could be brought up-to-date and, coincidentally, introduced to Agent Watkins.

For the second time that day, they assembled in the conference room. Jaime Carbajal and Ernie Carpenter had spent most of the day canvassing people from the Warren neighborhood nearest the ranch road, in case someone in that area had seen something. Not surprisingly, the detectives had come up empty.

With the help of Robin's boss, the FBI's agent in charge in Tucson, Frank Montoya had succeeded in obtaining a warrant that allowed investigators to access both victims' telephone records. Deb Howell had spent most of the day poring over call records from both phones and over text exchanges as well.

"Anything?" Joanna asked.

"Nada," Deb answered. "I can't find any point of contact between the two victims. Desirée doesn't seem to have many friends, or a current boyfriend, either, for that matter. Most of her texting is back and forth to her mother. Susan, on the other hand, did a lot of texting to her fellow teachers. She did some texting to the kids who are on her debate team, but nothing out of the ordinary or out of line. Times for coaching sessions; carpooling and busing arrangements for getting back and forth to tournaments; that sort of thing."

"No lovey-dovey stuff?" Joanna asked.

"Nope."

"But she's pregnant with a kid whose father most likely isn't her husband. That means she's carrying on an affair with someone, and that means there's got to be some point of contact somewhere."

"Unless she was doing it by code, it's not in her texting history, which is what I focused on today. Tomorrow I'll use the reverse directory to track down her most frequently called numbers. That's most likely where we'll find the boyfriend."

"You're probably right," Joanna agreed, "but you won't be able to get back to the phone issue until after we finish up doing the school interviews. In the meantime, I need you to let Desirée's mother know that Dr. Baldwin is prepared to release the body tomorrow morning. Since you're the one who spoke to her earlier, would you please handle that as soon as possible? At this point, calling her would probably be okay. It wouldn't require another in-person visit."

"I'll be glad to do a face to face," Deb offered. "Tonight happens to be Maury's and my anniversary. Ben has a sleepover, and I was planning to drive up to Tucson after work, have dinner with Maury, spend the night, and be in Sierra Vista tomorrow morning in time for the interviews. This way, I can mix a little business with pleasure. I'll stop by and give Roberta Wilburton the news probably before dinner rather than after."

Deb Howell had met Maury Robbins years earlier during a homicide investigation at an ATV park near Bowie in the northeast corner of the county. Maury was a 911 dispatcher for Pima County as well as an ATV enthusiast. The two of them had fallen in love and eventually married. Now Maury commuted back and forth between Tucson and Bisbee, spending four nights a week in Bisbee at the newly renovated home he and Deb had purchased at the far end of Brewery Gulch. The other three nights a week he spent at a home he still maintained in Tucson.

"Thank you," Joanna said. "Under the circumstances, mixing business with pleasure is fine with me. And happy anniversary, by the way. Speaking of those SVSSE interviews, however, what about them? Are they all set up, Detective Waters?"

"Yes, ma'am," Ian replied. "I don't know what kind of a kick in the butt you gave Mr. McVey, but after your phone call, he sent out notices letting all interested parties know that we'll be conducting interviews with students, faculty, and staff all day tomorrow. I expect that will amount to speaking to close to three hundred people, give or take. I suggested that we focus first on the kids most directly involved with Ms. Nelson, starting with members of the debate team. I asked Mr. McVey to plan on having ten or so kids come through at half-hour intervals and for him to ask faculty and staff to drop by when convenient—during planning periods, breaks, or whatever. Most of the interviews will be conducted on a fairly straightforward manner. Interviewees who don't know anything will be in and out in no time. For the ones who merit further scrutiny, we can schedule second interviews."

"Three hundred people sounds like a lot," Joanna said. "How long is this going to take?"

"School starts at eight thirty and gets out at three thirty. With five or six of us—including Chief Montoya—working the problem, I'm hoping we can get them all done in one day, but plan on packing a lunch. None of us will be getting time off for good behavior."

"Nobody needs to pack a lunch," Frank Montoya interjected. "My department will spring for coffee and doughnuts in the morning and sandwiches at lunchtime."

"Thanks, Frank," Joanna said. "One other thing, Detective Waters. How are you planning to handle parental involvement?"

"The notice Mr. McVey sent out specified that parents who don't object to their children being interviewed without their being present are advised to send signed permission slips to that effect," Ian told her. "Parents who wish to be present are being told when, during the day, their child is scheduled to be interviewed. No sense in someone having to take a whole day off work when we really need them for half an hour or so at most."

"Sounds like you've done a great job of organizing a complex set of problems," Joanna told him. "Thanks."

She called on Dave Hollicker next. "Why don't you give everyone an idea of what you and the K9 unit found at the crime scene today?"

He did so, telling them about the three pieces of solid evidence—the shoe and the hair as well as the blue fuzz. "Of the three," he concluded, "the most important is likely to be the fuzz. Casey was able to enhance those SVSSE security images enough for us to see that, at the time of the abduction, the perpetrator appeared to be wearing gloves, but with any kind of luck, he may not have been wearing gloves while handling the hoodie. And even if he was, there may be some cast-off DNA still present on the fuzz."

"If the fuzz came from the outside of the hoodie, the chances of finding DNA aren't all that good, are they?" Joanna asked.

"No, they're not," Dave agreed, "but even if it's a remote possibility, the fuzz and the hair, too, need to go to the crime lab in Tucson immediately. I can run both of them up there if you like."

"No need," Detective Howell offered. "I'll be glad to do that, too. Our place in Tucson is over on the far west side, only a mile or so from the crime lab. Dropping off the evidence will barely take me out of my way."

"Thanks, Deb," Joanna told her. "And if you're planning on doing all that before your anniversary dinner, you'd best grab those evidence bags from Dave and hit the road."

Joanna waited while Deb and Dave huddled long enough for him to hand over the evidence before resuming the meeting.

"Okay," Joanna said finally. "We're mostly finished here. I'd like to reinterview Drexel Nelson first thing tomorrow morning, before the school interviews start. I told Dr. Baldwin that I'd let him know that Susan's remains are ready to be released. Now that we've learned Susan Nelson was carrying a child that most likely wasn't his, a second chat with him is definitely in order, and I'll need someone along for the ride on that one—preferably someone who was there for the first interview."

"Since Deb will be coming from Tucson tomorrow morning, I'm guessing I'm your man," Ian Waters said. "When and where?"

"Thanks, Ian. What say we meet at the Nelson place in Sierra

Vista at seven thirty or so? That should give us enough time to finish with him before the school interviews start at eight thirty. And since we have Agent Watkins at our disposal, I'll have her come along, too."

"Sounds good," Detective Waters said.

Joanna looked out at the tired faces in the room and on the screen. Her people were pretty much done for, and so was she.

"Okay, folks," she said. "Enough is enough. Let's call it quits for today. Tomorrow is going to be a bear. You, too, Dave and Casey. Let's all head for the barn. As for everybody else? See you in Sierra Vista in the A.M."

People gathered up their things and filed out of the room. Agent Watkins lingered. "Do I need to change before dinner?" she asked.

"This is Arizona," Joanna told her. "Western attire is always appropriate."

"What are you going to wear?"

"I'd be wearing jeans too, if I had any that still fit."

"When are you due?"

"December?"

"With an election in November?"

"Yup."

"You don't believe in having a lot on your plate, do you," Robin observed.

"That's exactly how I like it," Joanna told her. "Wouldn't have it any other way."

CHAPTER 13

JOANNA'S PLAN TO USE ROBIN WATKINS AS A HUMAN SHIELD ENDED up working far better than she had intended or even wanted. It turned out that from the moment Robin and Bob Brundage were introduced, the two of them had settled into chatting as though they were long-lost buddies. During his years in the Pentagon, Bob had been in and out of the White House on numerous occasions, and he was quite sure he must have met Robin's brother at least once.

That initial point of connection soon evolved into a long discussion about the politics of government—not politics per se so much as the complexities of operating inside chains of command and inside governmental entities where no allowances were made for any kind of common sense. Bob and Robin might have been from entirely different agencies, but as far as dealing with inflexible command structures that seemed hell-bent on promoting waste and mismanagement, the two of them were definitely in the same corner.

Joanna had brought Robin home to dinner in hopes of deflecting some of the conversation about Eleanor and George's deaths, but she hadn't intended to deflect all of it. She went to bed feeling frustrated and annoyed, and awakened early the next morning—long before her alarm went off—feeling the same way. She crept out of bed, dressed quietly, and was in the process of tiptoeing out of the bedroom when Butch woke up.

"Where are you off to at the crack of dawn?" he asked, sitting up. "And what about breakfast?"

"I have to be in Sierra Vista by seven thirty," she said. "Since I'll be fighting rush hour for people heading on post, I thought I'd get an early start. As for breakfast, Sierra Vista PD is springing for that."

"All right, then," Butch said. "Be safe."

"Will," she answered, and hurried out.

In actual fact, leaving the house for a seven-thirty appointment at six fifteen was a clear case of overkill, but right that minute, she didn't want to discuss with Butch what had or hadn't gone on at dinner. One of the things that annoyed Joanna about Butch on occasion was his unfailing ability to see both sides of any given argument. There were times when she loved his penchant for playing devil's advocate, but only when the two of them happened to land on the same side. This wasn't one of those times.

Joanna was annoyed that Bob seemed to be exhibiting none of the grief over their mother's death that she herself was feeling. Of course, having outlived both his adoptive parents, Bob had already experienced this challenging process, and he had done so after becoming an adult. Joanna's father's death had come about while she was still a teenager. Inarguably, Bob had already been there and done that. Maybe that helped explain why he had been able to maintain dinnertime small talk in such a free and easy fashion, focusing on safe, theoretical topics and general philosophy without ever coming close to mentioning the emotionally draining reality of the upcoming funeral.

On an intellectual level, Joanna understood that the dynamics of the relationships Bob had shared with Eleanor and George had been forged in adulthood. Her own complicated relationship with her mother dated from childhood. In that two-character family drama, Joanna was forever cast in the role of "wayward teenager"—as the irresponsible girl who had "gotten herself in trouble"—as though Andrew Roy Brady had had nothing whatsoever to do with it.

As a consequence, even though Joanna had been right in front of Eleanor the whole time, Eleanor had never seen her daughter in the same light as, say, the voters of Cochise County, who had overwhelmingly elected her to a very responsible position twice over, and who, hopefully, would vote the same way again in a few months' time. The fact that Eleanor had ignored the steady presence of her levelheaded daughter and chosen Bob to function as her executor was something that rankled more than Joanna could say.

So even though she understood all those things on a logical level, it didn't mean she wanted to stand around while Butch explained it all to her in his perfectly reasonable and patient fashion. She was still driving and fuming a few minutes later when her phone rang.

"Hey, Mom," Jenny greeted her. "How's it going?"

"Fine," Joanna said. Of course, things were far from fine, but she hoped Jenny wouldn't be able to suss that out.

"Sorry I didn't get back to you yesterday," Jenny went on. "As soon as I got out of class, I went to work out with Maggie. By the time we finished up, it was too late to call. Did you need something?"

Yes, I needed something, Joanna thought. *I needed to hear the sound of your voice.* What she said aloud was, "I just wanted to say hi and see how things were going."

"Yesterday I went by to see the professors and instructors from my Friday classes," Jenny said. "I told them what was going on back home and let them know that I need to miss class on Friday so I can come to the funeral. The thing is, most of the lectures are available online these days, so I'll be able to listen to them coming and going. I'll leave as soon as my last class gets out tomorrow afternoon. I should be home by ten or so—no later."

Joanna's first instinct was to say, "No, you shouldn't," but she stifled it. She and Butch had decided between themselves that Jenny should ditch the funeral in favor of heading off to school on time. Now, though, Jenny was making a decision that suited her needs and was hers alone.

"What about Maggie?" Joanna asked.

"Mom!" Jenny exclaimed, sounding affronted. "Who do you think I am? Of course I've found someone to look after Maggie!"

Properly reprimanded, Joanna did an immediate about-face. "It'll be lovely to have you here," she said. "Dealing with all this is harder than I thought."

"So I heard," Jenny responded. "The situation with Grandma and Grandpa has to be hard enough, but adding a double homicide on top of that makes it that much worse."

"How do you know about the double homicide?" Joanna wondered aloud.

"Hello? Earth to Mom. Haven't you heard of the Internet? I read Marliss Shackleford's column first thing this morning, as soon as it was posted online."

"I hate to think what she said."

"Don't bother reading it," Jenny advised. "She interviewed Don Hubble, of course, and guess what? He thinks your being involved in an active homicide investigation when you should be off on personal leave is setting a bad example for your department. He also mentioned something to the effect that you should be wise enough to recognize that it's best for all concerned for you to stand down when you're caught up in an emotional turmoil that might cloud your judgment and cause you to be a less than effective law enforcement officer."

I solved Grandma and Grandpa's murder, didn't I? Joanna thought the words but didn't say them aloud.

"That figures," she said. "How very kind of Marliss to give Don Hubble an opportunity to spout his campaign rhetoric for free without his having to bother placing an ad."

"Is Marliss going to give you a chance to respond?"

"Not likely."

"Bitch," Jenny muttered fiercely.

Joanna couldn't help smiling. "My sentiments exactly," she said.

By then she had arrived in Sierra Vista, was driving down Busby Drive, and was about to turn into the parking lot at Holy Redeemer Chapel. She was early, but Ian's sleek Interceptor and Agent Watkins's Taurus were already parked and waiting so all three vehicles could approach the house together.

"I've gotta go, Jenny," Joanna said. "Thanks for the call. See you tomorrow."

"You're not going to give me any grief about coming home?" Jenny asked.

"Nope," Joanna said. "Not this time. Your life, your decision. You get to make the call."

"Thanks, Mom," Jenny said. "I love you."

Twang went Joanna Brady's emotional rubber band, one more time. Home and family versus work and murder. Maybe Don Hubble wasn't completely wrong after all.

CHAPTER 14

AS THE THREE POLICE VEHICLES CARAVANNED TOWARD THE house, another vehicle, a blue Ford Fiesta, came toward them, approaching the officers from the opposite direction. When it drove by, Joanna noticed a woman behind the wheel, but there was no time to grab a phone and photograph either the driver or the vehicle's license. Instead, she drove into the parking area in front of Drexel Nelson's house, hopped out of her Yukon, and hurried forward to knock on the door.

"What now?" Reverend Nelson demanded, banging open the door—which suddenly stopped moving in midswing. "Oh," he said. "I thought you were someone else. What do you want?"

Despite the fact that Nelson was looming over her in the same blue-and-white PJs Joanna had seen before, there was a visible trace of lipstick on his lower jaw. An unidentified female visitor had just driven away from his house at this very early hour of the morning. In other words, if the good reverend had already sought out female companionship for overnight visits, he wasn't exactly letting grass grow when it came to dealing with the grieving process.

By then the others had walked up onto the porch behind Joanna. "You've already met Detective Waters with Sierra Vista PD," Joanna said. "And this is Agent Watkins of the FBI. We wanted to speak to you for a few minutes about your wife's remains."

"What about them?" Reverend Nelson demanded, not opening the door any wider or showing any indication that he was about to invite his visitors inside.

"Dr. Kendra Baldwin, the ME, says she'll be able to release your wife's body today. She'll need to know which funeral home you'd like to have handle the arrangements."

"All right," he said. "Fair enough. I'll give her office a call and let her know."

He made as if to shut the door, but Joanna managed to insert the toe of her shoe between the door and the frame. "We'd also like to ask you a few additional questions."

"What about?"

"Wouldn't it be easier if we did this inside the house?"

With a reluctant sigh, he opened the door wide enough to allow the three officers to enter. As Joanna walked past him, she realized how tall the man was—six-four at least. Either she hadn't noticed that detail the previous night or she hadn't remembered it. In her autopsy overview, Kendra Baldwin had mentioned that Susan Nelson had been five-six. The male figure captured in the surveillance films escorting her from the school grounds was probably only four or five inches taller than she was—so six feet or maybe six-one at the most, including the hoodie. In other words, when it came to the kidnapping, Reverend Drexel Nelson was the wrong guy. That didn't mean, however, that he was completely off the hook.

It took a moment for the visitors to arrange themselves in the small, overly furnished room.

"So?" Nelson said impatiently once they were seated. "What is it you want to know?"

"Are you aware that most homicide victims are murdered by someone close to them—a husband or boyfriend, perhaps?"

"Of course," he replied. "Everybody knows that, and the husband is usually the one who did it."

"Did you murder your wife?"

"No, most assuredly not!"

"Are you aware that your wife was expecting a child?"

His jaw literally dropped. "She was what?"

"She was with child—as in pregnant." Joanna answered. "You mentioned last night that you had a vasectomy performed years ago, so presumably the baby isn't yours. If you, the husband, didn't kill your wife, then to our way of thinking, the boyfriend would be a good bet. Do you have any idea who that might be?"

"She let herself get pregnant by another man?" Nelson demanded in shocked disbelief. Before anyone in the room could react, he rose out of his chair, took a powerful swing at the wall behind him, and punched a fist-sized hole in the Sheetrock.

"That little bitch!" he exclaimed, rubbing his dust-covered, bleeding knuckles. "How dare she do that? Couldn't she see how shame from that would reflect on me? If word of her pregnancy gets out, it'll be a permanent stain on my reputation."

Speaking of stains, Joanna thought, *what about that visible lip-*

stick mark? The words "pot and kettle" crossed her mind about then, but she didn't utter them aloud.

"Please sit down, Reverend Nelson," she urged. "What we're wondering is if there was anyone inside your wife's circle of acquaintances with whom she was particularly close. A good friend, perhaps, someone in whom she might have confided?"

"I don't socialize outside the church, and I didn't approve of Susan doing so, either," Nelson countered. "I suppose she may have had friends—unsuitable friends—at the school, but her school life was outside my realm. I didn't know any of those churchless, godless people, and I didn't care to."

"You know of no one inside or outside the church with whom she may have been involved?"

"Certainly not! This dreadful news comes as a complete shock to me. Since I know nothing about it, you could just as well be on your way. If you wish to speak to me again, it will be in the presence of my attorney."

Now that he had invoked his right to an attorney, there was nothing more to discuss. Joanna and the others rose as one to leave.

"And about those remains," he added. "You can tell the medical examiner from me that I won't be bothering to claim them. As of this moment, I wash my hands of the woman. You can haul her off to the nearest landfill for all I care. I refuse to have anything more to do with her."

Joanna had been the first one in and now she was the last out. She was a cop, and she shouldn't have let Nelson get under her skin, but the man's blatant hypocrisy was more than she could stomach.

She paused in the doorway. "I should have thought a man in

your position would be more forgiving of his wife's transgressions. Isn't that what Jesus would have done?"

Reverend Nelson leveled a cold-eyed stare in her direction. "I'm sure He probably would have," he responded, "but forgiving sins is a little above my pay grade."

Joanna caught up with the others on the way back to the cars. "Other that learning that Reverend Drexel Nelson is a complete hypocrite, that visit wasn't much help," Agent Watkins grumbled.

"Not true," Joanna said, "because it did help. We know now that Nelson isn't the guy who walked Susan Nelson out of her classroom."

"How do we know that?" Robin asked.

"For one thing, he's far too tall, and for another, he's right-handed."

"So he's not our guy?" Ian Waters concluded.

"Not our guy so far as the abduction is concerned, but that doesn't clear him from having a hand in her murder."

"Why?" Robin asked.

"Because we've been thinking all along that both victims would have had to climb Geronimo under their own steam. Maybe that's not true."

"What are you saying?"

"Did you see the hole Reverend Nelson punched in that wall with his bare fist? Anyone strong enough to do that could probably throw someone over his shoulder and carry her fireman-style wherever he wanted to—including straight up Geronimo."

"But if he did that," Agent Watkins concluded, "he'd most likely need an accomplice."

"Who, given what he's told us so far, is also likely to be a member of Holy Redeemer Chapel."

"Right. Since he doesn't socialize outside the confines of his church, Reverend Nelson most likely wouldn't go shopping for a hit man outside it, either."

"So it still comes down to the boyfriend or the husband," Ian Waters suggested.

"Or maybe both," Joanna replied. "But first of all, whoever that boyfriend is, we need to find him."

CHAPTER 15

BY THE TIME THE EIGHT-THIRTY BELL RANG AT THE SIERRA VISTA School for Scholastic Excellence—it was more a droning buzzer than a bell—announcing the start of classes, members of Joanna's joint homicide task force were already situated in the library. Ian Waters's request for separate rooms had been nixed based on the physical reality of the school having no such rooms available. Instead, rolling whiteboards had been moved into the library. Those, when combined with the library's movable bookshelves and tables, created at least the illusion of separate interview spaces even if there was less privacy than anyone would have liked.

With five trained homicide investigators conducting the actual interviews, Joanna functioned as a self-appointed Harry Potter–style sorting hat, checking people off on a master list provided by school authorities, noting the kids who presented signed parental permission slips and keeping same. Kids who appeared with parental units present were given priority when it came to the interviews themselves. By the time one student left an interview appointment, Joanna had the next one checked in and lined up to take his or her place. Frank Montoya took it upon himself to move back and forth between the library and the office, ironing out any thorny issues that arose.

When Travis Stock showed up in Joanna's line, there was enough of a family resemblance for her to recognize him as Deputy Stock's son before he even gave her his name.

"You're here by yourself, Travis," she noted. "Do you have a permission slip?"

"No," he said. "My mom told me she's coming. She should be here any minute." He looked back over his shoulder. Following Travis's lead, Joanna did the same in time for them both to see Deputy Stock enter the room. Dressed in his sheriff's-department uniform and carrying his Stetson, he made straight for the sign-in table.

"Morning, ma'am," he said, nodding in Joanna's direction.

"What are you doing here?" Travis demanded. "I thought Mom was coming."

Joanna couldn't help but notice that there was something off in Travis's tone of voice—something uneasy—that indicated he would have much preferred that his mother be present for the interview. It was probably, she concluded, just some kind of family dynamic, a father/son sort of thing, not unlike some mother/daughter relationships, hers included.

"I'm hoping Sheriff Brady here will give me permission to go on duty late today," Jeremy explained. "This way Mom won't have to take any time off." He looked at Joanna. "If Allison leaves work during the day, her paycheck gets docked. I'm hoping that won't happen to me."

Joanna smiled. "Don't worry," she said. "It won't. Thanks for coming."

After checking Travis's name off the list, she looked up in time to see a solo student exiting Agent Watkins's interview area. Thinking it best to avoid even the appearance of favoritism, Joanna sent Travis and Deputy Stock straight to Agent Watkins. That way the interview would be conducted by someone with zero connection to Joanna's department and people.

Generally speaking, the interviews proceeded in an orderly and fairly efficient fashion. The first kids—the debate team students—mostly stayed for the full half hour and occasionally even longer. That made sense since Susan Nelson had been more than simply a classroom teacher in their lives. Kids who'd had her for one class or else no classes were in and out in a blink. Two hours in, Joanna called a fifteen-minute break in the action, giving the detectives an opportunity to visit restrooms or grab one of the quickly diminishing supply of doughnuts.

"How's it going?" she asked when Robin Watkins stopped by the check-in desk with a glazed doughnut in one hand and a cup of coffee in the other.

"All right, I guess," Robin answered. "I haven't turned up much so far, and I don't think anyone else has, either. I was a little surprised when you sent that deputy's son my way."

"You shouldn't have been," Joanna told her. "I thought it would be best to have a stranger-to-stranger interview there. If one of my own people had conducted the interview, someone looking in from the outside might think Travis Stock was given special treatment based on who his father is and what he does. I didn't want that to happen. I wanted the process to look and be both transparent and fair. Since you didn't know either him or his father, that seemed like the best plan."

"And the interview was fair," Robin agreed. "All the same, I think Travis is someone who's worth interviewing again. I suspect he knows more than he's letting on, and I could tell he was very uncomfortable being interviewed in front of his father."

"I noticed that, too," Joanna agreed. "Travis seemed taken aback when Deputy Stock showed up rather than his mother. Did anyone else strike you as being off or unduly uncomfortable?"

"Not really," Robin said. "Everyone else seemed to be shocked and distressed by what happened, but they also seemed to be fairly forthcoming."

With that, Robin returned to her makeshift cubicle, as did the others, and the game resumed. Most of the faculty members came through during their lunch hours while their students were in the cafeteria.

In the early afternoon, while the task force was dealing with kids who essentially had had zero contact with Susan Nelson, the process moved forward so swiftly that by two P.M., an hour and a half before school let out, the last of the student interviews had been completed.

"Okay," Joanna said, calling her troops to an impromptu meeting around one of the computer tables in the center of the room. "What, if anything, have we learned from all this?"

Ian Waters raised his hand first. "The kids in the debate club thought Susan Nelson walked on water," he said. "She took an active interest in their lives. She didn't just help them with debate and speech issues, she offered tutoring to them because low grades might result in their being dropped from the team."

"In other words," Joanna supplied, "it sounds like the general assessment is that she was a competent, caring teacher."

That statement was followed by nods of agreement all around.

"Agent Watkins found one student she thinks needs to be re-interviewed. Are there any others?"

"Not really," came the answer. As far as the other investigators were concerned, none of their kids seemed to have raised any alarms.

"How about Susan's fellow teachers?" Joanna asked. "No faculty-based feuds or turf wars?"

That question, too, was met with a circle of head shakes.

"Did any member of the faculty stand out as being especially close to the deceased?"

Again the visible responses were all in the negative.

Deb Howell raised her hand. "I spoke to a number of faculty members who all claimed Susan was a dynamic teacher who was well known for going the extra mile to help her kids," she said.

"Did anyone mention activities that might have gone on outside the school itself?"

"Not much. Evidently Susan showed up occasionally at TGIF or Girls Night Out bashes during the course of the year, but no one mentioned her being close pals with anyone in particular."

Jaime took the floor. "One of the math teachers, Mr. Briggs, mentioned that he and Susan Nelson were supposed to be advisers for last spring's junior/senior prom. They'd only had one meeting with the committee before Drexel Nelson showed up at school and raised hell with the principal, demanding that Mr. McVey remove Susan from the prom committee because it was his personal belief that dancing of any kind was the devil's own handiwork."

"What happened?" Joanna asked.

"Susan bowed out, of course, but Mr. Briggs said she told him later that although her husband may be a 'man of God,' he could also be a real jerk on occasion."

"Which is to say," Agent Watkins added, "Reverend Nelson is somewhat controlling."

"Make that very controlling," Ernie added. "To say nothing of hot-tempered and strong—all of which are elements often involved in domestic-violence-related homicides."

"Which this might very well be," Joanna agreed, "except for the presence of the second victim. If Susan Nelson and Desirée Wilburton maintained some kind of relationship of which Reverend Nelson disapproved, that might be motive enough for him to go after both of them."

"Yes," Deb said, "but so far we've established no direct links between the two women whatsoever. I can't find any connections between them via phone records, e-mails, or texts. There's nothing showing on social media, either. If the two of them were in contact, it would have had to be by smoke signals or snail mail because it's completely under the radar as far as electronic communications are concerned."

"Did Drexel Nelson grow up in Bisbee?" Robin Watkins asked suddenly.

The question seemed to come from way out in left field. All heads turned as one toward the newcomer in the room, the person who had asked the question. "Not as far as I know," Joanna answered. "Why?"

"Because yesterday, when we were on Geronimo, you told me that climbing the mountain is an iconic activity for young people growing up in Bisbee. It's pretty clear that Susan Nelson was abducted in Sierra Vista and then transported to the location where the homicide actually occurred. Why would that be? I think that suggests that either she or her killer must have had some kind of prior knowledge about or connection to that particular place."

At that juncture, Joanna's phone buzzed in her pocket. She had silenced the crowing ring tone during the interviews and hadn't turned it back on. After checking caller ID, she answered it anyway. "Hey, Larry," she said when Larry Kendrick, her daytime dispatcher, came on the line. "What's up?"

She listened for a minute. "Okay," she said. "I'll send Deb and Dave Hollicker. We're spread pretty thin around here right now, so one detective and one CSI are all I can spare." Breaking off, she turned back to the room. "We've got a domestic situation up in Sun Sites. Assault with intent. The victim is being transported to Tucson Medical Center. If he dies, the case may turn into a homicide, so deputies on the scene are requesting an investigative unit. Can you go, Deb, or should I send someone else?"

"I can go. Maury will be back in Bisbee this afternoon. He'll look after Ben once school gets out."

Joanna got back on the phone. "Did you hear that, Larry? Detective Howell is leaving now, coming from the far side of Sierra Vista. Once she's under way, you can radio her the details. And please go ahead and let Dave know that he's on a callout. Under most circumstances, I'd show up at the scene as well, but right now, when I'm caught between two confirmed homicides and one potential, I'm going to stick around here and deal with these. If anything changes on the other one, let me know."

By the time the call ended, Deb was already headed for the

door. Joanna glanced at her watch. She wanted to go home and change into something a little more dressy before dinner. "Anything else?" she asked, turning back to the others. "I believe we still have a secretary, a couple of custodians, and a groundskeeper that we need to talk to before we call it a day. The groundskeeper doubles as a bus driver, so he won't come in until after he drops kids off at the end of school."

"I'll handle the leftovers," Agent Watkins offered. "The rest of you probably have family obligations. I don't."

The room cleared at once with everyone but Agent Watkins hurrying out. As Joanna gathered up her goods to leave, a last straggling student, with her mother in tow, showed up to be interviewed. Joanna sent them to Agent Watkins, then she cleared out herself, stopping by the office, where she sought out Mr. McVey.

"I know this was a huge inconvenience for you and your people today," she said. "Thank you for making the effort."

"Did you find anything?"

"Nothing for certain," she replied, "but having the chance to speak to most of the people who knew Ms. Nelson in one place at one time, without having to chase them down individually, was a huge help."

"Very glad to be of service," Mr. McVey said, seeming to have forgotten that Joanna had threatened him with a media firestorm if he hadn't complied. "Any word on when and where Susan's services will be held? Most likely at Reverend Nelson's church, of course, but I'm sure a number of students and faculty members from here will be interested in attending."

With Drexel Nelson's declaration that he had no interest in claiming his wife's remains, the timing and place of a funeral service—if any—were entirely up in the air. Fortunately, that was one bullet that wasn't Joanna's to dodge.

"All of that is up to the family," she said. "I have no information in that regard at all."

She left then, heading for the Yukon. Because she had arrived just before the eight-thirty bell, her parking place was at the far end of the parking lot, near a basketball court. There was only one person visible on the court—a long, lanky kid, practicing dribbling and short jump shots. When Joanna clicked her key fob, the Yukon's lights flashed and a beep sounded as the doors unlocked. With her attention on the vehicle, she didn't notice at first that the dribbling had stopped.

"Sheriff Brady?" It was a young male voice—tentative, uncertain. "Can I talk to you for a minute?"

Stashing her purse on the front seat, Joanna turned around. The kid from the court approached her warily, holding the ball in front of him, almost as a shield. Out on the court, seeing him in the glare of the sunlight behind him, his features had been invisible. Now she recognized him. He had come to the Justice Center to interview her for an article he was doing as an assignment for his journalism class. It took a moment for Joanna to recall his name, but remembering names is something every politician has to learn sooner or later, and eventually it came to her.

"Kevin Thomas, right?" she asked, holding out her hand.

Relief at being recognized flashed across his face. He nodded gratefully. "That's me," he said. "I'm surprised you remembered."

"I trust you got a good grade on that assignment?"

"I did, thank you—something like ninety-four points out of a hundred. I sent you a copy, didn't I?"

"Yes," she answered. "I'm sure you did. The problem is, mountains of paperwork cross my desk on a daily basis, so please forgive me if I don't remember what it said. But what can I do for you today? Is this about your interview?"

Ducking his head, Kevin stared down at his feet. "I didn't exactly come in for an interview. I was out sick."

"Since you're well enough to be out on the basketball court this afternoon, you must be feeling better."

"Not exactly," he allowed reluctantly. "I mean, I didn't stay home today because I was sick. I stayed home because of the interview."

"Because you didn't want to talk to us or because your parents didn't want you to talk to us?" Joanna asked.

"My mom didn't know about the interviews," he said. "The school sent the notice to her home e-mail account, and I deleted it from her mailbox before she had a chance to read it."

"So you didn't want her to know about it?"

Kevin nodded. "That's right."

"Why?"

"Because I'm not a snitch, and because I didn't want to get someone else in trouble."

"But you want to talk to us now?"

"Yes."

"Why?"

"Because Mrs. Nelson is dead, and I may know who did it."

Joanna reached into the Yukon and retrieved her purse. "We'd better go inside, then," she said. "And we'll need to call your mother."

"But she's at work. Do you have to call her?"

"You're a juvenile, Kevin. When police officers question juveniles, the parents must be notified. Since you deleted the e-mail, your mother wasn't aware of this situation earlier. If she chooses not to come and allows us to interview you without her being present, that's up to her, but we have to give her the option. Okay?"

"I guess," Kevin said, in a very small voice. "If you have to."

CHAPTER 16

BACK IN THE LIBRARY, MOST OF THE OTHER WHITEBOARD BARRIers had been wheeled away. The only interview cubicle that remained relatively intact was the one belonging to Agent Watkins. Since there was someone still inside, Joanna stopped on the far side of the library.

"I need your mom's phone number," she told Kevin.

With a reluctant sigh, Kevin spit out a cell-phone number, and Joanna dialed it. "What's your mom's name?"

"Karenna Thomas, Karenna with two *Ns*," he said. "Colonel Karenna Thomas."

The female voice answering the phone clearly brooked no nonsense. "Colonel Thomas here," she said.

"This is Cochise County sheriff Joanna Brady," Joanna explained. "We're here at the school interviewing students, and we would like to speak to your son."

"He's not at school today," Colonel Thomas answered. "He was ill this morning and stayed home."

"He seems to have recovered," Joanna said. "He's here at school now, and we'd like to speak to him. Since he's a juvenile, you either need to be present during the interview or you need to send us a signed slip saying that we have permission to speak to him without your being in attendance."

"What kind of interview?" Colonel Thomas asked. "I know that one of his teachers was murdered over the weekend—Ms. Nelson. Everyone on post was talking about it this morning. Is this about that?"

"Yes."

"When did she die?"

"We believe the crime occurred late Saturday night."

"All right, then," Colonel Thomas said. "Put my son on the phone."

Clearly Colonel Thomas was accustomed to issuing orders, and she did so now without the niceties of either a please or thank-you. Joanna handed the phone over to Kevin, who grimaced as he placed it to his ear.

What followed was a very one-sided conversation during which Kevin murmured several subdued "no, ma'ams," and "yes ma'ams." Finally he handed the phone back to Joanna.

"She's on post," he said. "She'll be here in fifteen minutes, and she said I shouldn't say anything more to you in the meantime."

"Fair enough," Joanna said. "That's why I called."

She glanced at her watch. It was now verging on four o'clock. The dinner reservation at Café Roka was for six. Bisbee was close to forty minutes away. High Lonesome Ranch was closer to fifty, more like an hour if you took into consideration driving there, changing clothes, and then getting back uptown to the restaurant in time for dinner. Depending on how soon the interview started and how long it lasted, Joanna most likely would have to show up in her uniform rather than being properly dressed for an evening out.

A man in workaday khakis—most likely the bus driver/janitor—emerged from Agent Watkins's cubicle. He picked up a cloth push broom that had been leaning against a nearby table and then sauntered out of the room. Agent Watkins appeared, stretching her shoulders.

"That's the last of them," she remarked; then, after looking at her watch, she frowned in Joanna's direction. "Don't you have a dinner engagement?" she asked. "I thought you left a long time ago."

"I did, but something came up and I've been delayed," Joanna replied. "This is Kevin Thomas. Kevin, this is Agent Robin Watkins of the FBI. She's helping my department with the investigation into Mrs. Nelson's death. Kevin here skipped school today because he didn't want to talk to us. Now he does. We're waiting for his mother. She works on post and is on her way here now."

"All right," Robin said.

"Colonel Thomas gave her son strict instructions that he's not to speak to us until she arrives, but perhaps you and I could share a word in private."

Leaving Kevin alone, Joanna led the way into the cubicle.

"What's going on?" Agent Watkins asked.

"Kevin says he thinks he knows who did this," Joanna whispered urgently. "We need to handle him with kid gloves. We can't afford to spook him or his mother. If Colonel Thomas decides that her son needs to lawyer up, we may never hear what he has to say. He doesn't want to be a snitch."

"If he knows who did this," Robin agreed, "we definitely need to hear what he has to say. Do you know anything about him?"

"A little. He came to the Justice Center and interviewed me for a journalism-class assignment last year. Seemed like a good enough kid."

Robin nodded. "He looked a little skittish. Should we go out, chat him up a bit, and maybe break the ice?"

"Only if whatever is said can't possibly be construed as a formal interview."

"Remember me at dinner last night?" Robin said with a grin. "Breaking the ice is one of my best tricks."

They left the cubicle together. A dejected Kevin sat at a table loaded with four immense desktop computers—old-fashioned clunky things. With the basketball still clutched to his chest, he looked completely out of place and ill at ease.

"Do you play?" Robin asked, plucking the ball out of his hand and twirling it expertly on one finger for a moment before passing it back.

"Not really," he said. "I'm on the varsity team, but that's mostly because I'm tall rather than because I'm any good. SVSSE is a small school, and that's who we play—other small schools."

"What year are you?"

"A senior."

"Got plans to go to college?"

Kevin nodded. "My mom has me lined up to go to the University of Arizona," he answered. "She says ROTC is the only way to go. She says since it was good enough for her, it's good enough for me."

"Smart mom," Robin said brightly. "So the military is the family business. Same thing happened to me. I'm FBI because my dad was FBI. Or maybe in spite of the fact that my dad was FBI. That works sometimes, too."

Kevin frowned. "Really?" he asked.

"Yes," she answered. "That's the main reason I did it. He said I'd never make the grade."

"But you did anyway?"

"You bet."

"Okay, then," Kevin said.

For the first time, the boy seemed to relax. The smallest of grins appeared in the corners of his mouth. He stretched his long legs out under the table. Just as Agent Watkins had promised, the ice was officially broken. When Colonel Thomas, in full-dress uniform, marched into the library a few minutes later, she seemingly outranked everyone there, but she was definitely facing a united front of opposition. She might have arrived expecting to stifle the conversation, but everyone else, Kevin included, wanted to talk.

Colonel Thomas made straight for her son, without acknowledging anyone else's presence. "Just so you know, young man," she warned with a soul-searing glare, "there will be grave consequences for your having interfered with my receiving an official notification from the school."

"Yes, ma'am," he said.

"And if you ditch school again for any reason, I will be shipping you off on the first available flight, and you can spend the remainder of your senior year with your father at Fort Bliss. You got that, mister?"

"Yes, ma'am," he said.

"All right, then," she said, turning her glower full on Joanna. "You're Sheriff Brady?"

"Yes, ma'am," Joanna said. She couldn't help herself. Karenna Thomas was a woman whose very presence required "yes, ma'am" responses.

"Then let's get to it," Colonel Thomas said briskly. "I don't have all day."

There was no one else in the library at that point. Without any further discussion, Joanna and Robin made a joint decision to conduct the interview right where they were rather than returning to the last remaining cubicle. Kevin seemed to be at ease where he was, and they didn't want to do anything that would disturb him.

"All right, then, Sheriff Brady," Karenna said. "Before anything more is said, you need to know that Kevin and I were together all day on Saturday. We drove up to Tucson around noon so I could introduce him to an old classmate of mine who is the new commander of the U of A's ROTC program. We had a late dinner and came home around nine thirty or ten. I'll be glad to give you the particulars of our trip. I wanted you to know that up front."

"I'm glad to know you'll be able to account for Kevin's whereabouts on the day in question," Joanna said, "but he's not under investigation at this time. Your son actually sought us out, Colonel Thomas. He claims to have some idea of who might be responsible for Mrs. Nelson's homicide."

Colonel Thomas eyed her son. "Is that true?"

"Yes, ma'am."

"Since you were with me at the time, Kevin, you can rest assured that nothing you're going to say to these ladies here will be in any way incriminating as far as you're concerned."

"Yes, ma'am."

"But it's your duty as a responsible citizen to cooperate with law enforcement and tell them whatever you know. Is that clear?"

"Yes, ma'am."

It was equally clear from the get-go that Colonel Thomas was putting herself in charge of the interview. Cops conducting a conversation with a juvenile would, of necessity, have been more light-handed, but that kind of restraint was not required of mothers. With that in mind, Joanna sat back and let Karenna Thomas run with it. If necessary, she and Agent Watkins could always play good cop to Colonel Thomas's bad cop.

"What's this all about?"

"It's about Travis," Kevin said quietly.

"Travis Stock?" Colonel Thomas asked.

Kevin nodded.

At the mention of Travis's name, a bolt of electricity shot through Joanna's body. She sat up straighter in her chair, hardly believing what she'd just heard. Travis was Jeremy Stock's son—the child of one of her sworn deputies. Everything she had ever heard or known about Travis said that he was a good kid—a responsible kid. How was it possible for someone like him to have been caught up in Susan Nelson's kidnapping and murder?

"He and Mrs. Nelson were . . . well . . . you know . . ." Kevin ducked his head, looking miserable, while a bright red flush spread up his neck, past his bony Adam's apple, and onto his face.

"No, I don't know," Colonel Thomas declared. "How about if you tell me?"

"They were like . . . you know . . . doing it."

"You mean the two of them were involved?" Agent Watkins

put in gently, taking some of the pressure off the embarrassed young man. Kevin nodded gratefully.

"You mean they were having sex?" Colonel Thomas demanded, giving her son no quarter.

Joanna could tell that Karenna Thomas was a force to be reckoned with—a blunt force at that. The idea that she was putting her son through hell right then seemed to be the last thing on her mind.

"Yes," Kevin said in a small voice.

"And?"

"And she got pregnant," Kevin said. This time his words came out in a rush. "When it happened, Mrs. Nelson was furious with Travis. She blamed him for the whole thing. Said he must have screwed up with the . . . you know . . . the . . ."

"The condom?" Agent Watkins supplied, once again coming to Kevin's rescue.

Kevin nodded gratefully.

"What happened then?" Colonel Thomas demanded.

Joanna had to give the woman credit. The fact that she had zero doubt that her son had anything to do with the homicides gave her free rein, and she seemed determined to extract every bit of pertinent information Kevin might have to offer.

"Trav told me that he asked her to marry him. He wanted her to divorce her husband and marry him. He said he'd get two jobs or even three, if that's what it took. She just laughed at him. She said that if they did that, she'd never be able to teach again. Besides, as far as the world was concerned, the baby would be her husband's child—like a miracle child—because Mr. Nelson would never humiliate himself in public by divorcing her."

Yes, Joanna thought. *One of those very unusual post-vasectomy miracles*. "She thought that no one would be the wiser?" she asked.

"Yes," Kevin said with a nod, "except for Travis."

"What was his reaction?"

Kevin shrugged. "He was hurt, I guess, and confused. I mean she wanted things to go on just the way they had before. She still wanted to see him."

"So she didn't want to break off the affair?" Agent Watkins asked.

"Not at all. She didn't even want him to quit the debate team. The trouble is, Trav wouldn't take no for an answer. He told her that the kid was his, and he was determined to be involved in the baby's life no matter what. He usually had tutoring sessions with her on Saturday evenings, tutoring and other stuff. He told me that he was going to see her that night and tell her straight out that he was going to go to her husband."

"And spill the beans?"

"Yes."

"When did he tell you that?"

"Friday afternoon after school. Except he must have changed his mind. Instead he ended up going along with some friends to a U of A football game in Tucson on Saturday afternoon. That's one thing I couldn't understand. Trav wanted to be a father, but he still wanted to be a kid himself and go to football games and stuff."

"Did he go to the game?" Colonel Thomas demanded.

"I guess," Kevin said uncertainly.

"You and Travis must be very close for him to have told you about all this," Robin suggested quietly.

Kevin nodded. "He's my best friend—since we moved here

when I was in junior high. Me and Trav played on the same soccer team. His dad was our coach. This summer I could tell something was really bothering him. I kept asking him what was wrong, and he finally told me."

"Did you tell anyone else?" Joanna asked.

"He asked me not to—made me promise—so no. Except for right now. I haven't told anyone else."

"You do understand what was going on here," Joanna interjected. "If what you've told us about Travis's story is true, Mrs. Nelson was a pedophile—a child molester—who took advantage of her position of authority in Travis's life to exploit him sexually."

"But Travis said it was all his idea—that Mrs. Nelson just went along with it."

"We're talking statutory rape here," Joanna explained. "That's the legal terminology when an adult has sexual relations with someone who's under the age of consent. It's also against the law. Of course, that's what she'd claim—that their relationship was consensual. It's also predictable that she'd say that whatever had happened was somehow the victim's fault. That's how pedophiles work. They groom inexperienced young people and manipulate them into doing whatever the abuser wants. Mrs. Nelson was a woman in her thirties. How long ago did this start?"

"Last year," Kevin said, "just after Trav joined the debate team."

"So he was what, seventeen or so at the time?"

"Sixteen," Kevin said.

"The age gap between someone in her midthirties and someone in his midteens makes for a big difference in life experience," Joanna said. "What Travis thought was going on and what was really going on are probably two entirely different things. And I can understand completely why you didn't want to come talk to us this morning," she added, with a quick glance toward Colonel Thomas, who acknowledged the validity of what had been said with a brief nod.

"So Travis told you this on Friday?" Joanna asked.

"Yes," Kevin said. "We were shooting hoops after school, and then, all of sudden, he blurted it all out. Just hearing about it made me feel sick inside. And then I saw that message on Mom's e-mail—the one setting up the interviews. As soon as I saw that, I was sure Trav was the one who had done it."

"Believing your best friend may have committed murder is a big burden to carry around," Robin suggested.

Kevin nodded gratefully at that small expression of sympathy. "Yes," he agreed. "I was scared."

"Scared of what?" his mother asked.

"That Trav might do something drastic."

"Like what, kill her?"

"Like maybe kill himself," Kevin answered. "That's what Trav said he was going to do if she wouldn't agree to marry him—commit suicide. Now that she's dead and the baby's gone, too, I'm afraid Trav may kill himself anyway, just because."

With that, Kevin dissolved into a spasm of anguished sobs. What happened next took Joanna's breath away. In a split second, Colonel Thomas stopped being a tough-talking career army officer and transformed into a loving mother. Stepping up to her brokenhearted son, she gathered him into her arms.

"Shhh," she crooned over the top of his head. "It's all right, Kevie. It's all right. We'll take care of this. It's not your problem anymore."

CHAPTER 17

SOMETIME LATER, ONCE KEVIN THOMAS PULLED HIMSELF TO-gether, it was his mother, not the colonel, who gently escorted him from the room. Joanna followed the pair as far as the door.

"If you need anything more," Colonel Thomas said, "I want to be present when you speak to him."

"Of course," Joanna agreed. "He's already been through too much. But there is one more thing, Kevin."

"What?"

"How tall would you say Travis Stock is?"

The boy shrugged. "About my size, I guess," he said.

"So around six feet, give or take?"

Kevin nodded. "About that," he said.

Once Kevin and his mother walked out of the library, Joanna turned back to Robin Watkins, who had remained seated at the table. "Sounds like we have a new person of interest," she said quietly.

Joanna nodded. "Who happens to be the son of one of my deputies."

"What do you suggest?" Robin asked.

"Normally, due to conflict-of-interest concerns, I'd call in another agency to do a preliminary investigation. Except it so happens an officer from another agency is already involved—namely you. Unless I'm sadly mistaken, six feet is about the size of the guy who walked Susan Nelson out of her classroom on Saturday afternoon."

"Do we happen to know if Travis Stock is right- or left-handed?"

Closing her eyes, Joanna recalled the sign-in process earlier that morning during the interviews, but she couldn't remember. "I'm not sure," she said. "In any case, we're going to have to accomplish a preliminary investigation without tipping our hand to Deputy Stock. The best possible outcome would mean being able to eliminate his son as a suspect without ever having to bring Deputy Stock and his wife into the equation."

"Because you're not ready to tell them about their son's relationship with Susan Nelson?"

"Exactly," Joanna said, passing her hand over her eyes. "This is a nightmare. The possibility that he may have committed a double homicide is bad enough. The fact that the boy has previously been victimized by a pedophile makes the situation that much worse."

"Let's put first things first," Robin suggested. "If we can verify Travis's alibi for Saturday afternoon and evening—if he really did go to the game—then we know for sure that he wasn't responsible for the kidnapping and probably not for the homicides, either. I'm pretty sure it was a nighttime game, so it wouldn't have been over until ten o'clock or even later, which doesn't leave enough time for him to get back to Bisbee, a hundred miles away, and then be on Geronimo in time to commit the murders."

Picking up her iPad, Robin scrolled through her notes. "Here's what I was looking for. Travis told me during the interview that he and some buddies left for the football game early in the afternoon. They were planning to stop for pizza somewhere along the way, before they went to the game."

"Did he happen to mention the buddies' names?"

"Nate and Jack. No last names. My bad for not getting them in the first place," Robin said. "Do you remember seeing any Nathaniels or Jacks on the list of students here at the SVSSE?"

"Not right off the bat," Joanna answered. "That means that they may be friends from town rather than friends from school, which also means they wouldn't have been on our to-be-interviewed list."

"I'll see what I can do to locate them," Robin offered.

"Good," Joanna said. "I just wish there were some way we could get a sample of Travis's DNA without giving any of this away."

"Why?"

"Because before I drop any of the pedophilia issue on Jeremy and Allison Stock, I'd like to know for sure if their son is the father of Susan Nelson's unborn baby."

Shc paused for a moment, thinking, and then added, "Wait. Maybe there is a way. After the school shooting incidents, many schools, especially private ones, have taken the position that students are allowed the use of school lockers, but that the lockers are owned by the schools and therefore must be accessible to school officials at all times. It's almost five. With any luck, Mr. McVey will still be here, and with even more luck, this will be one of the schools that maintains legal authority over the contents of student lockers."

Joanna was relieved to find Mr. McVey still in his office and to learn that the school was indeed one of the ones she'd hoped it would be. In order to use a locker, each student at SVSSE agreed to use only school-approved combination locks. In addition, students were required to sign a waiver that allowed school officials full access to the locker at any time and for any reason. After a little convincing and a few minutes later, Mr. McVey led Joanna and Robin Watkins to the locker assigned to Travis Stock. Once there, Mr. McVey used a master key to open the padlock and swing open the door.

"What exactly are you expecting to find?" he asked.

Donning a pair of latex gloves, Joanna peered inside without answering the question. Books and notebooks were all neatly arranged. On the bottom of the locker, between the books and next to the metal wall, was an assortment of items—pencils, pens, a tiny pocketknife, and an unopened packet of condoms. Ignoring those, Joanna sorted through the items, finally selecting the well-chewed nub of a number two pencil.

"This will do," she said, slipping the pencil into an evidence bag.

"That's all?" Mr. McVey asked.

"For right now."

"Does this mean Travis Stock is a suspect in Susan's murder?" McVey asked. "He's a great kid—a scholarship kid—but still a real asset to the school. I can't imagine that he or any of our students, for that matter, could be in any way responsible for what happened."

"At the moment, Travis Stock may or may not be a person of interest in the homicides in question," Joanna replied. "And for the time being, I'd very much like you to keep that information confidential."

"Of course," McVey agreed. "I understand completely."

Joanna and Robin left the locker and headed straight back to the parking lot. "I'm not sure that's going to pass scrutiny as a legal search or if the resulting evidence will hold up in court," Agent Watkins said dubiously. "Yes, the school ostensibly has the right to search the students' lockers at any time, but I think a good defense attorney will be able to make a case for claiming that the school's property rights don't supersede the suspect's rights to the assumption of privacy."

"Presumably this pencil has Travis Stock's DNA all over it," Joanna said grimly, "and I do not intend to have whatever we find here end up in a court of law. This is for informational purposes only—my informational purposes. Sooner or later I'm going to have to show up at Allison and Jeremy Stock's house with the news that, without their knowledge, their son has spent years being victimized by a pedophile. When it comes time for that, I'm going to want to know for sure if Travis was also the father of Susan Nelson's unborn baby."

"But what if Travis committed the murders?" Robin asked. "What then?"

"At that point we'll have to find some other way to prove that he was responsible," Joanna said. "Because this pencil sure as hell isn't it."

It was ten after five by the time she got back into her Yukon. She called Butch the moment she was under way.

"You're still in Sierra Vista?" he asked crossly when she told him where she was. "Our dinner reservation is in less than an hour."

"I know," Joanna said. "I'm on my way, and I'll come straight to the restaurant, but I'm going to have to make one more stop before I do."

"Joanna," Butch reasoned, "can't you do whatever it is after dinner instead of before?"

"I'll be on time," she said. "I promise."

Her next call was to Kendra Baldwin. Since it was after five, Joanna didn't have to talk her way past Madge to reach the ME.

She got straight to the point. "We've learned there's a good chance Susan Nelson was a pedophile who was screwing around with at least one of her students."

"Whoa," Kendra said. "Not nice."

"You can say that again," Joanna agreed. "One of the possible victims, a juvenile, happens to be the son of one of my deputies. He may also be the father of that unborn baby."

"That's awkward."

"Yes, it is, and that's why I need your help. Before I approach the parents, I want to have some confidence that the story I've been told is what really happened. To that end, I've obtained a pencil, one I took from a school locker, that I'm pretty sure belongs to the boy in question and—"

"And you want me to see if I can get a DNA profile off the pencil and match it to the baby's without your having to use your own departmental channels."

"Exactly."

"Won't hold up in court," Kendra said, echoing the same concern Robin Watkins had expressed earlier.

"It doesn't need to," Joanna replied. "It only has to hold up for me. Before I drop by someone's house and break a pair of parents' hearts, I need to know if this is the real deal."

"When do you plan to drop it off?"

"As soon as I can get there. I'm just now leaving Sierra Vista."

"Don't speed and don't worry," Kendra said. "I'll wait right here until you show up. I've already sent tissue samples from the fetus to the crime lab. I'll make sure the pencil gets there tonight, too. Ralph Whetson was about to head out to Tucson to collect the other body. I'll have him wait here until you drop off the pencil—one trip rather than two."

"What other body?" Joanna asked.

"The one from Sun Sites. The guy from the golf course. I thought you knew about that."

"I didn't know there had been a confirmed death," Joanna said, "but I do now. See you in about half an hour."

During the interview with Kevin and while her phone had been turned on silent, Joanna had felt the buzz of a couple of incoming voice mails, ones she had yet to listen to. She checked the sources but didn't listen to them now, either. One was from Butch, no doubt worrying about her coming to dinner. The other one was from Detective Howell.

She called Deb's number first. "Sorry it took so long to get back to you," Joanna said when the detective came on the line. "What's up?"

"The domestic violence victim died," Detective Howell announced. "He's a guy who lived in Sun Sites. He was DOA at the hospital in Tucson."

"Right," Joanna muttered aloud. "Dr. Baldwin just told me."

Her two confirmed homicides and one potential had indeed turned into three confirmed, and she hadn't been there for the third one—hadn't shown up on the scene. As far as Joanna was concerned, that meant she had fallen down on the job.

"What happened?" she asked.

"According to witnesses, the couple was playing golf when the wife hauled off and cold-cocked the guy with her pitching wedge."

"What's a pitching wedge?" Sheriff Joanna Brady was great when it came to poker but was completely out of her depth concerning golf.

"It was a foursome," Deb continued. "Two couples, all of them retirees. The woman was lining up a wedge shot to pitch her ball up onto the green. According to witnesses, her husband was standing right behind her, explaining that she was doing it all wrong. Instead of hitting the ball with her club, she turned around and smacked him! Knocked him cold. When they couldn't bring him around, someone called for an ambulance. EMTs arrived on the scene and couldn't revive him, either. They summoned an air ambulance to transport him to Tucson. He didn't make it."

The whole idea of someone being killed over a golf game seemed almost laughable except for the guy who was dead, and most likely not for the woman who was responsible, either.

"Under the circumstances, Dave is doing as good a job as possible on the crime-scene investigation," Deb went on. "The guy who manages the course is understandably eager to know if he'll be able to be open tomorrow. I told them we'll have to let him know. In the meantime, we have the woman in cuffs in the back of my Tahoe. I'll be bringing her to the Justice Center a little later, probably leaving here in an hour or so, about the time it gets dark and after Dave finishes what he's doing. I'm expecting to do the official interview once she's booked into the jail."

"You've read her her rights?"

"Yes, ma'am."

"And she hasn't lawyered up?"

"Not so far," Deb replied. "She told me the only thing she's sorry about is that she didn't do it years earlier—that it would have spared her a lot of heartache and made her a better golfer."

"Sounds as though their golden years weren't especially golden," Joanna observed. "I have a dinner engagement in a few minutes, but call me when it's time for the interview. If the suspect still hasn't lawyered up by then, I'll want to be there, too."

"Okay," Deb said. "Will do."

CHAPTER 18

JOANNA REMEMBERED THAT AT SOME POINT IN THE DAY, A TRAY OF Subway sandwiches had appeared briefly on one of the tables near the back of the SVSSE library, but she had been too busy at the time to eat and had somehow missed the boat on grabbing one of them. She'd had a single doughnut, much earlier, but that was it. By the time she showed up at Café Roka, she was ten minutes late, still in uniform, and starving.

Housed in the space that had once been a Rexall drugstore, the restaurant still boasted some of the original fittings, including a tin ceiling that gleamed dully overhead. Butch, Marcie, and Bob were already seated and sharing a bottle of Monsoon Red, from the Flying Leap vineyard in nearby Santa Cruz County. There was a glass at Joanna's place, but she passed on wine for two reasons—she was pregnant and still working.

"You have to go back in tonight?" Butch asked with a frown when he heard that news.

"There was a homicide over by Sun Sites earlier today," Joanna explained. "Detective Howell is bringing the suspect into the Justice Center later, and I want to be there for the initial interview."

"A third homicide in addition to the two you were already working?" Bob asked.

Joanna nodded. "Homicides don't necessarily take any time off, not even when there's a death in someone else's family."

She waited to see if either Bob or Marcie would voice any objections to her working right then. Much to her relief, they did not. Settled in with a glass of iced tea, Joanna was mildly amused to find Bob was beyond impressed with how good the wine was, especially since it was grown in Arizona. If grapes could be grown in the vast desert valleys of California, there was no reason they couldn't be grown in Arizona's valleys, too, but Joanna didn't bother pointing that out. People from out of state often had peculiar ideas about Arizona's being nothing but an arid, uninhabitable desert. Most of the time Joanna was content to let those folks keep right on maintaining what she regarded as rather quaint misapprehensions.

The two couples had polished off their appetizers and had started on salads when Bob looked Joanna straight in the eye and broached the subject she had been dreading all along. "I'm sorry about the executor thing," he said. "I'm sure knowing that I'd been handed that job must have come as a shock."

There it was—the whole issue out in the open, just like that.

"It did," Joanna admitted, "but I'm sure it was Mother's decision. I don't see that you have any reason to apologize."

"I do, because I'm the one responsible," Bob explained. "She and George appointed me their executors at my suggestion. You see, I'd already been through the whole estate settlement issue several years earlier when my adoptive parents died. I can tell you, sorting out all those details was an immense, time-consuming pain in the butt. My parents were fairly well off, and I was their only child, but you'd be surprised at the number of cousins and shirttail relations who came crawling out of the woodwork looking for a handout.

"It took months to unload their properties and to get all the *Ts* crossed and *Is* dotted in settling their affairs. When George and Mother first broached the subject to me, I thought that since my current job is totally flexible and yours is not, I'd be better equipped to handle all those details than you, just in terms of the time and energy required, and that was before I had any idea that another baby was on the way. Congratulations on that score," he added with a smile.

Joanna tried to smile back—tried and failed.

"Of course, at the time, none of us knew that the need for an executor would arise so suddenly and tragically or so soon. When they were working on redrawing their wills last spring, I had no inkling that something like this would happen in only a few months' time. By the way, Burton Kimball let me know that the attorney for the shooter's family has been in touch. They're hoping to stave off a wrongful-death suit. His first offer was three hundred thousand dollars each—three hundred for George and three hundred for our mother. Burton says you might do better at trial. He also thinks he can move the settlement needle up a little from the original offer, but it's entirely up to you."

"Up to me?" Joanna asked. "What about you?"

"With a single exception, you're the sole beneficiary of both estates," Bob explained. "I made it very clear to both George and Eleanor that my adoptive parents had taken care of Marcie's and my needs, and that we lacked for nothing. I assured them that there was no need for me to come swooping in from out of the blue, seemingly at the last minute, to deprive you of your birthright."

"You're to receive nothing from their estates?"

"Not one thin dime," Bob answered with another smile. "And that's exactly how I want it."

Part of Joanna's anxiety about meeting up with Bob—something she hadn't shared with Butch—was her concern that Bob would inherit things that should have gone to her or to her kids. Suddenly ashamed that she had been both so greedy and so wrong, she was grateful to be in a shadowy, candlelit room where the hot flush that colored her face wasn't quite so visible.

"I don't want the settlement money, either," Joanna said. "It's blood money."

"As far as I can tell, George's only surviving relative is his nephew, Harold, his late sister's son. George left him a bequest in his will, but I've been given to understand that Harold's health is compromised, and he's living in rather straitened circumstances. The wrongful-death payment would count as a real windfall for him—a life-changing windfall. If you don't accept your share of the settlement, chances are that might compromise the nephew's receiving his."

"What do you suggest, then," Joanna asked, "about the shooter's settlement offer?"

"First off, give Burton a chance to move the needle, and then accept their final offer. You don't want to wind up in court. It'll take too much time, energy, and focus. I say take the money, walk away, and be done with it. And if you don't want to use the money? Fine. Put it aside. Use it to pay your kids' way through school so they don't graduate from college with crippling loads of debt. I think if our mother knew that's what was happening, she'd be thrilled with that kind of outcome—that she had helped guarantee her grandchildren's education."

Joanna gave it some thought. Finally she nodded. "Sounds like good advice," she said.

"As for the cemetery-plot issue?" Bob continued. "I just happen to have the certificate of purchase in hand, but now that you've come up with such a terrific solution, we don't really need the additional plot. How about if I leave the certificate with you? Once things settle down, maybe the Rojas family will agree to buy it back, or perhaps someone else will want it. In any event, with so much going on right now, there's no need to deal with any of that immediately. Those details can all be ironed out later."

The salad plates disappeared from the table and the entrées arrived. A still-famished Joanna was ready to dive into her steak and shrimp, but Bob held up his wineglass.

"First, I'd like to propose a toast," he said. "To Eleanor and George. I know I came as a bit of a surprise to you especially, Joanna, but thank you for sharing them with me. I wouldn't have missed getting to know them for anything."

They clinked glasses all around—three wineglasses and Joanna's iced tea. But then, before Joanna could pick up her fork and eat, she had to track down her purse and locate a tissue. She was embarrassed to be seen crying in public, especially while in uniform, but she cried anyway. She couldn't help it.

It turned out Joanna hadn't needed Agent Watkins to serve as a human shield in dealing with her brother. All she had needed was a little more faith in the kind of man he really was.

CHAPTER 19

JOANNA WAS BACK IN HER JUSTICE CENTER OFFICE WHEN DEB showed up in the doorway about eight thirty. Dinner had been delicious and far more pleasant than she'd anticipated. Where she really wanted to be right then was at home in bed.

"Katherine Hopkins is in the interview room," Detective Howell announced. "She's been booked and changed into a jumpsuit. There was blood spatter on her golf duds. We took them into evidence."

"She hit her husband with a golf club hard enough to cause blood spatter?" Joanna asked.

Deb nodded. "The victim's name is Hal—short for Halford Hopkins. She hit him twice, once going and once coming. And yes, there's definitely blood spatter. This wasn't a love tap, not by any means."

"And you've got eyewitnesses."

"Three of them—the other couple, the ones Katherine and Hal Hopkins were playing golf with, and a groundskeeper who was sitting on a mower nearby waiting to mow the green when they cleared it."

"And she still hasn't lawyered up?"

"Nope."

"Okay, then," Joanna said, rising from her desk, "let's get this over with."

They walked into the interview room together. The woman seated at the table was a grandmotherly-looking sort with white hair, hearing aids, and a bright smile that revealed a set of false teeth. In a grandmother-of-the-year contest, had there been a category for "least likely to commit murder," Katherine Hopkins would have been at the very head of the class.

"Good evening, Mrs. Hopkins," Joanna said. "I'm Sheriff Brady. My other detectives are busy working another case just now, so I'll be joining Detective Howell for this interview."

"Please call me Kay," the woman said. "My given name is Katherine, but as I told Detective Howell, I've never seen myself as a Katherine. It always sounded a little uppity to me. I'm more of a plain Jane kind of girl."

Joanna took a seat and then waited while Deb went through the formalities of starting the recording process, including announcing the time and date as well as the names of the people in the room.

"Just for the record," Deb said, "I would like you to assure Sheriff Brady that you have been formally read your rights and that you're still willing to talk to us."

"Absolutely," Kay said. "I'm perfectly willing to talk. Why wouldn't I? After all, it's inarguably clear that I did it, and it wasn't an accident, either. I meant to hit him, and I did. All I really wanted was for him to shut up for a change. I've put up with that man telling me what to do for the past thirty-five years. Today, when he told me how to line up my shot? It was the last straw. I buy the groceries, do the cooking, look after the house, and balance the checkbook. Lately, when he's been so sick he could barely lift his head off the pillow, I've looked after him, too. But there he was today, telling me that I was too dim to read the line on a putting green. It's geometry, for Pete's sake. I got straight A's in geometry. I just hit the end of my rope, that's all."

You hit the end of your rope, but you also hit your husband, Joanna thought. Then she remembered Drexel Nelson. What exactly had he said when she had come to tell him that Susan was dead? Something to the effect that having his erring wife murdered spared him the disgrace of having to divorce her.

Yup, Joanna thought. *As Yogi Berra would have said, "It's déjà vu all over again."*

"You and your husband—Halford—were married for thirty-five years, correct?" Joanna asked.

"Call him Hal, but yes. That's how long we were married—almost half my life. I was married once before when I was very young, but it didn't last."

"Given that," Joanna ventured, "you don't seem to be particularly . . . well . . . upset. In fact, you don't appear to be the least bit distressed by what's happened."

"I suppose you'd like it better if I were hysterical, tearing my hair, and crying my eyes out," Kay said. "That's what women are expected to do under circumstances like these—weep and wail and act like it's the end of the world. Well, it isn't. I'm something of a realist, you see. I did the crime, and I'm prepared to do the time. I'm willing to stand up and accept the consequences of my behavior."

"So before today on the golf course, had you and Hal been having any difficulties?" Detective Howell asked.

Kay sighed. "He'd been having some ongoing health issues lately, and he wasn't what I'd call an easy patient. In fact, today was the first time in several weeks that he felt well enough to play golf. After being locked up with him for weeks at a time, I was ready for an outing, too."

"What hole was this where it happened?" Joanna asked.

"Hole seven," Kay said at once. "It's a par three."

"What about the previous holes? Did the two of you have issues on any of the others?"

"Of course we had," she said. "He didn't like the way I drove the cart. I wasn't playing 'heads-up' golf. I was taking too much time. It was one thing after another, all the way along."

"And that's why you snapped?" Joanna asked.

"Exactly."

"Most people in your circumstances would have called for an attorney by now. They wouldn't still be talking to us the way you are. Why is that?"

Kay Hopkins shrugged. "I already said. I did it. There were eyewitnesses who saw me do it. My plan is to plead guilty and take my medicine."

"You're prepared to write out a full confession?"

"Of course."

"Why don't you go ahead and do that, then?" Joanna suggested. "Detective Howell and I will leave you to it."

It took Deb a moment to shut down the taping process, then

she followed Joanna out into the hall. "I guess that's that, then," she said.

"Not so fast," Joanna cautioned. "This is all way too neat and easy, and I'm not sure I'm buying it. A signed confession to murder should give us ample probable cause to search her home. I want you to get a warrant to do that first thing in the morning. And make sure that the warrant includes all electronic devices—cell phones, computers, everything."

"But why? The murder happened on the golf course," Deb objected. "She and Hal weren't even at the house when this all went down."

"Right," Joanna replied. "The way Kay tells it, she put up with Hal's bossing her around for thirty-five years, but today is when he finally pushed her over the edge? Why? I don't think this just happened out of the blue. Something led up to this fatal outcome, and I want to know what that something is. The way things stand right now, Kay can't be charged with anything more than manslaughter. I want you to go through her computer—every e-mail, text, and Internet search—and see what's there."

"You're thinking we'll find signs of premeditation—that she'd been planning on taking him out all along and this was her first opportunity?"

Joanna shook her head. "I've been in this job for a long time now. Maybe it's finally getting to me. Maybe I'm starting to see conspiracies where none exist. Maybe a whack on the head—even a well-deserved whack—is just that—a whack on the head. But all the same, Deb, humor me on this. Get the warrant and see where it takes us."

"Yes, ma'am," Deb said. "Will do."

"And while you're getting warrants, I want one for Susan and

Drexel Nelson's house. We had one for her classroom and for her electronics, but now I want one for their house as well. You have the address?"

"Got it."

"Okay, then."

Joanna glanced at the clock. It was almost ten. "I'm beat and heading home now. I'm scheduling a meet up with the whole team here in the conference room tomorrow morning at ten. We'll find out then where everything stands. I'll be off work on Friday for sure."

Deb started to walk away then changed her mind, stopped, and turned back around. "I'm so sorry about your mom and George," she said. "This week must have been awful for you, but I understand completely why you've been here at work. With everything that's gone on, if you had tried to stay home, you would have gone nuts."

"And maybe tried taking Butch out with a pitching wedge?" Joanna asked with a small grin. "No, wait. That wouldn't work because I don't own a pitching wedge, and neither does he. But thanks for the kind words, Deb. And thanks for understanding. Not everyone does, you know."

Deb nodded. "Most especially Marliss Shackleford," she said. "See you tomorrow morning, then, Sheriff Brady, ten o'clock sharp."

CHAPTER 20

BREAKFAST WAS ON THE TABLE AND DENNIS WAS MUNCHING HIS way through a stack of blueberry pancakes when Joanna stumbled into the kitchen the next morning.

"Sorry to be a slugabed," she said, dropping into the breakfast nook still wearing her nightgown and bathrobe.

"Robe day?" Butch asked.

Joanna nodded. "I left word for Kristin that I'd be there in time for a ten o'clock homicide briefing. I figure I can compensate for some of the extra hours I've worked this week by showing up late."

"That maybe works for you, but Denny still needs to be at school on time."

Butch brought over a cup of tea and a plate of pancakes. "You got home late."

"I know. Sorry. Deb brought in the suspect from the Sun Sites homicide. When the interview was over, I sent out e-mails about this morning's meeting. Time got away from me."

"How come you never mentioned that Jenny's coming home tonight?"

"I didn't? I thought I had."

"The only reason I know is that I called to see what her plans for the weekend were."

"She called yesterday morning as I was on my way to Sierra Vista. Things got so crazy after that that it completely slipped my mind."

"Anyway," Butch said, "it's a good thing she's coming. It'll be good for her to be here and be part of it—part of the funeral, I mean. Dying is an integral part of living, and our trying to keep her from facing that reality isn't exactly fair to her."

Joanna nodded. "I suppose you're right."

She'd taken only a single bite of pancake, but now she put her fork and knife down on her plate. She'd been so busy that she'd barely thought about the funeral since walking out the door of the mortuary days earlier. Now it was back staring her in the face.

"Speaking of the funeral," Butch said, "there's something I need to talk to you about."

"What? I thought it was all handled."

"I'm sure it is, but this is about after the funeral. I know you wanted the service itself to be private, and you'll get no argument from me there—none. But George and your mother were prominent people here in town, Joey. Important people. In a way the whole community is grieving, and you need to give them a chance to do so, the same way letting Jenny come home is giving her a chance to grieve."

"What are you saying?"

"Jim Bob called yesterday afternoon. As you know, he and George had been planning that big send-off barbecue for Jenny last weekend, and Jim Bob had already stocked up on beef brisket. He and Eva Lou proposed the idea of having a commemorative barbecue here tomorrow afternoon after the funeral."

Jim Bob and Eva Lou Brady were Joanna's first in-laws. Despite the fact that Butch was Joanna's second husband, Jim Bob and Eva Lou had remained fixtures in the family—being actively involved grandparents in Dennis's life just as they had been in Jenny's. It was not at all surprising that they would offer to do such a kind thing, but it was more complication than Joanna could bear that morning. She was already shaking her head before Butch finished speaking.

"I can't handle something like that," she said. "It's just not possible. I know my limits, and that's a bridge too far. God knows how many people would come. How would we manage the cooking and the cleanup?"

"That's the thing," Butch said. "Jim Bob said he'd talked to Lieutenant Wilson up at the Bisbee Fire Department. He says he and a crew of guys will come out and help with cooking, setting up, cleaning up, and breaking down. All you have to do is show up. If you had opened up the funeral to all comers, I'll bet five hundred people would have shown up. And maybe that many will come for this."

"Five hundred? Are you kidding? Jim Bob doesn't have that much beef brisket."

"We can always get more beef brisket," Butch said. "But listen to me, Joey. You're a take-charge kind of girl, and I love you for that, but there are times when it's important to let other people do for you, especially when doing so is better for the other people involved than it is for you. This is one of them."

"Why?"

"In the first place, there's an election coming up," Butch said. "One of the things people like about you—and one of the reasons they elected you to public office—is that you're a human being—a regular person. Your mom died. George died. You don't need to be a superhero right now. You don't need to conceal the fact that you're grieving over losing two of the most important people in your life. And sharing that grief with the people around you—not just those closest to you but with the rest of the community as well—is going to make voters like you even more."

"You're saying we're holding a memorial barbecue for Mom and George because it'll be good for my election prospects?" Joanna asked.

"No," Butch said with a grin. "Because it'll be good for you, because it'll give you a chance to see how much other people care. And we're also holding it because your mother would have absolutely loved it. Eleanor always adored being the center of attention. This will give her one more chance to shine as the queen bee."

"Are we going to have a party?" Denny asked. "A party for Grandma Eleanor and Grandpa George?"

"Not exactly a party," Butch said. "More like a celebration in their honor."

"Will there be balloons?"

"There can be," Butch said with a shrug. "If you'd like Grandma Eleanor and Grandpa George to have balloons, balloons there will be. Hustle up, now. Go brush your teeth and get a move on or we'll miss the bell."

Dennis did as he was bidden without a word of protest.

Once he was gone, Joanna gave Butch a dubious look. "Why do I get the feeling that I've just been played?"

"Maybe you have," he replied with a grin. "Just a little. Now let me give Bob and Marcie a call. They said that if more brisket was required, they'd be happy to drive to Tucson and pick it up."

CHAPTER 21

A FEW MINUTES LATER, AS JOANNA WAS STEPPING OUT OF THE shower, her phone rang with *Caller Unknown* showing in the ID window. At first she was tempted to let it go to voice mail, but the moment she heard Agent Watkins's voice, she was glad she had answered.

"What's up?"

"I have some probably not so good news," Robin said. "Remember Colonel Thomas told us to call her if we needed anything else?"

"Yes," Joanna answered. "So what do we need?"

"It occurred to me that since Kevin and Travis Stock are such close friends," Robin said, "maybe Kevin could lead us to those two no-last-name kids, Jack and Nathaniel. It turns out Colonel Thomas runs a very tight ship in terms of supervising her son's online presence. She was able to friend me, which gave me access to the people on Kevin's page. Sure enough, he does know the boys in question—Jack Stockman and Nathaniel Digby. I'm sending you a photo."

Joanna put the phone down on the counter long enough to dry off and wrap a robe around her body before the photo turned up in her message file. The picture showed a middle-aged man with two teenage boys—high-school-age kids from the looks of them—standing on either side of him. All three of them were decked out in standard University of Arizona football-game attire—red-and-blue baseball caps along with red-and-blue T-shirts, all of them bearing the standard Wildcat insignias. The caption on the photo read, *Me and dad and Nate at the game. Wildcats won walking away. Go CATS!*

Joanna put the phone back to her ear. "No Travis?" she asked.

"Indeed," Robin replied. "No Travis. In other words, Travis lied straight out when he told me he'd gone to the game instead of the tutoring session."

"Which means he no longer has an alibi for either the abduction or the two murders—at least not the alibi he claimed to have," Joanna breathed.

"Right," Robin said. "Since his father is one of your deputies, I didn't think you'd want this information dropped into the middle of that ten o'clock meeting, without my giving you some advance warning."

"Thank you for that," Joanna said.

"It's a delicate situation," Robin said. "How are you going to handle it?"

"As of right now I have no idea," Joanna admitted. "Are you coming to the meeting?"

"Wouldn't miss it," Robin said.

"Fair enough," Joanna said. "By the time it starts, I'll have some kind of game plan in mind. In the meantime, I really appreciate your keeping this under your hat."

"Wait," Robin said quickly before Joanna had a chance to hang up. "There's one more thing."

"What's that?"

"Colonel Thomas asked if it would be possible for us to view Kevin as a confidential informant and not reveal his name in public. She's worried that if word gets out on campus that he's the one who spilled the beans on Travis, he'll be treated as a pariah on the SVSSE campus and end up being shunned as a snitch the whole of his senior year. I told her that treating him as a CI was fine with me, but that ultimately it was up to you."

Joanna thought about that for the better part of a minute.

"Well?" Robin asked finally.

"As long as we have other ways of sourcing the information, I don't have a problem with giving Kevin Thomas CI status," Joanna replied at last. "It seems to me that this investigation is already blowing up plenty of people's lives. How about if we give Kevin Thomas a pass?"

"Good," Robin said. "Glad we're of the same mind."

Joanna ended the call, put down the phone, and then spent a few minutes drying her hair—thinking about Allison and Jeremy Stock, with her heart aching the whole time. Right now Travis's parents were most likely doing whatever ordinary things they would do on a perfectly ordinary day. She was pretty sure Allison Stock worked as a bank manager somewhere in Sierra Vista. Joanna didn't have a departmental scheduling chart handy just then, but since Jeremy had been working day shift yesterday, chances are he was working day shift today as well, unless, of course, it happened to be his day off.

So here they were, going about their day-to-day lives with no idea that their whole existence was about to be blown to smithereens. Joanna remembered someone mentioning that Travis had been on scholarship at SVSSE. Even so, with another son away at college, it had probably been something of a financial stretch for a pair of ordinary working people to send their second child to a private school in hopes of giving him the very best chance for making a success of his life. Instead, Travis's future had been hijacked when he was sexually victimized by someone who should have been a respected teacher and mentor.

Joanna had a hard time wrapping her head around the idea of calling what had happened to Travis rape, but as she had so carefully explained to Kevin Thomas, that's what it was legally—statutory rape. Travis was a juvenile and still under the age of consent, even though his relationship with Susan Nelson had evidently been ongoing for some time. Now, even worse than the fact that Travis had been victimized, Jeremy and Allison were about to learn that their beloved son was also a suspect—maybe even the prime suspect—in the murders of two women. One of those was most likely the mother of the boy's unborn child, while the other's only offense had been nothing more than being in the wrong place at the wrong time.

During the series of interviews conducted in the school library, all of the students—Travis Stock included—had been handled with kid gloves. The next time someone spoke to him, however, the gloves would be off. A whole new set of very pointed questions was likely to be posed to him in an official interview room at the Justice Center. No doubt one or both of Travis's parents would be present at the time, as would a defense attorney, court-appointed or not.

Joanna desperately wanted to have the DNA confirmation of

the dead baby's parentage in hand before she passed along any of this bad news to the family involved or to the remainder of her investigative team as well. The landscape of the case had just shifted substantially. Her handling of interviews with her deputy's family had to be spot on. If there was even the smallest appearance of special treatment in the way the Stocks were handled, there was always a possibility that the case against Travis might be thrown out of court. And much as she might have wished to pass this challenging task on to one of her underlings, that wasn't in the cards.

This is what you signed on for, Joanna told herself grimly. *The hard things as well as the easy things. So you'd better put on your big-girl panties and figure it out.*

On her way into the office, Joanna called the ME. Naturally Madge left her on hold for a time, but eventually Kendra Baldwin came on the line. "Yes," she said. "Yes, and yes."

"What does that mean?" Joanna asked.

"Yes, whoever chewed the hell out of that pencil stub is definitely the father of Susan Nelson's unborn baby."

The idea of having DNA results back so fast took Joanna's breath away. "How can you possibly know that already?" she asked.

"Because the state of Arizona ponied up some big bucks to have that new RapiDHIT™ DNA identification technology online in all their crime labs. You send in the sample, and they send you the results. Easy-peasy. Wham, bam, thank you, ma'am, if you'll pardon the use of that expression under these particular circumstances."

For good reason, the inappropriate and definitely politically incorrect comments cops and MEs routinely trade back and forth are usually not shared with anyone outside exclusive law enforcement circles.

"So that accounts for the first yes," Joanna said. "What's the second one?"

"After the autopsy, I found evidence of what may or may not have been consensual sex. I located a tiny trace of what appears to be semen on Susan's underwear—on her clothing rather than on her person."

"Like maybe the guy used a condom and some of the semen got away?"

"Exactly," Kendra said. "And just so you know, DNA from that matches up with the DNA from Pencil Boy, too."

"Wait," Joanna interrupted. "You said the sex might or might not be consensual?"

"If it had been rape, there would be signs of defensive wounds. There was nothing suspicious in the scrapings from under her nails. So either she was a willing participant or else . . ."

"Or else what?"

"She was unconscious at the time," Kendra answered. "So tell me about Pencil Boy."

"The pencil came from an SVSSE school locker used by Travis Stock, so we're operating under the assumption that the pencil belongs to him."

"Wait," Kendra said. "Did you say Travis Stock—as in Deputy Stock's son?"

"I'm afraid so—one and the same."

"That's terrible. The kid has been having sex with one of his teachers, and now he's apparently the father of her unborn baby?"

"That's what we were told by a confidential informant, and it looks as though your findings confirm it."

"Before this goes any further," Kendra cautioned, "we'll need to double-check those results with a properly obtained and documented DNA sample from Travis himself."

"I agree," Joanna said. "That's my next task."

"So where does all this leave the investigation?" Kendra asked.

"Agent Watkins and I were told that when Travis found out Susan was pregnant, he supposedly begged her to marry him, at which point she told him to take a hike—that marriage to him wasn't happening, ever—no way José."

"I can see why Travis might have had a motive to kill Susan Nelson," Kendra said. "But what about Desirée Wilburton? Why would he murder her, too?"

"That's a question with no obvious answer," Joanna replied. "As of now, we still haven't come up with any kind of direct connection between the two women—no texts, e-mails, or phone calls—at least none that we can find. But what we do know for sure is that everything Travis Stock told us about his whereabouts at the time of Susan Nelson's kidnapping and murder is entirely bogus. If he lied about his alibi, what else is he lying about?"

"But a teacher screwing around with one of her students?" Kendra asked. "The woman had to be a piece of work."

"Yes, she was definitely that," Joanna agreed. "Your basic sexual predator all the while passing herself off as a respected member of the community and the wife of a local minister, no less."

"Speaking of Reverend Nelson," Kendra said. "Did you ask him about his wife's funeral arrangements yesterday? If so, he never got around to contacting me about who will be handling them."

"Reverend Nelson didn't contact you because he has no

intention of making funeral arrangements of any kind," Joanna answered. "At least that's what he told me. Once he found out about Susan's unborn baby, he went totally ballistic. He told me quote/unquote that you're welcome to dump his wife's body in the nearest landfill."

"That's not going to fly and you know it," Kendra replied. "Would you please speak to him about this again? I can't keep Susan's body on ice indefinitely. Roberta Wilburton is sending someone from Flint Mortuary up in Tucson to collect her daughter's remains later on today. That will take some of the pressure off the morgue's occupancy rate, but with both Susan's and Hal's bodies currently on hold, I'm about to have to post a 'No Vacancy' sign. For the time being, nobody else around here is allowed to die, got it?"

Joanna couldn't help smiling. "Got it," she said. "I'll do my best."

At that moment, she was just slowing to turn into the parking lot at the Justice Center. "I need to hang up now," she said. "It's time for me to go inside and tell my team what's up. After that, we'll spend the rest of the day messing up other people's lives—starting with Deputy and Mrs. Jeremy Stock."

CHAPTER 22

DEB HAD OBTAINED THE SEARCH WARRANT FOR THE NELSONS' home and left it on Joanna's desk. Taking the warrant with her, Joanna headed for the conference room, where the entire team was already assembled. Bright-eyed, bushy-tailed, and expectant, they watched as she walked to the front of the room and took her place at the lectern.

"Good morning," she said. "We've got to stop meeting like this."

There were smiles and guffaws all around, and that's what she wanted. This was going to be a tough day for all concerned. She hoped that bit of lightness would relieve some of the tension in the room.

"We've had some developments overnight," she announced. "For one thing, we now have another unsolved homicide on our plate. Hal Hopkins, an Arizona Sun Sites resident, whose wife clobbered him in the head with a golf club yesterday, was DOA when he arrived at the TMC trauma center in Tucson. For the time being, Deb will be handling that case with Dave assisting with crime-scene investigation. I take it the autopsy is scheduled?"

Deb glanced at her watch. "In about forty-five," she said. "So don't be surprised if I have to rush out."

"Don't worry," Joanna said. "For once, the briefing is going to be brief. Last night, as Agent Watkins and I were preparing to leave the SVSSE campus, we were approached by a confidential informant. The CI is a close personal friend of Travis Stock, who, as some of you may already know, is Deputy Stock's son."

The room went dead quiet. It seemed to Joanna that for a time, people stopped breathing. After a moment, she continued. "The CI told us that for some time—a period of at least a year and maybe longer—Travis had been involved in a romantic relationship with Susan Nelson. According to the CI, when Susan told Travis about her pregnancy, he begged her to divorce her husband and marry him. She evidently found the suggestion laughable and made it blazingly clear that she intended to pass the baby off as her husband's. Again, according to the CI, Travis reacted badly to being rejected."

"Which sounds like motive to me," Ernie muttered.

"Possibly," Joanna agreed. "It seemed to me that the first step was to ascertain whether or not Travis was the father of the victim's unborn child. With the help of the school principal, Agent Watkins and I obtained an item from Travis's locker—a pencil stub we assume belongs to him. With Dr. Baldwin's assistance, the pencil was transported to the crime lab in Tucson, where it was tested for DNA. Dr. Baldwin reported the crime lab's findings as I was on my way here."

"And?" Jaime Carbajal asked.

"It turns out that DNA from the pencil belongs to the father of Susan Nelson's unborn baby."

"So Travis Stock is the father?" Ernie breathed. "Does Jeremy know any of this?"

"I have no idea what Jeremy knows or doesn't know," Joanna replied. "The crime lab's DNA findings will need to be confirmed with a properly obtained sample. The DNA we have now came from an item in Travis's school locker, which was opened by the school principal."

"Which may or may not constitute a legal search," Detective Howell volunteered.

"Exactly," Joanna agreed. "In other words, although it seems reasonable enough to assume that Travis is the father of the baby, I don't want any of this information being relayed to Deputy Stock or his family until they've been officially notified of their son's suspected involvement with the homicide victim. That's something I intend to handle personally. Is that understood?"

The people gathered in the room nodded in somber unison. "In addition, in the course of examining Susan Baldwin's clothing, Dr. Baldwin obtained a DNA sample from what she says 'may or may not be consensual sex,' and may or may not lead us to our killer. In any event, due to Deputy Stock's connection to the case, everything about our investigation into the Susan Nelson homicide must be handled by the book."

"If Susan Nelson was screwing around with one of her students," Jaime Carbajal muttered, "it sounds to me like she got just what she deserved."

Joanna sent him a frosty look. "Excuse me, Detective Carbajal. Since when is statutory rape a capital crime? Reprehensible as the victim's behavior may have been, her actions don't justify someone taking her life. This department isn't in favor of vigilante justice. You're all welcome to think those 'she deserved it' thoughts in private, but do not utter those words aloud. Understood?"

Jaime looked properly chastened. "Yes, ma'am," he replied. "But what are you suggesting—that Travis is the doer here? Just because he may be the father of Susan Nelson's baby doesn't mean that he killed her."

"No, it doesn't," Joanna agreed, "not for sure, but here's the next troubling piece of the puzzle. This morning Agent Watkins was able to access social media accounts that seem to indicate that Travis's alibi—his claim that he was in Tucson attending a U of A football game on Saturday afternoon and evening—is a complete fabrication. At this time we have no idea of his real whereabouts during the commission of the crimes."

"Which might give Travis both motive and opportunity," Ernie suggested.

"Exactly," Joanna agreed. "When we finish here, I'd like you two—Jaime and Ernie—to track down the kids Travis was supposed to accompany to the football game."

"What are their names?" Ernie asked.

"Nate Digby and Jack Stockman," Robin answered. "They're both students at Buena High."

"See if you can line up interviews with them—and with their parents, of course," Joanna added. "We need to know when Travis changed his mind about going to the football game. If it was Saturday during the day sometime, Nate and Jack may have been among the last people to interact with him before any of this happened. We also need to know his frame of mind that day—

was he upset or angry? And did he confide in either Nate or Jack concerning his situation with Susan?"

"How soon do you expect to speak to Jeremy and Allison?" Ernie asked.

"Later on today. For transparency's sake, I'll probably have Agent Watkins accompany me on that interview."

"You mentioned having a confidential informant," Jaime said. "Does the CI's information give us enough to go for a warrant?"

"Deb has already obtained a warrant for us to search Susan Nelson's residence and it will be executed later today. However, I don't think the CI's information gives us enough to justify a warrant for obtaining Travis's DNA. In addition, although Travis Stock may be the prime suspect in a homicide investigation, we have to remember that he's also a victim here—a juvenile victim of statutory rape—and his ID must be protected."

"What about the CI?" Ian Waters asked. "Shouldn't we have a formal sit-down with him?"

"For right now, no," Joanna answered. "I want to leave him as a CI. He and his mother are both worried about his being considered a snitch by his classmates and ostracized at school. If we can achieve the same ends without having to involve him further, that's how I'd like to proceed. One thing we could do is go back to SVSSE and reinterview just the debate club students. I have a feeling that some of Susan's sexual assignations may have occurred either on debate trips or else during her so-called one-on-one tutoring sessions."

"Pun intended," Deb Howell muttered.

"Yes," Joanna agreed, "pun intended. Those kids aren't stupid. I think there's a good chance that a number of students in addition to our CI may have been aware of what was going on between Travis and Mrs. Nelson. Jaime and Ernie, once you finish up with Nate and Jack, I'd like you to go back to SVSSE. I believe Mr. McVey will be somewhat more cooperative today than he was yesterday.

"This time around, I want you to focus on the members of the debate club in particular, and once again, bring parental units in for interviews wherever necessary. Make sure the kids feel at ease. Focus your questions strictly on Susan Nelson. How was she as a teacher and a coach? Did she apply any extra pressure to the people on the debate team? Did she play favorites? The more questions you ask about her and the fewer questions you ask about the kids, the better off we'll be."

"So maybe we should offer them sodas, water, and pencils for doodling?" Jaime asked sarcastically. He was still smarting from Joanna's earlier rebuke, and it showed.

"If that's what's required," Joanna said, "by all means break out the sodas. While you're at it, take any and all discarded cans, bottles, or straws into evidence, properly bagged and tagged. We may not be able to demand DNA samples, but we all know there's more than one legal way to collect them—and trash is always fair game.

"That's about all for now, but there's one more thing I need to mention. I know I announced earlier that funeral services for my mother and George are going to be private. Because of crowd limitations at the mortuary chapel and at the cemetery, some of you are on the invitation list and others aren't. Even though tomorrow's services will of necessity be private, we've scheduled a barbecue at High Lonesome Ranch for later on in the afternoon. Butch and my brother tell me there'll be plenty of food, and you're all welcome to come to that."

Most of the people filed out of the room, but Agent Watkins lingered behind. "What about me?" she asked. "Do you want me to work on the SVSSE interviews?"

Joanna shook her head. "No, for the time being, you're with me. First off, I need someone riding shotgun when it's time to execute the warrant at the Nelson residence."

"What about the interview with the Stocks?"

Joanna nodded. "For that, too. I think that when it comes time for delivering that bad news, Jeremy and Allison will appreciate having a relative stranger in the room as opposed to someone Deputy Stock has known and worked with for years."

"Yes," Robin agreed. "In a case like this, having a stranger present might well be the lesser of two evils."

CHAPTER 23

THE TWO WOMEN HEADED TOWARD SIERRA VISTA IN JOANNA'S YU-kon. The desert on either side of the highway was lush and green, especially when they dropped down toward the San Pedro River.

"This was all rich grassland once," Joanna explained. "Then two things happened. The Sonora earthquake of 1887 sent most of the river underground. Then Anglo ranchers overgrazed the land so much that the cattle ended up having to eat mesquite, leaving behind cow plops brimming with mesquite beans. Mesquite beans plus fertilizer worked their magic, and mesquite trees grew like crazy. When their root systems grabbed all the water, the grass went away. There's grass here now, but only because of the monsoons."

"I didn't know they had earthquakes here."

"That one was seven-point-six. The epicenter was across the line in Mexico. The only reason there weren't more casualties is that there weren't many people living here at the time."

"How do you know all this stuff?" Robin asked.

"My dad was a history buff, and he passed along what he learned to me."

"What happened to him?"

"He died when I was fifteen, wiped out while he was being a Good Samaritan and changing a tire for a stranded motorist."

"And now you've lost your mother, too," Robin mused quietly. "It must be hard."

"It *is* hard," Joanna admitted, "even though Mom and I were never close. My dad was another story. He and I were great pals, and Mom was always left on the outside looking in. After Dad died, things between my mother and me got worse and worse. There were times I wondered why it couldn't have been her who died instead of him. But then it never would have happened that way, would it? I don't believe Eleanor Lathrop Winfield ever changed a tire in her life."

"But wait," Robin said. "Didn't you tell me the other day that the two of you were growing closer?"

"That's true," Joanna answered. "Recently, things had been getting better. I guess that's why losing her now is hitting me so hard. We had reached a point where we were starting to see and accept one another's point of view. Given enough time, we might have been able to put the past behind us. The problem is we ran out of time."

"It's the same situation with my dad and me," Robin said regretfully. "Except we're still not ready to see the other's point of view, much less accept it."

"Well, then," Joanna told her with a half laugh. "I guess we'll both just have to soldier on, won't we?"

They rode on in silence for some time after that, each lost in her own thoughts. When Robin spoke again, it was on a different topic entirely. "Other than executing the search warrant, is there any other reason we're going back to see Reverend Nelson this morning?"

"We're doing the ME a favor. Remember that old song from *Oklahoma!* 'Pore Jud Is Daid'? It's the same thing here. Dr. Baldwin isn't running out of ice, but she *is* running out of space in her cooler."

"But yesterday Reverend Nelson told us that he had no interest in claiming his wife's body."

"That's correct," Joanna said, "and it's our job to make him change his mind."

When Joanna turned into the parking lot at Holy Redeemer Chapel, a single vehicle was parked next to the church—a blue Ford Fiesta.

"Wait a minute," she said, pulling up behind it. "Isn't this the car we saw leaving Reverend Nelson's house yesterday morning?"

"I believe it is."

Joanna was already on her radio. "I need you to run a plate for me," she told Larry Kendrick back at Dispatch. Once she gave him the number, it took only a matter of seconds for him to reply.

"The vehicle is registered to one Virginia Dycus with an address on Calle Veranda."

"Do we know anything about her?" Joanna asked.

"Running the name," Larry said. "Nothing. One traffic stop two years ago for going twenty-five in a school zone. Other than that, zip."

"I've got something," Robin said, consulting her iPad. "Ginny Dycus's LinkedIn page says she's the secretary at Holy Redeemer Chapel."

Joanna sighed. "Well, I'll be. If that isn't just a little too convenient! Susan Nelson is preying on kids at school while her husband is getting it on with the church secretary."

"Sounds like the Reverend and Susan Nelson were a matched set of cheaters who each deserved the other," Robin observed.

"Yes," Joanna agreed. "And poor Travis Stock got caught in the cross fire."

With that, she put the Yukon back in gear, drove as far as the Nelson house, and parked. "This should be fun," she said, unfastening her belt and climbing out of the SUV. "We weren't welcome yesterday, and I think we'll be even less so today."

Joanna knocked on the door. When it swung open, Drexel Nelson surged out onto the porch and into Joanna's space. "Why are you here again?" he demanded, leering down at her with eyes filled with cold fury. "I told you yesterday that you aren't welcome. I want you off my property, now!"

Tall people seldom take into consideration how the world appears when viewed by someone who happens to be relatively short. Without ceding any ground, Joanna stared up at Nelson's full crop of bristling nose hairs. Under other circumstances, it might have been funny, but in this case she worried that Drexel Nelson's short fuse made him an explosion waiting to happen.

"Actually, we happen to have a search warrant," Joanna said, retrieving the document from her purse and handing it to him.

Rather than looking at the paper, Nelson glowered at Joanna. "A search warrant? Why?"

"The reason for the warrant is one of the things we need to discuss with you, Reverend Nelson," she said reasonably.

"Oh, wait," he said, sounding sarcastic but nonetheless taking a step back. "Now I get it. You're back to thinking I killed Susan.

If that's the case, I shouldn't let you anywhere near me without my having an attorney present."

"At this point, Reverend Nelson, I can assure you that we have no reason to believe you had anything to do with your wife's death, but we do have reason to search through Susan's belongings."

"Why?"

"As I said, let's go inside, sit down, and discuss it," Joanna suggested. "Agent Watkins here can conduct the search while you and I have a civilized conversation about what was going on in your late wife's life."

Shaking his head, Nelson backed into the house, allowing Joanna and Robin to enter rather than inviting them inside. He ambled across the room and sank down into the same chair where he'd sat on their previous visits. A nod in Robin's direction from Joanna sent the FBI agent off to conduct the search while Joanna took a seat on the sofa, putting an expanse of glass-topped coffee table between her and Nelson.

"All right, then," he said. "Tell me. What's going on?"

Joanna took a deep breath. "It has come to our attention that your late wife may have been a sexual predator who was preying on at least one of her students and possibly more."

Reverend Drexel Nelson looked both shocked and utterly horrified. "Susan involved with one of her students? No," he declared, shaking his head. "That's just not possible."

"Unfortunately, it's all too possible," Joanna insisted. "We have DNA evidence that we expect will prove that she was sexually involved with at least one member of the SVSSE debate team."

For a long time Drexel Nelson simply stared at Joanna without speaking. "Is that why she died?" he asked finally. "As you said, it's usually either the husband or the boyfriend. Since I know I didn't do it, the boyfriend must be it."

"Perhaps," Joanna answered.

"Who all knows about this? I suppose it'll be in the paper or on TV and be all over town in a matter of minutes."

"It shouldn't be," Joanna replied. "The student involved happens to be a juvenile, so we'll do our best to keep his name out of the press."

"His name but not Susan's."

"I'm afraid she was well beyond the age of consent. The boy wasn't. At this point, Agent Watkins and I both know about it, as does the ME. Other members of my investigative team are aware of it as well, and now so are you."

"But it's going to become public knowledge eventually, isn't it?" he asked.

"Possibly," Joanna answered. "Especially if Susan's involvement with the boy turns out to be part of the motivation behind her murder. In that case, everything that happened between them will most likely have to come to light and may even end up being discussed in open court."

Before Reverend Nelson could respond, Agent Watkins entered the room with a look of utter triumph on her face. She was lugging what appeared to be a drawer of some kind. "Got it," she said. "I found what we needed in the second place I looked."

"Hey," Nelson objected. "Wait a minute. That's part of the linen closet. You can't take that."

"You're right," Robin replied. "This drawer is part of the linen closet, but we can take it. Have you ever bothered looking inside it?"

Drexel Nelson answered with a shrug. "Me? Why would I? Washing clothes and making beds aren't my responsibility around here."

They will be now, buddy boy, Joanna thought. "What did you find, Agent Watkins?" she asked aloud.

"The top couple of layers in the drawer contained exactly what you'd expect in a linen closet—sheets and pillowcases—but underneath those is a gold mine of material: handwritten letters and notes from what looks like a whole flock of lovesick boys. At least that's what the ones on the top of the stack appear to be."

"Letters?" Joanna asked. "As in snail mail letters?"

"Not exactly," Robin replied. "I think it's more likely that the notes were cloak-and-dagger stuff, dropped off somewhere and collected by hand rather than sent through USPS. But now we know why nothing incriminating showed on Susan's phone or computer. She must have known that was the first place someone would go looking for evidence—on her electronic devices. I'm guessing she carried on her romantic correspondence with these kids the old-fashioned way—using pen and paper. There are names, dates, and lots of envelopes, all of which should come complete with DNA."

"So not just one boy, then?" Nelson asked faintly.

"No," Robin answered. "From what I'm seeing here, I'd have to say there were several more than that."

A seemingly stunned Reverend Nelson buried his face in both hands. "The chapel will never survive this kind of scandal," he mumbled. "This will be the end of it. How could Susan do something so wicked? How could she?"

"Because she was too caught up in what she was doing to give any thought to how it might affect other people—you included," Joanna said. "But if you're worried about keeping Holy Redeemer Chapel afloat, I have a suggestion."

"What kind of suggestion?"

"Your church is supposed to be all about redemption, right? What does that mean exactly?"

"Being redeemed means being freed from sin."

"And presumably that freedom usually comes through some kind of forgiveness, correct?" Joanna asked.

Nelson looked utterly mystified. "I suppose," he said. "But what are you saying?"

"Yesterday morning when we came to tell you about your wife's unborn child, you told us that you were washing your hands of her—that, as far as you were concerned she could just as well be dropped off at the nearest landfill. Remember?"

Nelson nodded. "That's what I said, that's what I meant, and I still do."

"Maybe you should rethink that decision," Joanna suggested. "Maybe you should retrieve Susan's remains from the morgue and give her a proper funeral service right here at the chapel. Once what she did becomes public knowledge, I doubt the court of public opinion will ever forgive her, but I believe people will think more highly of you and your church if you make it clear that whatever sins Susan may have committed, you personally have forgiven her."

"You think I should forgive her? Why?"

"Because that's the only thing that will keep Holy Redeemer Chapel from folding—if you can convince people that you not only talk the talk, you also walk the walk. And by the way," Joanna added as she stood to go, "it might be a good idea for you and Ginny Dycus to cool it for a while. Let some time pass before the two of you become more deeply involved."

Drexel's ruddy face paled. "Wait," he said. "You know about Ginny and me? But it's nothing really. We're just friends."

"Sure you are," Joanna said. "But it turns out that if you're a man of a certain age, dealing with certain potency issues, however those symptoms can, as you mentioned earlier, be lessened with the aid of certain pharmaceuticals. You may claim the relationship between you and Ginny is strictly platonic, that may be true for no other reason than your inability to get it up. Platonic or not, whatever the two of you are doing or not doing certainly predates your wife's death.

"Once your relationship comes to light, as it's bound to, I doubt members of your congregation will believe your 'just friends' version of the story. Come to think of it, I'll bet you lied when you told us you didn't have an alibi for the night of Susan's murder. Supposing we checked security cameras and traffic cams between here and Ginny Dycus's place on Calle Veranda. What are the chances we'd find you motoring back and forth from her place to yours during the hours in question?"

Stunned, Drexel Nelson left off any attempt to voice further protests. He sat in stricken silence, watching as Joanna held open the door so Robin could carry the drawer outside.

"Where are we taking all this?" Robin asked.

"Straight back to the department," Joanna answered, her voice brimming with excitement. "If there are more boys involved in all this than Travis, we need to know who they are. Every piece of paper in that drawer needs to be analyzed, swabbed for DNA, copied, and maybe even dusted for prints. I'm willing to bet that we'll find our killer somewhere in that pile of correspondence—our killer and our motive. And if there is a connection between the two victims? I'm guessing that's where we'll find Desirée Wilburton, too."

"There's a lot of material here," Robin said. "And yes, it needs to go first to your department, where it can be properly logged into evidence. After that, though, how about if I take it to the FBI's lab in Tucson. Your department has a limited number of CSIs, and they're already overwhelmed. This would speed up the process immeasurably. I came here to help. Let me."

"Your lab can do it all, including DNA profiling?"

"Including," Robin answered.

"Let's do it, then," Joanna said. "The sooner the better."

CHAPTER 24

AN HOUR LATER, SHERIFF BRADY AND AGENT WATKINS WERE SIT-ting side by side on stools in the CSI lab at the Cochise County Justice Center. They watched as Casey Ledford—wearing latex gloves and using tweezers—carefully removed each individual piece of paper from the stack and held it up to be copied by a scanner before numbering the image and logging the paper itself into evidence. Once that was done, she used PowerPoint to display the scanned item on a nearby screen.

Item number one was a barely legible note, scrawled in pencil and written in awkward cursive on rough-edged paper torn from a student notebook. Reading the words broke Joanna's heart.

Please, please, please dont' do this. Its my baby too. I want to marry you. I want to be the baby's father. You know he doesn't love you, and I do. Please. I know you said your answer was final, but lets talk about this again.

Love you,

Trav

"Trav would be Deputy Stock's son?" Casey asked.

Joanna nodded. "One and the same."

"Do Jeremy and Allison know about any of this?"

"I doubt it," Joanna said. "Not yet, but it's almost word for word what our CI told us—that Travis thought the baby was his and had begged Susan Nelson to marry him. She apparently told him to get lost. And now, since Travis's alibi for Saturday afternoon and evening has just evaporated, we've moved him to first place on our prime suspect list."

"If Travis thought the child was his, Susan Nelson must have been teaching him lessons that weren't exactly speech or debate related," Casey said.

"No kidding," Joanna agreed. "DNA obtained from a pencil taken from Travis's school locker suggests that he's the father, but we'll need a properly obtained DNA sample from him to verify that information. In the meantime, I expect we're going to find the identities of any number of Susan's other sexploitation victims among the papers hidden in this drawer."

"You're saying there are more victims besides Travis?"

Joanna nodded. "Evidently."

"What can you say to the parents of kids who've been victimized that way?" Casey asked. "How on earth do you go about delivering that kind of awful news to anyone, let alone someone you know like Jeremy and Allison? And for them, it'll be a double whammy—not only is their son a victim of sexual assault, now he's a homicide suspect, too. Hearing about this is going to break their hearts."

"I know," Joanna said. "As of right now I have no idea of what I'm going to say to them."

Casey retrieved the next item—a second note. This one, written in the same hand and on a similar piece of paper, was only a few lines long:

> *Really? Are you kidding? Thats wonderful. When is it due?*
> *Trav*

Casey shook her head. "This just gets better and better, doesn't it."

Item number three turned out to be a plain white envelope with nothing on it—no name; no return address. The top had been slit open, so the flap was still sealed.

"We'll be able to get DNA from that flap with no problem," Casey observed as she carefully removed the piece of paper from the envelope and held it up to the camera. As she did so, item number four gradually came into focus on the wall-mounted screen on which Joanna and Robin had been viewing greatly enlarged images of each document.

"Oh my God!" Joanna exclaimed as the signature at the bottom gradually resolved itself into readable script—*Kev.*

"Who's Kev?" Casey asked.

"That's likely to be Kevin Thomas, the kid who's supposed to be our CI in all of this. The one who claimed he and Travis Stock were best buddies."

"Scroll back up to the top," Joanna directed. "We need to be able to read the whole thing." And doing that was enough to take her breath away:

I can't believe you'd just drop me like that and send me down the road like I'm some kind of worn out toy. Is that all I am to you? Is that all I was? And you still expect me to show up at Debate Club and act like nothing happened—like everything is just great?

I thought you loved me, but you don't. If I told people what you did to me, you'd lose your job. You might even go to JAIL!!

I know you won't take me back, but now I'm starting to wonder. Am I the only one or are there others? I feel so stupid. If my mother ever figures out what happened, I know she'll kill me, so I probably won't tell, even though I should.

What I don't understand is how you can look yourself in the face? How can you stand up in front of your classes and pretend to be such a great teacher and act like you care about all of us when you don't? Not at all. How can you go to that church of yours and sit there with all the other good people pretending you're good, too? You're not. You are evil. You deserve to die, and when you do, I hope you rot in hell.

Kev

"Holy moly!" Robin breathed. "This is a game changer. This guy threatened her, plain and simple. It says so right there in black and white. The whole time Kevin was pointing us in the direction of Travis Stock, he was really trying to make sure we weren't looking too closely at him."

"Does that mean we now have dueling prime suspects?" Casey asked.

"Maybe even more," Joanna said. "How many pieces of paper do you have in that stack of love notes?"

Casey shuffled through the documents. "Thirty or forty individual pieces of paper with what looks to be ten or fifteen distinctly different sets of handwriting. I'm guessing some of them are current students. Others may have already graduated."

"We'll need to identify and interview all of them," Joanna said. "Can we lift DNA from any of the notes?"

"Getting DNA from licked and sealed envelopes is easy," Casey answered. "Lifting DNA just by swabbing the surface of a piece of paper is a little more problematic than saliva on glue. Agent Watkins said we can make use of the FBI lab in Tucson. I suggest that she take the notes and letters themselves to the lab and let their people go to work on them. In the meantime, we'll send the envelopes directly to the state patrol crime lab."

"How many envelopes?" Joanna asked.

Casey sorted through the pile. "Six," she answered. "Most of them are just like the first one—still sealed because they've been slit open with a knife or letter opener."

"Would you like me to drop the envelopes off at the state crime lab when I take everything else to ours?" Robin asked.

"Sounds like a plan," Joanna said.

Her phone rang with the ME's number showing in caller ID. Not wanting to slow down Casey's analysis of the material from the linen drawer, Joanna excused herself and went out in the hallway to take the call.

"What's up?" she asked.

"You were right," Kendra Baldwin replied. "Hal Hopkins was suffering from arsenic poisoning. After what you said this morning, I ran a whole battery of tests, ones I might not necessarily have used on someone who died of blunt-force trauma. I'd say he'd been given low doses over some period of time. The amount administered wasn't enough to kill him outright, at least not yet, but it was getting there."

"During the interview, I seem to remember that his wife mentioned his being in ill health for some time—enough to require several recent hospitalizations."

"With flulike symptoms by any chance?" Kendra asked. "Low doses of arsenic will do that. Did she say where he was hospitalized? I can put through an official request for his medical records."

"I'd try the hospital in Willcox first," Joanna suggested.

"Will do."

"But this throws a whole new light on the subject," Joanna said. "It explains why Hal's nongrieving widow is so eager to confess to whacking the poor guy over the head with a golf club. She probably thought with blunt-force trauma, when you did the autopsy, you'd look at that and nothing else."

"Too bad for her, then," Kendra replied. "I suppose she thinks being charged with manslaughter or second-degree murder is preferable to being charged with murder in the first degree. The potential outcomes behind doors number one or two are better than the ones behind door number three."

"Does Detective Howell know any of this?" Joanna asked after a pause.

"Not yet," Kendra said. "At least not from me. You're the first person I called."

"I'll contact Deb now," Joanna said. "She's over in Sun Sites executing a search warrant. She needs to know that she should be looking for anything remotely related to arsenic. Before we're done, I'm hoping we'll be able to nail Kay Hopkins's feet to the ground."

Joanna ended the call and went back into the lab. While Casey continued to sort through papers, she reported what the ME had said.

"How much longer is this going to take?" she asked.

"We're only halfway," Casey answered.

"Okay, then," Joanna said. "You finish that so Agent Watkins can head for Tucson. In the meantime, I'm heading for Sierra Vista."

"To talk to Travis's parents?" Robin asked.

Joanna nodded. "To them first, and then I intend to have another chat with Kevin Thomas."

"You're talking to the Stocks on your own?" Robin asked. "I thought you wanted me along so you'd have someone from outside your department along with you."

"I do want an outsider," Joanna said. "Fortunately, with you fully occupied transporting evidence to Tucson, I have someone else in mind—Detective Ian Waters from the Sierra Vista PD. After I talk to Deb Howell, that's my next call—to Chief Montoya. I want to let him know what's up. When all this hits the fan and people know about not only Susan Nelson's pattern of abuse but the extent of it as well, it's going to come as huge news in Sierra Vista. It'll blow the lid off SVSSE, and Frank needs to know in advance exactly what's coming."

CHAPTER 25

WHEN JOANNA DIALED DEB'S NUMBER, THE CALL WENT TO VOICE mail. After leaving a complex message about the possibility of arsenic being involved in the Hopkins homicide, Joanna dialed Frank's number. "What's happening?" he asked when he came on the line. "Any news?"

"Yes, lots," Joanna answered, "and most of it bad. I need a favor. Do you know where Detective Waters is right now?"

"The last I heard he was on his way to SVSSE to let Mr. McVey know that there's another round of interviews coming. As soon as Ernie and Jaime finish talking to Travis Stock's friends at Buena High, that's where all three detectives are headed. What kind of favor?"

"I'm headed your way now, too," Joanna said, "and so's a whole crap storm. I want to have a word in private with you and Detective Waters before that happens."

"This sounds serious."

"It *is* serious," Joanna said. "Susan Nelson was evidently carrying on with a number of her students over an extended period of time, most likely over the course of several years. We have reason to believe that Deputy Stock's son was one of the boys involved."

"Travis?" Frank asked. "That's appalling. He's always seemed like such a straight-arrow kid. And when you say, 'carrying on,' does that mean she was having sex with them?"

"A definite yes to the sex question along with the added complication of having made at least one baby in the process," Joanna replied. "As I'm sure you saw in the reports, Dr. Baldwin's autopsy revealed that Susan Nelson was pregnant at the time of her death. Given the whole vasectomy/condom controversy from the other night, I'm relatively certain that one of her students, rather than her husband, was the father. We're attempting to ascertain which one."

"Any probable candidates so far?" Frank asked.

"Travis Stock seems to be under the impression that he's the father of the child, which may or may not be true. We'll need properly collected DNA from him to confirm that. In the meantime, I need to drop this whole batch of bad news into Jeremy and Allison's laps."

"Not an easy thing to do," Frank said.

"No, it's not," Joanna agreed. "I was hoping Detective Waters could go along with me on that interview. Given the fact that Deputy Stock has been with my department for years, I thought it might be easier on him and on Allison, too, if we do this in front of a relative stranger rather than in front of people he's worked alongside for years. At least I believe that's how I'd feel if our situations were reversed and I was in their shoes."

"You don't think either Jeremy or Allison has any idea about what's been going on at school?" Frank asked.

Joanna sighed. "Maybe," she said, "but I doubt it."

"Well, then," Frank said, "bringing in an outsider to deliver the bad news is probably a good call. I'll get on the horn with Ian as soon as we hang up. But, realistically, how many boys are we talking about here?"

"We found a hidden cache of correspondence," Joanna replied, "mostly handwritten notes. Casey came up with at least ten different handwriting styles on them, so the paper trail would indicate the involvement of at least ten to fifteen different kids. There may be more than that, however. We all need to be prepared for that possibility."

"So there will be other parents who'll need to be notified and interviewed as well?"

"Yes."

"Which means we'll need to think about ongoing counseling for the affected victims," Frank concluded. "That's going to create time and budget complications for both of our departments."

"Right," Joanna agreed. "In addition, once we've established who the victims are, we'll probably need help from your department to conduct whatever additional interviews are deemed necessary."

"Let me know what you need and you'll have it," Frank declared. "In the meantime, tell me about the notes you found."

"They're love notes, evidently, jotted on lined paper mostly torn from student notebooks. The notes are signed with first names only. It seems reasonable to assume that the one named Trav would be Travis Stock. Figuring out who the other victims are will be a bit more difficult. It seems unlikely that any of the kids Susan Nelson targeted will come forward on their own."

"I doubt that, too," Frank said. "If the victims were girls and the abuser turned out to be a male teacher or coach, the public would come down squarely on the side of the girls. With boys, it's a whole different ball game."

Alone in the Yukon, Joanna found herself nodding in agreement. "That was my first instinct as well. There's always a sense that girls are considered victims from the get-go, while boys are often regarded as co-instigators."

"How's it possible that she could get away with pulling stunts like this for so long?" Frank asked. "How come nobody caught on?"

"I believe Susan Nelson was a born manipulator," Joanna answered. "She seems to have convinced each and every one of those poor kids that he was her one and only—the true love of her life—right up until it came time for her to dump him. By then I would guess they were all too ashamed or embarrassed to come forward, leaving her free to move along and target someone else."

"Do you think one of those lovesick boys—Travis, for example—is responsible for your two murders?" Frank asked.

"That's certainly a possibility," Joanna answered. "The school surveillance tape made it appear as though Susan was being abducted at gunpoint. Or maybe knifepoint, but it turns out no weapon was used in the course of the attacks. No gunshot wounds or stab wounds were found on either body."

"If the killer turns out to be one of her juvenile victims," Frank suggested, "he might not have had ready access to a weapon, which would explain why no weapon was used."

There was a short silence on the phone. "What about the other people at the school," Frank asked, "the teachers and administrators? Do you think they knew about what was going on and simply turned a blind eye?"

"What do you think?" Joanna responded. "It's a small school. I suspect that, among the boys especially, what was happening may have been rumored about or, even worse, common knowledge. As far as the faculty is concerned, I'd be surprised to think that no one had any suspicions at all. For one thing, we already know Susan had a fling with a previous principal—one who was fired. Speaking of girls as victims and boys as co-instigators, here's an interesting question: Why did the principal get fired and Susan didn't?"

"That's easy," Frank replied. "It happens all the time. I believe it's called a double standard."

"But the real question—the one the boys' families should be asking—is this," Joanna added. "Did any members of the SVSSE faculty know or even suspect that this was going on right under their noses? If so, why didn't someone report it?"

"It's a hell of a mess," Frank said. "Once the news gets out, all the affected parents should probably go shopping for good trial attorneys. Susan Nelson may have moved beyond the reach of the criminal justice system, but there should still be plenty of soft targets out there for tort proceedings to move forward."

"Starting with the school and its board of directors?" Joanna asked.

"Indeed," Frank agreed. Then after a pause he asked, "So where are you?"

"Just now crossing the divide," Joanna answered. "I should be in your office in about twenty."

"I'll see to it that Detective Waters is here by then, too," Frank assured her.

"Thanks," Joanna said. "I appreciate it."

Off the phone with Frank, she tried reaching Deb Howell. When that didn't work again, her next call was to Larry Kendrick back at Dispatch. "Is Deputy Stock on duty today?"

"Yes, ma'am, he is. He's currently assisting a stranded motorist up by Kartchner Caverns."

"Let him know I'm on my way to Sierra Vista right now. As soon as he's finished with the motorist, tell him that I'd like very much to meet with him and with Allison, preferably at their house. Allison is probably at work right now, too, but tell him that we're meeting privately with parents of some of the SVSSE students. Let him know that it's important that we speak to both him and his wife ASAP. And, Larry, get their home address from Admin and text it to me. I know they've lived in Sierra Vista for years, but I have no idea exactly where. Call coming in. Gotta go."

When she switched over to the other call, Jenny was on the line. "Hey, Mom," she said. "How are things?"

Things were a mess, with three homicides and an outbreak of sexual abuse on her plate, but Joanna didn't want to go into any of that. After all, Jenny was only months out of high school. The idea of discussing a case that included a high school teacher having sex with some of her students wasn't a topic she wished to discuss with her daughter. Not now and most likely not in the near future, either. Maybe never.

"It sounds like you're in a car," Joanna said as a diversionary tactic. "Where are you?"

"Almost to the 101," Jenny answered.

A glance at her watch told Joanna it was just past one. "Already? I thought you had classes until noon and wouldn't be leaving Flagstaff until much later in the afternoon."

"I checked with my professor," Jenny replied. "He said it was no problem for me to leave early, so I did. And the guy who's watching Maggie knows to feed her tonight, too."

A welcome but fleeting moment of pride pulsed through Joanna's system. Jenny was coming for her grandparents' funeral because she wanted to, not because she had to. Not only that, before leaving for home, she had handled all her responsibilities regarding her classes and her horse as well. That was all to the good. Moreover, having Jenny at home meant that Joanna would have her daughter there to help ride herd on whatever guests turned up at the hastily scheduled barbecue.

"Great," Joanna said aloud. "I'm so glad you're coming."

"Do you know what's for dinner tonight?"

Joanna laughed. "You're asking me about dinner? I'm working, so I have no idea at all," she said. "You'll need to check with Butch. Why?"

"When I come through Tucson, I thought I'd get off at Speedway and pick up some tortillas and tamales from the Anita Street Market."

Years earlier, during the investigation into a grisly car crash involving an SUV loaded with illegals, Joanna had met a woman named Gabriella who had turned out to be the cousin of one of the dead victims. At the time of the accident, Gabriella had been working at the Anita Street Market, a tortilla factory in Tucson's Barrio Anita. In the years since, she had married. Now Gabriella Ortiz, she no longer worked in the back, making the tortillas. Instead, she was out front acting as the salesclerk. For Joanna and her family, no trip to Tucson was considered complete without stopping by the market to pick up a batch of freshly made tortillas and tamales and to say hello to Gabriella.

"Whatever we're having," Joanna said, "I can't imagine that tortillas and tamales wouldn't be welcome additions to the menu, if not for tonight, then for tomorrow for sure. But do check with Butch first."

There was a short pause on the line. "Are you okay, Mom?" Jenny asked. "There's a lot going on right now . . ."

"And you're wondering if I should be working."

"Well, yes," Jenny admitted reluctantly. "I guess I was."

Since when did our situations reverse? Joanna thought. *When did Jenny stop being the daughter and turn into the mother?*

"The original homicide case is a complicated one with two separate victims. And now there's a new one up at Sun Sites," Joanna answered. "Homicides are always important. Your grandmother wouldn't want me to neglect them, and neither would Grandpa George."

"Okay, then," Jenny said. "Be safe."

"Always," Joanna replied lightly. "Didn't you know? Safe is my middle name."

CHAPTER 26

JEREMY AND ALLISON STOCK LIVED ON PETERSON STREET IN AN area of modest, cookie-cutter houses that were within easy walking distance of the SVSSE campus. Hoping to create less of a neighborhood stir, Joanna and Detective Waters arrived in only one vehicle rather than two—Joanna's Yukon. When they pulled up out front, there were three cars in the carport and driveway—two sedans—a Honda and a Chevrolet Impala, as well as Deputy Stock's departmental Tahoe.

"Looks like everybody's home," Joanna said with a sigh. "Let's do this." She stopped at the back of the Yukon long enough to extract an evidence bag before leading the way toward the house.

Jeremy opened the front door to the house when they were halfway up the walk.

"Dispatch said this was urgent," he said. "What's going on?"

"Is Allison here?" Joanna asked.

"Yes, she took the afternoon off, but I don't understand. You already spoke to Travis about the murders yesterday. What do we need to talk about today?"

"Something else entirely," Joanna answered quietly.

Just then Allison appeared in the doorway behind him. She was an attractive woman, maybe a few years older than Joanna, and wearing a pantsuit with a long-sleeved blazer and a pair of high heels. Joanna remembered then that Allison Stock worked in a bank as a manager of some kind, and she dressed the part.

"What's going on?" Allison demanded, following her husband first out onto the porch and then down the concrete walkway. "From what Jeremy said, it sounded like an emergency of some kind. Is it? Has something happened to Travis? Is he hurt? Is he all right?"

Well, yes, Joanna thought, *something has happened to Travis. And it's going to be years from now before anyone will be able to figure out if he's all right.*

"This is Detective Ian Waters of the Sierra Vista Police Department," Joanna said, riding roughshod over Allison's questions. "Since we believe Susan Nelson was abducted from the campus of the SVSSE here in Sierra Vista, Chief Montoya and I have declared the homicide cases to be a joint investigation."

"I know all that," Jeremy said impatiently. "What I don't understand is why you have to meet with us again. Travis is at school. Should I go get him? Shouldn't he be here, too?"

"For now, I think it would be easier if Travis wasn't a part of this conversation," Joanna said. "I also believe we'd be better off doing this inside your home rather than out here in the yard."

Nodding, Allison Stock conducted them into the house and motioned Joanna and Ian Waters in the direction of a sofa. "Can I get you something?" she asked. "Iced tea, water?"

"Nothing, thank you," Joanna said. "This isn't that kind of visit."

"What kind of visit is it, then?" Jeremy asked. "If it has to do with the murders, Travis already answered those questions. He went to Tucson with some of his pals to watch a football game."

"That's the thing," Joanna said. "It turns out he didn't."

"Didn't what?"

"Attend the football game in Tucson. We saw postings on social media that showed both of Travis's friends—Nate Digby and Jack Stockman—at the game, but there was no sign of Travis in any of the posted photos. My investigators have since spoken to both Nate and Jack. According to Nate, Travis stopped by his house early Saturday afternoon and told him that he couldn't go to the game after all."

"Wait," Allison asked faintly. "Are you saying he didn't go?"

"That's right," Joanna replied. "Which means that what he told us about his whereabouts on Saturday afternoon and evening were all bold-faced lies."

"You're saying he doesn't have an alibi?" Jeremy Stock asked. "So what? As far as Travis was concerned, he thought Susan Nelson walked on water. Of all the teachers at school, she was Travis's hands-down favorite. He'd have absolutely no reason to harm her."

"That's just the thing," Joanna countered. "He does have a reason."

"That can't be," Allison began, but Jeremy held up a hand, effectively stifling whatever she was about to say.

"What reason?" he asked. "Is that why you're here, to accuse our son of murder?"

"We're not here to accuse Travis of murder," Joanna said. "But it's safe to say that he is now considered a person of interest along with several other SVSSE students. I hope you're right and he has some perfectly reasonable explanation for where he went on Saturday and why he lied about it yesterday morning when Agent Watkins interviewed him. But that's not the real reason we're here. There's something else."

Allison leaned back in her chair, holding one hand across her heart as if to ward off a physical attack. "What is it?" she whispered. "What haven't you told us?"

Joanna had to gather herself before launching into it. "It turns out that Susan Nelson, your son's teacher, was a sexual predator who was targeting young men and having multiple affairs with boys who were her students."

Allison's face paled. "You can't possibly mean that Travis was one of them!"

"That's exactly what I'm saying," Joanna said.

She glanced in Jeremy's direction. His mouth was set in a thin, grim line. "No," he declared. "That's impossible. It simply did not happen!"

"But it did happen," Joanna insisted. "We found a note—one written in what appears to be Travis's own handwriting—in which he admits as much. In addition, you need to know something else. It turns out Mrs. Nelson was pregnant at the time of her death."

"She was pregnant?" Allison gasped, her voice barely audible. "Are you saying that woman was carrying my son's baby?"

"We believe that to be the case," Joanna said. "We'll need a

DNA sample from Travis to ascertain that. From reading what he wrote, however, it's clear that Travis was under the impression that the baby was his. He begged Susan to divorce her husband and marry him. He didn't care how many jobs he had to work to support her and the child. He said he was the baby's father, and he wanted to act like it.

"The problem is," she continued, "Susan Nelson threw Travis over. She told him she had zero intention of getting a divorce. She said that if she claimed the baby was her husband's, no one ever would dare believe otherwise."

At that, Allison Stock simply doubled over where she sat, covering her face and weeping into her lap. Jeremy walked over to her chair. Perching on the arm, he leaned down and patted his wife's heaving shoulder. There may have been kindness in the touch, but his face was set in granite.

"How did this happen?" he demanded. "How could she get away with such a thing? And Travis wasn't the only one?"

"We have no idea how widespread the problem was," Joanna told him. "We have evidence that suggests there were a number of boys involved, including some who may have already graduated."

"Does that mean they're all persons of interest in the two homicides?" Jeremy asked.

"Yes," Joanna answered, "right along with Travis. Our first task will be identifying as many of them as possible. Once we know who they are, we'll start eliminating them one by one. So this is a courtesy call to give you a heads-up about the situation. It's also why we didn't want Travis present when we delivered this difficult news."

"To spare him from being embarrassed?" Jeremy demanded. "He damned well ought to be embarrassed!"

Joanna was startled by the obvious anger in Jeremy's voice—anger toward his son rather than his son's abuser.

"Please, Jeremy," she pleaded. "You have to remember that as far as the sexual assault is concerned, Travis is the victim. He was and still is under the age of consent. What Susan Nelson did to him constitutes statutory rape. But Detective Waters and I are here to suggest that the next time we speak to him, you may want to have an attorney present. In fact, there's a good chance an attorney will advise Travis to refuse to speak to us altogether."

"Is that because I'm a cop?" Jeremy asked. "Is that why you came here to tell us?"

"No," Joanna said. "I'm not playing favorites, and that's the reason Detective Waters is here—to make sure I don't give you some kind advantage that I withhold from the other individuals involved. Everyone will be given an opportunity to have both parents in attendance as well as to consult with an attorney before we conduct any additional interviews."

By then Allison had recovered enough that she was once again capable of speech. "When this all comes out, those poor boys' lives—and Travis's life, too—will be ruined forever," she declared. "I'm glad that awful woman is dead. That horrible bitch got what she deserved."

"The problem is, she didn't," Joanna replied. "Statutory rape is a crime, but it isn't a capital offense. In addition, Susan Nelson isn't the only homicide victim. A second woman died at the same time and place as she did. Her name is Desirée Wilburton, and she's from Tucson."

"Was she in on it, too?" Allison asked.

"Not that we know of," Joanna said. "So far we've not found any connections between the two women—not on social media, anyway. But then we've not found any electronic communications between Mrs. Nelson and any of the targeted boys, either."

Allison Stock remained unconvinced. "I'll bet she was doing the same thing Susan Nelson was—both of them together."

Somewhere in the back of the house, a door slammed shut. "Oh God," Allison uttered despairingly. "It's Trav. What's he doing here? They must have let school out early."

A moment later Travis appeared in the doorway between the kitchen and the combination dining room/living room. He stopped short when he saw the four people gathered there. "What's going on?" he asked.

"How about you tell us?" his father demanded grimly. "How long have you been screwing around with one of your teachers? What the hell were you thinking? You don't have the sense God gave little green apples!"

Travis's face turned ashen. He leaned against the doorframe for support. "You know about that?" he croaked.

"Yes, we do," Allison said, echoing both her husband's tone and sentiments. "How could you do such a thing? How could you?"

Their mirror-image reactions reminded Joanna of what Frank had said earlier—that when it came to juvenile sexual assaults, boys didn't qualify as victims so much as perpetrators, even as far as family members were concerned.

Without glancing at either of his parents, Travis stumbled into the room, sank into the only remaining chair, and then sat with his head bowed, staring at the floor.

"Where were you on Saturday?" Joanna asked. "Yesterday you told Agent Watkins that you had gone to a football game in Tucson, but you didn't, did you."

Travis shook his head.

"You lied about that, too?" Jeremy demanded in barely suppressed fury. "Where were you, then?"

"I went for a walk out by the San Pedro."

"Alone or with someone?" Joanna asked.

"Alone," Travis answered bleakly. "I needed to think. I knew what Susan and I were doing was wrong, but as soon as she told me about the baby, I wanted to do the right thing. I wanted to marry her. I begged her to get a divorce and marry me. Instead, she dumped me. Laughed at me to my face."

Had Joanna been a therapist, she might have asked, "How did that make you feel?" There was no need. Travis Stock was clearly devastated. The question she asked was a cop's question rather than a counselor's.

"Did anyone see you out by the river?"

"No, I came back by the school later—about the usual time I saw her for my regular tutoring sessions. I thought I'd try talking to her one more time and maybe convince her to change her mind, but her car wasn't in the parking lot. She was already gone."

"Tutoring sessions, my ass!" Jeremy muttered in the background.

"Did you go onto the school grounds?" Joanna asked, ignoring Jeremy and directing her question at his son. "If so, one of the security cameras might have picked you up."

Travis shook his head. "I only went as far as the edge of the parking lot. As soon as I saw that her car was already gone, I left."

"Where did you go?"

"I walked some more. For hours."

"Where?"

"Mostly right here in the neighborhood. I couldn't show up at home too early because I was supposed to be in Tucson at the game. I finally came home around midnight. Nobody saw me then, either. Mom was already in bed and Dad was at work." Travis paused long enough to look around the room, studying each face in turn. Finally, he settled on Joanna's. "You think I killed her, don't you?"

"Did you know there were others?"

"Other what?"

"Other boys—boys just like you—who were also involved with Susan Nelson."

"No," Travis declared. "That's not true. It can't be true."

"Unfortunately, it is," Joanna insisted. "It turns out you're only one of a long string of what older people might refer to as Susan Nelson's 'boy toys.' She was playing with you, Travis. She was never as serious about you as you were about her."

"There were others?" he asked faintly. "Really?"

Joanna nodded.

"I can't believe it," Travis said, shaking his head. At which point he buried his face in his hands and burst into tears. Allison's need to comfort her son finally overrode her disapproval of what he'd done. Rising from her chair, she hurried over to Travis and held him close, while a stony-eyed Jeremy stayed where he was, staring at them.

"So did you kill Susan Nelson?" Joanna asked when Travis finally quieted.

"No," he said. "I didn't. I couldn't. I loved her."

"But you don't have an alibi," Joanna pointed out. "Let me ask you this. Do you happen to own a blue-and-white hoodie?"

"Of course," Travis answered at once. "Almost everyone at school has one of those."

"Where's yours?" Joanna asked.

"In my bedroom."

"Would you mind getting it for me?"

"Look," Jeremy interjected. "I think this has gone far enough. If you want to ask him anything else, Sheriff Brady, we're going to have to insist on having an attorney present. And if you want his sweatshirt, we should probably see a warrant."

"Of course," Joanna agreed, but by then Travis had already sprung to his feet.

"No, Dad," he said. "I didn't do this. If there's a chance my hoodie will help clear my name, I want Sheriff Brady to have it."

He hurried out of the room, returning empty-handed a moment or so later with a puzzled expression on his face. "It's not there," he said. "I must have left it at school. It's probably in my locker. Sorry."

Except it wasn't in his locker. Joanna already knew that for sure.

"There's one other thing you can do to help us," Joanna said, reaching into her purse and extracting an evidence bag already stocked with a cheek swab. "The fact that Susan had sexual relations with a number of people besides you has given us a whole list of suspects that we'll need to eliminate. And with the baby involved, we need to establish paternity."

"But I'm the father," Travis insisted. "I already told you that."

"We'll need a cheek swab to prove it," Joanna said.

"A cheek swab?" Jeremy objected angrily, his eyes as hard as ever. "No way! I already told you, Sheriff Brady, if you want anything more from Travis, we'll need to see a warrant."

"No, Dad, they don't need a warrant," Travis declared, speaking for himself and reaching for the proffered evidence bag at the same time. "I'll be glad to do a cheek swab. The baby's mine, and I want to prove it. As for murdering Susan? I didn't do it, and I'll be glad to take a lie detector test to prove that, too. I intend to clear my name."

Jeremy sat with his arms crossed looking on in what appeared to be cold fury as Travis removed the swab from the baggie and ran it across the inside of his cheek. Finished, he returned the swab to the bag and handed it back to Joanna.

"Thank you," she said, slipping it into her purse. "Detective Waters and I will be going now. But for the record, Travis, are you right- or left-handed?"

"Right," he said, immediately raising his right hand in the air. "Why?"

"Just wondering," Joanna said.

When they let themselves out onto the front porch, Joanna was surprised to find that Travis had followed them. "I'm glad you told my parents about this," he said quietly as the front door closed behind them. "I wanted to tell them, but I couldn't figure out what to say. Now how do I go back inside and face them?"

"You have to understand that what Susan Nelson did to you and the others was utterly reprehensible," Joanna told him. "You're a juvenile. That means she was a pedophile and that makes you a victim of a crime called statutory rape. Recovering from something like this is never easy, and the only way to do it is to bring the whole mess out into the open. Keeping secrets is far harder on all concerned than letting them go. Your parents love you, Travis. Trust them. They only want what's best for you."

After a moment, Travis nodded. "I guess," he said, looking

and sounding unconvinced. "But tell me about the baby. Susan never told me what it was. She said it was too soon to tell. Was it a boy or a girl?"

Under normal circumstances it might have been too soon to tell, Joanna thought, *but an autopsy table was a lot different from a visit to your local OB/GYN.*

"A boy," Joanna answered. A wave of incredible grief washed across Travis's face—grief for an unborn child he would never have a chance to care for or hold or love. DNA had not yet confirmed the question of paternity, but Travis's grief was real enough. Joanna reached out and gave the boy a quick hug. Under the circumstances, that single hug didn't seem like nearly enough, but it was the best she could do.

As she and Detective Waters drove away from the house, Joanna watched in the rearview mirror. When they turned the corner, the devastated figure of Travis still stood, as if frozen solid, on the front porch. Joanna understood his delay. As long as he remained outside, he could put off facing his father's wrath.

Joanna glanced over at Ian Waters, realizing suddenly that he had said not one word during the course of the interview. "You've been very quiet," she said. "Why didn't you speak up?"

"Because you were handling it so well, and I didn't see how a contribution from me would make the situation any better," he replied. "But tell me. How many more interviews like this are we going to have to do?"

"Maybe as many as fifteen or so," Joanna told him, "and those are just the ones with the paper trail. There may well be more."

"Great," Ian muttered. "Is there a chance I can get Chief Montoya to pull me off the case before we have to do the next one?"

"No way," Joanna told him. "You're in this for the full-meal deal." She glanced at her watch. "It's only two thirty, which means there's probably enough time to do another one before we call it a day. In fact, I already have someone in mind."

"Awesome," Ian muttered.

Ignoring him, Joanna reached for her radio and called Larry. "I need someone to look in the murder book. Go through the SVSSE interviews from yesterday and find the contact information for Kevin Thomas and for his mother, Colonel Karenna Thomas. Text me their collection of phone numbers as soon as you can."

"Who's Kevin Thomas?" Ian asked once the radio transmission ended.

"Up until this morning, he was my confidential informant."

"What changed?"

"Remember all those handwritten messages I told you we found hidden in Susan Nelson's linen drawer? One of them was signed by someone named 'Kev,' who could very well be Kevin Thomas."

"So we need to tell his mother and probably get another swab?" Ian grumbled.

"That's right," Joanna said. "Come to think of it, I have a deal you're not going to be able to refuse. If you'll take Travis Stock's DNA sample to the crime lab in Tucson and then write up the Stock interview, I'll let you off the hook and handle the Thomas interview on my own."

"You're right," Ian said, sounding relieved. "If you're giving me a choice of writing up a report or putting another family through hell, that's a deal I can't refuse."

CHAPTER 27

JOANNA DROVE STRAIGHT BACK TO SIERRA VISTA PD. IAN IMMEDI-ately disappeared to do her bidding and write up the report, while she was ushered into Frank Montoya's private office. "How did it go?" he asked.

"Not fun," Joanna said. "Not at all. Jeremy and Allison are heartbroken, of course, and so is Travis. I don't think he had any idea there were other boys involved. Despite what we told him, he's still clinging to the belief that he was Susan Nelson's one true love. He's really broken up about losing her and about losing the baby, too. I think he genuinely wanted to be a part of the child's life."

A text came in just then, giving her a listing of Colonel Thomas's phone numbers. "I'm going to need to make a call," she said.

"To arrange the next interview?" Frank asked.

Joanna nodded. "Would you mind if I did it here?"

"No problem," Frank said. "Make yourself at home. I'll give you some privacy and find somewhere else to hang out for the next little while." With that, Chief Montoya got up from behind his desk and left the room while Joanna punched in the number listed as Colonel Thomas's office number. The secretary who answered the call immediately put it through.

"Colonel Thomas," Karenna said.

"Sheriff Brady here," Joanna replied. "Something has come up, and I'd really like to speak to you this afternoon if it's at all possible."

"You want to speak to me or to Kevin?" Colonel Thomas asked.

"To you," Joanna answered. "Preferably without Kevin."

"I thought we'd already put this matter to rest," Colonel Thomas objected. "As I told you yesterday, Kevin was with me on Saturday—all day Saturday. He couldn't possibly have been involved in what happened to those two women."

"This isn't about the homicides," Joanna said quickly. "Some other information has come to light, and I'd like to discuss it with you outside your son's presence."

"I'm working now. Is this really necessary?"

"Yes, it is. What we've learned may well jeopardize your son's position as a confidential informant. I want you to be fully aware of the situation before anyone speaks to Kevin again."

"This sounds serious."

"It *is* serious," Joanna insisted. "Very."

"Well, all right," Colonel Thomas said in grudging agreement. "Since it's such a hassle for civilians to get on post, it would probably be easiest if I met you somewhere else. Where are you?"

"I'm currently at the Sierra Vista Police Department. When you get here, ask to be shown into Chief Montoya's office. That's where I'll be."

Left to her own devices, Joanna dialed Casey's number first. "Thanks for tracking down that information for me. Now I need something else. Could you please sort through the scans from the linen-drawer papers and text me a copy of the one signed by Kev?"

"Sure," Casey said. "No trouble. Just let me find it. Okay, here it is. Sending now."

Seconds later, Joanna heard a satisfying *ding* as an incoming message arrived on her phone.

"Anything else happening there at the moment?" Joanna asked.

"Lots," Casey replied. "We're making progress. After getting your message, Detective Howell seems to have hit the arsenic jackpot up at Sun Sites. First she found a paperback copy of *The Poisoner's Handbook* hidden under the mattress in Katherine Hopkins's bedroom. She must have bought the book from a used-book store. Amazon sells the mass-market edition for more than twelve bucks. Inside this copy there's a penciled notation of one dollar. I'm guessing we'll be able to lift Kay's fingerprints from the chapter devoted to arsenic. As soon as Deb found a partially used four-pound container of rat poison under the kitchen sink, she thought she was home free."

"Thought she was home free but wasn't?" Joanna asked.

"Exactly. Arsenic used to be called 'inheritance powder' because it was so readily available back in the old days. That's also one of the primary reasons it isn't easy to come by anymore. I've spent the day checking with legitimate purveyors of the stuff to no good effect. None of them can locate any sign of purchases made by Katherine Hopkins of Sun Sites, Arizona. As for current rat poisons? These days most of them are made with warfarin rather than arsenic."

"Warfarin?" Joanna asked. "Wait a minute. Isn't that a medicine of some kind? I believe my mother was on that for a time after she had a blood clot in her leg."

"Right," Casey answered. "It's a blood thinner. The idea is the rats eat the bait and then crawl off somewhere else. When their blood gets thin enough, they die. Turns out that's the kind of rat poison Deb found under the sink—one that's warfarin-based rather than arsenic-based."

"So we're nowhere, then?"

"Not really," Casey said. "Wait for it. This gets better. Deb said that when she showed up with the search warrant, the Hopkins place turned out to be a seventy-foot double-wide mobile home stocked to overflowing with antiques—hundreds of them, maybe even thousands. She said it could have qualified as an antiques mall all by itself, with junk piled floor to ceiling: old clocks and radios; appliances; old containers of every kind—baking soda, soup cans, soda cans. In an in-home office, she found records that told her that's exactly what Hal and Kay Hopkins have been doing ever since they arrived in Sun Sites—running a thriving antiques business out of their home. Incidentally, while Deb was searching the office, she came across several small insurance policies. They only total about a hundred and fifty thousand dollars, but still, if your home is paid for, that much money could amount to quite a windfall—and Katherine is named as the sole beneficiary for all of them."

"When it comes to catching killers and finding motive," Joanna said, "it's always good to have a life insurance component in our corner."

"Right," Casey agreed. "So anyway, Deb and I were on the phone. I was in the process of giving her the bad news about the rat bait in the kitchen when she saw it right there in the living room. She was standing in front of one of those glass-fronted antique étagères. The shelves were full of all kinds of old-timey medicine bottles—Hadacol, Carter's Little Liver Pills, Mrs. Stewart's Bluing, you name it."

"Hey, wait a minute," Joanna objected. "Mrs. Stewart's Bluing isn't old. I buy it at Safeway. In fact, I keep a bottle of it in the laundry room at all times. It's great for scorpion stings."

"According to Deb, the bottles in the cabinet all came from a very long time ago rather than something you'd purchase recently at your local Safeway. At any rate, she was standing there studying the living room shelves when she noticed a tin canister up on the very top shelf—a red canister with three white skulls and crossbones painted on the sides. When she got it down, the top said 'Rat Rid: the Farmer's Friend.'"

"You're kidding," Joanna said. "An antique canister with arsenic still inside?"

"You betcha. Deb estimates there's about a pound or so of a powdery substance stored inside a Tupperware container."

"I doubt the Tupperware was part of the original storage plan," Joanna said.

"Probably not," Casey agreed. "Deb used her patrol car's chem-kit to test the powder. Turns out it's arsenic all right—showed up yellow on her test strip. It's most likely not pure arsenic. The powder probably contains a filler of some kind—cornmeal or flour, maybe—something to attract the rats' attention in the first place."

"No wonder Katherine Hopkins's name didn't show up among the lists of legitimate purchasers from one of the current arsenic sources," Joanna said. "She probably picked the canister up at a yard sale or an estate sale where the person selling it had no idea there was anything left inside. From where I sit, Kay was ready to be done with an ornery husband—and she had both means and opportunity. I'm guessing she tried using the arsenic—enough to put Hal in the hospital but not enough to kill him outright. So she gave up on that and whacked him with the golf club instead. The use of arsenic shows premeditation on her part. That should be good enough for murder in the second degree at least—maybe even first."

"You'd think so," Casey said, "but we have a slight problem with that."

"What problem?"

"According to Detective Howell, Kay's attorney has already reached out to the county attorney, asking for a plea deal."

"What kind of plea deal?" Joanna asked.

"Manslaughter."

"That's all?" Joanna demanded. "Shouldn't she also be facing additional charges of attempted murder?"

"That's what would happen if it was up to you or me," Casey answered. "Unfortunately, Arlee Jones gets to call this shot."

Arlee Jones was the local county attorney, and most of the time he and Joanna weren't necessarily in agreement. Arlee was a wheeler-dealer who was big on plea deals that sidestepped long-drawn-out courtroom proceedings. He liked getting results in a hurry rather than going to all the time, trouble, and effort of actually trying cases. Joanna knew at once that Casey was right. Arlee would be more than happy to take Katherine Hopkins's partial confession at face value because a simple manslaughter plea would get her off his docket with no muss or fuss.

"I'll call him as soon as we're off the phone," Joanna said. "Anything new on the Nelson case?"

"We've tentatively identified a couple of the linen-drawer boys," Casey said. "The Double C's are in the process of tracking down and speaking to the boys' parents. I told Ernie that you'd already handled the Stocks and would most likely take care of Colonel Thomas."

"All right, then, I'd better move on to Mr. Jones."

"Good luck with that," Casey said, "but I'm not holding my breath."

CHAPTER 28

WHEN JOANNA CALLED, ARLEE JONES WAS NOT THE LEAST BIT happy to hear from her. "I suppose this is all about the Sun Sites case," he grumbled. "Detective Howell has been in touch asking me to hold off on offering any kind of plea deal, but I don't see why I should. Supposedly, Detective Howell found some kind of rat poison in the Hopkinses' home, but that's hardly a crime. I happen to have rat poison in my home, too. The damned rats keep getting into the garage and eating everything in sight, including the wiring on my Porsche. It's evidently wrapped in some kind of vegetable-based plastic. Were you aware that's how they make some plastics these days? I'm sure it's all part of this newfangled all-things-green kind of thing. As far as I'm concerned, if it ain't broke, don't fix it."

Joanna wasn't in the mood to be sidetracked into a discussion of vegetable-based plastics. "Getting back to Katherine Hopkins—" she began.

"Look," Arlee interrupted impatiently. "I know all about Detective Howell's pet rat-poison thing. The problem is, with that we don't have a smoking gun. Yes, the ME found traces of arsenic in Hal's system during the autopsy—enough to suggest that it might have caused the flulike symptoms that put him in the hospital a couple of time in the recent past, but there's nothing that gives us a clear indication that Kay Hopkins is the one who administered it. As far as arsenic poisoning is concerned, we're dealing with a purely circumstantial case. With the blow to the head, we've got a smoking gun, which turns out to be a pitching wedge, for Pete's sake, and not a gun at all. In other words, manslaughter works for me."

"So you're willing to let her plead to manslaughter and walk on a charge of attempted murder, just to get her out of your hair?"

"She'll still be in jail."

"Not for nearly as long as she deserves," Joanna argued.

"Look," Arlee said, "this is not open to discussion."

"But it might be," Joanna said. "Suppose someone gave my mother's old pal Marliss Shackleford a call and mentioned—just hinted around—at the idea that perhaps you might be too old to cut the mustard and that making plea deals accounted for less wear and tear on a doddering old guy than actually taking criminal cases to court? How do you suppose that would go over with voters in an election year?"

"Young woman," Jones demanded, "are you threatening me?"

"Not threatening, exactly," Joanna replied. "Just putting it out there for your possible consideration."

"It sounds like slander to me!" Arlee declared before slamming down the receiver. Hanging up like that on a landline phone still worked. The resulting racket made far more of a statement than simply pressing end on a cell phone's keypad. One was high drama; the other wasn't.

Joanna was left sitting and staring at the phone in her hand in frustration. She understood that as far as Kay Hopkins was concerned, there was little she could do. Unfortunately, plea bargains amounted to business as usual in the world of criminal justice. Cops did the hard investigative work that, more often than not, ended up being undermined by the judicial system. Law enforcement caught the bad guys; prosecutors and courts gave them a slap on the wrist or let them walk.

Just then, the door to Frank's office opened, and Frank himself ushered Karenna Thomas into the room. Once she was inside, he backed out of the room and shut the door, leaving the two women alone. Colonel Thomas was in full uniform and high dudgeon.

"I still don't understand what's so important that I needed to be dragged away from work in the middle of the day!" she exclaimed. "If this isn't about the homicide investigation, why are you so determined to speak to me instead of Kevin?"

"This isn't exactly about the two homicides," Joanna said quietly, "although we have discovered evidence that supports what your son told us about Travis Stock."

"Does that mean he's the one who murdered Mrs. Nelson?"

"That's still under investigation. We have yet to determine if Travis was or wasn't involved in the homicides. Beyond what I've already said, I'm unable to disclose any details about our investigation. This meeting is about something else, Colonel Thomas, about what Kevin told us concerning Travis Stock's having been victimized by Mrs. Nelson prior to her death."

"Oh, that," Colonel Thomas said offhandedly. "The whole statutory rape thing. What about it?"

"We've come across evidence that suggests Travis Stock wasn't Mrs. Nelson's only victim," Joanna said quietly. With that, she turned on her phone, opened the text message app, and then adjusted the on-screen scanned image Casey had sent her until it was large enough to be legible. "Take a look at this," she suggested. "Does the handwriting appear to be familiar to you?"

Colonel Thomas picked up the phone and then donned a pair of reading glasses before studying it more closely. As she scrolled through the document, her eyes widened in dismay.

"Is this real?"

"I'm afraid so," Joanna answered.

"So that awful woman did the same thing to Kevin that she did to Travis! But how is that possible? When I enrolled Kevin at SVSSE, I was told it was the best possible school in the area as far as academics were concerned. And yet the school administrators were stupid enough to let something like this go on right under their noses? As for Susan Nelson, how could a monster like that be allowed to have a teaching credential? It's criminal, utterly criminal!"

Joanna was struck by the fact that unlike Jeremy Stock, Karenna Thomas was prepared to place the blame squarely where it belonged—on Susan Nelson's shoulders—rather than on her son's.

"Yes, it *is* criminal," Joanna agreed, "but you need to speak to your son about all this and let him know that you're aware of what was going on. I hope he was actually listening yesterday when I was explaining about Travis being the victim of a sex crime, because apparently Kevin has been victimized in exactly the same way."

For once, the usually cool and collected Colonel Thomas seemed to lose her composure. "What am I supposed to do about all this?" she asked, her voice nearly breaking.

"You'll need to try to bring that idea home to Kevin—that he was manipulated by a sexual predator. He's a victim and so are any other boys who were caught up in Susan Nelson's web. You'll also need to prepare him for the very real possibility that some or even all of this may eventually become public knowledge. Law enforcement officials are required to protect the names of juveniles, but this is a relatively small town. Word may leak out, especially if the families involved—including your own family, perhaps—decide to take the school to court and sue for damages."

An ashen-faced Karenna handed the phone back to Joanna. "Just because Kevin said he wanted Mrs. Nelson dead doesn't mean he killed her. As I told you yesterday, Kevin was with me in Tucson all day on Saturday."

"Yes," Joanna said with a nod, "but given the circumstances, we'll need to verify everything the two of you did on Saturday. We'll be doing the same thing with all the other affected families, once we ascertain exactly who all was involved. In the next few days, we'll be interviewing the boys and their parents together and most likely collecting DNA samples as we go. I expect those interviews will be more about eliminating suspects than they will be about finding one. I have every confidence that will be the case with Kevin—he'll be eliminated."

"What do I do in the meantime?"

"Go home and talk to your son. He's been through a shattering experience. He's going to need you. I'm telling you the same thing I told Jeremy and Allison Stock about Travis and the same thing we'll be saying to all the other families as well. Don't be afraid to seek counseling, for your son and for yourself, too. My department can put you in touch with the county's victims' advocate service, although you may want to seek out something more private."

"How is Travis?" Karenna asked, standing up to leave. "I've known him for years. He's a great kid. Is he okay?"

"He's pretty well shattered, too," Joanna answered.

"But is he going to be okay?"

Joanna thought back to the scene in the Stocks' living room and to how Jeremy had almost instantly leaped to the conclusion that Travis was somehow at fault.

"He'll probably be okay over time," Joanna said. "At least I hope so. Unfortunately, in situations like this it's easy for people to jump to the erroneous conclusion that the boys involved are somehow perpetrators rather than victims. That's why I believe counseling is so important for all concerned."

By then, Karenna Thomas was already at the door. She paused and turned back to Joanna. "Thank you for giving me this difficult news in person, Sheriff Brady. I'm sure you have plenty of other things vying for your attention right now, and you could easily have handed it off to someone else. I appreciate your going out of your way to do it."

"You're welcome," Joanna said. "Having to deliver bad news comes with the territory, but today has been especially tough—for everyone."

CHAPTER 29

JOANNA WAS TROUBLED AS SHE DROVE BACK TO BISBEE THINKING about the devastation her department's homicide investigation had now visited on at least two unsuspecting families, with probably many more to come. Her own unborn baby, of course, chose that moment of quiet reflection to start kicking up a storm.

"Settle down, Sage," she admonished the child aloud. "Hold your horses. We've got some time yet."

Because Butch was reluctant to sign off on naming their baby girl Sage, Joanna only addressed her that way in private. For Butch, sage was all about cooking turkeys and making dressing. For Joanna, it was different. D. H. Lathrop had loved Arizona history, but when it came to fiction, his favorite author had been Zane Grey, his favorite title being *Riders of the Purple Sage.* With Eleanor grumbling in the background that Joanna was far too young to be exposed to such things, D. H. had settled his daughter beside him on the sofa and read it aloud to her, stopping only when she drifted off to sleep. She still owned the book—her father's well-loved and very tattered copy. George Winfield had seen to it that the book had come to Joanna when he and Eleanor had sorted through the boxes in their garage. Whenever Joanna caught a glimpse of the book on the shelf over Butch's desk, that's what it evoked—a sweet memory of her long-absent father.

But just now, with the baby squirming in her belly, she couldn't help thinking about Allison Stock and Karenna Thomas. Back when the two women had been pregnant with their respective sons or when they had brought their infant boys home from hospital nurseries, had either of them ever considered the idea that only a few years down the road, the boys would become the victims of a sexual predator? For Joanna, that thought carried her right on to another.

The two women had reacted to hearing that dreadful news in almost a mirror-image fashion—first with shock and dismay, yes, but ultimately with compassion. Joanna had known Jeremy Stock for years—ever since she was elected to office—and yet she had been both surprised and dismayed that his knee-jerk reaction had been to place so much of the blame on Travis. Why would Jeremy do that? Why would *any* parent do it?

Then it hit her. She remembered how testy she had been with all the people who, in the course of the last few days, had been bold enough to suggest to her that, in view of her mother's recent passing and with the added complication of her pregnancy, perhaps Joanna should consider working less and staying home more. Shamefacedly, she realized now that she had more or less told them all to go to hell, mostly by snarling at them rather than thanking them for their concern.

Pot to kettle, Joanna reminded herself ruefully. The way Jeremy and Allison Stock raised their son was their private business and none of hers. And then, in order to take her mind off the Stocks, she reached for her phone and called Butch.

"What's for dinner?" she asked when he answered.

"Jenny called early enough to place her order. Evidently the cafeteria at NAU isn't big on green chili casserole, so that's what we're having. She picked up some tortillas and tamales on her way through Tucson, so that's the remainder of the menu."

"Who all is coming?"

"The usual suspects," Butch answered. "Carol and the boys, Bob and Marcie, Jim Bob and Eva Lou."

Carol was Carol Sunderson. Years earlier, when an electrical fire had burned her mobile home to the ground, she had been left a homeless widow with two young grandsons to support. She and the boys had moved into the original house at High Lonesome Ranch, the one where Joanna had once lived, paying a very affordable rent out of wages earned by working for Joanna and Butch as a sometime housekeeper/nanny. The grandsons, Danny, now eleven, and Rick, thirteen, were in and out of Butch and Joanna's house as much as if it were their own.

Joanna counted the guests off in her head. With the four of them, Carol's three, Bob and Marcie, and Joanna's original father- and mother-in-law, Jim Bob and Eva Lou, the dinner guests came to a total of eleven. She was glad that serving an impromptu meal for that many people posed no problem for Butch. It would have been a major cooking crisis for her.

"Where are you?" Butch asked. "And how's your day?"

She gave him a brief rundown. "I'm on my way back to the office now," she said when she finished. "Since I won't be in at all tomorrow, I need to clear up as many details as possible before I call it a day."

"Just don't be late for dinner," Butch cautioned. "I don't mind cooking, but I can't cook and entertain visitors at the same time. There's not enough room in the kitchen."

Joanna's chronic tendency to miss mealtimes was one of the few ongoing bones of contention in their otherwise relatively trouble-free marriage. Butch was good about her showing up late when it was just their family. He always left a plate for her to warm in the microwave when she did get home, but she knew it bugged him if she went AWOL when they were expecting guests.

"Yes, sir," she replied. "I'll be Johnny on the spot."

When she reached the Justice Center and pulled into her parking space behind the building, the one next to hers was occupied, which meant Chief Deputy Hadlock was still there. She went straight to his office and knocked on the doorframe.

"Busy day?" she asked, peeking inside.

"The media has been eating me alive. There are rumors out there that there's been some sexual wrongdoing on the part of an SVSSE faculty member, and everyone wants to know if Susan Nelson had anything to do with it."

"Who's asking?" Joanna asked.

"Who do you think?"

"Give Marliss the standard answer you give to everyone else—no comments on ongoing investigations. For right now, if Marliss gives you any more lip, send her in my direction. She's been invited to the funeral tomorrow, so that should keep her out of your hair for a while at least. As for the investigation? Between you and me, Susan Nelson was a pedophile who shouldn't have been within a mile of young male students, but we won't be making any statements to that effect until we have some idea of the full extent of her wrongdoing. And on the topic of the Geronimo homicides, we still haven't found a single connection between our two victims."

"I heard that you were doing a second interview with Travis Stock. Is he involved in all this? Do you think he's good for the two homicides?"

Obviously Tom had been keeping his ear to the ground all day in addition to dealing with media concerns.

"I'm thinking not," Joanna answered. "When Susan Nelson was frog-marched off the school grounds, the kidnapper was holding her with his right hand while presumably carrying a weapon of some kind in the left-hand pocket of the hoodie."

"Which would make the killer left-handed," Tom suggested

"And Travis Stock is right-handed," Joanna replied. "That's one thing in his favor. What's not in his favor is the fact that he and the victim were romantically involved, and she recently dumped him. Not only that, his alibi is crap, and his school hoodie has suddenly gone missing."

"So he's not out of the woods, then?"

"Nowhere near, and if we removed his name from the suspect list without investigating him more fully, we wouldn't be doing our jobs."

"Okay, then," Tom agreed before abruptly changing the subject. "Is it true that Let's-Make-a-Deal Jones is going to allow Katherine Hopkins to plead to manslaughter?"

"Probably," Joanna answered.

The chief deputy shook his head in dismay. "If that isn't enough to piss off the Good Fairy!"

In terms of their working relationship, having Tom Hadlock

feel comfortable enough to crack a joke with her amounted to big progress.

"It's our job to catch the bad guys and turn over our findings to the county attorney," she said. "What Arlee Jones does with them after that is on his head not ours."

Joanna turned back toward her own office.

"Are you heading out soon?" Tom asked.

"Not right away," she said. "Since I'll be off tomorrow, I want to clear as much paperwork off my desk as possible."

"Speaking of paperwork, duty rosters for the next month are done and sitting on your desk. I'm getting a little better at that, and I'll be at the board-of-supervisors meeting bright and early in the morning. I've taken a look at the agenda. I don't think they'll need me to say anything."

"If something comes up and you do need me," Joanna told him, "feel free to call. I'll be at a funeral. I won't be on the moon."

"Thanks, boss," Tom said. "Will do."

Joanna retreated into her own office. Once there, she gratefully stripped off the Kevlar vest her steadily expanding waistline had rendered too small and entirely uncomfortable. She had a larger one, out in the luggage compartment of the Yukon, but she was reluctant to make the switch. Wearing a vest large enough to accommodate her waist made it too big everywhere else.

Tomorrow, she told herself. *I'll change over to the other one tomorrow.*

With that, she turned to her desk. The expected paperwork was there waiting for her, all right, but she shoved it aside without a glance. There was something else that required her attention at the moment—something important that she had been holding at bay by keeping her mind totally focused on the two separate homicide investigations.

The night before, at the restaurant, Bob and Butch had ganged up on her and finally convinced her that she was the one best suited to stand up during the funeral service and deliver George and Eleanor's eulogies. Opening her computer, she sat staring at the blank screen for a very long time, wondering what to say. Her relationship with George was far less complicated than her dealings with Eleanor had been, so she started with him:

> *George Mason Winfield was a trusted colleague and friend long before he became my stepfather. Born and raised in Duluth, Minnesota, George was a physician who was helpless when it came to saving his own wife and daughter from the ravages of cancer. Those terrible losses, only a few years apart, left him mentally and spiritually depleted and unable to continue practicing medicine as he had done for many years. Instead, he sent himself back to school and trained to become a medical examiner.*
>
> *That's how I knew him initially—when he hired on to be Cochise County's ME. He was tasked with bringing what had been a shoestring operation into the modern world. He was easy to work with, didn't put on airs, and was always patient in dealing with investigators. What I liked most about him—what I respected most—was the unwavering kindness with which he treated the bereaved family members he came in contact with every day.*
>
> *I have no doubt that it was that very trait—his unfailing kindness—that attracted my mother to him in the first place. George never had kids who attended Bisbee schools, but he was nonetheless a big supporter. When someone came up with the*

idea of holding a most-eligible-bachelor auction to raise money for a new sound system in the high school auditorium, he signed up right away, and who was it who outbid everyone else? My mother, of course, Eleanor Lathrop Winfield.

It's easy, sometimes, to think that things will always be the way they've always been. My mother had been a widow for so long that it was impossible for me to think of her as anything else. When I first heard about her winning auction bid, I sort of laughed it off. And then, when she and George started going out, I figured it was nothing more than a passing fancy. But it wasn't.

George and I were on our way to a crime scene, driving between here and Douglas, when he told me that he and my mother had eloped to Vegas a few days earlier. When I heard the news, I very nearly wrecked my patrol car. And that's how George Winfield, the Cochise County medical examiner, became George Winfield, my stepfather.

Surprisingly enough, our working relationship didn't change that much, but my mother thought it was high time George quit working so they could enjoy their golden years—and that's exactly what they did, traveling back and forth to George's cabin on Minnesota's Big Stone Lake in an RV. Knowing how soon those golden years would be cut short, I'm sorry now that they didn't start enjoying them sooner.

So what can I tell you about my mother?

Joanna's fingers came to a sudden halt. The clicking keyboard went ominously silent. What should she say about her mother? What was it Marc Antony had said about his pal Julius? "I come to bury Caesar, not to praise him." The truth is, people expected praise during funerals, but right off the bat Joanna could think of very little to praise. She and Eleanor had been at war for most of their lives together. Was that something that should be acknowledged or glossed over? And what about her brother—a child born out of wedlock and given up for adoption long before her parents married? If Eleanor had been overjoyed to welcome Bob Brundage into her life, didn't he need to be publicly acknowledged, too?

And then there was Joanna's father's long-term mistress, Mona Tipton. After George and Eleanor married, George had come upon years' worth of journals kept by D. H. Lathrop. It was only through reading her father's diaries that Joanna had learned about his relationship with Mona. Only days before his tragic death, D.H. had come down on the side of hearth and home, breaking away from Mona in favor of Eleanor and Joanna. His sudden death had left behind two terribly bereft women who continued to live in the same town and who, of necessity, occasionally encountered one another in public. Eleanor's heartache over the loss of her husband had manifested itself more as anger than grief, while Mona, with no obvious justification for the depth of her loss, had simply suffered in silence.

At last Joanna's fingers moved again, more slowly this time and much more tentatively:

> *My mother was a woman of passion. My parents met when they were in high school. It was a first love that wouldn't be denied. Not even an unexpected pregnancy dissuaded them from pursuing that love. Their first baby, my brother, Bob Brundage, was given up for adoption all those years ago. He and his wife, Marcie, are here with us today, seated next to Butch and the kids.*

Once my mother was old enough to speak for herself, she defied her parents and married my father anyway. Her family immediately disowned her. I never knew my mother's parents, and I can't say that I'm sorry. As for Bob? When he came seeking his birth family a number of years ago, my mother welcomed him joyfully. He was raised by other people, good and loving people, but for my mother, he was always her firstborn, and for me he will always be my only brother.

Once again Joanna's moving fingers stuttered to a halt and then rested on the keyboard as she read back through the paragraphs she had just written. Yes, Eleanor had been angry when Joanna got pregnant with Jenny. Joanna could still remember that confrontation—the pinched expression on her mother's white face; the cold fury; the angry words.

But why wouldn't she have been angry? Joanna thought. Eleanor must have seen history repeating itself. Only it hadn't, Joanna realized suddenly and for the first time, because Eleanor Lathrop had seen to it. Her mother hadn't stood in the way of Joanna's marrying Andy. She had given her tight-lipped consent and had helped arrange what was regarded as a scandalous hurry-up wedding. Eleanor hadn't forced Joanna to leave town for the duration of her pregnancy nor had she insisted that Jenny be given up for adoption. Given her own history, Eleanor could very well have done unto her daughter what had been done unto her. But she had not. The buck had stopped right there—with her.

Joanna still couldn't help resenting the fact that in the course of those many years, the ones before Bob showed up in their lives, her mother hadn't once hinted to her daughter that she, too, had gone through the awful uncertainties of an out-of-wedlock pregnancy. But maybe that was her prerogative. People around town had been nice enough to Joanna and Andy and Jenny—at least to their faces. Eleanor, the parent left standing, along with Andy's parents—Jim Bob and Eva Lou—were the ones who had been forced to face down the gossip mills. Thinking back on those times, Joanna could guess what was said: "What a shame Eleanor Lathrop can't get that daughter of hers under control." Or maybe some version of that old saw about apples not falling far from the tree.

And what about Jenny? Right now, at age eighteen, she was already older than Joanna had been when her daughter was born. Jenny was young and naive in many ways, just as Joanna had once been young and naive. And that was the thing about being young—you did stupid things. Wasn't that what this whole day of investigation had been about—unfortunate young people who had been caught up in emotions that had gone horribly and stupidly wrong?

And if, as sometimes happens, another apple failed to fall far from its parental tree, what would happen then? If Jenny suddenly turned up pregnant and unmarried, how would Joanna react? Would she be more like Colonel Karenna Thomas or Allison Stock, or would she model her reaction after Jeremy's—with no forgiveness in his eyes or compassion in his heart?

It came home to her then, in a visceral way, that faced with that kind of turn of events, she could do far worse than follow in Eleanor's footsteps—by soldiering on, by facing down the gossips, by doing what needed to be done, and by helping a pair of scared young people make the best decisions for their lives, their futures, and their baby's future as well.

Joanna realized that she would have to stand very tall and

stretch very high to live up to her mother's example in terms of steadfastness and strength. When it came to kindness? Well, maybe not that so much. And perhaps, considering her own hurtful past with her mother, she would be able to help Jenny while avoiding being as unwaveringly judgmental as Eleanor had always been. Maybe.

Sudden tears clouded Joanna's eyes, eventually dripping off her chin and onto the keyboard. "Sorry, Mom," she murmured aloud. "I'm so sorry for everything."

Once her tears abated, she took a deep breath and returned to the keyboard:

My mother never really approved of my father's entry into law enforcement—or mine, either, for that matter. I think her objections in both instances were founded on a very real fear of losing us.

My mom was left to raise me on her own, and it wasn't easy. The other kids I knew all had two parents. I had only one. I was angry about that, and I'm afraid I took it out on her—blaming her for my father's absence, because she was alive and my father was dead. That wasn't fair of me. If I could take any of it back now, I would, but what I can tell you is this—whenever the chips were really down, Eleanor Lathrop Winfield was always there for me and always in my corner—whether or not I appreciated it or even noticed it at the time.

George and Eleanor died together last week when a troubled youngster decided to try out his sniper skills by shooting at moving vehicles on I-17 south of Sedona. They died as a result of injuries suffered in the incident. Subsequently the shooter died as well.

But standing here before you today, I can tell you straight out that having them go together, almost in an instant, was and is a blessing. It spared them both the longtime pain and grief that accompanied the losses of their first spouses.

Neither of them had to endure the long good-bye of a terminal cancer diagnosis or spend years alone after the unexpected loss of their beloved. At the time of the attack, George and my mother were together, doing exactly what they wanted, and traveling the country in that humongous RV of theirs. They were hurrying home to help host a barbecue planned as a send-off celebration for their granddaughter, Jenny, as she headed out for her freshman year of college.

Jenny is here today, and we've decided as a family that a barbecue is still the order of the day. It won't be at all the same kind of send-off party any of us wanted, but we're having it anyway. It'll be later on this afternoon and evening out at High Lonesome Ranch. You're all welcome to drop by, and I hope you will. Butch and Bob have assured me that there'll be plenty of food to go around.

When Dennis, my son, heard we were having a party in honor of his grandpa George and grandma Eleanor, he wanted to know if there would be balloons. We told him, yes. We're bringing lots of balloons, and you're welcome to do the same.

I think both George and my mother would approve.

A ringing phone—her private landline—startled Joanna out of her fugue of concentration. Looking around, she was surprised to see that the sun was down and the desert landscape outside her window had gone dark. The lights were off in the reception room, which meant Kristin had left for the day without interrupting her.

"Do you know what time it is?" Butch demanded. "As of right now, you're officially late for dinner. Again."

"I'm sorry," she said hurriedly. "I finally had a quiet moment to work on the eulogies, and I completely lost track of time."

"Come home now," Butch said. "Everybody else is already here, but they won't mind waiting a few minutes longer."

"I'm on my way," she said, hurriedly saving the document, closing the laptop, and reaching for her briefcase. "I'll be right there."

Once the laptop was stowed and the briefcase closed, she grabbed her purse and shut out the lights before stepping outside. She turned and started toward her car. She never got that far. When the Taser darts hit her in the back of the shoulder, Joanna had a split second in which she recognized what they were. She along with all her officers had been hit with Taser darts as part of their training.

So she knew what it was as it happened, but that was all she knew. She had no remembrance of her purse and briefcase flying out of her hands and into the air; of falling flat on her back; or of cracking the back of her head on the sidewalk. That's when everything went dark.

CHAPTER 30

JOANNA HAD NO IDEA OF HOW MUCH TIME PASSED BETWEEN THE time the Taser hit and the moment she came back to her senses. She was dazed and confused. She noticed the pain in her shoulder first—something was sticking her, and it hurt like hell. Then she remembered—she'd been Tasered, and the darts were still in her shoulder

With that realization, her confusion evaporated. *Oh my God,* she thought in growing panic. *What about Sage? Was she all right? Had she survived that terrible shock when thousands of volts of electricity had shot through both their bodies?*

Joanna knew that there were instances when Tasering had been blamed for inducing premature labor. Now she tried desperately to calm herself and slow her racing heart long enough to pay attention to her body. This was her third pregnancy. She knew something about labor pains, and there was nothing like that happening right now—no grinding pressure in her belly; no gush of water between her legs. But what terrified her even more was the fact that there was nothing happening down there at all—she sensed no movement from Sage whatsoever. In a matter of seconds, panic and despair changed to absolute fury and to a desperate need to take action.

Forcing her mind back to the present, Joanna tried to sort out exactly where she was—behind a wire-mesh screen, imprisoned in what she realized had to be the back of a speeding patrol car. Her hands were cuffed behind her back, most likely with her own handcuffs. Her service weapon was missing from its holster, and so, no doubt, was her phone.

Tentatively, she lifted her right leg a few inches off the floorboard, and a flood of relief washed through her body. With her pregnancy putting more and more pressure on the waistbands of her clothing, she had switched her reserve weapon from its usual place in a small-of-back holster to an ankle holster. Initially, walking with those extra twenty ounces attached to her right leg had been a problem, but then, like a prisoner forced to wear shackles, she had grown accustomed to the added weight. In his hurry to make good his escape, her unidentified captor had somehow overlooked the presence of her reserve weapon. Now, even though she couldn't reach her new Glock 43, she knew it was there, while the bad guy did not. That gave her a small edge—an edge with six 9-mm hollow-point shots—and that was far better than no edge at all.

It was dark, and Joanna was seated directly behind the driver. All she could see was the back of a head, outlined in the glow of the dash lights and the occasional headlights of an approaching vehicle. With no glimpse of a profile, she had no idea who her captor might be. He had to be a cop of some kind, obviously, or someone pretending to be a cop . . . Then she plucked a familiar voice out of the background chatter on a police radio—Tica Romero, her nighttime dispatcher. That awful moment of recognition sent a layer of gooseflesh skittering over her entire body. The guy wasn't a pretend cop, he was a real one, and most likely one of hers. That led to the next question: Which one? Who would do this, not just to her, but to Sage as well? Who?

"I was supposed to go straight home," she said, finding her voice and forcing it to remain steady. "Butch is expecting me for dinner. He's bound to raise an alarm. When they find my Yukon still parked behind the building, they'll put out an APB. As for the AFIDs from your Taser? Once someone examines the microdots, those little suckers will lead straight back to you."

"Doesn't matter," the voice from the front seat said calmly. "It's too late for that."

As soon as the man spoke, Joanna recognized his voice—including the unfamiliar hard edge that had been present the last time he had spoken to her. The guy behind the wheel of the speeding SUV was none other than Deputy Jeremy Stock.

"What the hell do you think you're doing?" she demanded. "Stop this vehicle and let me out."

"Not gonna happen," he replied, but even as he spoke, the vehicle slowed. For a brief moment, as he activated the turn signal, Joanna thought Jeremy had come to his senses and was going to comply with her wishes. Instead, he swung a fast left turn off Highway 80 and then sped south on the Warren Cutoff.

"What's too late?" she asked, going back to what he had said before.

"It's too late for me," he said. "My life is over. What is it people say sometimes—something about going out with a bang instead of a whimper?"

You're right, buddy boy, Joanna thought. *Life as you know it is over!* But that's not what she said aloud. Over the years she'd taken a number of hostage negotiation classes, without ever once thinking that at some time in the future she and her baby would be the hostages in question. Even so, the same rules applied: engage the guy in conversation, try to establish a connection, and get him to listen to reason.

"What happened to Travis is not your fault," she said quietly. "You can't blame yourself for that, Jeremy, and you can't blame Travis, either. All of that is on Susan Nelson's head, and she's dead."

"So at least I did something right," he muttered.

It was a throwaway comment, spoken under his breath and barely audible, and at first Joanna didn't believe her ears. Had Jeremy Stock just confessed to murdering Susan Nelson? But what good would a confession do if she was the only one who heard it? It took a moment to come to grips with the implication of that offhand confession. He had told her because it didn't matter what she knew or didn't know. This had to be a suicide mission, plain and simple. Jeremy intended to take his own life and most likely Joanna's as well. If that was the case, she could just as well go for broke. She had nothing to lose by trying to draw him out.

"You're saying you killed both of them?" Joanna asked. "Susan Nelson and Desirée Wilburton?"

"Had to," Jeremy replied nonchalantly. "I drove Susan in the back way, from the rifle range. I figured that made for the least chance of being spotted. I had no idea anyone else would be there. Susan screamed like crazy when I pushed her off the cliff. Pretty soon I saw a flashlight darting around down below and some other woman calling up, asking me what was wrong and did I need help? I told her I did. That my girlfriend had fallen and I needed help getting her down."

"So when Desirée showed up to help, you shoved her off the cliff, too?"

"Didn't have a choice," Jeremy said. "Had to. She had a phone with her. I couldn't risk having her calling 911. I needed to get away."

Joanna shook her head. That was the connection—that there wasn't one? Like Joanna's father changing the tire for a stranded motorist, Desirée Wilburton had perished for no other crime than trying to be a Good Samaritan.

They drove in silence past the looming darkness of the tailings dump, with the lights of Bisbee's Warren neighborhood brightening the sky ahead of them. Part of the heavenly glow came from the lights at the Warren Ballpark, where, no doubt, high school football practice was well under way.

When the left-hand turn signal came on again and they started up Yuma Trail, Joanna finally tumbled to what was happening. Suddenly she knew exactly where they were going. Some suspects are compelled to revisit the scenes of their crimes. Clearly the same thing was happening here with Jeremy Stock.

"You're taking me to Geronimo?" she asked.

"Sure thing," Jeremy answered. "When Grandpa Meynard used to take me and my friends up there, especially at night, he liked to tell us scary ghost stories. The ones he liked best were the ones that ended with the words 'the rest you know.' And now you do, too."

CHAPTER 31

BUTCH DIXON WAS PISSED—ROYALLY AND COMPLETELY PISSED. IN terms of travel time, it was less than ten minutes from Joanna's office at the Justice Center on Highway 80 to the house at High Lonesome Ranch. When she had told him on the phone that she was coming straight home, he had been dumb enough to believe her. He had gone ahead and put food on the table. For one thing, it was ready. Jim Bob and Eva Lou, longtime retirees, were used to eating earlier in the afternoon, so starting to eat at six thirty meant it was already well past their usual dinnertime. Bob and Marcie were still on East Coast time. As far as their interior clocks were concerned, it was verging on ten P.M. Jenny and Denny were hungry, too.

It wasn't as though he had spent the afternoon slaving over a hot stove. Making green chili casserole was duck soup to him. Heating up tamales, refritos, and tortillas and getting them on the table wasn't a big deal, either, but doing that while also greeting people, serving beverages, and trying to carry on three different conversations wasn't easy.

And now, with dinner almost over, Joanna's place at the table was still empty while he tried to entertain his wife's shirttail relatives—her former in-laws and the brother she barely knew.

When the landline phone rang just as Butch finished cleaning his plate, he was relieved to have a legitimate reason to jump up and answer it.

"Hey, Butch," Casey Ledford said, "I hate to intrude on your evening, but could I speak to Sheriff Brady, please? I've got some news she's going to want to hear."

"You'd be welcome to speak to her if she were here," Butch replied a little too curtly. "As far as I know, she's still at the department."

"That's funny," Casey said. "I just peeked at her office. Her lights are off."

Butch's throat constricted. Those were words cop-related families everywhere dreaded hearing—that for some reason their law enforcement loved one wasn't where he or she was supposed to be. Even more feared would be the awful late-night phone call or the piercing middle-of-the-night doorbell ring that always preceded the official arrival of the worst possible news.

Butch looked back toward the table. Jenny, smoothly assuming the role of hostess, was in the midst of an entertaining tale about dropping Maggie off at her new stable. Hoping that no one at the table was listening in, he tried to speak to Casey without letting his voice betray his roiling emotions.

"Maybe you could go back and check again," he suggested

quietly. "I spoke to her half an hour or so ago, and she told me she was leaving right then. She should have been here by now."

"Do you mind holding while I go look?" Casey asked.

"Sure," Butch replied. "I'll hold."

He waited—for a long time. There was no elevator music playing on the line with intermittent cheery-voiced announcements telling him, "Your call is very important to us." And the longer he waited, the more he understood that something untoward had happened—something bad.

When Casey finally returned to the line, she was breathless—as though she'd just run a sprint—and her voice was guarded. "I'm afraid something's terribly wrong," she said. "Sheriff Brady's Yukon is there, and so are her purse, briefcase, and phone—scattered all over the sidewalk. From the evidence I'm seeing on the ground, she may have been Tasered."

Butch's heart constricted. He wanted to speak, but didn't trust his voice to work properly.

"I need to go now," Casey continued. "We're seeing AFIDs on the sidewalk in front of her parking place, and I need to see if I can get someone from Taser International to help me identify them."

Butch understood that in cop-speak AFIDs were Anti-Felon Identification tags—tiny pieces of material that resembled confetti that could be used to identify each individual Taser.

"But where is she?" a desperate Butch demanded when he was finally able to speak, but by then the phone line was empty. Casey was already gone. For a time, he stood still listening to the buzzing hum of the dial tone before carefully returning the receiver to its charger. Something about his manner must have alerted Bob Brundage. When Butch turned around, Bob was eyeing him suspiciously. Then, without asking any questions, Bob rose from his chair. "You guys stay put," he told the others. "I'll help Butch clear."

Moments later, in the relative privacy of the kitchen and under the noisy cover of rinsing dishes, Bob asked, "What's wrong? What's going on?"

"It's Joanna," Butch managed. "She's gone missing from her office."

"Missing?" Bob echoed.

Butch nodded miserably. "It looks as though she was assaulted out in the parking lot as she left the office to come home."

Bob simply shouldered Butch aside. "Let me handle the dishes," he said. "You go do whatever you need to do. Marcie and I will stay here with the kids."

Butch didn't hang around waiting for a second offer. He poked his head into the dining room. "I have to go out for a while," he said, offering no further explanation. "I'll be back soon. You guys go ahead and have dessert."

Opening the garage door, Butch discovered Bob's rented Taurus was parked directly behind his Subaru. Rather than return to the dining room and ask Bob to move it, he grabbed the key fob to Joanna's Enclave from the collection of keys hanging on the laundry room pegboard. Moments later, he peeled out of the driveway in Joanna's SUV rather than his own, leaving behind a billowing cloud of dust.

Minutes after entering the highway, he rounded the barrier of low hills that separated the ranch from the Justice Center. Long before he could make out the buildings themselves, he saw the distinctive red and blue glow of emergency lights pulsing behind what he knew to be Joanna's office. Gripping the steering wheel that much tighter, he shoved the gas pedal all the way to the floor and drove like hell.

He didn't worry about being stopped for speeding. He didn't need to. He already knew that every cop in the immediate area was otherwise engaged.

CHAPTER 32

JEREMY STOCK HAD GONE TOTALLY SILENT, SO JOANNA SAT QUIetly, too, trying to evaluate her situation. She had a weapon, yes, but there was no way for her to reach it—not with her hands cuffed behind her back.

When she was little, she'd loved playing agility games with her dad. One of them had consisted of holding a broomstick at knee level and then trying to step over it forwards and backwards. Her father had been in his forties by the time Joanna was born. After years of working in the mines, his knees weren't as good as they had once been, and soon Joanna was far better at what they called the "broom game" than D.H. Lathrop. Back then she had been limber enough to step through the handcuffs, but not now—not with that bulging lump of baby stuck in her midsection.

The only way her Glock could come into play was if Jeremy

removed the cuffs. At the moment, as they bounced along the rough dirt track between Warren and the base of Geronimo, it seemed to Joanna the idea of his actually removing the cuffs was little more than a pipe dream, not unlike ponying up two bucks on a winning lottery ticket. The odds of either one happening were equally unlikely.

What else did she have in her favor? After a moment, she remembered. Months earlier, she had prevailed upon the board of supervisors to give her budgetary permission to invest in a fleet management program that came complete with an automated vehicle-location system and computer-assisted dispatch. The system's cutting-edge GPS capability made life easier for her Bisbee-based dispatchers. When faced with unfolding incidents throughout Joanna's 6,400-square-mile jurisdiction, the system made it possible for Dispatch to locate and deploy the nearest possible deputy. Only a few months into operation, the system had already cut departmental response times in half. From an administrative standpoint, it had the added advantage of allowing Joanna to know if one of her less reliable deputies was spending his working hours tucked away on some deserted side road, napping his shift away.

Right now Joanna understood that the new system had the capability of saving her life, but only if someone noticed she was missing, figured out that Jeremy Stock was the most likely culprit, and had brains enough to activate the high-tech system that could locate his vehicle.

Joanna had told Butch that she was coming straight home. However much time had elapsed, he must be worried by now, but how much longer would it take for him to sound the alarm? Once that happened, the AFIDs, from the Taser, could indeed lead directly to Jeremy's weapon, but how soon would that happen? When Joanna's CSIs had sent AFIDs in for examination previously, it had taken weeks for them to get results. This was a matter of life and death, but did anyone else understand that? And even if they did, would it make any difference?

And then there was the matter of the person in charge—Chief Deputy Hadlock. He was a good guy, and he was growing into his responsibilities as chief deputy, but this would be the first time he would be solely responsible for directing her department's response to a major incident. What would he do? How would he deploy his assets?

Tom wasn't a nuanced kind of guy. Joanna realized, with a sinking sense of dread that when it came time for a final confrontation with Jeremy Stock, Tom's most likely reaction would be an overreaction. She worried that he would come out in full attack mode—with lights flashing and guns blazing.

Joanna didn't doubt that a posse of well-armed officers could take Jeremy Stock down in a hail of gunfire, but she had no wish to be caught in the resulting cross fire. And if bullets were about to fly, where was her Kevlar vest at the moment? That would be back in her office, exactly where she'd left it!

I can't risk waiting around for someone to come riding to my rescue, she thought, giving herself a silent pep talk. *If it is to be, it is up to me. The Little Red Hen is going to have to do this on her own.*

Just then, as if to underscore her newfound resolve, Baby Sage stirred in her belly and delivered a surprisingly solid kick to Joanna's lower rib cage. It was exactly what she needed. The baby—

Joanna's baby—was in this fight to the death, too. Awash with relief at knowing Sage was still alive and kicking, Joanna smiled to herself in the dark.

Okay, then, she vowed silently. *I hear you loud and clear, little one. Make that the two of us, then. If it is to be, it is up to us.*

As the Tahoe continued to bounce along, Joanna turned her attention back to the problem at hand—the ongoing hostage negotiation.

"I didn't know you grew up in Bisbee," she said.

"I didn't," Jeremy answered. "What makes you say that?"

"You know about Geronimo. Locals know about Geronimo. Outsiders usually don't."

"I grew up in Sierra Vista, but my mother was from Bisbee," Jeremy answered. "Her folks, Gerald and Juanita Meynard, lived on Hazzard. Jerry was an underground miner; Juanita was a housewife. After my mother graduated from high school, she went to work at Fort Huachuca and ended up marrying a soldier she met on post. After my dad got out of the service, they stayed on in Sierra Vista.

"I used to come stay with Grandpa and Grandma for a few weeks during the summers when school was out. Grandpa and I hiked in the hills together; shot BB guns and his .22; did some prospecting. Then, the summer I turned eleven, he told me he wasn't up to hiking anymore. The truth is, he wasn't up to much of anything. A few months later, he was dead. It was years before I found out he got dusted. That's what killed him. His lungs gave out."

Joanna knew about the ugly reality behind the supposedly inoffensive sounding term "dusted." It was common usage in Arizona's copper-mining communities for career miners who developed lung problems. Most of the rest of the country referred to the ailment as the grimmer-sounding black lung disease. No matter how you said it, however, the outcome was usually the same—the miners sickened and died.

"Gramps always warned me to stay away from working in the mines, although they were mostly closed or closing by then," Jeremy continued. "That's one of the reasons I became a cop in the first place. Compared to being a miner, working in law enforcement was a big step up."

The fact that Jeremy had just volunteered some information cheered Joanna. Maybe she was making progress after all.

"But why did you bring Susan Nelson all the way out here to kill her?"

On the far side of the mesh screen she saw him raise and lower his shoulders as he shrugged. "Seemed like as good a place as any," he said.

"I know why you killed Desirée Wilburton—you said it was because she showed up unexpectedly and tried to come to Susan's aid, but you never told me why you killed Susan."

"She wouldn't get rid of the baby," Jeremy said. "She absolutely refused."

"That's what this is about—her baby?" Joanna echoed. "As I tried to explain to all of you earlier this afternoon, what happened with Susan Nelson was a crime against Travis. It wouldn't have mattered if she had gone ahead and had the child, kept it, given it up for adoption, or had an abortion. In the long run, no one would have held it against your son. In fact, if Susan hadn't died—if we hadn't become embroiled in a double homicide investigation—there's a good chance no one would have been the wiser."

"Shut up!" Jeremy ordered, pounding the steering wheel in sudden fury. "Just shut the hell up. I don't want to talk about this anymore."

And so Joanna did exactly what he asked—she shut the hell up.

CHAPTER 33

WHEN BUTCH PULLED UP TO THE ENTRANCE TO THE JUSTICE CENter, a cop car with flashing lights ablaze was parked across the roadway, blocking traffic. A deputy he didn't recognize stood next to it, waving traffic on. He seemed to be involved in an ongoing argument with a woman whose head was topped by a wild mane of hair.

Crap, Butch told himself. Just what I don't need right now—Marliss Shackleford!

He pulled over onto the shoulder just beyond the entrance, put the SUV in park, and vaulted out onto the pavement. He attempted to dodge past the deputy and Marliss, but it didn't work.

"Sorry, sir," the deputy said. "No one's allowed inside except sworn officers and first responders."

"I'm Butch Dixon, Sheriff Brady's husband," he explained. "One way or the other, I'm going to go find out what's going on."

"Please, Mr. Dixon," the deputy said. "I have my orders."

"What orders?" a female voice demanded. "What's going on?"

Butch turned in time to see Agent Watkins approaching from behind.

"It's Joanna," Butch told her. "Someone's taken her."

Unfortunately, Agent Watkins wasn't the only one listening in. "Someone's taken Sheriff Brady?" Marliss repeated breathlessly. "Are you saying the sheriff's been kidnapped?"

"Sorry, ma'am," the deputy began, this time directing his words in Robin's direction. "No one is allowed inside the Justice Center other than sworn officers."

In answer, she pulled out her ID wallet and snapped it open. "I believe that makes me a sworn officer," she said, "and Mr. Dixon is with me. Come on."

Together they walked past the deputy and onto the Justice Center grounds, while Marliss Shackleford's continued pleas for admittance fell on deaf ears.

"What the hell is going on?" Robin demanded.

While they threaded their way through the throng of cop cars, Butch told her what he knew, which turned out to be not much.

"All right, then," Robin said. "Stick with me and don't say a word. Let me ask the questions."

Rather than going to the back of the building, which was obviously the center of attention, Robin led the way toward the front door, which was locked. As soon as she spoke a few words into the intercom, the electronic latch clicked open and they were allowed inside. Approaching the front counter, Butch recognized the clerk behind the wall of bulletproof glass the moment he saw her.

Years earlier, one of Joanna's officers, Deputy Dan Sloan, had been killed in a line-of-duty shooting. His wife, Sunny, had been pregnant at the time of her husband's death. After the baby was born, Joanna had found a way to give Sunny a clerical job in the front office.

Robin was the one who approached the counter with her ID wallet still open, but Sunny's wide eyes were focused on Butch. "I'm so sorry about this," she said.

She was someone who knew exactly what Butch was feeling just then. He nodded in acknowledgment, but following Robin's orders, he said nothing.

"We already know there's a problem, with Sheriff Brady," Robin said. "But right now I'm here as part of the joint task force working the double homicides. This is urgent. I need to see Casey Ledford, and I need to see her now."

"With everything that's happened, Casey's pretty busy at the moment," Sunny stammered. "I'm not sure I should interrupt."

"Then get Chief Deputy Hadlock on the horn. Now!"

Cratering, Sunny turned and reached for her phone. Butch was about to ask what was so urgent, but Robin silenced his question with an imperious shake of her head. Sunny stood with her back to them, murmuring inaudibly into the phone. Finally, she turned back to face them.

"Chief Deputy Hadlock will be right out," she said.

The chief deputy who marched through the security door a few moments later was anything but a cool customer. His sparse gray hair, often worn in a self-conscious comb-over, stood on end. He looked more distraught than commanding and more than slightly overwhelmed.

He focused entirely on Butch. "This is a terrible turn of

events, Mr. Dixon," he said. "Unfortunately, someone evidently attacked Sheriff Brady, Tased her, and abducted her out in the back parking lot."

"Who?" Butch demanded. "This is the sheriff's department, for Pete's sake. Don't you have surveillance tapes?"

"We do," Tom Hadlock replied, "but the assailant was wearing a hoodie at the time of the attack. We can't identify him. Even so, this is an evolving situation, and you really shouldn't be here. Please go home. We'll contact you the moment we have news." With that, he turned his attention on Agent Watkins. "As for your request to see Casey? Ms. Ledford is quite busy at the moment trying to get a line on some AFIDs. It's mission critical that we ID them, but she's not getting much traction with Taser International."

"I believe I can help with that," Robin interjected. "Or, rather, my boss can. Bruce Ryder, Tucson's special agent in charge, went to college with one of the head honchos at TI. Roommates, I believe. That's one way to jump to the head of the AFIDs line. Now, do we get to see Casey or not?"

"Yes, ma'am," Tom said. "Right this way." He led them to a locked security door and keyed in the entry code. "Do you need me to come along, or can I get back to my crime scene?"

"Go do what you need to do," Robin told him. "I know my way to the lab."

By the time they arrived at the door to the laboratory, Robin had her boss on the phone and was bringing him up-to-date. Inside the lab, they found Casey seated at her desk with a telephone clamped to her ear while she used the eraser of a pencil to pound out an impatient drumbeat on the Formica surface.

"I'm on hold right now, and have been forever," she explained, shaking her head in annoyance. "And if I ever do get off the phone, I'm terribly busy."

In reply, Robin simply handed her cell phone to Casey. "It's on speaker," she said. "My boss, Bruce Ryder, the Tucson sector's special agent in charge, is on the line."

Casey attempted to pass the phone back, but Robin stepped out of reach. "Bruce, I'm putting Casey Ledford on the phone. She's with Cochise County Sheriff's Department."

"But what . . . ?" Casey began.

"If you want to jump-start your AFIDs search," Robin told her, "you're going to need some horsepower. Bruce Ryder is someone who can deliver it. He's longtime personal friends with the CFO of Taser International. They were college roommates."

"All right," Casey said with a resigned sigh. "But someone else is going to have to sit on hold." Once Robin had Casey's phone in hand, the criminalist immediately launched off on a detailed explanation of what had happened, but Ryder cut her short.

"Robin already briefed me," he said. "I fully understand the urgency of the situation. I take it you've already captured a legible image of one of the AFIDs?"

"Yes, sir," Casey replied.

"Good," Ryder said. "E-mail it to me. Robin can give you my address. Once I have it in hand, I'll get right on this."

"Thank you, sir," Casey breathed.

"Think nothing of it," he said. "We're all in this together. By the way, in my spare time, I'll be praying for Sheriff Brady."

"Thank you for that, too," Casey added. "We all are."

As the two women exchanged phones, Robin's rang again. "Agent Watkins here," she said. "Already? And there's a partial match?" She listened for some time. "All right, then. Yes, please forward all your results to Casey Ledford at the Cochise County Sheriff's Department, but I really appreciate the call."

"A partial match on what?" Casey asked.

"On one of the DNA profiles."

"Which one?"

"Between Susan Nelson's baby's profile and the DNA sample from Travis Stock, the one Sheriff Brady collected earlier today, and the same one I dropped off at the crime lab a few hours ago."

Casey frowned. "But you said it's only a partial match," she objected. "How can that be?"

"Because it turns out Travis Stock isn't the father of Susan Nelson's baby. Someone else is—a near male relative of Travis's—either his father or his grandfather. I'm taking a wild guess here, but it seems doubtful that even if the grandfather is still alive, he'd be the one responsible."

"Are you saying Jeremy is the father?" Casey asked in disbelief. "Wait just a minute." Hanging up on her endless hold, she turned away and pawed through the stacks of loose paper littering her desk. "Here it is," she said, picking up a single sheet. "This is it—a printout of the report Detective Waters wrote up concerning his and Sheriff Brady's interview with Travis Stock's family earlier this afternoon.

"When it came in, I barely scanned through it, hitting some of the high points, but it says right here that Travis voluntarily submitted a DNA sample over the strenuous objections of his father. And right above that notation, there's something else. Travis admitted to owning an SVSSE hoodie. He was willing to turn it over as well but was unable to locate it at the time. The surveillance footage of the attack on Sheriff Brady showed someone wearing a hoodie. And now we understand why Jeremy Stock was so adamantly opposed to his son submitting a DNA sample," Casey added. "He knew it would lead us right back to him." She reached for her phone again. "I'd better get Chief Deputy Hadlock on the line and let him know what's up."

"There's something else," Robin said. "If Travis's father came after Sheriff Brady, what are the chances he went after some other people, too?"

It took Butch a moment to fully grasp what she meant. When he did, it hit him like a blow to his gut. "Surely Jeremy Stock wouldn't harm his own family, would he?" Butch asked, but Robin didn't answer. She was already scrolling through her contacts list. Finally, she punched in a number and waited for someone to answer.

"Agent Watkins here, Detective Waters," she said. "Do you know what's going on here in Bisbee?" She paused. "Yes, well, actually it's probably a good thing you didn't hop in your car and race right over. Things are happening in a hell of a hurry, and I need you to handle something critical on your end. Travis's DNA sample has revealed that he is not the father of Susan Nelson's baby." Another pause. "Yes, that's correct—Travis is not the father. Most likely Jeremy Stock is. We're worried that Deputy Stock may have gone off the deep end. It's possible he's behind Sheriff Brady's kidnapping, and God knows what else. I'm worried his family may have come to grief."

There was another pause. "Yes," Robin said. "That's exactly what's called for—a welfare check at the Stocks' home. But please don't go alone, Detective Waters," she warned. "Be sure you have plenty of backup."

CHAPTER 34

THE TAHOE CAME TO AN ABRUPT STOP, FARTHER UP THE ROAD from where Joanna had parked three days earlier and close enough to the water hole for streamers of crime-scene tape to be briefly visible in the headlights. Jeremy switched off the engine. For a matter of moments—the better part of a minute—neither he nor Joanna spoke or moved.

"What happens now?" she asked at last, needing to break the silence.

"We go for a hike," Jeremy answered.

He exited the vehicle, opened the back door, and then roughly manhandled Joanna out onto the ground. In the glow of the dome light, she saw that he held the Taser in his left hand. In that brief instant, she realized this was a near replay if not an exact one of what must have happened to Susan Nelson. Jeremy had escorted his victim away from her classroom, gripping her with his right hand while holding the pocketed and hence invisible Taser in his left.

The Taser. Even though the darts had been deployed, Joanna knew the weapon could still function as a contact stun gun. After dragging her out of the vehicle, he shoved her face-forward up against the SUV's tailgate.

"We're going to climb up to the top," he said. "I know you can't do that with your hands cuffed behind you, so I'm going to fasten them in front. If you try anything at all, I'll knock you senseless. Understand?"

Joanna nodded mutely at this answered prayer. Having the cuffs in front of her would be far better than having them fastened behind, but it wouldn't be a big help in terms of weaponry. These days, with her protruding belly in the way, leaning over far enough to tie her shoes was a challenge. Ditto for grabbing the Glock out of her ankle holster.

A moment later, one of the cuffs clicked open. Jeremy spun her around while clutching the arm with the cuff still on it, then he slammed the back of Joanna's head against the car hard enough to leave her seeing stars and wavering drunkenly on her feet.

"Give me your other hand!" he ordered. "Now!"

Still swaying dizzily, Joanna could do nothing but comply. As the second cuff clicked shut, she found herself staring into Jeremy Stock's throat. There was no moon, but enough starlight beamed down on this empty piece of desert to allow nearby bushes to cast pale shadows on the ground. And there was also enough illumination for her to get a full-on look at her opponent.

Since Jeremy was a good eight inches taller than her five-foot-four, that meant she was facing the base of his chin. He still wore his uniform. A jagged cut of some kind trailed from the base of his chin and down to his collar, where a dark stain some two inches across marred the khaki fabric. Looking down as he struggled to refasten her cuff, she noticed that the backs of both hands were covered in a wild pattern of scratches.

Joanna was a cop. She had seen her share of those kinds of injuries and she knew what they meant—that the person wearing them had recently engaged in some kind of life-and-death struggle. Now, with sickening clarity, she understood what must have happened.

"What have you done?" she demanded. "Did you hurt Allison or Travis? Are they all right?"

"They're fine," he said. "They're totally fine."

But from the empty and coldly dispassionate way in which he delivered the words, she realized at once they weren't true—couldn't be true. Travis and Allison weren't "fine" at all. In fact, they were most likely dead. She remembered the hard-eyed stare with which Jeremy had regarded Travis during that earlier interview. Even then, his plan for what would happen next was most likely under consideration if not already in motion. What was it that had pushed him over the edge—the DNA sample, maybe? He had clearly been furious about that, but why?

Joanna had thought for a time that if she pleaded with Jeremy to spare her life for the sake of her baby's, maybe he would let them both live. Now she forced herself to let go of that tiny thread of hope. Pleading for mercy clearly wouldn't work. Granting mercy wasn't in Jeremy Stock's playbook. If he was so deranged at this point that he had sacrificed his own child, he certainly wouldn't hesitate to slaughter hers.

So rather than beg and plead, she went on the offensive, focusing on the scratches on the backs of his hands—scratches that hadn't been there earlier in the afternoon. The fact that there had been no defensive wounds on Susan Nelson's body had made Dr. Baldwin theorize that she had participated in consensual sex before she died. Joanna doubted that was true.

"We know Susan had sex shortly before her death," Joanna said. "Traces of DNA were found on her clothing, but how did that happen? Did she want to have sex with you or did you knock her senseless before you raped her?"

Joanna never saw the blow coming. Jeremy delivered a powerful slap that hit her full across her right cheek and sent her tumbling helplessly to the ground. The way the Taser darts pricked into her made her feel as though she had landed on a piece of cholla. Rolling over onto her side, she tried to cover her belly with her cuffed hands in case he kicked her, but he did not. Instead, grabbing her by the shoulders, he lifted her to her feet and shook her as if she were little more than a rag doll.

"Susan knew I was furious with her. She thought giving me a piece of tail would settle me down. It didn't work. When it was over, she got just what she deserved, and you will, too," he growled. "Now get moving!"

Still woozy from the blow, Joanna fought to remain upright and put one foot in front of the other. She tasted blood in her mouth and knew that he had loosened at least one and maybe several of her teeth. Already she felt the side of her face swelling. She'd look like hell tomorrow. And then she remembered. Tomorrow was the day of the funeral—her mother's funeral. If she somehow made it through the night and lived long enough to make it to the mortuary, she knew exactly what a disapproving Eleanor would have said.

During Joanna's childhood, there had been very few school or church or Bible school events at which Joanna Lee Lathrop hadn't shown up with at least one scraped knee or torn elbow or maybe even two of each. Her mother's comment had never changed.

"Wouldn't you know," she'd say, shaking her head in despair. "Here you are looking like something the cat dragged in. Aren't you ashamed of yourself?"

Joanna realized that if she and Sage somehow made it through this awful night and came out alive into the light of day, Eleanor would be totally justified in saying the same thing. Except since Eleanor wouldn't be there to deliver those words, Joanna would have to do so herself.

And suddenly, despite everything that was going on, she felt the beginning of a very inappropriate giggle bubble upward in her throat. She realized that if she could laugh in the face of all this, maybe she was as deranged as Jeremy. But the giggle came anyway. She couldn't stop it.

"What's so funny?" Jeremy demanded, shoving her from behind and making her struggle to retain her balance.

"Nothing," she said. "Nothing at all."

But she knew one thing about that inappropriate attack of laughter. It was symbolic of something else—of a determination to overcome and live.

One way or the other, Joanna Brady intended to do exactly that.

CHAPTER 35

"I'M GOING TO GO OUTSIDE AND SEE WHAT'S GOING ON," ROBIN ANnounced.

"I'm with you," Butch told her.

"No," Robin said. "You should stay here in the lab, out of the way."

"Like bloody hell!" he retorted. When he followed her out of the lab, Agent Watkins didn't object.

They never made it as far as the crime scene. The administrative end of the hallway was a beehive of activity as personnel from the cordoned-off crime scene outside hurried into the building and filed into the conference room. By the time Robin and Butch reached the doorway, the room was filled beyond capacity. With a standing-room-only crowd, Robin and Butch squeezed in barely far enough to allow Casey Ledford to tuck in behind them.

A grim-faced Chief Deputy Hadlock made his way to the

lectern. "All right, folks, quiet down, and listen up," he ordered, "I want everyone on the same page. We have reason to believe that the person who took Sheriff Brady hostage is one of our own—Deputy Jeremy Stock. In the course of the last several hours, a number of facts have come to light.

"We have evidence that suggests that for a considerable period of time, one of our homicide victims—Susan Nelson—was a sexual predator preying on young male students attending SVSSE. One of her victims, namely Travis Stock, believed he was the father of Susan's unborn baby. Through DNA profiling, we've now established that a near relative of Travis's rather than Travis himself is the baby's actual father. Jeremy's father has been deceased for years. That leaves us to believe that Deputy Stock fathered Susan Nelson's child. The same DNA profile turned up on clothing found at Susan Nelson's homicide scene.

"Sheriff Brady was abducted earlier this evening, apparently when she left the building to go to her car. We've found evidence that suggests that a Taser was used in the attack. Agent Robin Watkins of the FBI and the Tucson special agent in charge, Bruce Ryder, are assisting us in attempting to identify the AFIDs found at the scene. That will take time, of course, but for now the assumption is that Jeremy used his department-issued Taser in order to overpower her."

Hadlock paused momentarily to consult his notes while the room remained locked in hushed silence. Before he could continue, the jarring ring of a cell phone shattered the silence. The chief deputy looked on impatiently while Agent Watkins dug the offending device out of her pocket. She glanced at it. Then, rather than leaving the room, she took the call and listened for several long moments before nodding and hanging up.

"Well?" Tom Hadlock inquired. "Is it what we thought?"

Robin nodded. "They're dead," she said quietly.

"Both of them?"

Robin nodded again.

Tom Hadlock closed his eyes and gritted his teeth before speaking again. "A short time ago, officers from Sierra Vista PD were dispatched to Jeremy Stock's home. Apparently both Allison and Travis Stock are deceased."

Audible gasps shot through the crowded room.

"Quiet," Tom ordered. "Bearing that in mind, I believe it's reasonable to assume that the perpetrator behind all these atrocities, including the attack on Sheriff Brady earlier this evening, can be none other than Deputy Stock. I'm hereby issuing an APB. I cannot stress this enough. If you encounter him, Jeremy must be regarded as armed and dangerous. You may still consider him a fellow officer and friend, but he is to be approached with extreme caution.

"On the off chance that Jeremy might have been driving his patrol vehicle, I asked Tica Romero to use our fleet management system to locate his Tahoe. Just before I came into the conference room, she told me that the vehicle is currently parked at the base of Geronimo, the scene of both the Susan Nelson and Desirée Wilburton homicides. Tica has also been able to activate the system's theft deterrent. As of right now, Jeremy's vehicle has been rendered nonfunctional. If he attempts to leave the area, he'll be doing so on foot."

Hadlock paused and looked around the room. "I'm operating under the assumption that most of you are familiar with Geronimo."

There were knowing nods all around the room. "In case

you're not, here's a visual." He fiddled with a laptop, and a few moments later, a satellite view of Geronimo showed on a screen behind him. From his spot at the back of the room, it was difficult for Butch to make out the details as the chief deputy moved a cursor arrow around on the screen.

"This shows the west side of Geronimo, which sits east and a little to the north of the eastern edge of Warren. According to the GPS, the Tahoe is parked right here on the near side of this dark spot, which is actually a clump of trees surrounding the water hole at the base of the peak. This is the area where Desirée Wilburton was camped before she was killed. The spot where the two victims' bodies came to rest is right here, halfway down from the top." Again the cursor moved on the screen.

"As you can see," Hadlock continued, "this is an extremely isolated location. Any effort to approach it in vehicles is entirely out of the question. Jeremy would see us as soon as we left town and moved in that direction. We have a horse-mounted search and rescue team, but that's made up of volunteers rather than sworn officers. In addition, it would take too much time to assemble and deploy them—time we don't have.

"At the moment we have no idea of Jeremy's intentions, but given that he's most likely responsible for what happened to the two earlier homicide victims as well as the slaughter of his own family, we have to assume the worst—that he intends to murder Sheriff Brady, too. If we're going to effect Sheriff Brady's rescue, it will have to be done the old-fashioned way—on foot—and in a hell of a hurry."

Listening to the briefing, Butch was impressed. All the while Joanna had patiently been helping Tom Hadlock grow into the job of chief deputy, Butch had been one of the man's most unrelenting critics. In this roomful of people, all of them listening to the chief deputy's every word with rapt attention, he could understand, for the first time, what Joanna had seen in the man. Tom Hadlock had a commanding presence about him, and Butch had no doubt that the officers involved in this dicey operation would follow his every order to the letter.

"This is a potentially dangerous situation, but time is of the essence," Hadlock continued. "Do I have any volunteers?"

Hands shot up all around the room—twenty people in all, among them jail personnel who had been pulled away from their usual duties. Hadlock looked around the room, pointing as he went, focusing first on the younger and fitter officers, including the guys from the jail. "You, you, you, and you—you're to go with Detective Carbajal. I want you to approach Geronimo from the backside by way of the rifle range and take up defensive positions around the base. Do not attempt to climb the mountain. If Jeremy has the high ground and a rifle, he'll be able to pick you off with the greatest of ease. It's imperative that you wait for him to come to you.

"When you see him, avoid using weapons if at all possible. There will be too many friendlies on the ground out there to risk a shooting war. Jeremy has been operating in the dark long enough for his eyes to have adjusted to the lack of light. Once he's in range, shine your Maglites straight in his eyes. With any kind of luck, that should momentarily blind him.

"Everybody else? You're with me. Because Jeremy has his own radio capability, this entire operation is to be conducted with zero radio communication. I'll lead the group approaching from the front and take up a position near his parked vehicle. When we come up over the top of Yuma Trail, I'll leave my headlights on. Everyone else should douse theirs. I don't want Jeremy looking off over the valley and seeing a whole parade of arriving vehicles. That'll be a dead giveaway.

"We'll park at the end of Black Knob on the near side of the cattle guard and walk in from there. If we all rumble across the cattle guard, one vehicle after another, noise from that might travel far enough for Jeremy to hear us coming.

"Once you reach the mountain itself, deploy yourselves around the base of it with several people remaining in the vicinity of the disabled vehicle. We all know the Tahoe isn't drivable at the moment, but Jeremy doesn't. In other words, since that's his most likely means of escape, that's where he'll go. Let me repeat what I said earlier: no one is to go up the mountain looking for him. We wait below and let him come to us—with one exception."

As if needing to collect his thoughts, Chief Deputy Hadlock paused long enough to take a drink of water before turning his attention on the K9 unit. Terry Gregovich was seated on the last seat in the front row with Spike blocking the aisle beside him. The dog lay on the carpeted floor with his ears pricked forward and his grizzled gray and white muzzle resting on his front paws, as if taking it all in.

"Up to now, everything I've mentioned is all about catching Jeremy and successfully taking him into custody while he's trying to get away, but the real point of this exercise is to nail the suspect before he has a chance to carry out whatever it is he intends to do to Sheriff Brady. And that, Deputy Gregovich is where you and Spike come in.

"I know that the two of you were all over Geronimo the other day helping Dave Hollicker gather evidence. Tonight we need you to go up there again. Once we reach the Tahoe, I want you to give Spike a whiff of Jeremy's scent and send him off on the hunt. Does the dog have a silent mode?"

"Yes, sir," Terry answered.

"In this case, silence is golden."

"The problem is, sir," Terry objected, "Spike can get up the mountain a lot faster than I can."

"Is he capable of taking down a suspect on his own without your actually being present?"

"Yes, sir," Terry said. "Totally, but it's likely that the suspect will suffer worse injuries if I'm not there to call Spike off."

"What do you know!" Chief Hadlock said. "Now, wouldn't that just be too damned bad! Happy hunting, Spike. Go get him. As for everybody else? Hit it, people. Wear your vests and take along plenty of water. Be safe out there, but let's go get our old girl back," he added. "We need her."

Because they were nearest the door, Butch and Robin were the first ones out of the room and into the corridor. Without any discussion, they headed for the front lobby and set out across the parking lot.

"Do they call Joanna 'old girl' to her face? I wonder," Butch asked. "After all, Joanna's a hell of a lot younger than Chief Deputy Hadlock."

"Believe me," Agent Watkins assured him, "in cop-shop parlance, 'old girl' is a term of endearment."

When they reached the end of the Justice Center parking lot, the front entrance remained blocked by the idling patrol car. Marliss Shackleford was still very much in evidence, as were two additional people Butch immediately suspected of being reporters.

"Great," he muttered. "What's going to happen to this supposedly silent operation if a band of reporters gets in line behind the patrol cars?"

Just then, the first of a string of several vehicles approached the entrance and stopped facing the barrier patrol car. A moment later, the SUV's door opened and the hulking figure of Chief Deputy Hadlock stepped out into the otherworldly glow cast by the collection of flashing emergency lights. Once on the ground, Hadlock marched directly toward the deputy and the trio of reporters.

"Here's the deal," he said, loudly enough so everyone on the ground heard him. "At the moment we've got a serious hostage situation on our hands. In order to resolve it, we need to move quickly and under the cover of darkness. I'll be holding a press briefing once the operation is concluded and the crisis success-efully averted. In the meantime, if any one of you makes any effort to follow my people or to interfere with this operation in any way, I'm warning you, there will be serious consequences."

"What are you going to do," Marliss chirped, "put us in jail? You can't do that. What about freedom of the press?"

"What about it?" Hadlock returned. "Lives are at stake here, Ms. Shackleford. So let me say this one more time—there will be consequences. Anyone who interferes with this operation in any fashion will be automatically barred from attending all future departmental press briefings. Is that clear?"

With that, Tom Hadlock returned to his vehicle. Once the barricade patrol car was removed, the others drove away unimpeded. Marliss was still fuming in outrage as Butch and Robin walked past. When they reached her government-issue Taurus, Robin clicked open the trunk, reached for her vest, and began putting it on.

"You're going there?" Butch asked.

"Damned straight."

"Me, too," Butch said.

"No," Robin replied. "Absolutely not. Your son and Jenny already have one parent at risk. Don't give Jeremy Stock a chance to make it double or nothing."

Butch was going to object, but then he didn't. Agent Watkins had a point. If everything went south, someone needed to be there for the kids.

"You're right," he conceded. "I'll head home, but please keep me posted, one way or the other. Don't make me sit around waiting for someone to come knock on the door and give me the bad news."

"I'll need your phone number for that," Robin said. "And I promise, once this is over, you'll be the first to know."

CHAPTER 36

STILL STUNNED AND SHAKEN BY THE BLOW TO HER FACE, JOANNA moved forward slowly and unsteadily. Having her hands bound in front of her meant that she was unable to use her arms to help maintain her balance, and that extra twenty ounces on her ankle felt like an anchor.

Between the Tahoe and the grove of trees, she stumbled and fell three different times. Unable to break her fall, she landed hard each time, adding more scrapes and bruises to her already damaged face and body. After every fall, Jeremy grabbed her by the shoulders and hauled her back to her feet. Each time she was terrified that he would somehow spot the weapon concealed under her pant leg and take it away from her.

Once they entered the grove of trees, sheltering greenery blocked the starlight, leaving them in almost total darkness. Joanna stumbled along upright, occasionally colliding with an invisible tree trunk. Desolate as the surrounding desert may have seemed, this was arid pastureland. Not only did grazing cattle keep the earth denuded of grass, they also pruned the scrub oak as far up as they could reach. At five-four, Joanna was able to walk upright beneath the tree branches, while Jeremy, following behind her, had to duck his way underneath, cursing as he went.

This angry side of Jeremy Stock was something new, something Joanna had never encountered before today. She understood enough about domestic violence to realize that some abusers were monsters who managed to mask their ugly tempers in public all while venting their fury on loved ones behind closed doors at home. Had that reality been at work with Deputy Stock the whole time he had worked for her? If so, what could she have done to spot it and put a stop it. And if Allison and Travis Stock were dead, as she now feared they were, how much of that was her fault? She and Detective Waters had blithely driven away from the Stock family interview without any idea that they were leaving someone behind to die—make that, leaving two someones behind to die.

Beyond the water hole and still under the canopy of trees, Joanna tripped over a loose rock and tumbled to the ground. In an unavoidable chain reaction, Jeremy slammed into her and fell on top of her. As he dragged her upright again, her hip hurt like hell where the toe of his boot had hit her body full force, but at least he hadn't plowed head-on into her stomach. That would have been far worse.

"I could walk better if you uncuffed my hands," she said.

"Stuff it," Jeremy told her. "Keep walking."

"How did you find out about Travis and Susan?" she asked,

trying to initiate conversation as they emerged once more into pale starlight.

"I didn't," Jeremy said. "Until you showed up at the house this afternoon, I had no idea he was involved with her."

"Then how . . . ?"

Jeremy grabbed her by the shoulder and spun her around until they were face-to-face.

"Don't you understand anything?" he demanded furiously, shaking her again. "I thought Susan's baby was my damned baby! I had no idea anyone else was involved, much less Travis. I wanted her to get rid of it, and she wouldn't—she absolutely refused. As soon as Travis gave you that swab, I knew it was over and I was toast. I didn't want Allison and Travis to have to face what was coming, so I ended it for them."

"By killing them?"

He shrugged. "To my way of thinking, I did them a huge favor. That way they didn't have to live with the consequences of what I'd done."

"What about your other son?" Joanna asked. "Don't you have an older boy who's away at college?"

"You mean Thad? As far as I'm concerned, he's no son of mine. He turned his back on us when he went off to college. He can go to hell for all I care."

"And face all of this on his own?" Joanna asked.

"Yup," Jeremy said callously. "I guess them's the breaks."

Taken aback by the man's utter disregard for anyone but himself, Joanna rounded on him. "You're a coward, Jeremy Stock," she spat at him, "and a low-down, miserable excuse for a human being. Travis believed Susan's baby was his. Young as he was, he was willing to face up to the consequences of his actions. He wanted Susan to divorce her husband and marry him, but she evidently gave him the same answer she gave you—that it was her baby and she was keeping it, but I have to give Travis full marks. He didn't kill her for turning him down. Travis was man enough to take no for an answer. You weren't."

Jeremy said nothing. For a moment neither did she. They were stopped at the place where the game trail Joanna and Agent Watkins had followed veered off toward the left. "Which way?" she asked.

"Follow that," he said, gesturing toward the faint path. Joanna was relieved. At least that meant they were taking the side route rather than making a direct ascent.

"We're going up, I take it?" she asked.

"Yes, we are."

"Why?" she insisted. "What's the point?"

"The point is that this all ends at the time and place of my choosing. Grandma Meynard told me once that Grandpa always wished he could have climbed Geronimo on the last day of his life and taken a flying leap off it, instead of being locked up in that damned bed at the Copper Queen Hospital for weeks on end. He said if he'd known what was coming, he would have handled it himself while he was still able. I feel the same way, Sheriff Brady. No friggin' way I'm going to live out the rest of my days rotting away in prison."

"What about me?" Joanna asked.

"What about you?"

"Presumably I'm supposed to die, too?"

"Why not? You started it," he said. "I told you no DNA sample, and you took one anyway. I'm sick and tired of women not doing as they're told. Got it? Let's move."

Joanna moved, following the circuitous path as it wound its way up the mountain. The ground began to rise under her feet. As the grade grew steadily steeper, the only sound within hearing came from her and Jeremy's increasingly heavy breathing. In that noisy silence, she became aware that once again Sage was kicking away, reminding her mother of her presence and of her need and will to live.

Every forward step took both mother and child nearer to the brink. Joanna realized that she had to act soon. A moment or two later, she fell again, a faked fall this time rather than a real one, but one that sent her tumbling back down until she came to rest at Jeremy's feet.

"I can't do this," she pleaded, looking up at him imploringly and making her breathing sound more labored than it was. "Especially if we're going all the way to the top. It's too steep. I can't make it without using both hands. I can't."

For a time, Jeremy simply stared down at her, saying nothing. Finally, when he reached down to help her up, the key to the handcuffs was in his hand. As he bent to unfasten the cuffs, struggling in the dark to operate the lock, Joanna had a few seconds to peer out across the empty desert behind him, hoping against hope to see even the smallest sign that her people had somehow pieced things together and were coming to her aid. But there was nothing to see. The streetlights of Warren winked at her in the far distance, but between Geronimo and town, there was nothing but a pitch-black void.

When Jeremy straightened up, Joanna could tell from his defensive stance that he was braced for her to launch some kind of counterattack. Since that's what he expected, she didn't deliver. Better to lull him into a false sense of security. Better to let him think that he had drained all the fight out of her. Since Jeremy Stock thrived on reveling in his own power, she decided to give him an additional dose.

"Thank you," she said quietly, rubbing her abraded wrists. Then she turned back to the mountain and climbed anew, praying as she went—for strength and courage.

Somewhere during that steady climb upward, a familiar Bible verse came to mind. It was a passage from Deuteronomy that Marianne Maculyea had read aloud during Andy's funeral service:

> I have set before you the path of living and dying, good and evil. Therefore choose life.

I'm choosing life for both of us, she told herself and Sage, too. *But we're not getting out of this mess without a whole lot of help from the Man upstairs. Somehow, between here and the top of the mountain, I'm hoping He'll give us a chance to get away.*

CHAPTER 37

IT WASN'T UNTIL CHIEF DEPUTY HADLOCK WAS ALONE IN HIS TAHOE and speeding west on US Highway 80 that the whole situation threatened to overwhelm him. At that point, the shakes hit so hard he was afraid he was going to have to roll down the window and heave. He'd made it through the briefing, thank God, including running the damned PowerPoint presentation without a hitch and without losing his cool, either. But it wasn't just God he had to thank for all that, it was Sheriff Brady, too.

She was the one who had insisted that he spend a year joining a Toastmasters club and learning how to do solo public-speaking presentations. She was the one who had tossed him out in front of countless packs of clamoring reporters and forced him to figure out how to handle them. She was the one who had given him this job—one he had coveted but had hardly dared hope would ever be his.

Now it was, but with Sheriff Brady's life in jeopardy, Tom wondered if he was up to the task. Had he made the right calls? He had deployed his assets in the way that made the most sense to him, but were they being used in the most effective manner? And if they weren't—if he'd been wrong about any of it—chances were Joanna Brady wouldn't live through the night. If that happened, responsibility for her death would land squarely on his shoulders.

Tom remembered speaking to Butch Dixon out in the lobby. Under similar circumstances, he knew Joanna would have reached out to a frightened loved one and said something calming and reassuring. What was it he had said to Butch? He couldn't remember the exact words but he worried that he'd given the poor guy the dreadful news about his wife's situation in far too blunt a fashion and then more or less ordered him to take a hike.

Which Butch hadn't done, of course. Later on, Tom had noticed the man lurking in the back of the conference room during the briefing, and he'd been secretly glad to see him. At least now Joanna's husband knew what was going on not only with the investigation but also with Tom's course of action. These weren't things that would need to be explained later, if things went sideways, which they very well might.

Lost in thought, Tom approached the turn at the end of the cutoff going far too fast. He had to jam on his brakes in order to make the awkward left-hand turn onto Yuma Trail. Fortunately, the vehicle right behind him—driven by Terry Gregovich—was maintaining enough distance that he didn't slam into Tom's SUV from behind.

The dog, Tom thought as he accelerated up the narrow, winding street. Failure or success depends on nothing but a dog—a single damned dog.

He had seen Spike in action on occasion, usually in training situations where Terry was putting his canine partner through his paces. The dog was quick. He'd be able to charge up the mountain way faster than a human while making very little noise in the process. Unless, of course, he barked. Terry claimed the dog was capable of operating in silent mode, but could he really? Tom Hadlock had never owned a dog in his life, and he had no idea if Terry's claim was true. He hoped it was, but if it wasn't, one tiny bark from Spike could spell disaster.

Tom crested the top of Yuma Trail with enough speed that for a second or so his Tahoe went airborne. Behind him, one set of headlights after another went dark. Everyone appeared to be following orders.

So far so good, he thought.

Once the Tahoe was parked, Tom was the first one out of his vehicle, with Spike and Terry joining him before he reached the cattle guard. The three of them set off at a brisk pace, walking side by side toward the shadow of mountain looming in the near distance against a star-studded sky. Some of the younger guys—the daily workout guys—jogged around and past them. Tom kept walking with Ernie Carpenter trudging along behind. There hadn't been much discussion about who was going where, but since Tom himself would be left guarding the disabled escape vehicle, he was grateful to have an old hand like Ernie for backup.

A little over a mile later, the GPS coordinates provided by Tica led them directly to Jeremy's parked Tahoe. It was locked. There was enough of a signal that he was able to send a text to Tica back at the department, who was able to unlock it remotely. Before opening the door, Tom shielded his Maglite long enough to risk a glance inside the vehicle. Sitting there in plain sight on the front passenger seat was just what he had hoped to find—a clump of blue cloth. Standing in stark relief against the dark material were three four-inch-tall, white capital letters—SSE.

"Hot damn," Tom said to Terry as he doused the flashlight. "I think we just found the hoodie."

He removed a pair of gloves from his pocket. "I'm going to be tampering with evidence here," he told Terry. "We can't photograph it in place because we can't risk the camera flash. If need be, I may ask you to swear this is where we found it, and before you touch it, you'll need gloves, too."

While Terry located his own pair of gloves, Tom cracked open the door, grabbed the hoodie, and shut the door again as quickly and quietly as humanly possible. The dome light flashed on and off briefly. In that instant, it seemed incredibly bright compared to the relative darkness surrounding them. From Tom's point of view, the light seemed to linger forever—a telling beacon shining in the dark. He held his breath for several moments afterward, hoping but not knowing whether or not the light had attracted Jeremy's attention or if their intrusion would be met by a hail of gunfire.

Finally, Tom handed the hoodie over to Terry, who in turn held it down until it came in contact with Spike's eagerly twitching nose.

"Find, boy," Terry ordered. "Silent and find."

For a moment, Spike stood still with his muzzle raised in the air. Then with only the tiniest whimper of excitement, the dog set off at a dead run, heading straight toward the steepest part of the mountain with Terry Gregovich following to the best of his severely limited two-legged ability.

CHAPTER 38

AS JOANNA CONTINUED TO CLIMB, THE STARLIGHT GREW STEADILY brighter. With her vision now completely adjusted to the gloom, this could have been nothing more than a trick her eyes were playing on her. She could feel that she was tiring. Had she had lunch? Or even breakfast? She wasn't sure. Couldn't remember back that far. What she did know was that she had to keep going no matter what.

A couple of times she slipped for real and came very close to tumbling backward down the mountainside. One of those times was while pulling herself up onto the ledge where she and Agent Watkins had startled the horned toad days earlier. It was night-time now. Surely the toad was safely tucked away in a cozy underground burrow and out of harm's way. She hoped so.

Behind her, she heard the sound of Jeremy's labored breathing. He seemed to be having as much or even more trouble with the climb than she was, but then he had more weight to lift. She was counting on the chance that as he grew more fatigued, he would become more vulnerable to an unexpected attack. She hoped that her continued show of utter compliance would increase the effectiveness of her intended course of action. She needed to catch him completely off guard.

One thing in her favor was the fact that Jeremy had no idea she had ever climbed Geronimo or had even the slightest idea of the landscape on top of the peak. As she climbed, she tried to envision it—the placement of each of those thriving clumps of hedgehog cactus and their relative distance from the cliff's edge. Joanna was counting on that population of isolated hedgehogs—the very ones that had ultimately caused Desirée Wilburton's death—to help prevent hers. That was the crux of her plan—to either trip or shove an unsuspecting Jeremy hard enough to make him fall into one or more of those clumps of wicked thorns. And once he was distracted by that, she hoped to make good her escape. The chute down to the spring was still there—she had seen it herself. If she made it that far, the grove of scrub oak at the bottom of the chute would offer her some cover.

Yes, she still had her Glock, but she didn't kid herself about the prospect of surviving some kind of shootout at the top of the mountain. There was no such thing as a quick draw from an ankle holster. Jeremy would be all over her long before she could raise her weapon. Once she reached the relative safety of the trees, though, she might be able to pick him off when he came down the mountain after her.

Finally, Joanna scrambled up the last rise. She was several steps ahead of Jeremy by then, and she had enough time to hurry over to the small indentation that formed the dividing line between the mountaintop's two small humps, the spot that marked the top of the chute. She looked around, noting the distance between her and the nearest clumps of cactus.

Just then Jeremy topped out, too. First his head appeared and then the rest of him. He stood still for a moment catching his breath—a black shadow outlined against a starlit sky. And on that shadow she noted the distinctive bulge of a holster that told her he was carrying more weaponry than just his Taser. What if he decided to draw the gun and simply shoot her from the far side of the knoll? Well then, it would all be over, wouldn't it? For her last-ditch plan to succeed, she needed to draw him closer—closer to her and closer to the cactus.

"How did you do it?" she asked, speaking quietly between gasps as she, too, attempted to regain her breath. The ploy of speaking softly worked exactly as she intended. Jeremy came several steps closer before he answered.

"Do what?"

"Get Susan to go with you. How did you get her to leave the school in the first place?"

"That was easy. She was glad to go along for the ride. Like I said, she knew I was pissed and thought a quick roll in the hay would fix me."

"Surely she must have known you were up to no good and that she was in danger."

"When she caught on for real, that's when I threatened her with the Taser," Jeremy answered. "She was absolutely petrified of the damned thing and did everything I said. You're doing the same thing."

Yes, I am, Joanna thought. *But only up to a point.*

She remembered the earlier discussion back in the conference room after her officers had all watched Susan Nelson seemingly being force-walked off the school grounds. At that point there had been some speculation about whether her assailant had been carrying a weapon in his left hand—possibly a knife or a gun. Now Joanna understood that neither had been involved. Jeremy's weapon then had been his temper. Only later, when Susan had realized she was in real danger, had he employed his department-issue Taser.

When Tasers had been distributed to officers in her department, everyone who was given one—including Joanna herself—had been Tased as a part of their training. She remembered from then and also from only an hour or so ago that Tasers delivered a powerful punch that amounted to five seconds of exquisite pain followed by nothing at all. She suspected that the momentary dizziness she had experienced earlier had more to do with hitting her head on the sidewalk when she fell than it did with being Tased.

But Susan Nelson had been a civilian—someone who had never encountered the realities of Taser weaponry. For her, the prospect of being Tased must have been terrifying. No doubt Jeremy would have had talked it up some, too—exaggerating the effects enough to scare her into doing exactly as she was bidden. If he used the Taser as a stun gun on Joanna now, she knew that the effect would be much the same—not fun but not fatal, either. She'd get over it. She suspected that recovering from a fall into a batch of thorny cactus would take quite a bit longer.

"Why the duct tape?" Joanna asked.

Jeremy shrugged. "Why not? I couldn't risk having her kick her way out of the trunk between Sierra Vista and here."

Just then, out of the corner of her eye, Joanna saw a tiny

pinprick of light near the base of the mountain. The flash seemed to emanate from somewhere near where Jeremy had parked his SUV. It came and went so fast that once the spark was gone, she couldn't be sure she had seen it at all. She glanced in Jeremy's direction and saw no visible reaction. From where he stood, the flicker must have been outside his line of sight.

For the first time, Joanna felt a tiny burst of hope. If someone was out in the desert tonight—in the desert and in the dark—there was a good chance that whoever it was had come looking for her. That meant that, with any kind of luck, help really was on the way.

CHAPTER 39

"COME ON," JEREMY SAID, MOVING A FEW STEPS TOWARD HER. "ON your feet. It's time."

"Time for what?"

"What do you think? To do what we came here to do."

As he came nearer, Joanna saw him draw a weapon from the shadowy holster on his hip and point it in her direction. The starlight didn't offer enough illumination for her to make out exactly what it was, but she guessed he was most likely holding his service weapon—a Beretta. At that point the Taser and the Beretta offered unevenly bad options. A pulse from the stun gun would render her momentarily senseless, while a bullet from the handgun would render her dead. As for her cactus plan? He was still too far away.

"I can't," she whimpered.

"You can't what—you can't die?"

"I can't get up. I've got a cramp in my leg."

He came another step or two forward—reaching out to her with his right hand while still holding the pistol grip in his left. Just then, Joanna heard a sudden scrabbling noise that seemed to come from somewhere short of the crest of the peak. Something unseen was out there in the dark, speeding toward them and sending a cascade of rocks and gravel skittering down the mountainside.

Joanna first thought was that their presence on the mountain had most likely alarmed a wandering herd of javelina—boar-like creatures that roam the nighttime desert that tend to scatter in fear when faced with humans.

Joanna didn't care what kind of animal was out there, but the noisy racket was an audible answer to her fervent prayer for a desperately needed distraction. Jeremy heard the noise, too. He moved closer to the edge, peering into the darkness in an attempt to catch sight of whatever was down there.

Once he drew even with her, Joanna flew into action. She flung herself in his direction, head-butting him in the side of his knees. Arms windmilling in a futile effort to regain his balance, he fired off a single wild shot before tumbling to the ground. He landed just as Joanna had intended him to land—with his right cheek impaled on the spines of the nearest clump of cactus.

Jeremy howled in agony, but Joanna didn't wait around long enough to see if he had dropped his weapon. She was already on the move, making for the top of the chute. As she scrambled over the edge and started downward, a dark form shot past her. A bobcat maybe? A coyote? Whatever it was, the animal was Jeremy's problem now, not hers. Joanna hit the top of the chute hard with her backside. The trip down wasn't as smooth as she remembered, and it wasn't nearly as fast, either. There were numerous starts and stops. Expecting a bullet to slam into the back of her head at any moment, she maneuvered around the occasional fallen boulder and then pushed off again in order to keep her downward momentum going.

Behind and above her, Joanna heard Jeremy's scream change from one of agony to one of pure rage. "Get off me, you damn dog!" he yelled. "Get the hell off me."

Dog? Joanna wondered. *What dog?*

And then she knew. It had to be Spike. Someone had sent the K9 unit to rescue her, and Spike had arrived just in time.

At last Joanna gained the shelter of the trees and was able to tug the Glock out of its holster. With a weapon in her hand, things were a little more even. If Jeremy came after her now, she'd be ready and waiting.

But then, to her horror, she heard the sound of a gunshot, followed by the shocked yipe of an injured animal. That was followed by a long moment of total silence.

Joanna knew how her K9 unit operated. If Spike was here, Terry Gregovich would be somewhere nearby. That meant in terms of taking Jeremy down, it was now two to one, which made for better odds.

"You're surrounded, Jeremy," Joanna called up the mountainside. "Drop your weapon and show us your hands! Now!"

She caught the barest glimpse of him, peering down from above, trying to catch sight of her. But he didn't follow her order to drop his weapon. Behind and beneath her, she heard the sounds of someone else, another human, laboring up the mountain.

"Hang in there, Spike," Terry called. "I'm coming to get you."

Gazing back up toward the mountaintop, Joanna caught sight

of something that looked like an enormous night bird taking wing. A second or so later, her mind made sense of what she was seeing. The flying creature wasn't a bird at all. Jeremy Stock had made good on his threat and had taken a final flying leap off the mountain.

Time stood still. With his arms spread like an eagle, Jeremy seemed to stay airborne for a long time—as though he had been caught up in winds aloft. But then gravity took hold and he tumbled earthward. In utter silence, he did three acrobatic somersaults in the air before plunging headfirst into the ground.

He landed close enough to Joanna's sheltering grove of trees that she heard the sickening thud as his head smashed into something hard. It was the same sound she had heard earlier in the summer, when Dennis had accidentally dropped their Fourth-of-July watermelon.

There could be no doubt. In that moment, Joanna knew Jeremy Stock was dead.

Good riddance were the first words that came into her head. As for the second ones? *May you rot in hell!*

Just then Terry, panting with exertion and barely able to speak, stumbled into her protective thicket. "The son of a bitch shot Spike," he gasped as he rushed up to her. "Are you okay, Sheriff Brady?"

"I'm fine," she told him. "Go get your dog, Terry. Let's hope he's okay."

CHAPTER 40

BUTCH THOUGHT HE WOULD GO HOME AND MAINTAIN A QUIET VIGIL as he waited for Agent Watkins to call, but that was not to be. When he arrived at High Lonesome Ranch, the house and yard were both abuzz with activity. Inside, the dinner dishes had been cleared away. Denny was evidently in bed, but the kitchen itself was in full production mode, with all hands on deck preparing for the next day's post-funeral barbecue.

If we have *a barbecue,* Butch thought despairingly. If his precious Joey was gone forever, all bets were off.

Jenny, wearing an oversized apron and standing by the kitchen counter, was using the food processor to slice up cabbage for coleslaw. As soon as she caught sight of him, she abandoned her post and raced over.

"What's going on?" she demanded. "You left without saying a word. Tell me!"

Butch dropped onto the bench of the breakfast nook and buried his face in his hands. "It's your mother," he said. "She's been kidnapped."

He told the story then—as much of it as he knew anyway. A wide-eyed Jenny sat stone-faced across from him, staring and listening. The other women listened, too, but they kept on working, with Eva Lou and Carol mixing up and kneading batches of yeast dough while Marcie formed already raised dough into rolls and placed them on cookie sheets to rise a second time.

"Are you saying she could die?" Jenny asked at last when Butch finished.

He nodded miserably.

"And they're all out there right now trying to save her?"

Butch nodded again.

"Why aren't you out there, too?" Jenny demanded furiously. "Shouldn't you be helping them instead of sitting here doing nothing?"

Her angry words weren't questions so much as outright accusations.

Butch didn't want to own up to the real reason he had come home—that he hadn't wanted to run the risk of leaving both Jenny and her little brother fatherless and motherless. "I'm not a cop," he said instead. "I'd just be in the way. Besides, Chief Deputy Hadlock is doing a terrific job under the most dire of circumstances."

"Right," Jenny muttered sarcastically. "Of course he is."

With that, she got up from the table, leaving Butch sitting alone. She returned to her food processor, slicing up the cabbage heads with an impressive show of displaced fury. Jenny might not have inherited her mother's fiery red hair, but she hadn't missed out on Joanna's hot temper.

Having worn out his welcome in the kitchen, Butch retreated to the patio, where Jim Bob Brady and Bob Brundage, two guys with absolutely no blood ties between them, were keeping watch over Butch's propane-fired gas grill and tending to the several savory-smelling hunks of beef brisket that were already aligned side by side in the smoker.

"What's up?" Jim Bob asked. "The way you left without a word of explanation, it's got to be something serious."

And so Butch was obliged to tell the story again, from beginning to end. The whole while he was recounting the details, his eyes drifted off in the direction of Geronimo. With intervening hills between the mountain and High Lonesome Ranch, there was no way for him to see that far, but his heart and soul—his very existence; Joanna and his baby girl—were up on that unseen mountain. *What if they don't make it?* he wondered. *What if they don't come home to me? What if?*

Feeling lost and helpless and knowing the barbecue preparations were moving forward just fine without him, he opted for spending some time alone.

"I'm going to go check on the horses," he said.

With Jenny's black Lab, Lucky, at his heels, he went out to the corral and spent some quality time with Joanna's rescued mare, a blind Appaloosa named Spot, and Jenny's now-retired barrel-racing gelding, a sorrel named Kiddo. Butch was standing there, weeping silently into the smooth hair on Kiddo's neck, when his phone rang. With trembling hands, he wrestled the device out of his pocket. Caller ID told him it was an *unidentified caller.*

"Hello?"

"It's Robin," Agent Watkins said breathlessly. "It's over. She's safe."

Not trusting his ability to stand, Butch staggered drunkenly over to the nearest wooden fence post and leaned against it. Even though his head was shaved, he could feel his hair follicles standing on end. "You're sure she's okay?"

"I haven't seen her yet," Robin continued. "I've been told she has some bumps and bruises, but nothing too serious. It's still a very chaotic scene out here. Jeremy Stock is dead. He jumped to his death from the top of the mountain, but before he offed himself, the asshole shot the dog. My understanding is that Spike's still alive. There's a team up on the mountain right now, trying to bring him down."

"But you're sure Joey's okay," Butch said, as if he couldn't quite bring himself to believe it.

"Look," Agent Watkins said, "if you don't want to take my word for it, why don't you come see for yourself? The mop up from this incident is going to take time, but as of right now, the shooting war is over. If you happened to show up on the scene, I don't think Chief Deputy Hadlock would have balls enough to send you packing. Just don't you tell him I told you so."

"Thank you," Butch murmured. "Thank you more than I can say. I'm on my way."

His first instinct was to go straight to the garage and take off—do not pass Go; do not collect two hundred dollars. Then he thought better of it. He sprinted over to the patio and gave the wonderful news to the beef brisket guys before heading into the kitchen. Jenny looked up the moment he entered.

"She's okay," he announced.

Jenny fairly flew across the room and threw herself into his arms. "Really?"

"Really. Agent Watkins tells me processing the crime scene is probably going to be an all-nighter. I'm going to drive out there now. Want to come along?"

For an answer, Jenny whipped off her apron and headed for the garage. "Which car?" she asked. "Yours or Mom's?"

"Your mother's," he answered. "Bob is parked behind mine."

"What happened?" Jenny asked.

"I don't have the whole story, but somehow and for some unknowable reason, Deputy Stock took your mother captive and forced her to climb Geronimo."

"Why? What was he going to do to her up there, kill her?"

"I'm not sure, but probably," Butch said. "Maybe we should ask your mom that question the next time we see her."

"But why would he do something like that?" Jenny asked. "I mean, he's worked for Mom forever, hasn't he?"

Was this the time for Butch to tell her what he had heard in the conference room, that Jeremy Stock had gone on a crazed rampage and had murdered both his wife and son? He did a silent eenie, meenie, miny, moe, tapping his fingers on the steering wheel to the remembered words to the old counting rhyme. When the last word let him off the hook, he gratefully accepted that decision. After all, Jeremy Stock's murderous atrocities were police business. Talking about them outside of law enforcement circles was frowned on, even with family members.

"I don't know what set him off," Butch hedged. "That's something else we'll have to ask your mom, but I do have something to tell you. I wasn't being honest before."

"About what?" Jenny asked.

"About why I didn't go to the crime scene."

"Why?"

"Because I was afraid."

They were stopped at the stop sign at the turn onto Highway 80. When Butch glanced in Jenny's direction, he found her staring at him.

"Afraid of what?" she asked. "Afraid of getting killed?"

Butch shook his head. "What terrified me was the idea that if something happened to both your mother and me, you and Dennis would be left totally on your own. I may not be your real father, Jen, but I'm the only one you have. The thought of your possibly losing both your mom and me scared the living daylights out of me. So I was a good boy. When Chief Deputy Hadlock told me to go home, much as I didn't want to, I did as I was told. I came home, sat on my hands, and prayed a lot."

"And your prayers were answered," Jenny said softly.

Butch nodded. "Looks like," he said.

A moment later, Jenny reached across the center console and touched his hand. "Thanks, Dad," she said. "And for the record, coming home was the right thing to do."

CHAPTER 41

THE FIRST THING TOM HADLOCK HEARD WAS A GUNSHOT FOLlowed by a scream of some kind—the kind of scream that says someone is hurt—badly hurt. When another gunshot followed mere seconds later, it was all the chief deputy could do to remain upright. At that point, there was nothing to do but assume the worst. Sheriff Joanna Brady was dead—had to be. A shot at close range from what was most likely Jeremy Stock's Beretta? Even if a resulting wound wasn't instantly fatal, it would be by the time EMTs arrived.

Why the hell is that stubborn woman so dead set against using a helicopter—a free damned helicopter at that? he wondered. *That's what we need out here tonight in the very worst way—a helicopter!*

The silence following the gunshots seemed to stretch into an eternity. *Stay alert,* Tom thought, sending a dose of silent encouragement to his officers. He had directed them to stay in place and maintain radio silence until Jeremy Stock was seen attempting to flee or was actually in custody. With Joanna dead or dying, this was the time he would flee—running like hell and coming straight back to the spot where he'd left the car.

Then, to the chief deputy's immense relief, Terry Gregovich's panting voice crackled over the radio, speaking breathlessly into his shoulder mic. "Jeremy Stock is deceased. Repeat. The suspect is deceased. Sheriff Brady is okay. Going up to check on Spike. The son of a bitch shot him."

With shaking hands, Tom reached inside Jeremy's SUV and activated the radio. "Did everyone copy that? Jeremy Stock is down. Let's go find our sheriff and our dog."

Radio transmissions buzzed back and forth as Maglites flashed to life all around. From where Tom Hadlock stood, they looked like so many tiny lit candles surrounding the broad base of Geronimo and moving steadily toward it, gradually tightening the circle.

Weak with relief, Tom sank down gratefully onto the Tahoe's driver's seat and covered his face with his hands. He had done it. He had called the shots—all the shots—and they had worked. The tactics he had put in place had pulled it off. Sheriff Brady was safe, and Jeremy Stock was dead.

Finally, he picked up the mic again. "Tica," he managed with his voice still trembling. "Let Dr. Baldwin know what's happened. We'll need the ME out here." Then, after another pause, he added, "Deputy Gregovich. What's the word?"

"Spike's alive," Terry answered in a strangled whisper. "He's shot in the leg. I've got a tourniquet on it, but—"

"Hold tight, Deputy Gregovich. Where are you?"

"At the top. Up at the very top."

"Okay," Tom Hadlock said. "Stay where you are. I'm calling for a stretcher now. Did you copy that, Tica? I want some EMTs out here, ASAP."

"I doubt they'll come for a dog," Tica said.

"They by God will come for *this* damned dog!" Tom roared back at her. "Spike just saved Sheriff Brady's life, and now we're going to save his. If they give you any guff, put them through to me. Oh, and we're going to need that vet on the scene, too—what's her name?"

"You mean Dr. Ross?" Tica asked.

"Yes, that's right—Dr. Ross. Get her out here on the double."

Then another voice came over the radio—a welcome one Tom had feared he would never hear again. "Sheriff Brady here," she said. "Do you copy?"

"Yes, I do," he replied, brushing a tear from his eye. "I most certainly do. Where are you? Are you okay?"

"Up top with Terry and Spike. Climbing back up was a lot tougher than coming down. I'm a little worse for wear, but not bad. Terry tells me I've got a whale of a black eye, but I'm in better shape than Spike. We've got to get him some help. Bless that dog. He arrived in the nick of time—just when I needed him most. I never would have made it down the mountain alive if he hadn't been there to distract Jeremy. Spike blew right past me and gave me a chance to get away. Who was the brainiac who came up with the idea of sending him in?"

"I did," Tom Hadlock said modestly. "I'm glad it worked."

"You and me both," Joanna said.

Off in the distance Tom heard a siren—the distinctive wailing of an approaching aid car. Seconds later, he spotted flashing lights as the emergency vehicle sped northbound on Black

Knob heading toward the cattle guard at the far end of the ranch road.

"The EMTs are coming right now," he reported. "We'll send them up as soon as I can brief them and point them in your direction. In the meantime, guys, thank you, one and all. Some of you may need to assist in bringing Spike down the mountain. Everybody else, hop to it. We need to locate Jeremy Stock's body and get the area cordoned off as a crime scene. We're going to need lights, generators, CSIs—the whole nine yards. It's going to be a very long night."

"Great job, Tom," Joanna said when he finished issuing the spate of orders. "One hell of a job!"

"Thank you, Sheriff Brady," he replied. "Over and out!"

CHAPTER 42

CLIMBING BACK UP TO THE SUMMIT HAD BEEN FAR MORE DIFFICULT than Joanna would have thought possible. For one thing, she was terribly fatigued, but she felt a moral obligation to be there for Terry and Spike, come what may. After all, Spike had saved her life. She owed him. She owed them both.

Far below, there were suddenly swarms of flashing red lights all around and maybe even a faint siren or two, but up on the summit of Geronimo, it was unnaturally quiet. Terry sat cross-legged on the ground with Spike's head cradled in his lap. Whenever he reached out to touch the dog's forehead or ruffle his ears, Spike's long tail thumped gamely on the ground. Each time it happened, Joanna had to hold her breath to keep from crying, but crying wasn't allowed, not for her. After all, she was the sheriff, supposedly in command, and these were some of her troops—her very loyal troops.

Not knowing what to say, she simply sat beside them, saying nothing, and gratefully drinking water from the bottle Terry had pulled out of his pocket and given her.

"It looks bad," Terry said brokenly. "What if he loses the leg?"

"Then we give him a full medical retirement," Joanna promised. "Vet bills included."

"But he loves to work. It'll kill him if I go to work and he doesn't."

"He's done this job for a long time," Joanna said. "Longer than most K9s, right?"

Terry nodded. "He's always been such a good dog."

"He is *still* a good dog," Joanna assured him. "But Spike has earned his retirement, and you've earned yourself another partner."

Just then, bobbing lights off to the side indicated that someone was approaching and about to join them on the summit. Lieutenant Adam Wilson of the Bisbee Fire Department led the way. His head came into view first, topped by a light-equipped helmet. A medical kit thumped to the ground in front of him before he clambered the rest of the way onto the surface. Two more firefighters trailed behind him.

"I understand we have an injured patient who needs to be transported?" Wilson asked.

"Yes," Joanna said, getting to her feet. "Spike's over here."

"Okay, guys," Wilson said. "Bring the basket and let's get him strapped in. Your dog, sir?" The question was directed at Terry, who nodded mutely in reply.

"All right, then," Wilson said. "You stay close and help keep him calm. What about a muzzle? Will we need to put one on him? Injured dogs can be a problem sometimes. We may be trying to help them, but they don't understand what's going on."

"He'll be good," Terry answered. "Steady, Spike," he added as Wilson reached out an enormous gloved hand to pat the top of Spike's head. The dog didn't move.

"I could give him a little something for the pain, if you like," Wilson offered. "There may be a few bumps and jolts on the way down."

"Please," Terry said. "If you can, I'd like that a lot."

In the end, there were enough volunteers to pass the basket from hand to hand down the mountain rather than having to employ a block and tackle. Once Terry and the dog disappeared over the edge, Wilson turned back to Joanna and peered down at her with the light from his helmet shining in her eyes.

"If you'll pardon my saying so, ma'am, you look like hell. That's quite a shiner you have, and plenty of cuts and bruises as well. Maybe I should drag another stretcher up here and carry you down, too."

"Please don't do that," she said. "I'm fine. I can manage."

Wilson reached for her hands and examined them carefully. They were scratched and bruised all over as well. Some of the deeper cuts on her badly scraped knuckles still seeped blood.

It was at that precise moment, just as Lieutenant Wilson was studying her hands, when Sage asserted her presence with a vigorous series of kicks.

Wilson jumped back as though he'd unwittingly stumbled over a rattlesnake. "What the hell was that?" he demanded.

"My baby," she said. "A girl. I'm due in December."

"Jesus Christ, woman!" he exclaimed. "You're out here acting like a mountain goat and you're expecting a baby?"

"I didn't exactly come here of my own volition," she told him.

"Maybe so, but you're sure as hell not climbing down on your own, either—not on my watch. Understood?"

Joanna started to argue but stopped. Wilson was doing his job, and she needed to let him do it.

Turning abruptly, Wilson walked over to the edge of the summit. "Hey, guys," he called down. "Once you deliver that dog to the vet, I need a couple of you to come back. There's a pregnant lady up here who doesn't think she needs any help getting down, but I'm saying otherwise."

He sounded so fierce that it tickled Joanna's funny bone. A moment later she was giggling uncontrollably.

Wilson spun around to face her. "What's so funny?"

"Nothing," she said, silencing her laughter. "When you're right, you're right. Thank you."

It was humiliating being passed from hand to hand, but Joanna realized partway down that she really was in no condition to make the descent on her own, especially not in the dark. The first two faces she saw once her feet were on *terra firma* were the ones she wanted to see the most—Butch and Jenny's.

"Oh, Mom," Jenny whispered, pulling Joanna into an impassioned embrace. "I was so scared!"

"So was I," Joanna admitted. "Believe me, so was I."

She turned away from Jenny into Butch's welcoming arms and let him hold her for a long, long time. When she drew away at last, she saw that she had left several bloody imprints on his shirt. "You're bleeding," he said. "You're hurt."

"It's nothing," Joanna replied, trying to downplay his concern. "But how did you get here?"

"Agent Watkins called me the moment Jeremy Stock bit the dust. I wanted to come here along with everyone else earlier, but she talked me out of it. Said it was too dangerous and that I should go home."

"It *was* too dangerous," Joanna said.

"Agent Watkins promised that she'd call me the moment you were safe, and she did. But, Joey, you look awful. Your face is a mess!"

Just then someone walked up behind Butch and tapped him on the shoulder. "May I cut in?" Tom Hadlock asked. As Butch stepped away, Tom swept Joanna into a smothering bear hug.

"Boy howdy!" he exclaimed, pushing her away finally and examining her face. "If you aren't a sight for sore eyes!"

"I'm a sight all right," Joanna replied with a laugh. "Everyone keeps telling me so, but thanks, Tom. Thank you for everything you did tonight. You made some really great calls, and I wouldn't be here talking about them if you hadn't."

"Thank you, ma'am," he murmured. "Appreciate it."

Lieutenant Wilson approached Tom Hadlock. "Okay, Chief Deputy," he said. "We're done here. Dr. Ross has taken charge of the dog, so we'll be heading out."

"This is Lieutenant Adam Wilson," Joanna told Butch. "With the Bisbee Fire Department, and this is my husband, Butch Dixon."

"He's the guy who helped you down off the mountain?" Butch asked.

"The very one," she replied.

Butch held out his hand to shake Wilson's. "Thanks," he said. "Thanks for rescuing my wife and our baby, too."

Wilson glanced back and forth between them. "Is it possible your wife is slightly stubborn?" he asked.

"Not slightly," Butch answered with a grin. "Very."

"You might want to have her visit the ER after she finishes up whatever she needs to do here," Lieutenant Wilson suggested.

"Those cuts and scratches need to be cleaned by professionals, and at least one of them—the cut on her right cheek—should probably be stitched up if she doesn't want to be stuck with a scar. Oh, and a word of advice," he added. "If I were you, I wouldn't bother asking her opinion on the subject. I'd just put her in the car and take her there."

"Good idea," Butch said. "I'll do that very thing, the first chance I get."

CHAPTER 43

THE EVENTS OF THE DAY—AND OF THE NIGHT AS WELL—HAD LEFT Joanna in an odd position. She was still the sheriff, yes, but she was also both victim and witness. By virtue of the latter two, it was necessary for her to leave her chief deputy in charge of investigating the incident, especially since, by all accounts, he was doing a great job. That left her strictly on the sidelines and at somewhat of a loss. She was glad to have Butch and Jenny there with her, but still . . .

Joanna learned that the EMTs had loaded Spike and the basket as well into Dr. Ross's van so he could be taken directly to the vet's clinic, where the injured dog was currently undergoing surgery. Dr. Ross had given Terry a lift back to his parked SUV so he could follow her back into town. Joanna had no doubt that Terry, and probably Kristin as well, were both sitting vigil in the vet's waiting room.

With Joanna no longer on the mountain to direct the search, it took close to an hour for deputies to locate Jeremy Stock's body. They found his shattered remains just as the ME's van arrived on the scene. As Dave Hollicker told Joanna later, Jeremy had crashed to earth only feet from the spot where they had determined he had shoved both Susan Nelson and Desirée Wilburton to their deaths.

Kendra Baldwin got out of her van, spotted Joanna, and came right over. "What are you doing here?" she asked.

"Where else would I be?" Joanna asked.

"The hospital maybe? I heard what happened. You got Tased and cracked the back of your head. You need to go to the ER and be checked out for a possible concussion. In addition, your face is a mess."

"I've been trying to tell her—" Butch began.

"Don't bother," Kendra advised. "Just take her."

"Come on, Mom," Jenny urged. "That's at least five to one, all of us telling you the same thing. When are you going to give in?"

"About now, I suppose," Joanna agreed grudgingly. "I'll go tell Tom that we're leaving."

She found Chief Deputy Hadlock overseeing the towing of Jeremy's Tahoe to the impound lot. "Have you spoken to Frank about the homicides out in Sierra Vista?" she asked.

Tom nodded. "The bodies are still where they were found, waiting for Dr. Baldwin to make the trip out there after she finishes here. According to Frank, it looks like both Allison and Travis died of a choke hold. That's not certain, of course, until Dr. Baldwin gives us the final word."

"A police choke hold?" Joanna asked.

Tom nodded grimly. "What the hell happened to the guy?" he

demanded, glancing around to see if anyone else was in earshot. "I mean you and I worked with Jeremy for years—we all did— and I never saw any of this coming. Wouldn't have guessed it in a million years. What did we miss?"

"We missed what was going on behind closed doors," Joanna said. "Once we go digging into the family situation, we may find that there was a certain level of domestic abuse going on in the Stock family for a long time without it ever being reported. Jeremy expected his wife and son to do whatever he said, no matter what."

"Make that *sons*, not *son*," Tom corrected. "I've just been informed that there's a second one, an older boy named Thad. He's going to school somewhere in Texas. I've got law enforcement people there reaching out to let him know what's happened."

"Jeremy mentioned Thad earlier," Joanna said. "He indicated there was some bad blood between them."

"Not surprised," Tom muttered. "This kind of crap probably explains why Thad is in school in Texas rather than somewhere closer to home."

Joanna nodded. "When Jeremy issued an order, he expected instant, unquestioning obedience. That's what happened to Susan Nelson. When she refused to abort their child, he went off the deep end. This afternoon, when he found out that she had been screwing around with Travis, too, that was the last straw."

"Wait," Tom interjected. "You already knew that Jeremy was the father of Susan Nelson's baby? We didn't find that out until late this afternoon, and you weren't in the conference room for that briefing. How did you know that?"

"I heard it straight from Jeremy himself. And this afternoon, when Travis insisted on giving me that voluntary DNA sample, he did so in defiance of his father's direct orders, ones issued no doubt because Jeremy knew that his son's DNA would be his downfall and lead straight back to him."

"Which is exactly what it did," Tom said. "What's unbelievable is that by giving you that sample, Travis signed his own death warrant, his mother's, too, and very nearly yours." Joanna nodded in agreement.

"Are there other cases like this?" Tom wondered aloud. "Other people inside the department who are pulling the same kinds of stunts at home?"

"Maybe," Joanna said. "And maybe it's high time we had some departmental meetings focused on that very topic—for both our officers and their respective spouses."

"Right," Tom said. "I suppose we should, but right this minute, it seems like way too little way too late."

Those words hung in the air between them for a moment before Tom continued. "Bruce Ryder, the FBI's Tucson special agent in charge, came through for us in a big way. He lit a fire under one of his buddies at Taser International. Casey just had a call back from them. The AFIDs we found out in the parking lot did come from Jeremy's Taser."

"No surprises there," Joanna said.

"No, but it'll be an important piece of evidence as we start putting the sequence of events together. Speaking of which, the Arizona Department of Public Safety is sending an investigation team to conduct impartial interviews with everyone involved. They'll be at the Justice Center in about an hour or so. Will you feel up to talking to them tonight, or do you want me to ask them to come back some other time? Not tomorrow, because of the funeral, of course, but maybe over the weekend."

"I'd rather get the interview over with tonight and not have it hanging over my head all weekend long," Joanna told him. "Butch and Dr. Baldwin are both insisting that I stop by the hospital to be checked out. Depending on how long that takes, maybe I could go home and change into different clothing before the interview."

Unfortunately, her first pair of specially modified, expanded-waist trousers had literally bitten the dust, and on their very first day of use. Climbing up and down Geronimo twice in the course of one day had left her uniform very much the worse for wear.

"By all means, stop by the ER," Tom urged. "Incidentally, have you ever heard of arnica?"

"What's that?"

"A plant of some kind which they use to make a salve. I forget the name of it—Arnicare maybe—but it's great on bruises of any kind. Helps with the pain and reduces the swelling. Have Butch pick you up some of that. You've got a fat lip at the moment, and that black eye is a doozy."

"Thanks," Joanna said. "Will do."

Something to reduce the swelling was probably a good idea, she realized as she walked back to where Butch and Jenny waited beside the Enclave. There was an extra bump of cheek sticking out under her right eye and distorting her vision. Yes, there was definitely some swelling.

The ER visit took less time than expected. The doctor determined that there was no concussion. That was the good news. The bad news was that Lieutenant Wilson was right. The scrapes and abrasions all needed to be properly cleaned, and the cut on her cheek did indeed require several stitches.

When she and Butch finally arrived at the house at High

Lonesome Ranch, just after midnight, lights were on all over the place and barbecue preparations were still in full swing. Joanna stepped out of the passenger seat into the arms of a stream of people who hurried into the garage to welcome her home—Carol Sunderson; Jim Bob and Eva Lou; Bob and Marcie.

They greeted Joanna as if she were some kind of conquering hero, but she didn't feel very damned heroic. She was bruised and battered, stitched and sore, but she was still alive. Maybe that was part of what it meant to be a hero—being the one who lived to tell the tale.

At the hospital, suspecting that Joanna's blood sugar was at an all-time low, Butch had sent Jenny off in search of a vending machine. Jenny had returned with a much-needed Snickers bar, but when Joanna stepped into a kitchen alive with the aroma of freshly baked yeast rolls, she realized she was beyond famished.

"Go shower and change," Butch admonished her. "I'll drive you back for your interview, but not until after you've had something to eat."

"You don't need to drive me," she objected. "There's no telling how long the interview will take. I can drive myself."

"I will drive you," Butch insisted even more firmly. "Go shower. Driving yourself is not an option, Joey. That's an order."

"Yes, sir," she said, giving him a mock salute. "On my way."

When Joanna returned to the kitchen, showered and dressed, a bowl of green chili casserole, a still-warm yeast roll, and a glass of milk were waiting for her in the breakfast nook. The food was there and so was Butch, but no one else was in evidence.

"Where did everybody go?" she asked.

"Jenny went to bed and everyone else went home," Butch

said, sinking down beside her on the bench. "They were all hanging around to make sure you were okay. I told them, but they wanted to see it with their own eyes, and I don't blame them for that. I felt the same way. That's why Jenny and I showed up at the crime scene—to see for ourselves."

He reached across the table and covered one of her bruised hands with his own. "I'm so glad you're here, Joey," he said, his voice cracking with emotion. "The idea of you and the baby being Tased? I can hardly imagine something so awful. You're sure she's all right?"

For an answer, Joanna lifted both their hands from the tabletop and placed them side by side on her belly, where Sage was once again pummeling her lower ribs.

"See there?" she said. "Sage is just fine."

"Thank God," Butch breathed.

"Thank God and dog," Joanna told him with a smile. "Spike had a paw in saving me, too."

Half an hour later, they were in the Enclave and on their way to the Justice Center. Joanna, sitting with her head against the headrest and her eyes closed, tried to imagine how she could possibly manage to make it through the rigors the next day. When Butch's voice drew her out of her reverie, she realized he must have been speaking to her without her having heard a word he'd said.

"Sorry," she said. "I was half-asleep. What were you saying?"

"About the name—the baby's name."

"I know," Joanna answered. "You don't like the name Sage."

"I don't mind it all that much," Butch replied, "but wouldn't it be better as a middle name? What if we called her Eleanor Sage Dixon—Ellie for short?"

As soon as he spoke the name aloud, a chill ran up and down Joanna's legs. Knowing how incredibly right it was, she momentarily lost her ability to speak.

"That's perfect," she breathed at last. "Absolutely perfect. Eleanor Sage Dixon it is!"

CHAPTER 44

THE INTERVIEW ITSELF WENT PRETTY MUCH AS JOANNA EXPECTED. The DPS detectives wanted to ascertain where everyone was at the time Jeremy Stock had gone airborne. Since at least two gunshots had occurred in the course of the incident, they wondered if anyone had administered GSR tests the night before. Joanna smiled when they asked that question.

"Yes," she answered. "My chief deputy, Tom Hadlock, made sure that our CSI team did Gunshot Residue Tests on my K9 officer, Terry Gregovich, on me, and on the dog, too, before any of us left the scene."

Go, Tom, she thought to herself. That was something else—a big something else—that her chief deputy had gotten right under the most challenging of circumstances.

In the course of the interview, Joanna laid the whole thing out, from the original homicides to the deaths of Jeremy Stock's wife and son, and on to Jeremy's suicide. She told the detectives as much as she knew about the ongoing investigation involving the Susan Nelson sexual-abuse scandal, something which, in the next hours and days, was bound to set all of southeastern Arizona on its ear.

Halfway through the interview, her phone rang . . . well . . . crowed, really. The DPS guys exchanged disparaging glances, but Joanna wasn't exactly a suspect, and they had no grounds to forbid her taking the call. With Kristin's name showing in caller ID, they would have had to physically wrestle the phone out of her hands to keep her from doing so.

"How's Spike?" she asked at once.

"Out of surgery," Kristin answered. "Dr. Ross thinks she's managed to save the leg, but it's still touch and go. Terry's really broken up over it. He says that without Spike he's ready to quit the department and look for some other kind of work."

"Of course he's broken up," Joanna said. "Why wouldn't he be? He and Spike have been partners for a long time. They'll both have some grieving and adjusting to do. As I told Terry while we were still up on Geronimo, Spike has earned every minute of his retirement."

What came to her then was something she would later regard as a moment of divine inspiration. "While Spike is recovering and while we're finding a new partner for Terry, maybe you could bring the dog along to work with you. That way Spike will feel like he's still on the job, and maybe Terry will, too."

"What a wonderful idea," Kristin said. "I love it, and so will Terry. I'll go tell him."

When the called ended, Joanna turned back to the DPS detectives, "Okay, gentlemen. Where were we?"

The interview ended at 2:45 A.M. Joanna and Butch made it back home just after three. Falling into bed, Joanna slept a deep, dreamless sleep. When she opened her eyes in the morning, Butch was long out of bed and the clock on the nightstand told her she had overslept. Thinking she was about to be late for work, she started to scramble out of bed and then stopped. Everything hurt. There was no part of her that wasn't stiff, sore, and aching, and all of that reminded her of everything else—everything that had happened yesterday and everything that would happen today.

Joanna Brady was alive this morning, but George and Eleanor Winfield were still dead. Yesterday she had fought a life-or-death battle with a stone-cold killer. Today she had to get through the aftermath of another double homicide.

Squaring her aching shoulders, Joanna got up finally and limped into the bathroom, where a brand-new tube of Arnicare stood front and center on the bathroom countertop. Seeing her face in the mirror was a shock to the system. Her right cheek was purple from her eyebrow to the bottom of her nose. Where the bruise ended, the line of stitches began. Not a pretty picture. Taking Butch's pointed hint, she opened the box, took out the tube, and spread some of the soothing ointment over everything that hurt—at least over everything that hurt that she could reach. There were scrapes in the middle of her back where applying salve simply wasn't an option.

Summoned by the unmistakable scent of baking waffles, Joanna donned her robe and headed in that direction, only to come to a sudden halt in the living room. Most of the ceiling was covered with an array of brightly colored helium balloons, bunches and bunches of them, all tied together with strings.

"How many balloons did you buy?" she asked Butch when she reached the kitchen doorway.

"Morning, gorgeous," he said with a smile as he looked up from his steaming waffle iron. "I bought as many as Safeway had on hand. I believe that's called cornering the market. I wanted them here at the house before the funeral rather than having to go pick them up afterward."

"Good idea," Joanna said. "I should have gone along."

"Not enough room," Butch said. "It turns out that balloons take up a lot of space, especially when you're transporting them in a vehicle."

Dennis sat at the table staring at her. "Mommy," he said finally. "What happened to your face? You look awful!"

"Out of the mouths of babes," Butch said with a grin.

"I was out hiking and I fell down," Joanna answered. It was a long way from the truth but it was close enough to do the job.

"Did you see the balloons?" Denny continued enthusiastically, paying no attention at all to his mother's truth-dodging explanation. "Do you know how long it takes to fill that many balloons? A long time. They ran out of . . . What's it called again, Daddy?"

"Helium," Butch answered, setting a plate with a waffle on it directly in front of Denny's place at the table and a mug of tea in front of Joanna's.

"They ran out of helium," Dennis finished. "Good thing they had another . . ."

"Bottle," Butch supplied. "It looks like a tank, but I believe they call them bottles."

"When we let them loose, will Grandma Eleanor and Grandpa George be able to see them?" Dennis wanted to know.

"Yes, they will," Butch answered preemptively, before Joanna could say otherwise. "Of course they will."

When Joanna's waffle came, she ate it gingerly, chewing on the left side of her mouth only. There were definitely some loose teeth on the other side.

"The service starts at eleven," Butch said. "What time do you want to leave the house?"

"Probably around ten," Joanna answered. "There are always last-minute details that need to be attended to."

Jenny appeared in the doorway, wearing PJs and sniffing the air. "Waffles? Goody. I love waffles."

"If Mom and I go uptown early, can you get Dennis ready and bring him along?"

"Sure thing," Jenny said. "No problem."

Minutes later, Joanna excused herself and headed back to the bedroom. She had to admit that the salve had helped some with the swelling. She did the best she could with makeup, but there was no way to cover up the worst of the damage. She dug her only black suit out of the closet and put it on. She was able to zip the skirt most of the way, but she couldn't fasten the button. She used a safety pin to close the placket, but the jacket was two inches shy of closing around her ample middle.

Yes, she thought, appraising herself in the mirror. *No way Mom would ever give me a passing grade on this outfit.*

Butch came in just then to get ready, too. "Do you know what you're going to say?"

"Pretty much," she said. "I wrote something down. It's on my iPad."

"You won't need your iPad," he told her, handing her the freshly pressed lace-edged handkerchief Dennis had given her for Mother's Day. "All you have to do is speak from your heart."

Joanna and Butch drove from the house to the mortuary mostly in silence because, right then, filling the car with words simply wasn't necessary. While Butch negotiated with one of Norm Higgins's sons about the best place for them to park and who would ride in the limo from the mortuary to the cemetery, Joanna went inside the chapel.

Marianne Maculyea was already on hand. Had the final arrangements been left to Eleanor, no doubt she would have chosen the pastor from her church, First Presbyterian, to officiate. The problem was, the new minister, Reverend Donald Graham, had come on board after George and Eleanor had left town for their summer-long RV adventure. He would have been a complete stranger to them, just as he was to Joanna.

As a consequence, Eleanor's preferences simply didn't apply. After all, funerals were for the living rather than the dead, and Joanna wanted someone she knew officiating at the ceremony and issuing the words of comfort. Of course, there was that other important part of the equation—the one that included Marianne's troubled relationship with her own mother. That meant Marianne had a far better understanding of Joanna's current storm of conflicting emotions than anyone else on the planet.

"I heard what happened," Marianne said, hurrying forward as if to wrap her arms around Joanna's shoulders.

"No hugs, please," Joanna said, warning her away. "I hurt all over."

Since Marianne functioned as a local police and fire chaplain, it was hardly surprising that she was aware of what had gone on.

Still, when she saw the stitches on Joanna's face, she visibly recoiled.

"How are you?"

"I'm okay," Joanna admitted. "A little stiff and sore, but you're welcome to go ahead and tell me how awful I look. Everyone else does."

"Considering what you went through yesterday, you're entitled to look the part," Marianne said. "By the way, Marliss was on the phone early this morning complaining right and left that Tom Hadlock had scheduled a press briefing for eleven A.M. She was wondering if since she would be missing the service, could I possibly make arrangements to tape it. I told her no, by the way."

"Thanks," Joanna said. "I suspect there may have been a bit of malice aforethought on my chief deputy's part when he scheduled the briefing for the same time as the funeral. On the face of it, he's giving news outlets from out of town a chance to get here on time. Even so, with that eleven A.M. start time, he may have been sticking it to Marliss just a little."

Norm Higgins appeared silently at her elbow. "May I show you to the family meditation room?"

With a nod, Joanna allowed herself to be led away. She sat alone for several minutes, studying what she'd written of the eulogies on her iPad. When Jenny, Dennis, and Butch filed in a few minutes later, she turned the iPad off and put it in her purse.

She'd do exactly as Butch had suggested, she decided—speak from the heart. And when in the course of the service, it came time for her to step forward, the iPad remained exactly where she had left it—stowed and closed in her purse.

"My mother, Eleanor Lathrop Winfield, would be appalled to see me standing here like this today—bruised and battered and looking like, as she would have said, 'something the cat dragged in.' Some of you may have heard that there was a serious incident out on Geronimo last night. It came about as part of an investigation into several homicides. As sheriff, I was involved in that incident, and I've got the stitches and bruises to prove it. I remember a limerick I heard once:

As a beauty, I'm not a great star;
There are others more handsome by far.
But my face—I don't mind it,
For I am behind it.
It's the people out front that I jar.

"On behalf of my mother and her husband, George Winfield, I offer my apologies for how I look today, but in this case, what you see is what you get."

There was a small titter of laughter from the audience before Joanna continued. "What can I say about George? He was terrific. When he was appointed to be Cochise County's first-ever medical examiner, he and I soon became trusted colleagues and later friends.

"I was a bit surprised when he and my mother took up with one another. Mom had been a widow on her own for a very long time. When they put George's name up as one of the 'most eligible bachelors' in a school district auction, I was surprised when Mom ponied up the kind of money she did. I thought it was a whim. Turns out it wasn't. George and I were working a case and driving to Douglas on the day he happened to mention that he and my mother had eloped to Las Vegas the previous weekend. I didn't total my patrol car that day, but it wasn't for lack of trying."

Another whisper of laughter rippled through the room.

"As I said earlier, my mother had been widowed for a long time when George showed up in her life. He put a smile on her face and a sparkle in her eye that I never remember seeing before. For that, I'm forever grateful.

"And then there's my mom—Eleanor. If any of you ever had the misfortune of tangling with her, you know she was a force to be reckoned with—a 'my way or the highway' kind of person. She was tough, yes, but she was tough because she had to be. I was fifteen when my father died, leaving her to finish raising a teenage daughter—a willful, stubborn, and defiant daughter, I might add—one you could easily call a handful. I can't tell you how grateful I am that my daughter, Jenny, sitting there at the end of the second row, isn't a chip off the old block—at least not off this old block. That's something for which I count my blessings every day.

"My mother didn't have a smooth, trouble-free life. She and my dad were high school sweethearts back in the day. When their romance got a bit out of hand, she ended up having an out-of-wedlock child—a baby boy she was forced by her parents to give up for adoption. That baby grew up to be my brother, Bob Brundage, seated next to Jenny.

"After giving up that first child, she and my father waited until she no longer required parental consent to marry. At that point and despite her family's disapproval, my parents did marry and finally, years later, had me, but I believe she always felt like a piece of her heart was missing. When Bob came looking for his birth family a few years ago, my mother welcomed him and his lovely wife, Marcie, with all her heart.

"Some of you may still remember my dad, Sheriff D.H.

Lathrop. When he left the mines to work in law enforcement, my mother wasn't exactly thrilled. I spent years thinking that she didn't want him to be a cop out of sheer contrariness. I'm older and wiser now. She didn't want him to be a cop—or me either, for that matter—out of an abiding fear that she might end up losing us. Considering what almost happened yesterday, I can tell you those fears were not ill-founded.

"Mother wasn't just against my following my father's footsteps into law enforcement—she was adamantly opposed. Even so, when push came to shove, she was right there door-belling, licking envelopes, and campaigning with the best of them. My mother and I may have wrangled from time to time, but she was always in my corner. She never came right out and said aloud that she was proud of what I do, but I know now that she was.

"Last week, after a shooting incident on I-17 left George dead and Mother gravely wounded, I went to the hospital hoping to see her. I arrived thinking I'd be able to tell her good-bye, but I was too late. She was gone long before I ever reached her bedside. In speaking to one of her doctors, however, I learned that even though she was in terrible shape when they brought her into the ER, she roused herself enough to ask the doctors and nurses to give me an important message—something about a red dot. Because I'm in law enforcement, I understood the importance of that single clue. She was letting me know that she and George had been forced off the freeway by someone wielding a high-powered rifle with a laser sight.

"Having that clue made it possible for me to help solve her murder and George's, too, and giving me that deathbed clue was a true gift from Eleanor Lathrop Winfield to her daughter, the cop. It's one I'll always treasure.

"George and Eleanor died within hours of each other. Both had lost previous spouses and spent years grieving over those losses before they found the courage to love again. Their time together was far too brief, but it was all good.

"George had the words 'Happy Trails' painted on the back of their RV. Some of you may not recognize it, but I understand Happy Trails was the theme song from one of George's favorite boyhood TV shows, one starring Roy Rogers and Dale Evans. The words 'Happy Trails' worked for Mom and George as they traveled back and forth from Arizona to Minnesota, and it still works for them now.

"Happy trails, George and Eleanor. We'll miss you."

CHAPTER 45

THE POST-FUNERAL BARBECUE WAS A LOAVES-AND-FISHES KIND of affair. People hadn't been asked to bring food, but they did anyway—and it was a good thing. So many people showed up that they had to park not only all up and down the ranch road, but also out onto High Lonesome Road as well.

For Joanna, that afternoon and evening were nothing short of a revelation. If people thought she looked like hell, they mostly didn't mention it. Instead, they came by and offered their condolences. That was to be expected. What amazed her were the countless number of people who told her stories about how Eleanor had been kind to them once when they'd been down on their luck; how she'd assisted a family whose two sons had died in a car wreck and had helped pull together funeral arrangements; how, when a small church in Naco, Sonora, burned to the ground, she'd organized a group to replace the organ.

This was all news to Joanna. Her mother had always sniffed in disapproval at people who went around "tooting their own horns," as she liked to say. In that regard, she had certainly practiced what she preached. Joanna had no idea how Eleanor had quietly woven herself into the fabric of the community. Yes, George had been a great guy—a wonderful guy—but Eleanor, her stern and perpetually disapproving mother, was the one the mourners remembered fondly. There were times when it seemed to Joanna as though they were talking about a complete stranger.

Marliss showed up early on, with her hair standing on end and a brittle smile plastered on her face.

"What a great turn out," she said.

"Yes, it is," Joanna agreed noncommittally. She wasn't sure where this conversation was going, but probably nowhere good.

"I was so disappointed not to be able to attend the funeral itself," Marliss continued. "It was horrid of Thomas Hadlock to set the press conference for the exact same time as the service. The least he could have done was throw the local media folk a bone so we could have had a head start on everybody else. I think he scheduled it that way deliberately, just to make us look bad."

Even though Joanna suspected that was indeed the truth, she nonetheless came down firmly in Tom Hadlock's corner. "It's been a tough couple of days around here," she said. "I'm sure Chief Deputy Hadlock has been running to keep up right along with everyone else. He probably needed some extra time this morning to pull his remarks together."

"I suppose," Marliss allowed disagreeably. "But I do wish the local cop shops could show us a little courtesy. Once in a while they might even hand us a scoop."

As a still-fuming Marliss started to walk away, Joanna

remembered how her father always told her that carrots were more effective than sticks.

"About that . . ." she called after her.

Marliss stopped and turned. "About what?" she asked suspiciously.

"About scoops, Marliss. You're a journalist," Joanna said. "Does that mean you don't reveal your sources?"

"Absolutely not," Marliss declared. "I wouldn't give out that information, no matter what—never in a million years—not even if they sent me to jail. Why?"

"You know that lady from Sun Sites, the one who clobbered her husband with her pitching wedge?"

"He died, didn't he?" Marliss asked.

"Yes, he did," Joanna answered. "His wife's in our lockup right now. The problem is I've heard rumors that Arlee Jones is considering offering her an election-year plea deal—manslaughter most likely, not even second degree."

"So?" Marliss asked.

"Plea deals are shortcuts—ways to clear cases and win elections."

"What are you saying?"

"That there's a good possibility that there's more to the story than just a pitching-wedge crime-of-the-moment. I think some enterprising reporter might want to start doing a little digging, like maybe asking about how many times Hal Hopkins wound up in the hospital in the last several months—always with flulike symptoms which might or might not be similar to symptoms suffered by someone being given low doses of arsenic."

Marliss's eyes widened. "Arsenic?" she asked. "Are you saying his wife was poisoning him?"

"She might have been," Joanna said, "and if that's the case, shouldn't she also end up being charged with attempted murder? Hal Hopkins's death may have been nothing more than a spur-of-the-moment deal, but doesn't the presence of arsenic in his system suggest a certain amount of premeditation?"

"You're serious about all this, aren't you," Marliss said.

Joanna nodded. "But I'm taking you at your word. Remember, if it gets back to me that you let on I was the source of this information, I'll make good on Chief Deputy Hadlock's threat."

"Which threat is that?"

"The one about your never being allowed to attend another departmental briefing. And make no mistake, Marliss, I can deliver on that threat for as long as I'm sheriff. Is that clear?"

"Perfectly," Marliss said. "I understand completely."

She trotted off, groping for her cell phone as she went. Joanna wasn't aware that Tom Hadlock had been observing them from the sidelines until he appeared beside her.

"What was that all about?" he asked. "Marliss was all over me this morning about how I'd scheduled the press conference when I did just to get under her skin and make sure she couldn't attend the funeral. Which is true, by the way," he added, "but I did it as a personal favor to you, to keep her out of your hair."

"Thank you," Joanna said. "You're getting better at your job all the time."

"But she took off just now grinning like the Cheshire cat," Tom continued. "I don't think I've ever seen Marliss looking that smug. What did you do to her?"

"I decided to give her a carrot for a change—a carrot instead of a stick," Joanna said. "It turns out she liked it."

"I came over to tell you that I just got off the phone with Thad Stock," Tom added.

"And?"

"It's just as we suspected. Jeremy was a good guy in public and a bullying tyrant at home. Thad had a full-ride football scholarship to the U of A, but Allison begged him to go to school somewhere out of state. A couple of months before he graduated from high school, Thad had tried to intervene on her behalf when Jeremy was beating on her, and she was afraid something bad was going to happen."

"She was right," Joanna pointed out. "Something bad did happen,"

"Yes, it did," Tom agreed, "and poor Thad seems to think it's all his fault—that if he'd stayed around home, maybe he could have prevented it."

"In that case, chances are he would have wound up dead, too."

"Right," Tom nodded. "Probably so."

"Does he have someone in his corner right now?" Joanna asked. "Someone to help him through all this?"

"I asked him that very question. He said he's staying with friends in Sierra Vista at the moment, but he gave me his number. I'll check in with him from time to time to see how he's doing."

"Thanks, Tom," Joanna said. "He's going to need all the help he can get."

Toward midafternoon, the day turned cooler as puffy cumulus clouds promising a late-afternoon thunderstorm appeared overhead. As people started clearing away the barbecue debris, Butch and Bob, along with several others, went inside to collect the balloons. Dennis was allowed to carry only two of them. He wanted to carry one of the big bunches, but he didn't weigh enough, and Butch worried he might be picked up and carried away.

Out in the yard, Butch turned on his megaphone-style voice. "When Dennis understood we were having this party for his grandpa and grandma, he wanted to know if there would be balloons. As you can see, we have balloons. Since I know George was a huge Roy Rogers and Dale Evans fan, as we send the balloons up to heaven, I'm hoping anyone who remembers the words will join me in singing 'Happy Trails to You.'"

As the cloud of balloons soared skyward, so did a chorus of voices. When the song was over, there wasn't a dry eye in the house.

CHAPTER 46

THERE WERE PLENTY OF HELPING HANDS TO MAKE LIGHT WORK OF the cleanup. By the time the rain started coming down in earnest, everyone was gone. The storm was furious but brief. An hour after it started, it was over.

"I'm going to go out and say good night to the horses," Jenny said. "I miss them."

"Okay if I come along?" Joanna asked.

"Sure," Jenny said, looking surprised. "Come right ahead."

They walked through puddles of water across the driveway toward the barn and corral. "It's a good thing it didn't rain like this last night," Jenny offered.

"I'll say," Joanna agreed. "That would have made for an even worse mess, especially since reinforcements would have had a devil of a time getting there in time."

"I was scared when I found out what was going on," Jenny

said. "And I was mad that Dad just took off without telling us."

"He was trying to protect you."

"I'm a grown-up now," Jenny reminded her mother. "I don't need protection. And at least, once it was over, he took me with him to the crime scene."

"That counts for something, doesn't it?" Joanna asked.

"I guess."

Out in the barn, Jenny produced some carrots, pulling them out of her pocket and feeding them to the horses as she scratched their necks and ruffled their muzzles.

"You're good with horses," Joanna observed.

"And you're good with people," Jenny countered. "I really liked what you said about Grandpa and Grandma today—especially what you said about Grandma."

It was as though a flashbulb exploded inside Joanna's head. She was just as guilty of protecting Jenny as Butch had tried to be. Maybe now was the right time to stop doing that.

"What I said was true," she said after a moment.

"Even the part about you being willful and defiant?"

"Especially that part. I was a regular pain in your grandmother's you-know-where." She paused again, wondering how she would say what was coming or even if she should.

"Did you know your father and I were pregnant with you when we got married?"

"Sure," Jenny said with a shrug. "I figured that out a long time ago. We even talked about it once, but it was right after Dad died. Maybe you've forgotten."

Is that possible? Joanna wondered. *Could I have somehow misplaced such a momentous conversation?*

She took a deep breath before continuing. "She and my dad were just kids when they fell in love. When your grandmother turned up pregnant, abortions weren't an option, and her parents insisted that she give the baby away."

"That must have been awful for her."

"I'm sure it was awful for both of them," Joanna said. "But they were still in love, and as soon as they could, they got married anyway."

"Is that why I never met anyone from Grandma's side of the family?" Jenny asked.

"That's why. And it's also why, when I turned up pregnant with you, Grandma was devastated. She saw history repeating itself and blamed herself for not doing a better job of raising me. But history didn't repeat itself, Jenny. My mother didn't force me to give you up. She helped your father and me make it through. And the moment you turned up on the scene, she loved you like crazy."

"I loved her, too," Jenny said. "She was prickly at times, but I still loved her."

"Prickly," Joanna said, nodding. "She certainly was that. But she set a good example for me, Jen—a powerful example. And I want you to know whatever choices you make—good or bad—Butch and I will be there for you."

"No matter what?"

"No matter what."

"Thank you, Mom," Jenny said. "You're the best."

CHAPTER 47

FOR THE FIRST TIME IN PRETTY MUCH FOREVER, JOANNA STAYED home for an entire weekend. Everyone who had wanted to drop by had done so on Friday afternoon. Bob and Marcie left on Saturday morning to fly back to DC. On Sunday, Jenny left early to drive back to Flagstaff.

Joanna spent a lot of time that weekend soaking in her own beautiful tub. As the pain of her aching muscles eased in the hot water, her overwrought emotions seemed to dissipate just like the mountains of bubble floating on the water's surface.

At some point in the middle of Sunday afternoon, she was sitting in the tub, almost dozing, and thinking about her mother's many unsung acts of kindness, when another piece of divine inspiration came to her. She crawled out of the bath, dressed, and went looking for Butch and Denny. She found them in the dining room working on what looked like an impossibly complex LEGO project.

"I'm going out for a while," she said.

"Promise me that you are not going into the office," Butch said.

"I promise. But where's that purchase agreement from the cemetery—the one Bob gave you?"

"On my desk," Butch answered. "In the in-box. But why do you need it?"

"Because I think I know someone who would love to have it—make that someone who deserves to have it."

She drove past the Justice Center without even being tempted to turn in. She drove past the traffic circle and Lavender Pit and wound her way up into Old Bisbee. Only when she put the Enclave in park in front of Mona Tipton's modest clapboard house on Quality Hill did she have second thoughts. Maybe she should have called ahead. Maybe she shouldn't have come at all.

Too late to reconsider, Joanna told herself. *It's now or never.*

She climbed up the wooden stairway. The handrail was a bit rickety. It probably needed a handyman's attention. She punched the button on the old-fashioned round doorbell and heard it buzz inside the house. A few seconds later, slow footsteps creaked across linoleum-covered floorboards.

The woman who opened the door was the same one Joanna had seen some time ago when she had come here to let Mona know that Joanna's father's death—Mona's lover's death—long thought to be an accident, had actually been murder-for-hire.

Mona was dressed the same way she'd been on that other occasion. Even on a hot and quiet Sunday afternoon in early September, she looked as though she was ready to walk out the door and head off to work. She wore a neatly pressed white blouse and a long-out-of-fashion double-breasted suit that was fraying at the cuffs. Sensible heels and a pair of panty hose completed her ensemble. What was different was her hair. It had been gunmetal gray the last time Joanna had seen her. Now it had gone completely white.

"Why, Joanna," Mona said in genuine surprise, pushing open a flimsy wood-framed screen door. "What in the world are you doing here? I should think you'd have your hands full this weekend."

"I have, but things have quieted down a little," Joanna replied. "I have something I wanted to drop off. May I come in?"

"Of course. Please. What can I get you?"

"Nothing, thank you," she said.

Inside, a noisy swamp cooler kept the house reasonably cool.

Mona settled slowly into a swaybacked easy chair. "Is something the matter?" she asked.

"Not really the matter, no," Joanna said. "It's just that when my mother and George died, there was some confusion about cemetery arrangements. It turned out we ended up with an extra burial plot, one that wasn't needed."

"An extra plot?" Mona asked with a frown.

"Yes, my mother and brother were arranging to purchase one without my knowledge, and now we have this one." She reached into her purse, pulled out the purchase agreement, and held it out to Mona over the shiny wooden surface of an intervening coffee table.

"I want to offer it to you," Joanna said, "if you're interested, that is. I know how much you cared for my dad, and I know he cared for you, too. If you'd like to be buried in the family plot with him, now's your chance."

"Why on earth would you do such a thing?" Mona asked. "And what would people say?"

"After all these years, does it matter what people say? And I'm doing it because it seems like the right thing to do."

Tentatively, Mona reached for the piece of paper. Once it was in her hand, she put on a pair of reading glasses and scanned it all the way through.

"I don't know what to say," she said finally, clutching the paper to her breast. "I think this is the kindest thing anyone has ever done for me. Of course, I'll accept. It means the world to me. Thank you."

"You're welcome," Joanna said. "But there is one small detail that may make you change your mind."

"What's that?"

"The Rojas plots are on the far side of my mother, so you wouldn't actually be next to my dad, you'd be next to Eleanor."

There was a moment of silence before Mona Tipton's face broke into a sad smile. "I can't think of anything more appropriate," she murmured. "Eleanor always came between D.H. and me. This way she still can—forever and ever."

Joanna drove home feeling as though a huge weight had been lifted from her shoulders. For dinner, they had leftovers from the barbecue. Not long after Dennis hit the hay, they did, too.

"It's been a hell of a couple of weeks," Butch said as they lay side by side in the dark. "I'm glad it's over."

"Me, too," she said. Butch hadn't asked about the purchase agreement, and she hadn't told him. Maybe it was time to take another page out of her mother's playbook—do good works and keep quiet about them.

"Much as I hate to admit it," Butch said, "I was dead wrong about Tom Hadlock being your chief deputy. When the chips were down, he really stepped up. You always said you saw something in him that nobody else did, and I'm here to say, you were right."

"Thanks," Joanna said. "He did step up, and now, with a fully functioning chief deputy in place, when Eleanor Sage Dixon is born, I intend to take a whole month of maternity leave, whether or not I win the election."

"Sure you will," Butch replied with a laugh, "but only when hell freezes over."

ABOUT THE AUTHOR

J. A. JANCE is the *New York Times* bestselling author of the J. P. Beaumont series, the Joanna Brady series, the Ali Reynolds series, and five interrelated thrillers about the Walker Family as well as a volume of poetry. Born in South Dakota and brought up in Bisbee, Arizona, Jance lives with her husband in Seattle, Washington, and Tucson, Arizona.